CHARACTERS
OF
HUFFINFIELD

by

Tina Marie L. Lamb

ISBN: 978-1-7374391-3-4

Published by Oak Contemplations
Springfield, Massachusetts

Author website: www.lipstickonjenga.com

This book is printed on acid-free paper.

Printed in the United States of America

For Henry, Ann, Allen and Rosanne

Week One

Chapter 1. Close Encounter

Garish images flashed through her mind and shook her body. She hugged herself and considered. Perhaps the shifting light and the blowing wind tricked her eyes. Perhaps she imagined the old man's squirming snake-like scarf and that open gash on the little girl's cheek. Her spine straightened. She didn't have that much imagination.

She needed to stay calm, focus on the facts and take steps. Her call to the police was her first step. After doublechecking the door locks, she made a cup of tea and pondered. It was their hats that prompted her to investigate. She closed her eyes to collect her thoughts. She wanted to make sense when the police arrived.

On her daily walk to the pond, Lady Carmella was surprised to see a crowd gathered just a block off her route. She counted fifteen. She saw no sign of an accident. Observing no bicycles or motor vehicles, she wondered how they came to cluster on this rural road.

As odd as their presence was their look. A curious mix of ages and hats, these people seemed to be in costume for a picture show.

Straining her eyes, she recognized a beret, a straw hat, a jester cap, a turban, an Easter bonnet, a Fedora, and a pillbox hat. Lady Carmella took a moment to revel in memories of her favorite hats. People didn't wear hats much these days. Most people that is, these people clearly did.

She took a step closer and hesitated. Perhaps she had best mind her own business.

Lady Carmella bristled at her cowardice and proceeded toward the crowd. They seemed oblivious to her. Some were practicing elocution; others were turning in circles; one seemed to be sobbing. Most were looking down at something in the cow pasture by the side of the road. She stopped within thirty paces of the crowd and tried to discern what was on the ground. She wanted to take a photo but didn't have the nerve.

Lady Carmella could see nothing amiss. She advanced further until the crowd turned toward her with a perplexed stare. She smiled slightly and pushed her scarf back to better reveal her face. The characters responded by smiling benevolently upon her. Their attention turned to a flapping bird, tethered to a little girl's hat. The girl was covering her cheeks with her hands. An older woman was working to pry the girl's hands away. Lady Carmella wondered if she could be of help and stepped closer.

She stopped when she caught a whiff of something putrid in the field. Was it an animal of some sort struggling in the ditch, perhaps kicking up fresh manure? She blinked. It looked like a large pig sewn into a sack. With the tall vegetation, she couldn't be sure.

From this closer proximity, she was better able to observe the crowd and noted their clothes were once of even brighter hues. The floral arrangement in one woman's basket, so pretty from afar, was less than pleasing now freshly cut pig tails were visible amidst the flowers. A bald man's tartan scarf squirmed beneath his collar, and her blood went cold as she realized a snake was slithering around his neck. "People keep the strangest pets these days," she muttered.

She was distracted from further contemplation by the wailing of the little girl. When the bird pecked a bloody hole in the little girl's cheek, the crowd roared with approval. Lady Carmella emitted a short shriek before muzzling herself with her hand.

Wide-eyed, the crowd looked back at Lady Carmella and in quick unison, stuck out their tongues and stepped toward her.

Lady Carmella screamed and dropped her sunglasses. She ran on the desolate pond road. The crowd's roars of laughter prompted her to run faster. Miraculously, she reached home unscathed. Once inside, she bolted the door. She telephoned the police to report the crowd as a frightening public nuisance. An apathetic voice intoned, "Someone will be out to take a look."

Chapter 2. Inspector Deighton

Inspector Mitch Deighton was a tall, stalky man, in his early fifties. He wore his short sandy hair in a side flip. His attire was business casual with a navy blazer and khaki slacks. He generally left his neck tie in the car's glove box. Most of his white button down shirts had blue pinstripes. His shoes were laced-up brown oxfords he found at the orthopedic shop, recommended by his podiatrist. He had a wide, clean-shaven face and usually wore an earnest look on it. He kept dark brown reading glasses in his shirt pocket. His hands weren't calloused, but they weren't manicured either. His voice was neither high nor low. He bore a feint scent of Pepsodent. Inspector Deighton's presentation was almost pleasant, but nondescript was the better adjective. Indeed, it served him well.

Inspector Deighton heaved a sigh as he turned off the car's ignition. The report sounded like a prank, but the new superintendent insisted on a follow up to each report. It bulked up the police blotter if nothing else. He opened the car door and reminded himself this job paid his bills.

He walked up the winding stone path to the front door. It was an impressive looking Queen Anne style house with a lovely landscaped garden. Inspector Deighton liked detailed gardens. His retirement was coming up in a few years, and gardening was something he wanted to explore.

Upon ringing the doorbell, he heard a loud, deep chime. Through the intercom, a crisp female voice told him she would be down presently. Inspector Deighton shifted his feet and admired the decorative, arched door.

Two minutes later, the door opened and a middle aged woman in jeans and a yellow, short-sleeved sweater, beckoned him in. She introduced herself as Lady Carmella Bennett.

He complimented her on her home. She said she had lived at this address for almost a year, moving in upon her retirement. He found her pleasant enough.

They sat in a small but elegant parlor. Lady Carmella arched her back and then leaned into her chair. "I know this will sound bizarre," she explained, "But I feel obliged to report what I saw to authorities."

Inspector Deighton leaned forward with his pen in hand and his pad on his knee and looked into her expressive eyes. So far, she seemed on the level and not at all like the dispatcher's report.

Lady Carmella pressed her fingertips together and knitted her brow. "Let me try to be concise. I'm sure you're a busy man."

She took a deep breath. "On my walk to the pond this morning, I noticed a crowd at the junction toward Allen Road and walked over to investigate. A young girl was standing in the crowd when a bird pecked at her cheek, causing her to bleed. The crowd cheered the bird with no concern for the little girl. My disapproval prompted, what I perceived to be, the group's threatening demeanor so I returned directly home and phoned the police."

Lady Carmella bent her head and momentarily covered her face with her hands. She hesitated, "I thought I owed it to the little girl."

"Of course," assured the Inspector. "Can you recall what it was about them you perceived as threatening?"

Lady Carmella turned her head and swallowed hard. She turned toward the inspector and softly related: "All in unison, they turned toward me, stuck out their tongues and stepped toward me. I was at least ten paces away so I'm not sure if my fright was rational, but I was frightened."

Inspector Deighton hedged, "I see."

He scribbled on his pad and asked, "Was there anything else, Lady Carmella?"

She shook her head, no.

Inspector Deighton cleared his throat and related, "The dispatcher mentioned 'a floral arrangement with freshly cut pigs tails' and a 'gent sporting a live snake around his neck." He looked at her quizzically.

Lady Carmella stiffened and looked at him squarely. "It is all true," she asserted. "No apparent harm in any of that but yes, it did strike me as odd."

Inspector Deighton nodded his understanding and scribbled on his pad. "Anything else distinguishing about the crowd?"

She rattled off her observations. "Varied ages. Colorful hats and costumes. A few turned in circles and others recited. Most were fixated upon a thrashing burlap sack. I am not making a complaint about any of that."

"Quite," agreed Inspector Deighton.

He put down his pen with a start. The Houdini act! He looked up and grinned. It was the circus troupe who lived in the large farmhouse at the end of Allen Road. Some performers appeared very old and others very young, and their slights of hand and off color stage pranks caused a quite a stir when they first moved to town.

"This is all making sense in a way," assured the Inspector.

It was Lady Carmella's turn to stare quizzically.

As Inspector Deighton relayed the group's history and how they came to be her distant neighbors, she laughed nervously. She wasn't sure she believed him.

Lady Carmella wanted to believe.

Chapter 3. Blurry and Dark

Lady Carmella twisted and turned in her bed. Should she get up and pour herself a drink? Should she call a friend and relate the day's events? In talking to Inspector Deighton, she realized how insane it sounded when she described her encounter.

Carmella couldn't keep the little girl from her mind. Why was she imagining the worst when the Inspector found it made perfect sense? Something did not seem right, though Inspector Deighton seemed on the level. Or was he even one of their crowd sent over to appease an old woman?

Damn it, she knew what she saw. The girl wore a bonnet to which a small bird's foot was tethered and the bird pecked at the girl's cheek so it bled. The girl shrieked in pain and quivered in fear. If that had been an act, wouldn't the girl have taken a bow? It wasn't a circus act and something was unwholesome about that crowd by the side of the road. The way they stared and stuck out their tongues and stepped toward her, all in unison, was unnerving. Then to learn the squirming burlap sack held a human trying to escape…She shuddered.

Carmella sat up in her bed. She turned on the light, found her robe and headed to her desk in the adjoining room.

She sat with a pad and pen. She would pay a visit to that farmhouse to put this drama to rest. After all, now she knew they were neighbors. Perhaps she made a poor impression today. She could bring a batch of cookies to make amends. She would leave an email for her cousin, a clue as to her whereabouts should anything go amiss.

Her imagination was running wild again. Perhaps she should inquire about part time jobs. She made a note and returned to bed.

The next morning, Carmella baked a batch of lemon cookies. At about ten o'clock, they seemed cool enough to pack. With nothing else to wait for, she took a deep breath and took the cookies out to her car. As she settled in behind the wheel, Carmella wondered if this was a smart move. She closed her eyes. She didn't see it could cause any harm. She turned on the ignition and soon headed toward the farmhouse at the end of Allen Road.

She drove up the long, straight drive to the farmhouse. It looked well-kept. She couldn't tell if anyone was home. She took the cookies and headed for the front door. She rang the bell. Within seconds, a tall, slender man opened the door. He was pale with dark, straight hair reaching just below his shoulders; he wore a black three-piece suit. He had an amused grin and inquiring eyes. She didn't recognize him from yesterday.

Carmella became nervous. She shifted her feet and blurted out she was a new neighbor and wanted to say hello. She smiled slightly and held out her box of cookies. He grinned again and nonchalantly beckoned her to enter. She slowly poked her head in the door and saw he wasn't alone. An older woman sat at a Baby Grand piano; a young child sat on the rug and played jacks, a younger woman braided her long red hair, and an older man sat at a table building a house of cards. They all turned and smiled at Carmella so she stepped inside.

"Good morning," greeted Carmella.

"Hey ho," they chimed in unison.

The tall, slender man invited her to sit on a stuffed chair by the piano. The woman braiding her hair volunteered to see about a pot of tea. The man building a house of cards, asked her what she had on her lap. Carmella started. She had not given her cookies to the tall, slender man! She put her box on a nearby table. She cleared her throat. "I'm new to the neighborhood and thought a batch of freshly baked cookies might get me a cup of tea." The pianist began playing and they all sang, "Tea for two."

Milena, the woman with braided hair, returned with two other women wearing her same dress. Carmella raised her eyebrow when she noticed all three women were identical. One raised a finger to her lips and whispered, "We're triplets!" and more loudly announced, "Tea is on its way." All three turned away from Carmella and headed toward a nearby couch.

Carmella returned her attention to the tall, slender man in black. She breathed, "Lady Carmella from around the bend."

He beamed, "Charmed."

In less than a minute, another man, sporting a Robin Hood cap, entered. He was carrying a tray with a tea pot and cups. That was fast, thought Carmella. She reintroduced herself for the sake of the newcomer. The room beamed at her and smiled. She wondered if they might be a religious cult.

To break the ensuing silence, Carmella asked, "How many people live at this farmhouse?" Instantly regretting her question, she offered, "Just the right amount?"

The woman at the piano turned to face her. With a wink, the pianist giggled, "You guessed it!" She watched the pianist turn back toward the Baby Grand, pull a fascinator veil over her face, and begin to silently move her fingers over the keyboard.

The older man at the card table rose and approached. Carmella held her breath. His gray hair was cropped short, and he sported a dark suit with a cummerbund and bow tie that matched his faded blue eyes. At a respectable distance, he bowed and clicked his heels together. "May I try a cookie?" he coaxed.

"Yes, please do," gasped Carmella as she struggled to remove the box cover.

Milena brought her a cup of tea. It smelled like an herbal brew. Carmella was intrigued. "What sort of tea do we have here?"

Milena paused and intoned. "What sort of tea is this, Daryl?"

The tall, slender man moved closer and sat on a chair next to Carmella. He took a cookie and confided, "This is a tea straight from our garden and bound to make you feel like you're out of this world." He grinned at Carmella and bit into the cookie.

Carmella felt he looked right into her soul, but he didn't stare. He made her feel safe, and now she knew his name, Darryl. Carmella grinned back and took a sip. It wasn't too hot and it tasted delicious. She realized she was thirsty and took a longer sip.

Darryl stretched back in his chair and smugly inquired, "Do you like your tea?"

The room twittered.

Such strange people, thought Carmella, as she nodded, "I like it very much." She felt as though she was holding onto her cup for balance with this crowd.

She closed her eyes and took another sip. When she opened her eyes, suddenly everything became blurry and dark. She blinked a few times and shook. With tremendous effort, she put her cup on the table. "I'm-m n-not sh-sure wha-what is raw-wrong with m-me," she stuttered. The room filled with laughter and Carmella became dizzy.

Chapter 4. Stumped on the Stoop

The next morning, Carmella's cousin Nancy was concerned. Carmella wasn't responding. It was unlike Carmella to send an email about her plans, and even more so to ask Nancy to follow up. If all was well, asking another to check on Carmella may create problems between them. After re-reading the email, Nancy called work to say she had a family emergency.

As she waited at Carmella's front door, Nancy Mapother stamped her foot. It was nine o'clock on a work day and she didn't have all day. If she knew her cousin, a house key lay under the mat outside the back door. Nancy marched over the lawn and down the side of the house. When she turned the corner, she thought she saw a trash bag on the steps and shook her head at her cousin's carelessness. Seconds later, her eyes grew wide and she stopped in her tracks. It looked like a person. It looked like Carmella! Nancy began to run.

Carmella was slumped in the middle of the three back steps. Her feet were straight out along the second step, her hands were folded in her lap and her head was hanging over her thighs. "Carmella," bleated Nancy. Carmella seemed to sway a bit but said nothing. Nancy reached her side, full of questions.

"Did you fall?"

"Are you all right?

Nancy put her hands on Carmella's shoulders and whispered, "Are you alright?" Carmella fumbled for Nancy's arm and squeezed it. Nancy smelled her breath. No liquor. Nancy looked into Carmella's face and saw she was wide-eyed.

"You are going to be OK," Nancy firmly assured her.

Carmella was breathing hard. She was trying to say something. Nancy quietly admonished, "Save your strength; we will get this sorted out."

Carmella shook her head back and forth as though she was either having a seizure or indicating disdain for her predicament. Carmella squeezed Nancy's arm again and turned her head to face Nancy. Her lips seemed to form words. Nancy held her tightly. She could have sworn Carmella was telling her to be careful. "I'll be careful. Did you take a fall on the stairs? Were they slippery?"

Carmella blinked and shook her head no. She struggled and barely mouthed her words. "This is their doing. Be wary of them."

"Of who?" whispered Nancy. Carmella went limp. Nancy swallowed hard and looked around. She saw no one else. Just the same, Nancy felt vulnerable. Instead of calling for help, she returned Carmella to her slump and searched under the mat for a key. She quickly unlocked the back door.

Nancy was shaking. She put her pocketbook on the table. Back outside, she grasped Carmella by her hands and legs, pulling and then heaving and then pulling her inside the door. With Carmella sprawled on the mudroom floor, Nancy jumped over her and bolted the door. It was the chemistry between them. Even as young girls, their giggling and story-telling would frequently turn to joint paranoia. It was happening all over again but Carmella was unconscious, leaving Nancy alone to deal with this unease.

Nancy wanted to call the police, but called Carmella's doctor. Perhaps there was a medical condition Carmella had not shared. This might be as easy as giving her an injection or smelling salts even. There was no need to make a public fuss. But when the doctor's answering service wanted to know the reason for the call, Nancy blurted out, "It's an emergency!"

It seemed like an eternity until Nancy was connected to Carmella's doctor. Dr. Darcy said she saw Carmella only last month and found her a very healthy woman. The doctor suggested Nancy call the police. Nancy considered driving Carmella to hospital's A&E, but she was too nervous to move outside the house. Nancy telephoned the police. The dispatcher assured her an ambulance would arrive soon.

Nancy sat by Carmella. When a bird screeched, Nancy jumped. She pulled the shades in the mudroom in case someone was watching. Nancy put a chair cushion under Carmella's head. She didn't know what else to do.

What had befallen her cousin? Given her posture, it didn't seem like she fell. Carmella was afraid. Who were the people Carmella warned her about? They didn't seem to be here now. Nancy recalled Carmella's email, something about going to visit neighbors at the end of Allen Road and wanting Nancy to check she returned home. Were those the people Carmella was warning her about?

Carmella groaned. Nancy bent low. "I'm here. We are going to be OK. An ambulance is on its way and I've alerted the police."

Nancy looked at Carmella's wide-eyed face. Carmella was almost wheezing but still managed to gasp, "The sack in the ditch was no Houdini act." Nancy put down her head and closed her eyes. Had her cousin developed dementia in the short time since she last saw her?

"No Houdini," Carmella gurgled as though she may be choking.

Nancy took charge. "Stay calm, concentrate on your breathing. I heard you, the sack in the ditch was no Houdini act. Now save your strength and concentrate on your breathing. An ambulance is coming soon." Once again, Carmella fell limp.

Nancy felt tears running down her cheeks. She had no idea what happened or if Carmella would ever be well. Carmella was so smart and independent. Was that all in the past? Nancy was angry with her emotions. She knew she needed to get a grip, but Carmella was not one to warn without good reason. Finally, she heard a siren.

Inspector Deighton put down the phone and scribbled. *Lady Carmella - found unconscious on her stoop by her cousin- found nonresponsive after visiting the neighbors at the end of Allen Road yesterday - adamant about a sack in the ditch being no Houdini act. Cousin at wits' end – unclear if accosted or demented.*

He needed to research this circus troupe so he could ask better questions, or perhaps provide better answers. Deighton was on medical leave when the circus troupe first moved into town, but he knew the troupe prompted a brouhaha of untold proportions. He recalled reading about it in the newspaper.

He pulled up the police records for that year and queried Allen Road. "No records found." Searches for "circus" and "Houdini act" did not find any records. Deighton knew he had the right year. He googled the town newspaper and found numerous articles about the circus troupe and the litany of allegations against it. Inspector Rodstrum led the investigation. Jack Rodstrum was retired, and retirees were generally talkative. He googled Rodstrum and learned he moved to Paris but went missing over a year ago.

Inspector Deighton turned from his computer screen and looked out the window to stretch his eyes. Staring at his reflection, he felt uneasy. Missing police inspectors would likely make a police inspector uneasy, he reflected. Or was it about the sack not being a Houdini act? Didn't Lady Carmella say yesterday she thought it was a pig in that sack? He would find the police records later. Deighton rose from his desk and snatched his coat from the wall. He would talk to Lady Carmella's cousin if he could find her.

Unfortunately, Tompkins Hospital didn't record the cousin's name.

Chapter 5. Worried and Waiting

Nancy's head was spinning. The last thing she expected was to be spending her morning in the Tompkins Hospital's A&E. Throughout the morning, her nerves had frayed, reconnected and now felt limp. In retrospect, Nancy wished she had acted before morning.

Her name being spoken aloud jolted Nancy from her reverie. "Here," she croaked. A woman, in blue hospital garb, beckoned her from just outside the waiting room. The doctors wanted to speak to her.

Next, she sat at a large table across from the Social Worker. The young man, in a dark suit, looked sleep deprived. Staring into Nancy's eyes, he asked about Carmella's marital status and dutifully noted, "Widowed." He took notes on Nancy's relationship to Carmella and the approximate time Nancy found her. In somber tones, he explained preliminary tests indicated a drug overdose. After thanking her for her cooperation, he asked if she could stay to speak with the substance abuse consultants. Nancy agreed. She wasn't sure where this was going. Before departing, the Social Worker promised those doctors would arrive soon.

In the ensuing stillness, the walls seemed to get closer. In the pit of her stomach, none of this felt right. Nancy unwrapped a Werther's lolly and tried to think.

Only years apart, they were an off and on team throughout life, the blond and the brunette, generally up to no good. Nancy remembered how Carmella took Ipecac syrup as a freshman in college, just to keep a chum company. Nancy had laughed at Carmella's outrage over being unable to stop the ensuing vomit. That was the last she knew of Carmella experimenting with any drug. Nancy was more inclined to think this was some sort of mental breakdown. She wished she had visited more in Carmella's first year of retirement.

The door opened and three women stepped inside. One looked to be in her fifties and the other two looked to be in their late twenties. Once seated, the older woman took the lead. "The NHS is seeing an explosion of older people suffering mental problems after taking drugs. The Opioid crisis affects members in all strata of society."

Nancy shook her head, "My cousin didn't use drugs."

A younger doctor chimed in, "We see no evidence of a prescription. In fact, she doesn't seem to have seen any doctor on a regular basis."

The older doctor explained that was why they were hoping Nancy could supply missing information. Nancy rested her jaw on her hands and nodded. Nancy was frustrated by their questions. These sporadic bits were not painting a relevant picture of her cousin. Then, the doctor asked her to describe the last time she spoke with her cousin.

"It was two months earlier, at a funeral. Carmella looked good. She retired earlier that year---moving to the country, fixing up an older house, taking up gardening. Many changes from her fast-paced, urban life. She seemed ready to tackle retirement with her usual intensity, but expressed a bit of longing for the hustle and bustle of her work life. Carmella spoke of daily walks and experimenting with new kitchen recipes. I suggested she may want to get a dog for company. She seemed perky. I remember wanting to see her new home, but life became busy."

Next, the doctor asked, "How is it you came to find your cousin at her home this morning?"

Nancy exhaled. She wanted to get this right. "Carmella sent me an email yesterday morning, saying she was going to visit her neighbors. She mentioned their first encounter, on the day before, gave her a start and she wanted to clear up any misunderstanding. Carmella asked me to check on her later in the day to make sure she returned home safely. This sort of request was odd, implying a level of caution that was abnormal for my cousin."

The three doctors murmured their thanks. Nancy was alone again. Furious, Nancy wondered if she had sealed her cousin's substance abuse diagnosis. Carmella had no such problem. But Nancy didn't know what to do.

Chapter 6. Nancy Finds Her Voice

Nancy was desperate. Her cousin was drifting in and out of consciousness, and hospital staff assumed she had a drug addled cousin. Her mind screamed, Carmella is not a drug addict! Unable to calm down, Nancy's mind raced in circles. At mid-morning, she left the hospital wing. Outdoors, she stormed around the carpark. Carmella seemed to think she was in danger from the neighbors she had been to visit. How could she protect her?

A series of fire trucks raced toward hospital. Outside hospital doors, a squad of firefighters alighted. More sirens, in the distance, filled her ears. Nancy returned inside. She went to Carmella's room and found nothing amiss. Nancy walked to the window and regarded the scene below. She went to the nurse's station to ask what was happening, but learned nothing. Ready to return outside, Nancy walked toward the elevator and pressed the button. When the doors opened, an athletic fellow, flushed with alarm, rushed past her and into the hall. Nancy followed him.

Gregg Armstrong wore a taupe, two-piece suit and a red necktie; he wore his hair cropped short, his aftershave lotion sparingly and his shoes shined. He was quick on his feet. Nancy had to work to keep up with him. He sped past Carmella's room and turned the corner. When Nancy turned the corner, a portly security guard attempted to stop her. "I'm with him," she panted and kept jogging after Gregg. The guard called in a message over his radio, turned white and then ran after the both of them. All three turned into the room of an elderly man, who looked asleep. Nancy leaned against the wall, panting. The security guard filled the doorway. The athletic fellow, Gregg, bent to look over the sleeping patient, as though to assure himself nothing was amiss. Nancy pondered. He's like me, worrying about this man, thinking the man may be in danger. Perhaps she would get some notion of what to do by learning what this fellow intended.

Gregg turned on Nancy and demanded, "How long has he been alone?" Nancy froze. He thought she was a member of the hospital staff, and she had no good explanation for why she was there. She couldn't speak.

At that moment, Gregg's attention riveted to the uniformed man in the doorway. Clearly winded, the security guard swallowed and clutched his chest. He fumbled to unbutton the neck of his uniform and then held up a hand toward Gregg and finally managed, "The Director is on his way." Nancy wondered if he meant the Hospital Director Nevels; then she heard his imperious voice coming down the hall.

Gregg turned his attention again to Nancy and hotly inquired, "What is your role here?"

Almost immediately, Troward Nevels brushed past the security guard and into the room. He was a trim, middle aged man, clean cut, polished, with a distinctive diamond stud in his left ear. Nevels looked hard at the patient. To no one in particular, he asked, "Is he all right?"

Gregg grimly responded, "As far as I can tell." Then Gregg crossed him arms and pressed his cupped hand to his mouth; he stared at the patient and his eyes teared.

Nevels exhaled and gushed, "We've been on red alert since we heard of the threat."

Nevels noticed Nancy, who earlier in the day, had furiously protested that his doctors were making vacuous assumptions about her cousin. Nevels turned to snarl at Nancy when Gregg stormed, "Then why wasn't a guard or a nurse or someone posted in or by his room when you learned of the threat?"

"A meeting is ongoing at this moment to determine what protocols should be put in place," minced a chastened Nevels.

Incredulous, Gregg almost shrieked, "They knew he was in room 1231 and you didn't send someone to his room immediately?" As livid as he was scared, Gregg reached out to place his hand on the sleeping man's arm, as though to reassure himself the man was breathing regularly. The man did not wake.

"We will assign a security guard outside the door right away," hushed Nevels.

"But they are looking for him here. Why don't you move him to another room and then post a security guard at both doors?" Gregg's tone turned from rage to pleading.

Nevels looked at Gregg and quietly explained, "We have no vacant rooms in this section and this is the section best suited to his treatment."

Gregg raised his head to the ceiling as if seeking strength. When he lowered his head, his voice was choking with emotion. "My grandfather's life has been threatened by white supremist thugs and your whole hospital has no place for him other than this room?"

Nevels met his gaze and then stared at the man in the bed. With considerable effort, Nevels maintained, "That is the case, Mr. Armstrong."

Nancy didn't believe him and blurted, "My cousin is on this floor and she has an empty bed in her room. You could move him there."

Nevels ignored her and shook his head to let Gregg know this was not a possibility. Gregg turned and looked at Nancy closely. Glaring at the security guard, Nevels snapped, "Get her out."

Gregg took a step toward the security guard, who then retreated. Gregg pleaded, "Wait! She has offered an option. Why are you so sure that can't be done?"

Nancy was still leaning against the wall.

Nevels hissed, "As far as we know, this woman may be in league with the white supremist group."

"I am no such thing," retorted Nancy.

Turning to Gregg, Nancy pleaded, "My cousin has been drifting in and out of consciousness all day. I can't think she would raise any objection. Besides, I would prefer it if my cousin had a security guard posted outside her door. From what I can tell, she is concerned her neighbors may mean her harm."

"Oh please," scoffed Nevels. At the same time, Nevels was imagining double the carnage and did not want to involve someone as prominent as he believed Lady Carmella might be. He needed to say something quickly to put a stop to this idea.

Nevels punted, "This man will hardly be better off if we put him in a coed room alongside a drug addict."

Nancy stopped leaning against the wall and snapped, "How dare you! My cousin is not a drug addict."

Raising his hand, Gregg interjected, "Wait. Let's think this through. Where is this other room?"

Nancy pointed, "It's around the corner and two doors down; your grandfather won't need to be moved far."

Gregg pursued the sticky topic. "Why is your cousin in hospital?" he asked.

Nancy looked at the floor and exhaled. Looking into Gregg's eyes, she recounted, "My cousin emailed me yesterday that she planned to visit neighbors and so unlike her, wanted to tell me of her plans should anything go amiss. I was unable to reach her all day so I drove out this morning and found her almost incoherent on her back steps. My cousin was afraid of someone and then she became unconscious."

Empathetically, Gregg looked at her and asked, "Have they checked if she was drugged?"

Nevels interjected, "Our doctors are providing the best of care."

Ignoring Nevels, Nancy replied, "Not that they told me. I have been so concerned for her safety but couldn't think what to do. I followed you because you looked like you had the urgency I was seeking."

Nevels was looking daggers at her. Nancy backed against the wall again.

Gregg sized up Nancy. She didn't have a local accent and looked like an office denizen, dressed in a pale blue sweater over a black skirt and matching pumps. She wore small silver earrings and a matching necklace. He discerned her hazel eyes were in earnest. Gregg slowly muttered, "Well, if this is the only option..."

"Rubbish," Nevels snapped, "Your grandfather will stay where he is."

"Perhaps you are the one in league with the thugs," challenged Nancy. Nevels bristled and looked at the security guard. Gregg admired Nancy's spunk; he had been wondering the same thing.

Before Nevels could speak, a slender woman appeared at the doorway. Her graying hair fell to her shoulders and her eye glasses hung from a chain she wore around her neck. Ms. Minders bit her lip as she reported, "Director Nevels, they left another threatening message. We are keeping the police presence in the parking lot but…"

Paula Minders was a no-nonsense Assistant Director. Seeing her shaken was unnerving to Nevels. "Out with it Minders," bellowed Nevels.

"They say they are getting closer to him," Ms. Minders whispered urgently.

"They are blustering," Nevels retorted.

"But who are they? Are they even inside the building now and we don't know it?" Ms. Minders looked panicked. Nevels was at a loss.

Ms. Minders regained her composure and quietly asked, "Who can we trust?"

Nancy wanted to rush out and check on Carmella, but instead she stepped over to the clearly strained Gregg and softly asked. "Who is your grandfather?"

Gregg sighed as he looked down upon the man and replied, "Reginald Atwater is an ordinary man, who stood up for a black man when a bunch of ignorant people were attacking him. Those same ignorant people are after him now, calling him a race traitor."

Nancy sighed, "My cousin is a retired financier. She moved to this county almost a year ago. She has never been the sort to be afraid of anything, do drugs or make up stories. I'm worried for her."

Still tense, Nevels looked at Ms. Minders who grumbled, "The police seem to be braced for visible trouble. Invisible trouble seems to be up to us."

Turning to Gregg, Nancy offered, "You are very welcome to move your grandfather into the empty bed in my cousin's room, if that may make him safer."

A bit abashed that Nancy suggested he may be part of the plot to harm Gregg's grandfather, Nevels crossed his arms and contemplated the floor. He looked at Gregg, then at Nancy and then back at Gregg. "It is your decision," he told Gregg, "We will put our hospital security on alert and we can post a guard at both rooms. As Ms. Minders has pointed out, we are not sure who or what to guard against."

Nancy found her voice, "Could you set up a protocol where no staff person would be permitted to enter their room alone, and an additional guard would be at the door when two or more staff persons did enter the room? And could the meal trays be prepared and served by staff, specially vetted? Could their visitors be limited to us? Could visitors to the floor be screened and limited?" Gregg nodded to show his agreement with Nancy's ideas.

Ms. Minders nodded affirmatively and looked at Director Nevels. Turning to Ms. Minders, Nevels quietly instructed, "Start by vetting the staff who will be moving the patient to his new room, then the security who will be guarding the rooms, and then turn to meal preparation. In addition to implementing these protocols, we need to ensure the nurse's station understands what needs to be done." Nevels raised his head erect, turned smartly and left the room.

Nevels hated to be caught short. In the absence of any lans coming from his staff, that woman's ideas seemed reasonable. Guerilla warfare had arrived on his home turf.New protocols needed to be ramped up carefully and quickly.

Chapter 7. Cold Consideration

Darryl remained irritated with himself about the staging of the most recent Spectacle, the one that prompted Carmella's attention. In the aftermath, he found himself tested in managing disgruntled troupe members.

The triplets cornered him, pressing against him and grumbling about his decision to allow that Carmella character to leave, suggesting a re-evaluation of their relations may become necessary. The monthly deaths, and the preservation and sale of the corpses, could have been handled in a private manner. It was the triplets, who liked the notoriety of the Spectacle and everyday macabre. Damn them, grated Darryl.

The child-like waif, Karolina, was a mean clown, both respected and feared for her skills in torture. Her expertise included injuries that slowly become intolerable. Darryl considered the notion of arranging for Karolina to visit Carmella's hospital bed. When Karolina informed him it was only a short time before the "cup of tea" would have its desired effect on that Carmella bitch, her menacing expression told him Karolina was not going to be a team player on this.

One wearisome acrobat protested it was only fair if he should run at the first sign of trouble. Darryl responded with his trademark, penetrating stare and the acrobat clammed up. Others huddled and whispered in groups which quickly disbanded when Darryl showed himself. Though he shared none of his angst, it seemed to spread like wildfire.

Darryl was unaccustomed to such affronts and found himself wandering through the kitchen and out the back door. He needed time to himself, or more exactly, a bit of time away from these emboldened third rate players. He walked down the garden path and toward a wooded area.

In his mind, Darryl was juggling and judging the morning's reactions and filing each least movement away into his overall picture. It was what a KGB strategist was trained to do, and he was good at it. Darryl (known as Dennes Dorokhin in those years) had quickly risen through the ranks in KGB surveillance and control operations, but then the Berlin Wall fell and he needed to adapt to a new world. It was heady, outmaneuvering all those who sought to blame, ensnare, kill or remake him. Now, he sensed it was again time for reinvention and new adaptations.

After climbing a forested hill, Darryl's perspective widened. His mind stretched as he sought to formulate his purpose, weigh options and prioritize tasks. Minutes later, he came upon a small clearing where the pianist and the strong man were silently seated. Darryl was pleased to find them together today. Their analytical minds and close attention to detail proved invaluable. With their help, his purpose might revert to fixing the current threat to the troupe's viability.

Darryl paused to look at the interesting pair. The strongman Bogdan was in his circus attire: a bright blue leotard, a thick black belt, short red leggings and high black boots. The pianist Swaeger wore a sequined, black dress with a long, side slit and hugged at skirt-covered knees. Darryl strode toward them, found a seat and with an audible harrumph, sat down to join them. Typical of these two, neither acknowledged Darryl.

Finally, the pianist raised the fascinator veil on the sideways-perched pillbox hat and spoke softly, "We have a situation that needs fixing."

Bogdan remained still and in a deep base voice, responded, "We need to clear the premises."

"I don't think it prudent to move just yet," cautioned Swaeger.

In an irritated manner, Bogdan put both hands on his knees and in a hushed voice, explained, "I mean it is reasonable to assume if that nosey woman articulates any complaint against us, it will likely prompt a search of the premises. We need to dismantle labs, pause experiments and remove unseemly decorations."

"As well as relocate records and clean the premises," urged Swaeger.

Darryl pondered aloud, "Creating an alternate base of records and equipment could stymie an accurate analysis."

The others nodded. "Leave the physical premises to me," declared Bogdan.

Darryl asserted, "I will talk to Otto to ensure our finances are fluid."

"A search will prove nothing," huffed Bogdan.

Swaeger leaned in. "To ensure questions don't resurface, Carmella needs to be dead." After a pause, the pianist managed a wry grin. "People often die in hospitals."

Darryl glanced in Swaeger's direction and said, "Perhaps an unobservable injection with the result to mimic a mundane condition…while the mundane is being addressed, the true danger might take effect before its detection."

Bogdan turned up his palms and searched Swaeger's face. Swaeger weighed the matter, and then softly concluded. "I can provide your substance, but who will inject it?"

"It is paramount it not be traced back to us," growled Bogdan.

"Rouben may be able to get to her without detection," floated Darryl.

"But will he understand how to make the injection?" quizzed Bogdan.

Darryl looked at Swaeger.

"Yes, it will be a simple matter. I myself will review it with him," declared Swaeger.

Decided, the elder triumvirate proceeded to the farmhouse. They paused briefly to solemnly nod at the archer Ned, and continued toward the garden.

When they were out of sight, Ned scratched an itchy bug bite until it bled.

Chapter 8. Rousing Rouben

Rouben was an expert at stealth. At sixteen, he ran away from his drunken father and found work smuggling cigarettes, alcohol and drugs, from Lithuania to Russia and back again. He didn't belong to any one criminal organization but worked as a freelancer, known for his youthful looks and hutzpah. Owing to his quick mind and fleet feet, Rouben survived that precarious life and kept two steps ahead of most everyone. On his eighteenth birthday, the KGB recruited him as an informant. His shocking atrocities garnered respect and promotions, but led to his undoing in the aftermath of Glasnost. Rouben was on the run when he met Darryl. It perplexed him how Darryl seemed to know everything about him when they first met.

With Darryl at the helm, life was good and money was easy. Though he had options, not the least of which was a position in Russia's Red Coyote Forces, Rouben followed Darryl in flight from the Continent. They made a bargain---Darryl would provide protection and Rouben would render his services. Over the years, both lived up to those terms with ease.

Leaning against the barn door, Rouben pondered. The unexpected interruption of the Spectacle by that Carmella woman, followed by her visit to the farmhouse, unnerved him. As Darryl walked toward him, Rouben pushed his questions away and made eye contact from under his jester cap.

Darryl gazed upon Rouben and skimmed his mental catalog until he found the entry: Medium height, a brunette with brown eyes and fair skin. Socially adept, but a penchant for perfectionism hinders growth. A baritone, gifted in music and language. Runs an easy six-minute kilometer at age forty-two. Nimble and discrete.

Within ten paces, Darryl nodded and in his deep voice, called, "Rouben!"

Rouben straightened and put his hands on his hips. "Yes, Darryl," was his expectant response. Despite his anxiety, he admired Darryl.

Within two hours, Rouben was reviewing a dissolvable syringe with the pianist. Rouben didn't mention it, but he would have bet his father's life the pianist was a man.

An hour later, Rouben was dressed in street clothes, on a local bus toward Tompkins Hospital.

Rouben entered hospital. At the reception desk, he learned Lady Carmella was in Room 1224, but she was only to have one approved female visitor and they could not name her. Other patients on that floor could have one visitor at a time, but each first needed to be vetted by the Patient Services Desk on the second floor. Rouben moved along.

It required all of Rouben's wiles to reach the twelfth floor. There, he was disappointed to see two security guards at Room 1224. Walking past, he noted another guard inside. The staff bringing in her meal trays required carefully checked photo identification to enter. Other staff permitted in her room needed to approach in pairs with prior approval from the nurse's station. The security guards were on edge and there was no getting past them.

As an exploratory venture, Rouben wandered over to the basement where patient meals were prepared. He learned Carmella's meals were prepared by only select staff, required to undergo a retina scan before preparing each meal. He noted hospital rooms had wall vents, and the windows could be opened or locked only from the inside. Rouben determined this plan to reach Lady Carmella was folly. Instead, he made a copy of the hospital's protocols for Room 1224, as well as the lists of selected security guards and meal preparers. Rouben consoled himself that Darryl would be pleased to learn the hospital had yet to correctly diagnose Lady Carmella's predicament.

Carmella's tea included heroin. Her positive screen for heroin led the hospital staff to discontinue further testing. Nancy pleaded. She left messages for the hospital's Director. She appealed to the first trio of doctors. She spoke with prominent politicians. She consulted medical experts. Not until the next afternoon did hospital staff advise they would be testing Carmella for additional drugs. Whether they relented only to mollify her, Nancy didn't care.

With Gregg's grandfather sharing Carmella's room, Nancy had Gregg's company and support.
Police came to interview Gregg about his grandfather, but no police inquired about Carmella.

At the Patient Services Desk, Nancy learned a man, who inquired about Lady Carmella, withdrew when told no visitors were permitted. Nobody could remember what he looked like. Nancy made a note of it. She was irritated police did not appear interested.

Nancy had a quick supper at the cafeteria, called a neighbor to take in her mail and then called work. Upon entering her hotel room, Nancy fell onto the bed and fell asleep.

Technicians read and re-read the test results. Carmella showed high doses of Tubocurarine, Aconite, Lobelia and Yohimbine hydrochloride. At three o'clock in the morning, the doctors revised their treatment. Six hours later, Nancy cornered the lead doctor for Carmella's care and demanded an update

"It is amazing she's still alive!" the doctor exclaimed. He shared the test results and maintained the substances were most uncommon in patients. The doctor was pulled away before Nancy could ask more questions. Staring at the white walls and the gray bed rails and the white bed covers, and the translucent intravenous bags hanging from the gray metal supports, Nancy felt alone. Gregg arrived to check on his grandfather, and Nancy updated him. Though the outcome remained unclear, both voiced agreement that Carmella was bound to pull through.

The Patient Services Desk notified Nancy that Inspector Deighton was in the lobby. Nancy found Deighton, seated in a high-backed stuffed chair, sipping his coffee. Once he spotted Nancy, Deighton rose to greet her.

Nancy was not impressed with the look of him. His rain-soaked hair and the bags under his eyes, suggested one with less vigor and decorum than she had hoped. Deighton seemed to have grasped her impression and hastened to show her his credentials and note his thirty years of police experience. He told how he met her cousin just days earlier, regarding her concerns about the people living in the farmhouse at the end of Allen Road. He extended his condolences to hear her cousin was unwell.

Nancy put her hands on her hips and stamped her foot. In a hushed tone, she fumed, "My cousin believes it is those same neighbors who are responsible for her current condition. If you had prior knowledge of her concerns, it is curious no police precautions were taken to protect my cousin, then or now. I would expect authorities to take my cousin's plight more seriously." Breathless, Nancy looked at Deighton expectantly.

Deighton straightened and consciously kept his hands by his sides. Looking directly at Nancy, he placatingly explained, "I have been assigned to look into this matter. At the current time, we have no evidence linking your cousin's condition to any action by her neighbors. She has shifted to and from consciousness since arriving at hospital, and you say, though incoherent, your cousin indicated to you that she was afraid of these neighbors. We will take precautions to protect your cousin if and when it appears there may be a valid threat to her safety." Deighton could see his attempt to diffuse her anger failed.

Seething, Nancy bit her lip and nodded as though weighing the matter. She held up her hand to suggest she needed a moment, and then calmly spoke, "Let me tell you a bit about my cousin and why I am concerned. My cousin emailed me that she planned to visit her neighbors and so unlike her, wanted to tell me of her plans should anything go amiss. I was unable to reach her all day so I drove out yesterday morning and found her almost incoherent on her back steps. My cousin was afraid and then became unconscious."

Nancy took a deep breath and continued, "My cousin is a retired financier. She has never been the sort to be afraid of anything or make up stories. Finally, the doctors pinpointed the poisons in her system. Her roommate has received threats so the hospital agreed to safeguard her room and meals. But an unknown man inquired about visiting her yesterday and that concerns me. Police need to take this more seriously."

Deighton cleared his throat and remarked, "Clearly, you know more than me. Yesterday, the hospital said your cousin overdosed on heroin."

Nancy nodded, "That was their conclusion. I told them they were wrong. After calling everyone I could think of, the hospital relented and conducted additional tests. In the night, they found multiple uncommon drugs in her blood. Carmella doesn't use drugs. Carmella tried to warn
me this was the work of those neighbors." Her eyes widened, "I want professionals working on this."

Deighton let that last shot pass. He ventured, "You say a man wanted to visit your cousin. How do you know this?"

Nancy sighed, "The Patient Services Desk mentioned it. He came in the early afternoon and none of them could recall his face."

Deighton pulled a small pad from his blazer pocket. He made a quick note, returned his pad, and asserted, "Ms. Mapother, I'll mention my personal support for the precautions, but we don't have enough yet to warrant police precautions, particular to your cousin."

Nancy tried to interrupt but Deighton continued, "I have been looking into these neighbors. Years ago, there was a prior case with them. I've been looking to talk to the inspector who handled that case. I've searched for the files on that case. I hope to access them today. Efforts to speak with farmhouse residents are ongoing. Other than your testimony, we don't have much to work on here. I'll follow up on the most recent drug tests and the mention of a visitor.

"Thank you," said Nancy. She turned to return to Carmella's room and didn't look back.

Deighton sat for a bit and considered what Nancy had said. Given the current Police Superintendent and his own proximity to retirement, he would leave no clue unturned.

Upon meeting with Assistant Director Minders, Deighton made his pitch in support of security for Lady Carmella. In reviewing the security camera footage, he found only one man approached the Patients Service Desk yesterday afternoon and obtained a clear head shot. The medical record showed Lady Carmella tested positive for multiple substances.

On his way to the office, Mitch Deighton stopped at a favorite pastry shop of Rodstrum's. As he ordered a freshly made éclair, Deighton inquired of the owner, "Joey, you remember Jack Rodstrum?" Joey nodded.

Deighton asked, "Seen or heard from him lately?" Joey shook his head slowly. Deighton paid for his éclair.

"I'm looking to pick his brain about a case, and he has all but disappeared," declared an exasperated Deighton before pleading, "If you see him, tell him Deighton could use his help."

It was ten o'clock by the time Deighton reached the police station. Grabbing a mug of coffee, Deighton crossed over to the mailroom. He got an earful, but it was mostly gossip. He learned Rodstrum did not update his address as anything sent by the mailroom was returned. They promised to keep their ears to the ground for him.

Back at his office, Deighton stared into his computer screen. He sent the head shot to the Forensics Unit. He took out his éclair and looked up the drugs referenced in the medical record. After wading through lists of similar names, he found perfect matches. These drugs were unusual, but most could be extracted from plants that were possible to grow in the area. Ingesting them separately caused incoherence and delusion.

Nancy seemed adamant Carmella would not intentionally use drugs. Perhaps Carmella mixed herself an herbal tea, thinking it would be harmless. If in fact, Carmella visited the farmhouse only the day before, that might have remained on her mind. There was nothing to cast suspicion on that farmhouse crowd. He recalled the prior cases determined these nonconforming people were being persecuted for no good reason. Deighton sighed. It was time to begin the battle to see the records on the prior cases.

Chapter 9. The Superintendent's Edict

Inspector Deighton spent hours searching the Huffinfield Police Department's electronic records system for mention of the farmhouse crowd. When he rose from his desk, he felt cramped and defeated. After a late lunch, he prepared an investigation plan and set about tracking the paper records. Hours later, after finding all file locations empty of files, he headed to the break room. He generally avoided this dismal spot, but tonight it was convenient.

Deighton pushed the heavy door open and entered. After selecting a reasonably clean mug from the cupboard, he poured some old coffee and put his coin in the tin. He selected a candy bar from the vending machine. The door creaked open.

Sam Willey was a lithe and wiry constable with a quick smile and sparkling eyes; he wore his red hair flipped over to one side, to give his thinning hair a fuller look. Wiley was as sharp as he was experienced, and Deighton held him in high regard. As Wiley bounded toward the coffee pot, he gave Deighton a sidelong glance. "Don't you work the day shift now, Deighton?" smiled Wiley.

Deighton grinned, "I'm salaried now so all shifts are game."

Wiley was about to say more when Pete Privitt came in with his lunch box. Pete was a stocky constable, as down to earth as they come. His face had more lines than his years deserved, yet he had an easy smile. Privitt reached into his lunch box, removed a loaf stuffed with the remnants of the week's joint, slammed it on the table and announced, "Now it's dead."

Privitt eyed Deighton and asked, "What did you do to get put to work at this time of night?"

Deighton grinned, "I just can't get enough of the place."

They all paused to watch Sergeant Kevin Cathcart enter the break room. Tall and straight, the bespectacled Cathcart was well-read;

he was quick to provide statistics, easily piqued by inefficiencies, but still a well-liked man. He went directly to the vending machine to get his fix of chocolate before pouring himself some coffee. Cathcart muttered, "Late night last night and I'm knackered."

Wiley joked, "Been there, done that."

Cathcart raised his eyebrow and questioned, "Stayed up to re-read War and Peace?" Then throwing a look at Deighton, he gaped, "We have an Inspector in our presence."

"Bring it on, Mr. Sergeant," smirked Deighton. Then he inquired, "Hey Cathcart, you know everything that goes on around here, do you remember Rodstrum? He retired two years ago."

Cathcart nodded. Deighton continued, "Do you recall what Rodstrum was up to before he retired?"

"Not exactly," replied Cathcart as he unwrapped his candy bar. "I do know his most memorable case before retiring had to do with that circus troupe at the Allen Road farmhouse."

Deighton asked, "Did he solve the case?"

"I remember that case," interjected Privitt as he chewed furiously on a big hunk of sandwich, "It started with a bunch of hoopla and then just petered out; nothing solved and I'll be damned if I can remember what started it even. The papers had a field day about it."

Wiley asserted, "It was a bunch of freaks, dressed in sci-fi clothes, scared the neighbors."

Cathcart raised his finger as he slowly munched on his chocolate bar. "Criminal allegations, and for some reason, child abuse comes to mind. Case closed when the Bench got involved. Determined the freaks, as Wiley says, were being persecuted for no good reason. A good deal was happening then and now I'm not sure of the details," admitted Cathcart.

Deighton ventured, "I've got this assignment now about them, a lot about colorful hats, something thrashing around in a burlap sack and a little girl whose face was pecked by a bird. I told this lady they were a circus troupe and that was part of their act, but now she's hospitalized, with intermittent consciousness, and implies it's their doing. I can't find any records from Rodstrum's case. The storage locations are all empty."

After a brief pause, his three companions howled in unison.

"That will be the Superintendent's edict stymying you," divulged Cathcart.

"How's that?" Deighton queried. He wasn't partial to Superintendent Sykes but wasn't sure he had heard of this particular edict.

Cathcart massaged his brow and took a deep breath. He explained, "She wants us to use the new computer records system, which is slow and fiendish. She had the paper records locked up when it came to her attention that busy people were reviewing physical records, instead of spending hours at a computer with nothing to show for it."

Wiley added, "We are all praying she finds a new job and leaves us in peace."

Deighton shook his head and complained, "I spent four hours looking for computer records today."

"Welcome to the club," smirked Privitt, "You'll have to call IT in the morning.

Wiley widened his eyes, pursed his lips and leaned in, "If that seems too long a wait, we can tell you what they'll tell you. That IT crew always says it's because of how you're querying their system."

Cathcart tapped his fists on the table and ranted, "But their system doesn't know how to respond to a query. Too many people are 'incorrectly using this system.' It's the system that's the problem. But the Superintendent is convinced we are all averse to change and not to be believed." He dropped his head.

"Who has the keys?" angled Deighton.

Cathcart shrugged, "Only yesterday, we heard of the lock up. Other than the Superintendent, I don't know yet."

Wiley intoned, "Yes, we all know. It's unbelievable." As he rose to return to work and quipped, "But it's a job."

Deighton looked at the time. He would see Lady Carmella first thing in the morning.

Chapter 10. Finding the Box

Deighton checked in at Tompkins Hospital to learn Lady Carmella was unconscious and her cousin was preoccupied with doctors. Deighton turned out of the hospital carpark and drove toward the farmhouse at the end of Allen Road. He figured if they were cooperative, he would ask if Lady Carmella visited the other day, explain she was rushed to hospital and ask if they noticed anything amiss with her.

When Deighton pulled into the drive, the place looked deserted. He opened his car door and took a deep breath. After ringing the doorbell, Deighton stepped back a pace, he saw no movement in the farmhouse. He rang the bell again. He knocked and hollered, "Hello, in there."

Deighton walked the porch to the rear of the house. He saw nobody but glimpsed a curtain being quickly drawn. Deighton left the porch, muttering about returning with a search warrant. Little did he dream anyone overheard, but standing aside of the screened window, Karolina heard him. The triplets, with their hands on their hips, watched Deighton from a second story window.

After Rouben's account of the obstacles to reaching Carmella; Darryl decided to wait and see if she survived. If she did, Rouben could visit Carmella at home. Nothing incriminated the circus troupe. When the doorbell rang, he was trying to persuade the strongman Bogdan and the pianist Swaeger of his plan. On the second ring, Darryl excused himself and headed downstairs.

The cook Helga met him at the bottom step and with a pointed look, pushed him back toward the stairs, rasping, "The trouble is up there." She waived three fingers toward the second floor room overlooking the door.

Darryl bolted up the steps. He turned the corner into the room where the triplets looked out the window and barely managed to stop Staska from throwing a dagger at Deighton. Staska's sisters were too fixed on Deighton to intervene. Once Deighton was beyond her range, Staska sneered. Darryl thought it best to discuss the matter later.

That would have been too easy, Deighton thought as he left the farmhouse with nothing to show for it. Behind the wheel, Deighton drove on auto pilot. He recalled the alarm when that circus troupe first moved to town. He wondered if Jack Rodstrum's disappearance involved a Spectacle sack. Jolted by the upcoming sign, "Chester 200 KM," Deighton recalled Rodstrum had family in Chester and decided that would be his next stop.

He drove on. His stomach felt almost uneasy. His chest felt like he may be coming down with low level heartburn. It was as though the silence was making too much noise. Deighton took out a piece of chewing gum and turned on the radio. Something unnerved him. The grey blotched sky looked like an endless Rorschach Test, taunting him to name it.

Deighton knew Jack Rodstrum was a good inspector. He would have filed reports that met more than the minimum requirements. Rodstrum was a mate. They lunched together and chatted at the water cooler. Deighton figured Rodstrum would still have family living in the family home at the edge of the park. A blue moon ago, he gave Rodstrum a ride to that home and remembered the family's hospitality.

Deighton found the Rodstrum home just as he remembered it. He sat and considered what he wanted to accomplish. Upon opening his car door, his ears told him the Rodstrum family's dog was home.

Back on the road, Deighton was somber and pensive. Jack Rodstrum's family was unanimous it was unlike him to go off to Paris. They didn't know what to make of the report Rodstrum went missing either. They didn't believe Rodstrum was dead, but wondered if he had been lured somewhere, perhaps in retribution for one of his many arrests. The authorities' response to their concerns was to say, "Rodstrum is an adult who can go where he pleases." Deighton was determined to find Rodstrum's investigation reports.

At the office, even the IT Specialists couldn't locate the electronic records. Unfortunately, this wasn't reason enough to permit access to the hard copy. Deighton tried various angles: medical urgency, profiling unusual drugs, potential to identify the head shot, a prominent complainant and potential bad press. Administrators empathized, but told him it wasn't within their authority. Finally, his Chief Inspector intervened with the Superintendent. Fully four hours later, Deighton obtained permission to see the paper records of the prior cases. Only now, those with the necessary keys were in meetings. Deighton had a headache. He guzzled a glass of water in case it was dehydration.

Grabbing his blazer, Deighton walked out into the sunshine and charged around the block. His mind was racing in a rant of frustration, but then he caught himself. Channeling his inner will, Deighton focused on breathing in and out, as he stormed down the sidewalk. Slowly, he let go of his frustration. He had a list of those with keys. He would get access to the records today. Now it was time for a late lunch. He knew of a counter that stayed open until three o'clock.

Refreshed and focused, Deighton returned to the office. Key in hand, he sped to the storage room. The key worked; the door opened; he stepped in. Immediately, his spirits fell. The records were in hundreds of unmarked boxes, crammed into the room and stacked almost as high as his head. He would have to check each box. After looking around, he concluded the room had no free space. He decided after checking a box, he would move it to the hallway. He started at the left wall.

At quarter past eight that evening, Deighton found Rodstrum's reports on the Allen Road farmhouse. A large box held those records along with news clippings and related materials. Relieved, Deighton returned the cover to the box and brought it directly to his office. He spent the next forty-five minutes returning boxes from the hallway to the storage room. Once the boxes were stacked so they fit inside, he locked the door.

In his office, Deighton sat down and covered his face with his hands. He felt another headache coming on. He reached for his water bottle, blessedly full, and drank. Then he splashed a bit of water on his hands and rubbed his face. It would be good to get a sense of what was in that box and write a work plan for tomorrow. Deighton uncovered the box and pulled everything out, taking stock of what he had as he repacked it.

As hoped, Rodstrum's files looked detailed and organized. In a red folder, he found copies of each of the charges brought against the troupe, with the dates and pertinent details highlighted. News clippings were organized by date with highlighted text; each was in its own plastic pocket and fixed into a binder. Court documents included several affidavits. Notifications and investigation write-ups indicated Social Services' involvement.

He came to a folder marked "Confidential." It was stapled shut. After pulling open the folder, Deighton went through the papers, one by one. It looked like records of finger prints, affidavits in foreign languages, maps of Eastern Europe on which certain cities were highlighted, foreign newspaper clippings, and what looked like court docket rosters. He found a stack of photographs and wondered if he could match any circus troupe members.

Lastly, he noted an unopened envelope with a smudged postmark, addressed merely to "Police" with a return address from the U.K.'s Consulate in Bulgaria. Deighton slit open the envelope and pulled out the letter to read, "Experienced and ruthless criminals. Take all precaution." He scanned the full letter and then re-read:

This criminal outfit has been together for almost a decade, moving from place to place and leaving corpses and mayhem in its wake. Reports have confirmed its operations using fronts including a funeral home, a dance school, and a troupe of street players. It is believed this group last operated as house painters before leaving the Continent. However, in tracing their movements, local authorities came across unidentified naked corpses in a lake, and later identified the dead as members of a traveling circus troupe.

Deighton opened his email. He alerted Special Services that Lady Carmella needed protection; he scanned the Consulate's letter and sent it to the Chief Inspector and to the Sergeant's Desk; he added a short note about the statements by Lady Carmella and her cousin Nancy. He didn't know if this circus troupe on Allen Road was the group referenced in the letter, but it seemed prudent to err on the side of caution. Noting the clock, Deighton sighed and made a note to request a search warrant.

Chapter 11. Over a Cup of Tea

Back at the farmhouse, the childlike clown Karolina furrowed her brow at the mention of a search warrant. She did not like the man's nonchalant manner, prowling around the porch. Had not Darryl dealt with the police so they knew to stay at a discrete distance? Obviously, she had misjudged Darryl's precautions. Karolina needed allies. She walked into the kitchen, a place she had barely entered before, and found a blue apron to cover her gingham and lace dress. Karolina busied herself making scones. After placing the scones in the oven, she filled a kettle. That was the easy part.

Karolina marched to the garden where she spotted the pink hair, piled high like candy floss. This could only be the head of Helga, the Cook. Helga was in loose blue jeans and a striped blouse. Her tall and plump figure was in stark contrast to Karolina. "Looks like the sunshine will be victorious today," ventured Karolina to Helga. Helga nodded before raising her sunglasses, and giving her a sharp look.

Karolina dryly announced, "It is time for tea. Be on the porch in a quarter hour." Karolina tilted her head as if asking whether Helga understood.

After a curt, "I'll be there," Helga lowered her sunglasses and resumed pruning tomato plants.

Back inside, Karolina found an upside-down triplet, dressed in black leggings and a matching exercise bra, practicing yoga in the side parlor. Karolina put her hands on her hips and inquired, "You saw or heard this morning's visitor?"

Milena moved to an upright stance, and announced. "My sisters, as well, saw this."

Karolina dryly declared, "It is time for tea. Be on the porch in a quarter hour." Karolina tilted her head and looked at Milena.

Milena nodded once and without any expression responded, "We three will be there."

Karolina turned away. That finished the invitations. She returned to the kitchen and set out a tray for the scones and tea.

At ten thirty, Helga and Karolina were seated and the triplets (Alina, Milena and Staska), now in matching navy dresses, stepped toward the table. Helga poured the tea. Once all were settled, Karolina straightened in her chair, thanked them for coming and paused for a long breath. "That man, who came by this morning, is bad news," she declared.

"Certainly not good news," retorted Helga.

Karolina continued, "I heard the man say he would return here with a search warrant." The triplets straightened in their seats at this news.

Alina was adamant, "We will be ready."

Karolina folded her hands. "I would rather arrange it so the police do not return."

Helga nodded her agreement. She trusted Darryl to handle matters more than she trusted these four, but Helga was in favor of avoiding police.

Staska folded her arms and declared, "It is incredulous Darryl would not have a plan. I believe he is keeping us in the dark."

Alina frowned, "An outrage! We have given him no cause to distrust us."

Karolina looked around the table and asserted, "We know what happens to people who are no longer trusted."

A wave of fear enveloped Helga, who bleated in a barely audible manner, "What do we do?" Karolina wondered how much help they could expect from Helga.

Milena responded, "We devise our own plan and implement it. We target the police inspector."

Karolina considered the triplets and asserted, "We need to be specific."

Staska pondered, "We should target the police inspector. Let Darryl consider Carmella."

Alina examined her teaspoon and droned, "We need to instill fear. This is the first order of business."

"But perhaps first, it would be helpful to identify this man," suggested Karolina. Helga rattled off the make and model of his car, as well as its license plate number. Karolina nodded, now pleased she had included Helga.

Over the course of the scones and tea, the five women agreed on a plan to deal with this man. In their home countries, it was customary to first frighten police and then pay them a pittance for their silence, with the understanding that breaking their silence would lead to broken necks.

Meanwhile, Darryl took his midmorning tea in his room. It was a large and tastefully decorated suite overlooking the gardens behind the farmhouse. The walls were lined with built-in bookcases which served as a sound barrier. Darryl was alone in his room because he was too angry to trust himself with a public display. Obstacles were arriving in bunches.

Yesterday, Rouben's news about hospital security around Carmella was a blow to an easy solution. After supper, Helga informed him of an inquiry about a missing person, a former participant of the Farm and Circus Experience for Disadvantaged Youth. Late last night, Swaeger informed him Bogdan suffered a mild heart attack. Then this morning, he barely stopped a triplet from stabbing a police inspector.

Darryl rose from his chair, paced a bit, glanced out the window and then lay down on a nearby divan. He closed his eyes. He would figure it out, but the timing of these distractions was infuriating. He should turn to the triplets first, before any hair-brained plans arose or hard feelings festered.

Toward the morning's end, Darryl found the triplets in a side parlor. Sensing Darryl's approach, they moved quickly. All sat on the same stuffed chair, one on the seat and one on either arm rest. They pulled open an old issue of Vogue and looked to be flipping through the pages together. After this morning, it didn't pay to look threatening.

Darryl paused at the room's entrance, and hesitated, "Mademoiselles, may I join you?"

The triplets looked up at him and nodded approvingly. Alina slowly closed the magazine and placed it on the damask ottoman in front of her. Darryl casually seated himself on the velveteen couch to face them. With his arm stretched over the seatback and his head tilted with a mischievous grin, his presence, to those who didn't know him, appeared laid back and friendly.

"Crazy morning," offered Staska.

"Police knocking at the door can be unsettling," commented Darryl. He ventured, "You all seem to have rebounded wonderfully."

"We know you have our backs, Darryl," grinned Milena.

Alina raised her eyebrows and coyly asked, "Don't you?"

"You're breaking my heart," pouted Darryl.

They went back and forth for the next five minutes. Darryl found it grueling. Eventually, he felt he had played long enough. He pointed at the triplets, and cajoled, "You are to leave this Carmella business to me."

Staska leaned in and demurely replied, "Carmella is all yours." The other two nodded their agreement.

Knowing that was the best he could get, Darryl trod lightly. "Thank you as always," he persevered before slowly exiting the room. The triplets smirked. They were handling the police inspector.

Chapter 12. The Chief Wants a Report

The next morning, Deighton called for an update. Lady Carmella had regained consciousness, but it was uncertain if this state was merely temporary. On his race out the door, Deighton filled his water bottle, double-checked for his notebook and pocketed a spare pen. Once he reached the car, the rain started to pour. Thunder cracked loudly and the windscreen became blurred despite the frantic wipers.

Waiting for his security escort, Deighton saw Assistant Director Minders step out of an elevator. Deighton rose from his seat and greeted her. "Good morning Ms. Minders."

Minders inquired, "Were you able to learn anything about the man who asked at the Patient Services Desk for Lady Carmella?"

Deighton frowned, "Unfortunately, no."

On the twelfth floor, Minders stopped at the nurse's station to sign the access log for Room 1224. They peered in the door, watching a group of doctors evaluate Carmella. As the minutes ticked on, Minders interrupted and addressed the team, "Inspector Deighton is here to get a statement from Lady Carmella."

The lead doctor stepped forward. In a hushed tone, he addressed Deighton, "Please, Lady Carmella has not turned the corner yet. It would be advisable to hold your questions and let her rest." Deighton nodded and left with Minders.

Back on the elevator, Deighton cleared his throat. "It is important I speak with Lady Carmella. Ms. Minders, please contact my office once the doctors are willing to give their approval." He gave Minders another of his cards.

"Understood," replied Minders.

Within the hour, Carmella was unconsciousness.

Deighton unlocked his office, removed his jacket and rolled up his sleeves. After submitting a request for a search warrant on the farmhouse, he cleared his desk top and page by page, reviewed the box of records. He carefully jotted notes and made a time line.

At three o'clock, Deighton rose from his desk, cramped and stiff. He gently stepped around his desk while holding the desktop for support. He discovered much, but was far from connecting the records with Lady Carmella. Once he felt sure of his cramped feet and stiff hips, Deighton grabbed his blazer and headed outdoors. Deighton was starting to get a headache. At the corner store, he purchased one of the meat pies hidden in the refrigerator and an extra-large bottle of fruit juice.

As he devoured his lunch, Deighton recalled a masseuse Rodstrum had recommended. He headed that way and recognized the sign. Deighton popped in, showed his badge and asked if the masseuse knew when the retired Inspector Rodstrum might be in town again. The masseuse checked his calendar and found Rodstrum had an appointment scheduled in another three weeks. Deighton's heart leapt. Jack Rodstrum was alive and local!

In the late afternoon, the Chief Inspector summoned Deighton. The only good part about going to the Chief's office was Carol, a middle aged, plump woman with a gray pageboy hairstyle, twinkling blue eyes and an ever-present grin. Carol sat in the foyer in front of the Chief's office. She made a grimacing face to warn him the Chief was in a bad mood. Deighton knocked on the frame of the opened door. The Chief gave him a sideways glance and directed, "In and shut the door."

The Chief's office was of medium size with little decoration, except for the line of coffee mugs on the bookcase. In front of the Chief's desk, were two chairs and behind it was a bookcase with next to nothing in it. At the far side of the room was a round table with four matching chairs. Deighton was disappointed to find the window's decent view blocked by high stacks of file folders on the window sill.

Chief Inspector Gerald Jenkins was a bearded, wiry fellow, a bit short for a copper, and always in a dark suit with a solid, silk tie. He rose and motioned for Deighton to sit at the table beyond his desk. Jenkins arched his shoulders and sighed, "So tell me more about your email."

Deighton proceeded with his account.

"How does the group of Continental criminals come in?" interjected an impatient Jenkins.

"This gets interesting. Lady Carmella is sharing a room with Reginald Atwater, that man who was jumped by the white supremist mob the other day. He is still unconscious but anyway, his nephew wanted maximum security and the hospital gave it. Part of that package was placing him in Lady Carmella's room, a request by her cousin."

"The short version, if you please," interjected Chief Jenkins.

Deighton nodded. "Give me three minutes. I pulled the records for the prior cases you helped me obtain yesterday. In an unopened envelope from the Consulate in Bulgaria, it referenced a dangerous group of criminals on the lam on the Continent, operating under various covers, and last believed to have drowned the bodies of a traveling circus troupe."

Chief Jenkins interrupted, "Why wasn't I told of this immediately?"

Deighton patiently reminded him of his email. The Chief was silent and then thrice tapped his index finger on the table, indicating Deighton was to get on with his story. Deighton continued, "I went to the Allen Road troupe's residence, somebody pulled a curtain but nobody came to the door. It is still unclear whether these people are the ones referenced by the Consulate. I put in a request for a search warrant through your office, per protocol, but I've received no word on that as yet."

Jenkins, who had not reviewed his in-basket, huffed, "It has been a whirlwind of events around here."

Deighton had his doubts.

In the end, the Chief ordered Deighton to report to the conference room in twenty minutes to summarize what was known thus far.

Deighton returned to his office to make a list of talking points. He cancelled his dinner date, thinking how impossible it was to plan a life in this job.

Twenty minutes later, he arrived at a conference room where six other inspectors and the Chief were already seated. Deighton headed to the front of the room and promised to be brief. Almost twenty-five minutes later, Deighton asked, "Any questions, gents?"

After a pause, the chief responded wearily, "Not at this time. Get me a written report first thing tomorrow."

"Yes sir," Deighton replied and left the meeting dejected. He was still processing the information and the Chief already wanted a report. He knew he was onto something big and the higher ups wanted to make sure they stayed ahead of it, but they weren't staying up all night.

By eight thirty, Deighton was exhausted and accomplishing next to nothing. Disgusted, he grabbed his jacket. As he walked outside, it was starting to rain again. Deighton drove home by way of the local supermarket, arriving home after nine o'clock with a package of sushi and a bottle of wine for his supper. He opened the large umbrella and headed toward the steps to his door. Déjà vu, he thought. If he could have a bottle of wine for each time he arrived home after a thirteen-hour day, he wouldn't have to buy wine again.

At almost ten o'clock, he heard a knock on the door. Unsure if the door was locked, Deighton sprinted to his kitchen junk drawer, removed a chain collar and quickly wrapped the collar around his left knuckles. Then he grabbed his blazer hanging over the chair. They didn't knock again. Deighton looked through the peephole and saw nothing. He put his left hand in his blazer pocket and opened the unlocked door to find a man on his stoop. It was Rodstrum!

Chapter 13. Inspector Rodstrum

"Rodstrum!" exclaimed Deighton, elated to find retired Inspector Jack Rodstrum at his door.

"Expecting someone else?" asked Rodstrum.

Deighton pulled his left hand from his pocket, showing the metal chain collar, and admitted, "Wasn't sure."

Rodstrum admonished, "I've heard from more than one person you were looking for me today. Is that so?"

Still wide eyed with relief, Deighton beckoned, "Yes, yes. Come in please." This time, Deighton locked the door. He led Rodstrum to the kitchen and poured him a glass of wine.

"The only thing going this evening," he explained as he handed him the glass. Rodstrum hesitated, and then accepted with a nod.

Rodstrum was a sturdy character, tall enough, and known to be quick on his feet. His green eyes flitted in every direction and missed very little. His gray moustache oversaw a mouth known for its caustic wit. His face, young in the outside darkness, held many lines in the kitchen light. His hands were sunburnt and calloused, and he wore his school ring from decades earlier.

Deighton peppered him with questions. "How did you hear I was looking for you?" and "What is this about you going missing in Paris?" He barely noticed Rodstrum gave no answers. He was still giddy from relief of having encountered Rodstrum rather than a circus freak.

Rodstrum knew Deighton enough to know he wouldn't have been asking for him if it wasn't serious. He repeated that he was told Deighton was asking for him. Deighton nodded. Rodstrum looked Deighton in the eye, and in a deep bass, boomed, "So what's up with that?"

Deighton sighed, "It's about a case I'm working on and a case you worked on before you retired. Let's get a more comfortable seat."

Deighton quickly organized a tray holding a pitcher of water and an opened box of ginger snaps before moving to the living room. He put the tray on the coffee table and sat on a faded love seat.

"Where to begin?" Deighton muttered as he leaned toward the coffee table and ran his hands through his hair. Rodstrum put their wine glasses on the coffee table, sat in a plush recliner and put his feet up. Deighton closed his eyes.

Rodstrum, seeing Deighton was tired, gave him a moment and then quietly suggested, "Start at the beginning, why don't you?"

With a lopsided grin, Rodstrum added, "I'm quite comfortable here. Take it from the top."

Deighton looked at him and chuckled. Rodstrum was a seasoned Inspector; he would appreciate the details and nuances of a case. Deighton started from the time of his assignment to Lady Carmella's complaint.

Then Deighton was spent and it was Rodstrum's turn to talk. After a pause, Rodstrum sighed, "I'll be." After a longer pause, Rodstrum held up his hand for more time and lapsed into another long silence.

"Devil of a case," muttered Rodstrum as he stretched in his chair.

"My investigation was shut down, but I have firm suspicions the so-called circus troupe was up to no good," declared Rodstrum before asking, "Do you want the long or the short version?"

"Give me the details," replied Deighton.

Rodstrum said, "They attracted a bit of attention when they moved in. I talked to loads of people who had something to say about it. I wrote it all up for the record."

Rodstrum looked around like he didn't know where to begin and then pressed onward, "I recall unusually large orders for taxidermy supplies; they claimed it was a hobby aimed at birds and rodents. One of them, a woman, produced a taxidermist licensing certificate from Romania. Community gossip included comment on large orders of machinist equipment. Turns out they had their own designs for some optometry equipment. Didn't seem like they planned to use any of it for commerce or research; they claimed it was just a hobby, an expensive hobby."

Rodstrum's face lit up as he recalled, "I caught wind of this Farm and Circus Experience for Disadvantaged Youth. I found no written advertising or even business permits. They kept no records. When I pressed, they claimed it was part of their fledgling philanthropy project."

Rodstrum shook his head. "I tried tracking down the Farm and Circus participants to see what they thought of their time at the farmhouse. Of the two dozen I could identify, I couldn't find a one. Not many people seemed to keep in touch with these ones, eighteen and nineteen years old, no intact families, nobody to take notice of them once they finished school. When I saw two had records and completed probation, I checked in with their probation officers. Sure enough, both had kept in touch with their former parolees; both told me the last they heard was their young man was accepted for this Farm and Circus Experience."

Rodstrum paused again. He tapped his finger on his forehead, and sighed, "It has been a while"…then Rodstrum's eyes widened as he recalled, "Wild tales about orders for burlap sacks, big enough to fit a man, started dark rumors. They claimed that was for practicing circus stunts. They said they moved to the U.K. without bringing along all their circus trappings. They were a flamboyant bunch, colorful costumes and posturing…the lead spokesperson for the group wasn't what you'd call flamboyant. He was Darryl Dorokhin, cooperative but close-lipped; he appeared well educated."

He winced, "It frustrated me that beyond their foreign passports and questionable immigration status, I never was able to track down exactly who these people were and why they ended up on Allen Road. Records were impounded. Unknown people seemed to sway the higher ups against pursuing these details. My investigation was shut down long before the advocacy groups cried foul about the group's persecution." Rodstrum stretched and looked over at Deighton.

Deighton was taking notes. After a moment, Deighton asked, "Did you receive news from any Consulate about these people?"

Rodstrum shook his head and noted, "I followed protocols for making inquiries to a number of Eastern European consulates. I don't know if the inquiries were ever made or answered. Like I said, it seemed like people didn't want this information on record."

Deighton told him again of the unopened package, with the smudged postmark from the Consulate in Bulgaria, warning of dangerous criminals who may be using the cover of a circus troupe.

"I did not see that," declared Rodstrum. "Perhaps your complainant having a title will make a difference in what you get to see."

Deighton shrugged. "I don't think anyone thought I even would locate the records and like I say, this package was unopened."

He wanted to ask about Paris and the reports that Rodstrum had gone missing, but it was too late. It was three hours until Deighton's alarm would ring. He extended an invitation to Rodstrum to take his spare room for the remaining hours of darkness.

"This chair's all right," mumbled Rodstrum.

Deighton rose and pointed to a room off the hall. He said, "The sheets were last changed a year ago after my cousin slept there, but it should be clean enough. The half bath right next to it has towels in the cupboard."

"Offer accepted," Rodstrum replied and was down the hall before Deighton reached the light switch in the living room.

Deighton was exhausted.

Chapter 14. Remembering

Carmella opened her eyes and smiled at Nancy. Without warning, two nurses bustled into the room and fussed around Carmella as her pulse rate and blood pressure rose higher. By the early evening, Carmella's condition improved. At nine o'clock at night, Carmella was sitting up in bed. Carmella was tired but wanted Nancy to tell her everything. Nancy wanted to know what had happened. Carmella said she was sipping tea and became very dizzy. She didn't remember much more.

Ned Carraway remembered it clearly. On the day Lady Carmella visited the farmhouse with her box of lemon cookies, Ned watched as the triplet Milena served her tea.

Ned leaned against the living room wall, awaiting the sign to hoist up this Carmella lady and take her to the other side of the house.

The pianist played stark and jarring chords. Ned straightened. That Carmella character was stuttering and twitching. The musical accompaniment mimicked her jerking motions. Poor form, in his opinion. There was no need to mock the old woman now.

Though Ned wanted to close his eyes and take a break from this sordid scene, he needed to maintain total awareness. He turned to look at the room through the reflection of the gilded mirror in the corner.

Through the mirror, Ned noticed Darryl nod to the young-looking person sitting on the rug with her ball and jacks. (She had not aged a day in Ned's four years there so her youth was questionable.) Knowingly, the youngster rose and walked over to Lady Carmella. She smiled ever so sweetly and climbed upon her lap. Then the child crinkled up her nose and reached into her apron. When she removed her hands, she grinned and then in a burst of speed, stuffed metal jacks into Carmella's ears and nostrils. Carmella remained twitching and wide-eyed; she squeaked in pain. Ned winced and wished they would just cudgel her.

A loud gurgling sound prompted Ned back to attention. He turned just in time to watch Lady Carmella go limp. The piano stopped, followed by a collective sigh of contentment. Without thinking, Ned joined in. With a comatose body in the parlor, he stood ready to receive direction.

Darryl vividly remembered Carmella's visit. He slept in fits and starts the next two nights. His emotions were full of self-recrimination. He should have taken the container of cookies and slammed the door in her face. At dawn, he rose and dressed.

In a dark corner of the den, he considered the recent events. That Carmella woman proved to be an exceptionally strong character. They should have kept her here. But she was gone now.

To help him think, Darryl picked up the deck of cards on the end table, snapped the deck in half, made a bridge and shuffled. Perhaps he had grown too comfortable in this quiet hamlet. His mind drifted to the journey that led him to this site.

After two decades of evermore sordid experiments, their cover as home contractors had grown thin. At first, the accusations prompted their move from Warsaw to Prague. Later, a string of accusations led to their mass exodus from the Continent. Harrowing weeks of stealth while tramping through the Alps had been demoralizing. The survivors developed physical strength and stamina. The rest were tasty enough.

With their mug shots everywhere, they barely escaped detection upon encountering a circus troupe in transit. In a defensive move, they stripped each body, stole the accoutrements and sunk the dead in the river. A circus seemed like a gig worth trying. They rummaged through the circus trunks and developed new characters. Days later, they presented a convincing circus act in a mountain village. They performed whenever a populated site was unavoidable. At last, they came to

Brussels where they boarded an overnight train to Paris, found their way to Dover by ferry, and regrouped in London.

Away from the acute hunt by Continental police and within London's ever moving sea of people, the troupe kept up the circus charade, performing a variety of street acts in the evenings at Piccadilly Square. Among the multitude of buskers, they received no more attention than desired. In the daytime, they spread out, lying low in dead end alleys or under bridges.

Darryl scoured the real estate listings. With the loot they stole at each circus performance and then on each night of the train journey, they could afford a substantial residence. He circled this country farmhouse with hectares of land; it looked promising.

It was a cloudy, cold day in November when Darryl travelled alone to see the property and inquire about a price. Conning a local solicitor, Reed Crimson, proved helpful in processing the purchase through normal channels and having the circus gear forwarded by lorry. One act at a time, the troupe departed the Piccadilly Square scene for the farmhouse.

At the start, Reed Crimson connected Darryl with Dr. Miles Middleton. The troupe members each needed two personal references for perfecting their immigration status. Dr. Middleton met with each member and delivered on a reference. Upon Dr. Middleton's introduction to the triplets, they learned of his connections to the Eugenics Society and his interest in human body parts. Within hours, Darryl learned of the triplets' agreement to Middleton's request for a Black and White set of specimens. Darryl raged at the triplets' indiscretion. He prevailed upon Crimson to obtain the second personal references without introductions. Crimson produced a second set, each with a signed attestation by a prominent resident. After setting up a trust to pay for the taxes and regular expenses at the farmhouse, the helpful solicitor was no longer needed. Crimson's death was attributed to natural causes.

Darryl preferred the troupe keep its distance from the local inhabitants, but this was not always possible.

In their third month in town, Darryl learned the farmhouse deed included a renewable lease agreement, permitting a local man's lease of three fields and an adjoining greenhouse at the far end of the property. Darryl was caught unaware when this man, Edgar Ward, paid a visit to the farmhouse to pay his substantial rent cash in hand. As it turned out, Edgar Ward proved very discrete about the lease arrangement, making it easier to abide. Once arrangements were made for direct deposit of the rental fee, there was no reason for either to make direct contact again. So they didn't.

Then at the end of the troupe's first year in town, Dr. Miles Middleton stopped his car outside the farmhouse door. Minutes later, Darryl stepped outside. "To what do we owe this surprise pleasure?" quizzed Darryl.

Dr. Middleton stepped closer to relate, "I have an acquaintance, who after admiring my purchases, the studies in black and white, is interested in purchasing a specimen of his own. How can I connect the two of you?"

"You have his name and contact information?" asked Darryl. Dr. Middleton handed him a business card.

"We'll handle it from here," nodded Darryl as he took the card. That was the first of Dr. Middleton's referrals. Darryl was reluctant to make local sales at first. But each local buyer was well vetted, and the vetting cost was built into the price. As time went on, the Middleton connection proved quite lucrative.

Finally, there was Gordon Butler. Darryl recalled it was toward the end of their first year that this prominent local resident, sent a car to the farmhouse and requested Darryl's presence. After carefully arming himself and placing a beacon onto the car, Darryl got in. At the end of a long drive, Darryl was escorted through a lovely garden and into a large three-story brick house. (Mr. Butler made his fortune in the chemical industry. His father built a small business focusing on laundering products. By his late twenties, Mr. Butler had expanded the business with an emphasis on weed killers.) Darryl was escorted to Mr. Butler's study. His escort disappeared behind a closed door.

"Good day to you mister," bellowed an old man from behind a mahogany desk. "I've heard rumors of these Spectacles at your place. My informants have investigated. It appears our interests may dovetail here and there."

Darryl raised an eyebrow. Mr. Butler snatched a post-it from a stack.

"A troublemaker is intent on slandering my company with an environmentalist campaign. We can deliver him to your farmhouse for Spectacle fodder. The matter is to be handled confidentially so no questions ever arise. Name your price, cash or deposit, and we'll deliver it with the troublemaker at your preferred date and time."

Darryl drawled, "Always a pleasure to meet new faces. I'm sorry to hear of your business predicament. If I come across any options, I'll let you know."

Mr. Butler leaned back in his chair. "Contact me within the week," he murmured before pressing an intercom button and announcing, "Our guest is ready to return."

Back at the farmhouse, their research was fast and furious. Darryl satisfied himself this character had sufficient weaknesses to exploit, if needed. (Initially, these quarterly Spectacles involved bounty hunters from the Continent and sought to reinforce the troupe's sense of safety. Darryl failed to discover how Mr. Butler obtained his information, but assumed the private satellite owned by Butler's company was responsible.) Ultimately, this business from Mr. Butler expanded to include union organizers, racial justice advocates, and community organizers. It was all the same to Darryl.

Unaccustomed to local ways, the troupe members were less careful than intended that first year. The more watchful neighbors raised alarm, alleging criminal misconduct. Those who complained the loudest, were moved to care homes, saving much work for Darryl.

Adding an articulate Brit to their ranks increased their English proficiency. A civil rights group came to their aid, believing them victims of society's unfair judgment on their nonconformity. Darryl let that play out and by the end of the second year, all was quiet.

At the end of five years at the farmhouse, this Carmella character caught him off guard. The Spectacle should have been kept away from the public road. He cursed his carelessness. Calculating a clean and quick end to this potential witness, Darryl returned the woman and her vehicle to her home address. But she wasn't dead yet

A black storm raged in Darryl's eyes.

Chapter 15. Contemplating the Prelude

There wasn't much Sweager didn't remember. The stately pianist sat at the grand piano in the parlor. Overseen by green eyes below a pillbox hat, the nimble fingers played Beethoven's Egmont Overture. In the room's far corner, the man in the dark suit studied his next move in constructing a house of cards. The music's repetition was wearing on his concentration. Three times, four times. To his relief, the keyboard cover banged closed.

The pianist sat still and then slowly fitted long, black gloves over long, thin fingers. Memories harkened back to another land and a time when these fingers were famed for deft surgery. But that didn't lend itself to a circus act, so it was piano playing these days. Still, at this time of year, the restless memories of the metamorphosis awoke.

The evening soiree at the Medical Society seemed to go well. In the wafting cigar smoke, the officers lauded the thirty-minute presentation that took days to prepare. The caviar was particularly tasty. Rustling, long skirts murmured approvingly. A piercing whistle shrieked, upsetting the moment. Men in military uniforms invaded the room. He sensed he was slowly falling down. Fast forward to swinging in a wire cage inside a dark, cold tower. An unseen pulley mechanism grinded as the cage descended. Just as the taste of blood became noticeable, the grinding stopped and the wire cage landed on a cement floor with a thud.

Staring out at the beady eyes and red cheeks filling the face of an obese man, in a uniform threatening to burst, provided no answers. Still, it did not seem prudent to speak. Locks clicked and doors slammed. Footsteps became louder. Four tall, hooded men, all in black, came into sight and walked closer. The obese uniform clicked his heels and left.

The first man pushed back his hood, but his face was unfamiliar. In a hushed and deep voice, the man snarled, "We have a very special patient for you, Doctor. And a very particular surgical operation." The other three hooded figures nodded their agreement.

The lead man warned, "Cooperation is the wise choice. Otherwise, you shall lose your fingers and eyesight before leaving here."

After the quickest nod from within the cage, the man pulled up his hood and loudly commanded, "Bring him."

Within minutes, a dozen soldiers arrived, escorting a stretcher, bearing a white-haired man. The wire cage opened and the stretcher was pushed closer. A hooded figure stepped forward to pull the sheet cover off the man's bare chest. Another stepped forward to whisper, "Remove his beating heart." Yet another placed a set of assorted blades on the stretcher and stepped back. Then the four hooded figures nodded it was time to begin. No gloves. No sanitized implements. Their Gregorian chant seemed inappropriate, but he didn't mention this. He ascertained the man on the stretcher was unconscious.

After removing the still beating heart, cameras flashed at the organ being held over the recently vacated cavity, as blood and other organs sloshed forward to fill the void. Shaking with fear and bewilderment, the surgeon endured the rush of the hooded figures who tore at the suspended heart. Almost immediately, the obese uniform prodded him, with a sword at his back, toward the door and the surgeon ran for freedom.

After a day of running and hiding in the rural hills, mud covered most of the blood that had splattered over him. The hours felt unreal as if surely a nightmare. The next morning, the surgeon came upon a hiker.

In a scandalized tone, the hiker divulged, "After efforts to defrock the bishop failed, his detractors had his heart pulled out of him, even while he breathed life. The brazen perpetrators took a picture of the deed."

The hiker paused, "The police are looking everywhere." The surgeon was stunned and thanked the hiker for the news.

"Keep a look out, the picture is soon to be printed," advised the hiker.

The surgeon could have surrendered and attempted to explain the cruel twist of events. But people would focus on the photograph. Such an offense against the Archbishop meant certain doom, torture to reveal accomplices and a cruel execution. Running was the only sensible option.

The surgeon improvised. Keeping to the underground, ample abortion work presented itself. Upon regaining stability, he used his skills to make huge profits. His finger tissue implants resulted in alternative fingerprints, and his kaleidoscopic contact lenses thwarted retina scans. Connecting with Darryl brought steady work.

Though the disgraced surgeon (known as Shkodra) disappeared long ago, that missing person checked in on life's trajectory at this time of year. The pianist (known as Swaeger) sensed the surgeon's approval at living in the countryside in one's middle age. Now, ostensibly part of a circus troupe, deft finger work was still a dependable strength. Admiring his gloved hands, his eyes counted ten fingers. As he rose to walk on velvet heels, the pianist knew he had made the correct choice.

Chapter 16. The Circus Troupe

The archer Ned Carraway felt he too had made the correct choice. He didn't know the official backstory of the other seventeen people in the troupe, but he had a good sense they didn't want police poking around the place either. It was fair to say he fit in with this circus crowd, but never comfortable enough to lower his guard. He wondered if any of them did. Given the grizzly expertise of many of these characters, he felt certain he wasn't the only one on the lam. The crowd, or troupe as newspapers called them, gave him a measure of protection. It was the promise of a hideout that kept him loyal.

Four years ago, Ned was running, with the law in hot pursuit, when he came upon this circus troupe on parade in front of a farmhouse. It looked like the perfect ruse. He inquired as to whether they might consider an expert archer who was willing to fill in with odd jobs here and there. To his relief, the tall and thin man, Darryl, stepped forward, looked him over and nodded his approval. Then a muscular man, attired as a court jester, ran toward him, stopping just short of him. Jumping and squealing in delight, the jester pointed to a shed. A cluster of characters sang out that Ned could find all he needed inside the shed. Ned's inquiries about the pay met with silence. Without much time to dicker, Ned ran toward the shed. He rummaged through their costume trunk and came out in a Robin Hood costume, attired with a bow and a quiver of arrows. Darryl pronounced him as "one of us." Ned never did get more information about the circus.

Ned learned survival tactics. Staying in character was all important. He wore his cap most of the time and engaged in elaborate archery practice twice a day. Asking questions was frowned upon at all levels, though circumstances often begged answers. Visitors rarely left the way they arrived. Body parts, displayed in a vase, decomposed and then disappeared. Though he maintained an apathetic posture, the particularly vicious attacks on weaker members made his hair stand on end. At monthly intervals, the entire crowd gathered for the Spectacle, in which a muffled creature fights to free itself from a sealed burlap sack before succumbing to exhaustion to be buried alive. He didn't hoist those sacks, but he had his suspicions about those sacked creatures. This crowd had no qualms about operating outside of the law and uncannily, operated under the radar of law enforcement. That last piece was good enough for Ned.

In addition to the ringmaster Darryl, the troupe's intriguing characters included the strongman Bogdan, the Triplet Gymnasts (Staska, Milena and Alina) and the child-like clown Karolina. Perhaps the juggling clown Otto could be included on the list, thought Ned. There was much he still didn't know about this troupe. Why did the Cook Helga have a revolving door of help? Why did Darryl seem to hold Otto in such high regard?

Then there was Rouben, a stalky man who wore a jester's cap and practiced magic tricks, including appearing out of nowhere. Rouben's stealth made Ned uneasy. Ned knew the gymnast triplets were an integral part of the recurrent Spectacle events. He believed it possible the thrashing sacks held humans. Ned was useful as an English teacher for the troupe, but now most members were fluent. Would Ned find himself thrashing in a sack? Ned kept to his archer character and made himself useful wherever he could. He tried to ignore the ever-present question---Who were these people?

Bogdan, the strongman, practiced his routine in the early morning and early afternoon. Unlike Ned, Bogdan put his costume aside when not practicing, and instead wore a three-piece suit with a silk bowtie and cummerbund. In his suit, Bogdan spent time in the drawing room building houses of playing cards. Ned heard Bogdan used the numbered cards to spell out code, and practiced to maintain his fluency. Bogdan's two distinct personal presentations intrigued

Ned. He knew Bogdan was consulted in most major maintenance jobs around the farm, but Bogdan did not directly work on the farm.

The identical triplets Staska, Milena and Alina, practiced their routines twice a day. When not in gymnast costume, they wore identical dresses but individualized jewelry. Ned thought they liked to confuse people about which triplet was which. Ned could tell Milena was the best gymnast, and he felt most comfortable in her presence. Staska gave him the creeps but every so often her comments inspired Ned to persevere. Alina was a very quiet person and usually found between the other two. Darryl paid great deference to the triplets so Ned made sure to be on his guard around them.

The child-like Karolina practiced eating fire, pushing a sword down her throat and throwing knives. She devised painful experiments and tested them on herself. He had seen her viciously attack those much larger than herself and her victims inevitably cried out in surprised pain. Curt in her speech, Karolina used the parlor whenever so inclined. Ned kept his distance from her.

Otto was lean and lanky like Darryl. He seemed to relish his colorful stage costumes. Ned had not seen him dressed in anything else. Otto was a juggler and could be seen juggling a variety of objects, either outside or in the barn, at most any time of day. He was quiet but had a kind grin. Sometimes, Otto would disappear into a far room of the farmhouse for up to three days. He didn't seem to use drugs, none of them did. From snatches of conversation between Darryl and Otto, it sounded like Otto worked out puzzles.

The cook Helga was the glue that seemed to keep the troupe---and whatever its operations might be---running in synch. Ned was sure there was nothing Helga did not know, but she did not speak other than to give direction or make pleasantries enough to keep the place running smoothly. When new people came or went, Helga knew. When a new garish object was placed in the farmhouse, Helga knew. When Otto would be absent for days, Helga knew. When Darryl was in meetings, Helga knew. When the triplets had lists of procurements that needed attention, Helga knew. Only Helga seemed to grieve after the Spectacles. Helga congratulated Ned when he progressed to expert archer but never said how she knew. Come to think of it, Ned had never seen Helga cook.

Ned felt it best not to learn more about these people, lest they perceive him as a threat.

What Ned didn't know would have explained much.

The identical triplets were key players in the Spectacles. Staska, a psychiatrist, adept at playing on people's fears, used the Spectacle in a way to instill silent compliance within the Troupe. Alina, a chemist specializing in traceless poisons, devised poisons specific to the monthly mark. Milena, an experienced coroner who turned to taxidermy, prepared corpses and body parts to fill purchase orders. Darryl made sure her stuffed corpses sold at a high price on the underground market.

The meticulous Helga Nikitina ran the Farm and Circus Experience for Disadvantaged Youth. In three weeks, the youth learned how to milk a cow, collect eggs, clear out horse stalls, perform on a balance beam, ride a unicycle and juggle a variety of objects. The Farm and Circus Experience served as a pipeline of sorts. At the end of each term, Darryl found a buyer for that month's program participant, in a placement of a sort not mentioned in the Farm and Circus Experience brochure. But if a youth was particularly good looking, he was spared bondage and instead sacrificed for the monthly Spectacle.

Helga had experience in human trafficking. She had been the marketing manager for a Russian mogul's illicit business. When her boss was gunned down, Helga fled. She ensured tight administrative protocols within the troupe. It was Helga who made connections with Carlson Applegate, a local trafficker, who paid highly for the troupe's deliveries.

The Strongman Bogdan pulled more than his weight, whether or not in costume. He started his professional career as a mechanical engineer and oversaw the mechanical operations at the farmhouse. He proved brilliant in the design and maintenance of equipment, air brush systems and hydraulic design. Bogdan procured the parts and manufactured the equipment that optimized the "advanced operations" at the farmhouse and ensured only he could repair particular machinery.

Bogdan had the body of a strongman all his life, but he had been through hard times. In his early thirties, he published a fictional book, a coming of age story, much like his own. Declared a government dissident and charged with anti-government agitation and propaganda, Bogdan was forced to flee. Ultimately, he found the criminal underground where he could sell his inventions and crafty replicas of technology, especially those dealing with artificial intelligence. It was a rough and violent existence. Once Darryl found him, Bogdan was freed from the banal bargaining of his expertise to focus on his work, and surprisingly earned more.

The clown Karolina was trained by a Stasi Interrogator in East Germany; she was overlooked for promotion because of her height so she took her skills elsewhere.

The juggler Otto was a computer expert who, in his teens, devised software enabling the free download of pornography, a feat that landed him in jail. Now Darryl obtained high prices for Otto's work running interference in national elections.

Inspector Deighton knew none of this.

The farmhouse remained in a quiet uproar so Darryl felt it no longer prudent to await Carmella's hospital discharge. He decided it best to dispense of this matter swiftly. With Otto's computer savvy, he made a deep dive into hospital security information provided by Rouben. One man, scheduled to stand guard inside Carmella's room, starting at six in the morning, had a height and build similar to that of Rouben. That was their mark.

Otto reviewed the current security schedule on the hospital's system and confirmed this guard's schedule was still current. That guard's Facebook page even noted he would have to skip a pancake breakfast because he was scheduled to work that morning. A review of the other guards' social media indicated no incident to impact the work schedule. Ultimately, Darryl agreed this corroboration was sufficient.

Rouben was up at four o'clock to prepare for his mission. The triplet Milena, the mortician, applied the makeup to Rouben's face. Rouben himself had "borrowed" the security officer's uniform. Otto provided a video showing this guard's movement on his last security shift. Rouben studied. He had a left twitch every so often, took measured medium steps, and darted his eyes about every other minute. Rouben practiced until he looked much like the real guard. (Rouben depended on Darryl to ensure the real security guard didn't make an inopportune appearance.)

Rouben stopped at a car lot near the bus stop, just one stop away from hospital, gave one last look to his badge and departed the car. He stepped off the bus at quarter to six. With his practiced gait, Rouben walked through the hospital carpark. He didn't sense anything amiss. He didn't see the anxious man, clutching a notebook and looking around constantly.

Keeping watch against the nameless thugs threatening his grandfather, Gregg Armstrong remained alert in the far corner of the hospital carpark. The hospital's lack of a plan to keep his grandfather safe made him uneasy. He was sure the current plan was implemented more for his grandfather's new roommate, a titled woman. Gregg was convinced, other than for this patient's title and concern about bad press, Director Nevels would have whined, "This is not our problem."

Gregg considered. That was a security guard entering. The regular shift starts at seven o'clock, but the guard in his grandfather's room is scheduled to change at six o'clock. After his visit to the Security Office last night, the desk supervisor wrote a description of exactly what to expect on the changing of the guards for the next twenty-four hours. It was purely to mollify Gregg, but the supervisor made a copy for himself and promised to advise of any changes.

Gregg skimmed his finger down the morning's security schedule to find Joseph Rodden was the guard's name. He looked at the handwritten notes now; this incoming guard was to arrive in a motor car with plate #AB344, not step off a public bus. His stomach tensed. Had anyone inside noted this departure from the protocol? Gregg ran toward the hospital door.

Inside, that new guard was now nowhere in sight. Gregg yelled, "Security!" He saw no one. He started toward the stairs and then decided on the elevator.

"Hey," yelled a security guard, who had just turned a corner to see the cause of the commotion. Gregg pressed the elevator button.

"Hey," yelled the now running guard. The guard caught up with Gregg just as the elevator doors opened; the guard put his hand on Gregg's shoulder as Gregg was entering the elevator.

"I'm worried my grandfather on the twelfth floor may be in trouble," thundered Gregg. The security guard followed him into the elevator.

"Calm down and talk to me," directed the security guard.

Gregg pressed the button for the twelfth floor and said, "Security officer, starting at six, came by bus, not the vehicle per security protocol."

"Maybe the car didn't start; maybe his wife took it to buy milk…slow down. We'll check it out. There may be nothing to harm your grandfather. We're almost there." Gregg bounded out of the elevator, followed by the guard. Halfway to his grandfather's room, Gregg saw the guards huddled at the door.

"Stop him from entering!" shouted Gregg. The guards looked at Gregg.

"The new guard taking over at six o'clock…don't let him in the room," panted Gregg as he jogged closer to room 1224. One of the three guards in the hallway returned inside the room, faced his replacement, Rouben, and matter-of-factly stated, "You're needed outside. I'll cover here."

Rouben looked questioningly. The guard shrugged, "Maybe they need your signature again. They're strict on the protocols, you know." He grinned, "Please don't be long."

Rouben nodded and surreptitiously returned the syringe to his pocket. As he reached the doorway, Rouben heard the voice over the radio, "I'll be right there, I can vouch for Rodden." He stepped outside the room where Gregg and the three other guards were waiting.

The guard, now closest to Rouben, stated, "Rodden, we've got a complaint about noncompliance with protocols."

Rouben stayed still save for darting his eyes around. Then he shrugged, tilted his head and asked, "Mind if I check out the loo?" The guard shook his head no.

Rouben headed down the hall. He knew this direction was headed for the farthest of the toilet facilities, but still it was a legitimate destination. He turned the corner and bolted down the stairwell. His effect might appear genuine to most, but not for one able to vouch for the true Rodden. He hated returning to Darryl with another failure, but he didn't see much help for it. Rouben was confident Darryl would have another plan.

Chapter 17. Blast

Deighton awoke to his five thirty alarm. He sat up in bed, slowly remembering the night before. Just as he was rising, a loud blast shook the flat and he fell back onto the bed. "Jesus," he heard Rodstrum shout. Deighton grabbed his jeans as he flew from his bedroom. Rodstrum was already on the phone, making a report. From the window, Deighton watched the remnants of his car glimmer in orange flames and felt thankful for taking his blazer and large umbrella from the car last night.

Rodstrum pointed to a chalked message, "STOP NOW" scrawled on the steps to his flat. "You don't think this is them?" asked Deighton.

"I wouldn't put anything past them," deadpanned Rodstrum.

Deighton phoned his insurance company. When he looked outside again, fire trucks were pulling up at the corner and the local news cameras were across the street. "Isn't anything else happening today?" muttered Deighton.

"Flames of this height don't happen every day," responded Rodstrum, "Mind if I make us some coffee?"

Deighton shook his head. In no time, the scent of perking coffee brought Deighton a semblance of normalcy. By the time Rodstrum brought him a mug of coffee, Deighton was ready to continue the evening's conversation.

He began, "Rodstrum, I'm hoping you'll fill in a few gaps. When I was looking for you, I saw documentation saying you went to Paris and went missing, and then your family in Chester didn't believe it but hadn't heard from you."

"There's a sleuth," pouted Rodstrum as he settled into a chair.

"You really want to know?" he asked in a taciturn tone. Deighton paused and then nodded. Rodstrum rolled his eyes and put his mug down. Then he put his hand over his mouth and looked as though he was trying to decide how to respond.

Rodstrum recalled, "When the higher ups shut down my case on the circus troupe, I was getting these bad vibes. Bad vibes about locals with crazy ideas. That patient sharing your Carmella's room is an example. I got the notion people, who didn't like the mixing of races in our rural community, were doing more than thinking about it. No hard evidence; just a gut feeling, as they say."

After a sip of coffee, he continued, "It was my sense this circus troupe, if I may call it that, was being protected because they were white. I know that must make no sense. Let me go back. A philanthropic organization, serving refugees from Somalia, I believe, had inquired about purchasing the farmhouse on Allen Road, and it caused quite a stir. A quiet stir, but a rumbling no less. In less than a month, with no advance warning, the farmhouse and all its accompanying land was sold for a pittance to this circus troupe."

Rodstrum added. "When I looked for the seller, I found it was an elderly woman in a care home. The woman was in such arthritic pain that she was barely coherent." Deighton raised his eyebrows but said nothing.

Rodstrum looked at Deighton. "I'm getting to your questions now," he stated in a matter-of-fact manner.

Rodstrum looked into his coffee mug as he spoke, "After the Chief Inspector closed my case on the circus troupe, I got the strong sensation I was being watched, being watched closely. My nerves were on edge. It felt like someone had decided I knew too much. You don't do this work for decades without sharpening your antennae. Mine were vibrating twenty-four, seven. So I retired. I was lucky enough I could. The sensation didn't let up so I took a trip to Paris. Still, that sense of being watched held on. So I went missing. Best thing, my antennae were on holiday. I didn't want to make contact with my family and possibly bring danger to their door. Just last month, I returned. I was trying to keep a low profile."

"Sorry," apologized Deighton. Then he looked at Rodstrum and grinned, "Are you going to help me?"

Rodstrum sucked in his breath. "Hell yeah," he muttered.

The police knocked on the door. By the time the police left, the news service knocked. Once the news service left, it was ten o'clock. Deighton saw he had a phone message from the Chief Inspector and a phone message from Nancy. He phoned Nancy.

Nancy jumped. She must have fallen asleep in the waiting room. It was finally Inspector Deighton returning her call, more than thirty minutes later. Nancy rose and walked to the carpark so she could relay the morning's events more privately.

"And it was Gregg Armstrong, not the security guards, who recognized the security breach. The imposter disappeared just before a man who knew the true guard arrived on the scene. That expected guard, Rodden…I hear he was in a car accident on his way to work, and his phone went missing when he went out to inspect the damage to his car. I've been waiting to tell you," she snapped.

Nancy paused to catch her breath. It was Deighton's turn. He wanted to say this was his first time since waking at five thirty that he had the chance to check his phone, but instead, he thanked Nancy for the information, asked if Carmella was conscious, and promised to check on her cousin later that day.

Nancy was beginning to realize the only evidence Deighton had was her description of what she thought her cousin tried to tell her. She was unsure what else she could expect him to do. Nancy mulled over her initial exchange with Inspector Deighton. Thirty years on the force, he said. Perhaps she misjudged him. Nancy wasn't sure what to do anymore, but knew Carmella needed an advocate.

Deighton returned the Chief Inspector's call. By then, Chief Jenkins had heard of Deighton's car explosion. Deighton admitted, "I'm a bit shook up" and mentioned, "The insurance company should provide a rental car by five o'clock today."

In a surprise, even to himself, Chief Jenkins responded, "Be sure to submit that report by tomorrow morning."

Deighton said, "Thank you Sir," and disconnected before the Chief had time to change his tone. After a brief consultation with Rodstrum, Deighton left for the office, eager to complete his review of the documents waiting in the box. Rodstrum left to conduct undercover reconnaissance at the Allen Road farmhouse.

Darryl learned of Rouben's aborted mission and Deighton's car explosion. He was incensed the car was bombed without consulting him. This slop did not meet his standards. Darryl's drive for self-preservation was burning.

After four nights at hospital, Carmella became strong enough to resent being there. She was piqued by what felt like being ignored by Inspector Deighton. If the police weren't going to take action on her behalf, then she would exact her own revenge. Those people would pay for using her as their play thing.

While Carmella fretted, Nancy spent the rest of the morning and early afternoon in tense negotiations. By the mid-afternoon, Nancy obtained Carmella's discharge, albeit a discharge against doctors' orders.

As they reached her car, Nancy threw her phone into the boot, and shouted, "I feel like that thing is trying to become an attachment to my ear." Carmella chuckled. Carmella had Nancy drive them directly to the farmhouse. It looked deserted, but Carmella wasn't so sure it was. Both of them were feeling uneasy about going in so they returned to Carmella's house.

After a careful review, Deighton was inclined to believe the photographs of the circus troupe members matched those of the Consulate's criminals. From what he could tell, most of these criminals led brilliant professional careers before being branded as Soviet dissidents; fleeing the consequences of this branding led them to live outside the law. He was perplexed by the number of intriguing reports. He wondered who closed Rodstrum's investigations, and why.

Deighton saw his electronic case log had another assignment. The Chief assigned him to the assault and battery involving the elderly Reginald Atwater, now days after it happened. As this was highly irregular, Deighton phoned Carol to inquire. Carol told him the new Inspector, a favorite of the Superintendent, threw a tantrum about the case being too difficult so the Superintendent reassigned it. Rolling his eyes, Deighton asked Carol if she would print out the case record for him. He had spent enough empty hours on the blasted electronic records system.

Late that same morning, Jack Rodstrum slipped into the rear grounds of the farmhouse. He observed a man practicing archery; then another practicing knife throwing; and yet another practicing power lifting. He poked around a deserted barn. He could discern no surveillance cameras. By the early afternoon, he was getting closer to the farmhouse. He studied the wrap-around porch as a potential point of entry. At a table on the porch, he spied a woman, with a pink beehive of hair, who seemed in deep conversation with a man in black.

Rodstrum dashed into the shrubbery and then crept on his stomach between the bushes just beyond the porch, getting close enough to better hear. She spoke in loud Russian, but she spoke slowly. As best as he could make out, it was something about…not wanting police to return with a search warrant, only trying to scare off police. Rodstrum couldn't hear what the man was saying. Then the woman spoke again. It sounded like people were already at Lady Carmella's house, lying in wait for her return. There was a pause in the conversation. Then she went on to speak of rescheduling the next Farm and Circus Disadvantaged Youth participant. Rodstrum didn't dare move.

Meanwhile, the triplets stood on the second-floor veranda. Alina pointed and all three craned their necks to better see Rodstrum, stretched out on his stomach under the bushes. "We have a snake in the grass," hissed Milena.

"Perhaps we should attend to the homecoming ourselves," suggested Staska. The other two nodded their agreement. The triplets made no effort to alert Darryl to the intruder. Their destinies and his were no longer on the same path.

At four o'clock, Deighton and Rodstrum reconvened. Deighton had a draft report ready for the Chief. Once they swapped information, Deighton excused himself as he was overdue to meet with Lady Carmella at hospital. On route, he learned she was discharged. Given Rodstrum's news, Deighton didn't think returning to her home was a good idea, but he didn't know if that was her plan. He called Nancy and left a message. Deighton headed for Lady Carmella's house. He felt nothing was right about any of this. "Lady Carmella would have been safer in hospital," he muttered.

On route, Deighton phoned Rodstrum with an update. Rodstrum suggested, "Park a bit away from the house, just in case I understood that woman correctly. And think about approaching from the side rather than going directly to the front door. Oh, you know all this." Rodstrum couldn't see it, but Deighton was nodding in agreement.

Nancy parked in Carmella's drive. They sat for a good five minutes, still feeling uneasy after their return from the farmhouse. It was at this house that Nancy had found an incoherent Carmella on her back stoop. Instead of entering the house, they decided on a walk to the pond. From behind the house, crouching figures raised knives and moved closer toward the house. Nancy and Carmella walked toward the road, unaware of this movement.

Deighton was painfully aware. He watched the car in the drive. Once the two women exited the car, Deighton needed to warn them. He entered the grounds from the rear side, a good distance from the drive. He approached the house, crouched down by a rose trellis and looked around. Knives flew in the air. "Get back in the car," shouted Deighton as he ran toward the drive. Once out in the open, Deighton was soon overwhelmed by four bodies crashing down on him. When he looked up, the triplets surrounded the melee and pointed their pistols straight at him. The triplets gave a nod to one of the grunts on top of him. Deighton was promptly bound and gagged. So much for that rescue mission, he mused.

Stand watch," the triplet Staska directed Ned, but Staska didn't say what to watch for. He was a bit unsure of what he was supposed to be doing. While he didn't have a reason to refuse Staska, this was his first directive from anyone other than Darryl. Ned stood about thirty paces from the front walk of Carmella's house and leaned against a large boulder surrounded by gargantuan lilac bushes. He guessed members of the troupe were inside the house, but Ned did not observe anyone enter. In fact, he neither saw nor heard anyone as he stood watch. He hoped Staska would not forget him.

Nancy and Carmella approached the house. They noticed the still-as-stone Ned, nodded their acknowledgement and kept on. Ned nodded back. Ned listened. They recounted their good fortune to encounter wildlife along the pond. Then they slowed and came closer together. A curtain blew every so often in an open window, but they did not recall any opened windows when they studied the house from the car. The wide tire tracks in the mud puzzled them too.

Carmella was pulling Nancy toward the house and in an exasperated tone, whispering, "Oh don't be a twit."

Nancy cringed, "Do you think it's safe to enter?"

Ned cleared his throat. He had their attention. Then Ned shook his head. "Likely better if you stay away," he mumbled.

Nancy gave a faint smile at Ned and commandeered Carmella back toward the pond. The two of them became more nervous with each step. Finally at the pond's edge, they threw off their outer clothes and swam. In late May, the water was still and cold. Swimming quickly, they reached the far shore and climbed onto the rocky beach. They sat in their wet underwear and panted for breath, more from fear than exertion.

"Not bad for someone discharged against doctors' orders," grinned Carmella.

Minutes passed and they didn't know what to do next. They hoped Inspector Deighton would be looking for them.

Chapter 18. Dire Straits

Back at the farmhouse, the bound and gagged Deighton was propped up in a wheel barrel and paraded to the barn. Everyone at the farmhouse turned out to investigate the commotion. The triplets presided over the events. Deighton was blindfolded and stuffed into an underground compartment beneath the dirt floor. He heard the compartment door click. He felt the crash above him when the false floor hit the ground with a thud. He heard the crowd roar with approval.

"Fine enough for them," silently huffed Deighton as he tried to remain sane. The underground compartment may have been roomy enough for a contortionist, but Deighton was having a hard time enduring the pain of his folded neck and limbs. He concentrated on trying to breathe in that cramped space. He hoped they would let him out.

Darryl was aghast that Deighton was taken to the farmhouse, and then again to see he was without a blindfold. "Amateurs," he scoffed under his breath.

The triplets watched Darryl seethe while Deighton was blindfolded; they giggled and stepped toward Darryl. "But he isn't going anywhere," soothed Alina. Darryl nodded in agreement while he inwardly raged at such idiocy. It was sloppy. He had no intention of letting the triplets bring trouble to his door. But he needed to think. Kidnapping a police inspector! Clearly, the triplets did not think.

Darryl considered. This was an all-hands-on-deck moment, but he didn't see Ned. He spied Helga and strode over to inquire. She had not seen Ned. The triplets, thought Darryl. This would be nauseating. Darryl meandered his way toward the triplets and found Milena looking a bit lost. Darryl purred, "Congratulations on your trophy." Milena glowed.

"Do tell me how your game trophy was won," he coaxed.

"We agreed Staska would tell you," pouted Milena.

Darryl sighed, "I'll be patient," as he shrugged his shoulders and grinned. Darryl moved closer to Milena and as though he was just noticing, squinted a quizzical eye and inquired in a hushed voice, "Do you see Ned anywhere?"

Milena frowned and furrowed her brow. "I'll bet that fool is still standing guard where we left him." She spun away to find her sisters and then whispered in their ears. Alina bellowed at the goon that Deighton had gifted with a black eye, and he ran outside. Darryl watched it all.

"Break it up," interjected Helga, in an attempt to disperse the crowd. She banged a broom handle against a metal tack box and announced, "Lights will be dimming soon. Please get to where you want to be for the evening."

At first, this had no impact, but eventually, people moved. Within twenty minutes, Helga was directing a crew sweeping and raking down the barn floor. By the time Ned arrived at the farmhouse, nothing remained to indicate any break in the troupe's protocol. Ned spotted Darryl and strode over to him.

"I hear it is you I have to thank for being relieved from guard duty this evening. Thank you Darryl." Ned was at his most earnest. At his most earnest, Ned was as earnest as they come. Darryl gave him a faint grin and motioned with his head for Ned to come closer.

"Yes sir," responded Ned as he took a step closer to Darryl.

In a smooth tone, Darryl addressed him. "I apologize you weren't relieved earlier. I didn't remember scheduling you for guard duty this evening." Darryl raised one eye brow.

Ned stammered, "No. Staska directed me to that Carmella lady's house to stand watch, but she didn't say what I was to watch for. I just assumed she was relaying a directive from you?" Ned wondered if he was being reprimanded.

Darryl put up his hand and beamed, "Don't think twice about it. It won't happen again." He added, "Thank you for your service, Ned."

Ned mustered another, "Yes sir." With a quick tilt of his head, Darryl motioned for Ned to go. Ned almost raced to his room. This was not normal.

Carmella and Nancy were wet and the sun would soon be going down. They spotted their clothes setting on the rocks across the pond and wished they had hid them under a rock. Carmella hissed, "If we can swim the pond, a farmhouse denizen can swim it too."

Being wet was no longer their biggest problem. They were sitting ducks on the open shoreline. They stared briefly, as their predicament dawned on them. Nancy broke the silence. "Come on," she urged.

The cousins rose from the shore and bolted into the closest bit of tree cover. About twenty paces in, they spotted a large boulder. They dashed to the boulder and crouched behind it. Next, they needed to decide on their direction. Since moving to the area, Carmella had walked all the way around this pond a few times. In her mind, she was tracing the route and making note of any landmarks along the way. Her eyes lit up. "About twenty-five minutes in that direction," she announced.

"You're sure?" asked Nancy.

"There is a boathouse," she told Nancy. "The one time I had a look in it, I recall seeing a Bunsen burner and a hammock."

"We could cover ourselves with the hammock," suggested the shivering Nancy.

Without shoes and still wet, the tenacious cousins arrived at the boathouse in just under twenty-five minutes. The door was stuck, but the handle wasn't locked. The window was open. Carmella looked expectantly at Nancy and declared, "Well, I've been in hospital."

Nancy gritted her teeth, put her arms over the sill and jumped.

"I'll need a boost," she groaned. Carmella collected Nancy's suspended legs, stretched them long and then heaved them upwards. Nancy wailed as she crashed into a hard object inside the boathouse.

"Are you still with us," asked Carmella in a loud whisper.

"As far as I can tell," Nancy muttered, as she then tripped and clamored in the noisiest of fashion.

The noise stopped and then Nancy's strained voice reached Carmella. "I can't see much in here. Which way is the door from where I fell in?"

"It should be on your left," hissed Carmella, who was getting nervous they may be discovered by the wrong people in the wake of the noise. Minutes later, Nancy was pushing outward on the door. It didn't budge.

"Try it again and I'll help," encouraged Carmella.

Nancy braced herself and directed, "On the count of three; one, two, three." Carmella was pulling on the door from the outside and Nancy was pushing from the inside. With a loud grind, the door slowly opened just enough for Carmella to pass through. Having seen the interior in the daylight, Carmella recalled a pull cord dangling from the ceiling. She felt her way along the oars and pontoons until she felt she was in the center of the room.

"Let me use your shoulder," whispered Carmella. Nancy found her way to Carmella's side. Carmella put her left hand on Nancy's shoulder for balance, as she reached upward for a dangling cord. After a brief yank, the light was frighteningly bright, but now they could get their bearings. There was much to see, including a set of antlers suspended over the ceiling light bulb. Nancy gasped and pointed. It was a red, rotary-dial phone on the wall. Working their way around the equipment and gear, they reached the red phone.

Nancy reached the phone first. In a silent flash of hope, Nancy paused to wonder if it could be this easy. "Pick it up," hissed Carmella.

Nancy raised the receiver. It had a dial tone! Nancy phoned Gregg Armstrong's number and he answered. Carmella gave him directions and they turned off the light. As they waited in a huddle, they shook more from fear than from the damp chill. Gregg sent a caravan of neighbors to their aide. Then Gregg reported the cousins' predicament to the police. By nine o'clock that evening, both Carmella and Nancy were at hospital for evaluation. Nancy asked that Inspector Deighton be told of their whereabouts.

The farmhouse lights were dimmed at the usual hour. Darryl sat alone and pondered. Swift stealth was required. Darryl considered his options and made his selection. Closing his eyes, he realized his plan needed computer support. He walked up the stairs to consult his computer expert. He knocked on Otto's door. No answer. Darryl slowly pushed open the door. Otto's room was empty. Nothing on the walls. His closet was bare. His bureau held only his clown costume. His laptop was no longer by the bed. The set of computers remained on the desk. Darryl closed the door and sat at the desk; he typed in his password but the screen remained blank. He typed his second password, devised for situations requiring stealth. A message typed itself on the screen, "TRIPLETS GONE RENEGADE. RUN!" Darryl thrice pressed the escape button and the screen went blank.

Chapter 19. Deighton's Fate

The roosters crowed at dawn. Unfortunately, Deighton was already awake. Impossibly, he stayed conscious each minute within that cramped underground compartment. Bound, gagged and blindfolded, he wondered where the air was coming from. What he couldn't see was the compartment's connection to a series of oxygen tanks, with enough oxygen for only three more hours. Except for Deighton and a few barn animals, the barn was empty. No telltale marks indicated Deighton's subterranean compartment.

Inside the farmhouse kitchen, seventeen people crowded around four long, rectangular tables, set in an open square design. Over a family-style breakfast of smoked sausages, pickled vegetables, hard-boiled eggs and bread, their animated discussion was jovial and boisterous. The topic of the hour---what to do with the police inspector in the barn. Darryl wasn't at the table, but only Helga and Ned seemed to notice. In fact, the pianist Swaeger noticed too. All three wondered what his absence meant for them. Bogdan was too infatuated with the triplet Milena to notice Darryl's absence. The triplets were still obsessed with their moment of triumph, parading the police inspector into the barn.

"While he's alive, he would make a fine target for knife throwing practice," suggested Rouben. "We could take turns with it."

"What about stuffing him and using him for a mailbox?" joked Karolina.

"We could stretch him on a rack and then use him as a scarecrow in the garden," guffawed another."

"Perhaps we could make a meal out of him?" considered Helga.

"For the pigs, perhaps," responded Swaeger. Sitting next to him, Bogdan looked at Milena and pointed to his wrist watch. She looked at her sisters.

Alina sat back in her chair and grinned. "Do we have any burlap bags handy?" she asked to no one in particular. The table roared. Soon the crowd was banging cutlery on the table and chanting, "Spec-ta-cle, Spec-ta-cle."

Milena raised her coffee mug and loudly pronounced, "Done!" The crowd roared. Ned was roaring too; his roar was driven by his quest for self-preservation rather than any approval or anticipation. Swaeger had a splitting headache but you would never guess it by looking at his gleeful demeanor. With a big smile, Helga was pumping her clenched fists over her head.

Milena rose, as did her sisters. With an air of confidence and strength, they marched toward the barn. The majority of the crowd followed the triplets into the barn. Swaeger and Ned returned upstairs. Helga cleared the table.

Back in his bedroom, Ned was at loss. He had nothing in his bedroom. How could he run and where would he run to? Ned found himself automatically looking for the outfit he was wearing when he first went into the barn to look for a disguise in that big, colorful circus trunk. He found it in back of the bottom bureau drawer. What else did he have? He had a torch, a pencil and a small package of tissues in his night stand. He opened his closet, not much there but a few pieces of archer attire but on the top shelf, he found walking shoes from years ago. He put the shoes with his clothes in the bottom bureau drawer and searched the rest of the bureau. He found a nylon bag that might work as a travel bag. He put in the socks and underclothes provided by the Troupe.

In the top drawer, Ned found an envelope he had not seen before. Inside were a few pound notes and two train tickets, first to London and then to Edinburgh. The first train left that evening. "Thank you God," he prayed fervently. Ned stuffed the envelope at the bottom of his bag, stuffed the bag in the bottom bureau drawer, and dashed downstairs. He needed to be in the barn before his absence was noticed.

Swaeger returned to his room to make preparations. He knew he must show up in the barn soon or he would be missed. He pulled a hanging black bag from the rear of his closet. Inside, he found the man's suit, dress shoes, and socks were still there. He put his wallet and wrist watch in the jacket pocket. He found a cell phone and set it to charge. He removed a laptop from his desk and put it in an overnight bag with toiletries, a shirt, a change of underwear and night clothes. With a smirk, he tossed in swim trunks and then a portable charger. He slipped off his dress and changed to men's underclothes. He grabbed the dress from the bed, held it up to gaze upon it, and then redonned it. Swaeger checked his look in the mirror, glanced around his room and quickly headed downstairs.

Helga worked to maintain her composure as she filled the trolley car with empty breakfast dishes. She sent her regular help to enjoy the shenanigans in the barn. This gig had come to an end for her. She could only hope Darryl had destroyed all incriminating records. The question was how to extricate herself in the moment without creating a stir. She counted the young lives lost to the Farm and Circus Program; she knew things would not go well for her should the triplets' rash measures bring a bad end to the farmhouse. She pulled the trolley toward the sink. On the edge of the sink, sat a vial. She had not put it there. She knew it was a strong hallucinogenic. She bet all odds this was Darryl recommending she drug the witnesses before leaving the scene. She could do that.

In the barn, the triplets walked over to the piece of floor over Deighton's compartment. Milena stamped on the floor with her foot. She looked around and announced, "It's time."

Two goons, a trapeze artist and a tightrope walker, approached and set about raising the floor boards so the compartment was now visible. Bogdan stepped forward. He held the compartment's handles and raised the compartment above ground and onto the floor. He flipped open the compartment's lid and stepped back. Alina stepped forward and looking down, she kicked at Deighton's form. Deighton's reaction assured the watching crowd he was alive. On the mime artist's cue, they went wild.

Milena addressed Deighton so the crowd could hear. "We are going to unbind you, little man." She motioned to one of Helga's helpers to get something from the kitchen. The helper ran.

In the kitchen, Helga was ready. She took a cup from the counter and held it out. "Take care with this. We don't want it spilling," Helga directed.

The runner held it with two hands and hurried back to the barn. Deighton's gag was already off. Swaeger stepped forward to take the cup from the helper. Bogdan held down Deighton while Swaeger professionally tipped his head and told him to drink. Deighton emptied the cup and thought it tasted like cherry Kool Aid. Deighton's gag was re-fastened. Swaeger held onto the cup and stood back, looking expectantly at Milena. She looked at Swaeger as though she had forgotten what happened next.

"In another five minutes he'll be ready," Swaeger intoned as he focused on Deighton. Best not to highlight the fact Milena was confused, he figured.

The crowd, a dozen strong, grew restless and chanted. "Push him in, tie him up. Push him in, tie him up."

The barn door opened wider and a decorated horse pranced in. An equestrian was standing atop the horse and waving a burlap bag like a banner. Swaeger left the barn to return the cup to the farmhouse. He did not return.

Ned watched Swaeger go and wished he could leave the barn then, but he stayed on. The trapeze artist and tightrope walker stepped forward. "Unbind him," Milena commanded.

Now Deighton was free except his hands were tied together, his mouth was gagged and his eyes were blindfolded. Deighton was so cramped he was unable to move. The equestrian leapt from his horse and presented the burlap bag to the triplets. (Ned gulped as he realized the prior burlap sacks truly were stuffed with people! He started to shake.) The crowd was swaying back and forth and clapping their hands as they continued their chant, "Push him in, tie him up. Push him in, tie him up."

The clown in the yellow tweed jacket coaxed his pet Peruvian Python from her cage and then stepped forward. He put the long snake around his neck and then extended his arms. The crowd quieted as the snake slowly stretched out over the arms of his jacket. Once the snake had stretched its full length, the clown raised his arms and gave a piercing screech. Most clapped and stamped their feet. Four clowns turned in circles, in jarring motions, measured to the beat. As Ned considered this strange congregation, he found its attention turning in his direction.

Milena nodded to Rouben and Ned. They stepped forward and took the burlap bag. The shaking Ned took his cue from Rouben. They opened the bag wide and held it toward Deighton. Then Bogdan lifted Deighton over his head. The crowd went wild as Bogdan stuffed Deighton headfirst into the raised burlap bag. Rouben and Ned each pulled a cord clinching the bag shut. Then Bogdan lifted the bagged Deighton over his head with a flourish. He turned in a circle as Rouben and Ned backed away. The crowd roared. The trapeze artist and tightrope walker came back into sight, pulling a wheel barrel. Bogdan put the bagged Deighton atop the wheel barrel and pushed it out of the barn. Then he turned and waited for the triplets to lead the parade.

As the procession passed the farmhouse, Ned skipped inside and into the loo and waited there until the noise abated. Then he ran to his room.

The parade took a winding route. The initial enthusiasm of the crowd waned. The woman, who tossed flowers and pig offal, emptied her basket. The man with the Peruvian Python lowered his arms and proceeded with the snake hanging over his neck. The clowns turning in circles now marched straight ahead. The clapping petered out. The crowd continued to follow Bogdan, who pushed the wheel barrel with the sacked Deighton. The beaming and untiring Bogdan followed the triplets.

The triplets had not planned. As they led the parade, the triplets walked in a huddle, debating their destination. (Darryl generally took care of such details, but the triplets assumed he was still sulking.) After leading the procession on what seemed like an overly long walk, the triplets decided to return to where the last Spectacle had taken place, the one interrupted by that nosey Carmella character. As the destination became clear, the crowd's excitement returned.

That same morning, Darryl stepped off a plane and onto a jet bridge. He was one of many in a stream of passengers heading inside New York's JFK Airport.

Jack Rodstrum spent a sleepless night after Mitch Deighton failed to return from his visit to Lady Carmella. Deighton had phoned to say he was heading to her residence. At mid-morning, Rodstrum drove to Lady Carmella's residence. He walked around the premises. The house appeared to be empty, and a window was left open. He saw a parked car about a block away, and wondered if it was Deighton's rental car.

Rodstrum decided on a walk to the nearby pond, hoping to unwind and perhaps think more clearly. As he walked, he heard the sound of a boisterous crowd. He froze in his steps. He ran off the road and into the brush. He wormed his way on the ground about fifty paces until he reached the front of a large boulder. He peeked around it to find the circus troupe, all decked out in colorful attire. They all wore hats. He was wishing he had a hat on this bright sunny day. Then only about a hundred paces from the boulder, the troupe stopped and dumped a sack from a wheel barrel and kicked it into the ditch. This was a burlap sack spectacle, like the ones he received complaints about when he was a Police Inspector. He muttered "That best not be Deighton." Then a cold shudder ran down his spine.

Chapter 20. Circus Scatters

Jack Rodstrum ran back to Carmella's house. From a concealed vantage point, he surveyed the scene. Nothing looked amiss. Returning to his car, Rodstrum grabbed his phone and called the police. He waited, keeping his head down.

A quarter hour passed in silence. He collected his thoughts so he could explain himself more clearly. Twelve minutes later, he heard motor cars. He looked out and saw the tail end of three police vehicles. Rodstrum jumped from his car and ran, hoping he was wrong about what was in the burlap sack.

Another police vehicle came from behind. He pointed toward the crowd, already beginning to disperse. Officers from the front vehicles were beginning to step onto the scene. He requested an ambulance but didn't see one coming. Should he make a second call to 999? "Work with me people," he grimaced.

The crowd disappeared by the time Rodstrum reached the ditch. The lumpy, burlap sack remained still. "I think Deighton is in that sack," he gasped. An officer sliced the sack's cord with a pocket knife while Rodstrum held his breath. It was Deighton. Rodstrum felt sick. An ambulance was approaching. An officer removed the gag and blindfold, better revealing Deighton's bloodied face. Rodstrum closed his eyes in prayer. The ambulance pulled up and parked. Deighton was still alive. Rodstrum understood no more than that, as the ambulance pulled away with Deighton.

A frantic bunch arrived at the farmhouse. At first, the mood was one of relief they escaped the police. "I counted six of them," exclaimed a clown.

"They were coming right for us like they knew we were there," wailed a trapeze artist.

"Do you think they installed cameras, you know, A.I., since that Carmella lady's complaint?" wondered the contortionist.

Bogdan silently sat on the couch and looked at his shoes. He clenched his fists and breathed, "The damned burlap bag."

"Where is the Police Inspector now?" demanded Karolina.

"Don't tell me he is still in the ditch," muttered Rouben.

The crowd swapped recriminations about the bagged Deighton. Panic struck. The trapeze artist loudly accused the triplets of recklessness. The triplets stood on the staircase, silently aloof, as they looked upon the scene. The contortionist wailed, "Where is Darryl?" But Darryl was not to be found, and Swaeger was not at the piano.

Irked by Ned's shakiness in opening the burlap sack that morning, Rouben looked for Ned. He recalled Ned had fallen back on the route from the barn. He wondered if Ned called the police. He went to Ned's room. When his knock went unanswered, Rouben opened the door. The room was sparse, though the closet held a dozen archer costumes. The bureau was next to empty. With Ned, that didn't prove much. Rouben collected orders for the troupe's quarterly supply runs, and he knew Ned did not order much in the way of material goods.

Downstairs, Rouben could hear pandemonium breaking out. The triplets failed to show any leadership. The troupe was used to working in concert. With no direction, each was left to wonder whether to run or hide or be ready to fight. Stepping into the void, Helga rang the dinner bell to get their attention. She parked a tray of dixie cups and was filling the cups from a jug. While pouring, she explained this milkshake was "fortified with vitamins and electrolytes to keep you strong."

She emptied a cup in one swallow. "Not bad tasting," she opined. Helga crumpled her paper cup and surreptitiously stuffed it in her pocket while placing another crumpled cup, one emptied of the milkshake, into the bin.

As she backed out of the living room, Helga hollered, "I'll leave the tray and anyone, who wants to fortify themselves, is welcome to take a cup." Recovering from their shortness of breath after fleeing the police, many drank the milkshake that would leave them groggy and hallucinating within the hour.

Her task completed, Helga hung her apron on a peg as she went out the back door. Heading toward the rear vegetable garden, she grabbed a garden hoe from the root shed. The hoe was for self-defense as much as subterfuge, but no one seemed to notice her. At the edge of the garden, she raised a mountain bike from under the leaves. Helga pedaled through the wooded paths and didn't look back.

In the farmhouse, the crowd was fixated on the seated Bogdan. He looked like he was trying to mute the hiccups as he arched his back, then he slowly keeled forward. His face color was gray stone. Alina commandeered an able-bodied trio to carry him to his bed. After dumping Bogdan on his bed, the trio fled.

Alone with Bogdan, the triplets gathered his sheets and moved him toward his closet. Staska commented how unfortunate it was so few survive a heart attack of such magnitude. Placing Bogdan in a hidden recess beyond a fake closet wall, the triplets ensured Bogdan would die of this heart attack. Milena commented Bogdan would have made a fascinating taxidermy specimen. Her sisters debated the price Bogdan's body might fetch. That was the last conversation Bogdan heard.

After the ambulance pulled away, Rodstrum pulled himself together and gathered the reporting police around him. Most knew him and had worked with him in the past. He explained how Deighton was investigating the farmhouse when he came across a Consulate's warning that the inhabitants may be a group of hardened criminals, wanted on the Continent. The responding police called for reinforcements.

Rodstrum figured he would sit out the rest of the mission until it seemed everyone had this same idea. Police had not detained even one of the circus crowd for questioning. "We need to catch up with them while they are still in town," Rodstrum shouted and ran toward the farmhouse.

The farmhouse looked deceptively deserted. A knock at the door prompted no response. In a booming voice, one officer shouted, "Open up for police!" A rock hit him on the temple and he staggered back. Police cars lined the drive by now. At Rodstrum's suggestion, the police threw tear gas canisters through farmhouse windows. They could hear people shrieking and cursing inside. After donning gas masks, the police moved in closer. People stumbled out. The police took seven people to the police station. Bogdan remained undetected under the false door inside his bedroom closet. The triplets fled by way of the cellar, where a freezer room was linked to an underground tunnel.

Ned was standing at the bus stop. He leaned against the bus stop's sign pole and prayed. When he opened his eyes, he was facing Rouben. It was uncanny how that man could appear out of nowhere.

Rouben sneered, "I should've known by your shakes you were up to no good."

"Leave me alone," snarled Ned. Rouben responded with a left hook onto Ned's chin, a knee to his stomach and then he crashed both fists down on his head. Ned breathed. Still bent low, Ned reached out and grabbed Rouben's ankles, toppled him backward and twirled him in a circle before throwing him down. Then Ned ran. (Ned was a fast runner, a track champion in his school days.) He got a good head start, but the incensed Rouben ran after him. Once Rouben had Ned in his sight, he pulled a knife from his boot and let it fly. The knife landed in Ned's left shoulder and penetrated to his armpit. On hearing a bus plodding ever closer, Rouben fled.

Emboldened by fear, Ned removed the knife, retrieved his bag and managed to board the local bus before the blood on his clothes became overly noticeable. In a back seat, he wound a pair of socks around his shoulder and pulled on another t-shirt. At the train station, he purchased two bottles of water and boarded the train. On the train journey, Ned was uncomfortable but gritted his teeth and managed to change trains in London. On the sleeper car to Edinburgh, Ned lost so much blood that he lost consciousness.

Karolina escaped the tear gas but in so doing, left herself exposed to the many police officers waiting on the perimeter of the farm. The police called in Social Services to take charge of this apparent minor. Late that afternoon, Karolina was handed over to Social Services as an unsupervised child. It was late in the day and she was uncooperative so the best that could be done was to find her a bed for the evening and renew their efforts with her in the morning. At almost eight o'clock, a van pulled up to a nondescript house. Karolina climbed out and was welcomed inside. After the required formalities, she was shown her bed.

Later that evening, Karolina left her bed. The foster parents were not wealthy, but she did find meager change to pocket. Also unfortunate, the foster home was located far from town and had no working vehicle, so Karolina walked.

Congratulating herself on having worn sensible shoes that day, she took a wooded path and eventually spotted a bus stop on the parallel road. She caught the early morning bus. As she observed her surroundings, she mused on this hiccup in her life's trajectory. Minutes later, Karolina was dead when her bus was struck by a lorry. The newspapers reported a drunken lorry driver, moving at a substantial speed, failed to heed a stop sign and plowed into the side of a local bus, leaving a number of passengers dead and more injured. The road was closed for the rest of the day.

Chapter 21. Deighton in Hospital

The next morning, Mitch Deighton awoke to find himself in a white room on a white bed. Jack Rodstrum sat next to the bed and chuckled at Deighton's bewildered expression. "You made a spectacle of yourself and survived it," he quipped. Just then, a nurse bustled in and informed Rodstrum that visitor hours did not start for another hour.

"It's this newfangled watch, hard to tell the time on its face," muttered Rodstrum as he left.

"How are we feeling today Mr. Deighton," the nurse cooed. He gave her a faint grin and promptly fell asleep.

Jack Rodstrum stopped at his favorite pastry shop. The owner Joey bounded over, all questions about that inspector asking for him earlier in the week. Rodstrum assured him everything worked out.

"A Gloucester tart and cuppa for you," Joey declared officiously.

"You know it. And I'll be joining those two gents," pointed Rodstrum. At a corner booth, two police cronies bent over their well-earned tea, having just come off the night shift. Rodstrum sauntered over to their booth.

Gazing down at them, he demanded, "What are you two still doing up?"

"Rodstrum!" declared Pete Privitt, the stockier of the two. Sam Wiley moved in to make room for Rodstrum to join them.

"We heard all about your heroics yesterday," declared Wiley.

"Good on you," approved Privitt.

"Any news on the circus troupe members they took in yesterday?" asked Rodstrum.
"A bunch of addicts," announced Wiley. Rodstrum raised an eyebrow.

"A waste of police time, is what it was," continued Wiley. Rodstrum looked at Privitt.

Privitt sighed. "They provided us with a good deal of incriminating testimony, supported most of the worst rumors. But when all was said and done, six of the seven tested positive for oddball hallucinogens." He shook his head.

"That leaves one unimpaired witness," counted Rodstrum. Privitt and Wiley looked at each other.

Wiley leaned in. In a hushed manner, he explained, "The Superintendent was saying the witnesses should not have been questioned without her direct approval. Cathcart was in fine form over that. We may find he got the sack tomorrow."

"Odd even for her," added Privitt.

Rodstrum looked into his tea and opined, "Seems like yesterday raised more questions than we got answers."

"We did get answers, just none from those seven brought in yesterday," grinned Wiley. He thumped his finger on the table. "We found what became of Ned Carraway, you remember him?"

Ned survived Rouben's knife. After being lifted unconscious from the train and rushed to hospital, he received life-saving medical treatment that killed his hope of escape. Ned was recognized as the missing Father Ned from Essex Parish.

In the midst of a pedophilia scandal, Father Ned disappeared. Multiple parishioners filed charges of child sexual abuse and statutory rape. In the ensuing years, additional charges, spotlighting the unexplained deaths of three troubled youths, arose at his former parish in Somerset. Now the authorities were holding Ned Carraway on the four-year old warrant. To his astonishment, Ned was offered a plea bargain in return for information on human trafficking and corpse desecration! Alas, Ned knew nothing.

Rodstrum returned to hospital later that morning. Deighton was still sleeping when the hospital's director, Troward Nevels, stepped into his room. He looked at Rodstrum, who was seated by the bed, and quietly asked, "Is that the copper?"

"That is Police Inspector Deighton," Rodstrum replied in an amused tone. Rodstrum paused. The silence was deafening. Rodstrum inquired, "Who are you?"

Nevels bridled, then asserted, "I am Director Nevels, the Hospital Director."

"Inspector Rodstrum," replied Rodstrum.

Nevels felt conspicuous. He cleared his throat and attempted to explain himself. "My Assistant Director spoke with Inspector Deighton just this week when he was checking on Lady Carmella. I was a bit curious to hear he was admitted himself now. I'm sure it's unrelated."

"But it is related," corrected Rodstrum. Sensing Nevels was agitated to hear this, he added, "They're both victims of that troupe in the farmhouse at the end of Allen Road."

"Oh my," Nevels gushed, as he bit his lip. Nevels covered his mouth with his fist and stared at his knuckles.

"You know something about the troupe in the farmhouse?" Rodstrum dryly inquired.

"No," responded Nevels. It was a bit too emphatic of a reply, he realized as Rodstrum tilted his head.

"Of course, I know what has been in the papers," Nevels backtracked.

As he leaned toward Nevels, Rodstrum slowly enunciated, "What else do you know?"

Nevels arched his back and set his face in a grimace; he looked as though he was about to make a vicious retort. Then, as if short of breath, Nevels mumbled, "I know nothing more about the troupe. I know a bit about the farmhouse." Nevels looked desperate, like he knew he should say nothing but so much wanted to finally say something. Nevels shut the door to Deighton's room and walked over to Rodstrum. He leaned back against the window.

"Maybe I don't know anything you don't already know," Nevels whispered quickly.

"Try me," Rodstrum demanded.

Nevels leaned closer. "I only know this. It was property owned by an old lady, the ward of a local solicitor. It was property worth much more than the asking price and that was because...it seemed like it was because a philanthropy group, some type of racial justice advocates, inquired about purchasing the farmhouse for a handsome price. Their idea was to teach tolerance of immigrants, especially Somali immigrants, as I recall. It was about six months before that...there had been a slew of horrific crimes, racially motivated, targeting an extended Black family, from here in the UK, who were traveling on holiday. Their injuries were treated at this hospital. Somehow those crimes were hushed up, not a word made it into the papers. But months later, this philanthropic group wanted to purchase the farmhouse; that created an uproar in the more bigoted parts of the community. The circus troupe was all white. Their accents were bothersome, but the head man assured people, saying they were working on their English language skills and wanted to merit the community's acceptance. It was the circus troupe or the philanthropic bunch. The circus troupe attracted supporters from people who knew nothing more about them than their skin color. The solicitor, Reed Crimson, sold it for a sorry price and was found dead soon after the purchase was recorded. That's all I know." Nevels stood and quickly crossed the room; he opened the door just enough to fit through the opening and left.

A minute later, Deighton opened his eyes and looked at Rodstrum. "Quite an earful," he asserted.

While Rodstrum was bringing Deighton up to date and swapping ideas about what to do next, a similar conversation was happening in New York City.

In a fourth floor room at the Sourgate Hotel, Darryl sat on a stuffed couch and held his brandy glass tightly. The former clown Otto had news, bad news. Otto related Bogdan's massive heart attack, Swaeger's absence, the police interrupting the Spectacle to find the inspector's body in the burlap bag, and the police raid on the farmhouse. Otto guzzled his bottled water and looked at Darryl. "No, it's not good news but it is news you should know."

Darryl snapped into character and with a charming grin, he tilted his head and lightly said, "But of course. Thank you so much."

Otto was exasperated. "I'm telling you because I think you are the person best suited to extinguish these fires." After a pause, Otto ventured, "I am at your service, if you want me."

Leaning forward and looking into Otto's eyes, Darryl intoned, "Can you find out who the police took and what they said, and tell me the current posture of each troupe member?" Otto nodded.

"Tell me what is happening with our Lady Carmella now," added Darryl. Otto grinned.

Darryl put down his glass and declared, "Good. We'll talk soon." Then Darryl rose and let himself out the door.

It was just before dawn. Otto felt relieved to have survived the ordeal. He feared Darryl but remained confident in his decision to contact him. Besides, Darryl was not a person from whom one could hide.

Chapter 22. Taking Stock

After a quick walk about the bowels of Madison Square Garden, Darryl stepped back into the outdoors. He soon stopped in a delicatessen for coffee but could not think with all the noise and bustle. Without emptying his cup, he left for the crisp outdoors and crossed over to Fifth Avenue. Darryl walked briskly amongst the throng of hurried people. The exercise helped clear his head. Almost an hour later, he paused at the Public Library flanked by two large, marble lions. Darryl climbed the library's steps and found it wouldn't open until nine o'clock. Turning back he saw a large cathedral. He crossed the street and slowly entered. This was the solace he was seeking. Darryl slowly walked along the side walls. His gaze found the Lady of Czestochowa, surely a favorable omen from happier days. Stopping at a quiet side altar, Darryl knelt in silence.

Darryl's mind raced through a list of considerations. In retrospect, there was the troupe. Otto would have a report on each of them today. There was the farmhouse with the underground laboratories and incriminating evidence strewn throughout the living quarters. The latter was sloppiness and he regretted it. There was the police inspector who was kidnapped and stuffed in a sack; all very unfortunate. There was the long list of allegations and notoriety recorded on the Continent. Otto erased much of it, but no doubt pen and ink write-ups existed in places. And not to be underestimated was the persistence of that Carmella lady, who seemed convinced she had witnessed child abuse. Prospectively, he needed a new base. Perhaps he needed a new scheme. He needed to decide whether to let Otto ride or dispense with him. Perhaps he would need to change his look.

In the next hours, Darryl determined his first order of business was to address the remnants of his old life. An outline of options and chronologies shimmered in his mind. At two o'clock, he departed from the cathedral. He found himself on Lexington and Fifty-Second Street and stopped for a late lunch. Thinking the sugar rush might do him good, he had cheesecake for dessert. He felt optimistic.

Late in the afternoon, Darryl met Otto at the John Lennon Memorial in Central Park. They stood at a distance and lingered as if paying their respects to the dead. After a respectable time, Darryl strode away. Otto soon caught up with him and pleaded, "Slow down so I can talk without gasping for air!" Darryl slowed a bit.

Otto hugged himself and raised his eyes; he shook his head and muttered, "Where to begin?" He told Darryl of Karolina's death and then of Ned's arrest. He told of Helga's apparent escape, as she was nowhere to be found. He told of Swaeger's passage on a cruise ship, from Southampton, scheduled to land in Boston next week. The triplets' whereabouts remained unknown. The police took in seven troupe members, but Rouben somehow disappeared prior to being booked. The police obtained statements from the remaining six, who were now being held without bail. These six tested positive for hallucinogens. (Darryl gave a faint smile as he realized dependable Helga followed through on his direction.)

Darryl gave a sharp look and demanded, "And what of the police inspector found in the sack?"

"That police Inspector is looking like he will survive but is still in hospital. He has not given any statement on what happened to him. But I'm sure he will," cautioned Otto.

Otto shook his head and raised his shoulders; his voice became hushed, "Then this gets interesting. Even with a police inspector found bloodied in a sack, local voices are advocating for charges against troupe members to be dismissed, saying it is specious evidence connecting the troupe to the bagged inspector!"

Darryl dryly replied, "Curious."

Otto ignored that comment. He recounted, "And that Carmella lady left hospital in the afternoon but returned at night, diagnosed as suffering from dehydration and exhaustion; she got potassium, iron and glucose via an intravenous drip for twelve hours, and now she is staying with her cousin Nancy at a London flat."

Darryl intoned, "At a flat, you have the address, no?"

Otto snapped, "I'll get it."

They walked on in silence until Otto asked glumly, "So what is next?"

Darryl tilted his head. "I seem to recall more than a few glass houses in that county, perhaps we might lob a few well aimed stones," posited Darryl.

After firmly grasping Otto's arm and leaning toward him, Darryl confided, "This is what I want you to do…"

In his hospital bed, Deighton awoke to find he had slept through lunch. It was now three o'clock. His head was swimming with questions. What were these unreported crimes mentioned by Nevels? What happened to Reed Crimson? Does his ward still live and deserve recompense for her loss? What happened to the other writhing burlap sacks, reported in the past? Was there any follow up at the farmhouse on the cramped compartment in which he spent an overnight? What was the purpose of placing victims in burlap sacks? Is it a scare tactic to keep troupe members in-line? Is it a cult ritual?

Deighton raised his head and gingerly leaned on his elbows. Perhaps a cup of coffee would do him good. He pulled the cord to request assistance. Nobody came. He counted to one hundred. He returned to a horizontal position and closed his eyes.

The questions kept swimming in his head. Where was Lady Carmella now? What happened to Lady Carmella before she was found on her back stoop? If the circus troupe is no longer at the farmhouse, where are they? Did Rodstrum follow up with Cathcart to learn exactly who was questioned and precisely what they said? Was Gregg Armstrong's grandfather still in hospital? Why is the Police Superintendent upset about police questioning the troupe members?

Did Rodstrum say a decomposed human hand was stuck in a vase of flowers?

A nurse's aide stuck her head in the door and chirped, "Be right with you!" But it was a very long time before she returned.

At the farmhouse, the triplets cautiously re-entered the cellar's freezer room, through the same underground tunnel used in their escape from the police. They were so pre-occupied with Bogdan, they fled with only the clothes on their backs. Uncharacteristically disheveled, and tense from the realization of how much they relied on Darryl, the triplets moved silently. Their moment of usurpation and glory had upended them.

Alina motioned for help to pull the nails from a false door leading to a concealed stairway to their laboratory. Staska found a hammer and Milena found a screwdriver. At the top of the stairs, Milena found the laboratory door was locked. Odd, she thought as she withdrew a hairpin to pick the lock. As the door opened, the motion sensor turned on the lights.

Alina went directly to a low drawer beneath a cabinet. She reached into the depths of the drawer and removed a box of disposable plastic gloves; she pulled out all the gloves, uncovering the three cell phones at the bottom of the box. Milena retrieved a multiport charger stuffed at the bottom of a pencil holder, and Alina set the phones to charge. Staska checked the specimen collection drawers only to find them empty. "I don't think this was the police," she whispered, "I think this was Darryl."

When Milena attempted to wash her hands in the sink, they discovered the water was turned off.

"Hold on," Staska whispered and went directly to a stash of water bottles, hidden behind the fire extinguisher.

Milena accepted a bottle and took a long sip. "We need a plan," she sighed.

"We need money," countered Alina.

"Let's get to our room and get clean clothes," urged Staska.

After unlocking three more doors, the triplets entered their ransacked room and surveyed the disarray. Beds were turned over, bureaus were emptied onto the floor, and the contents of the medicine chest were heaped in the tub. The linen closet was empty and a hot water bottle was stuffed into a lampshade. The blinds were drawn but the curtains were open, letting in plenty of light. "Let's see what we've got," suggested Alina.

Starting in separate corners, the triplets scavenged for anything salvageable that might help in their plight.

Flight seemed their best option but to do that, they needed money. Hours later, the triplets decided to target Carmella.

Week Two

Chapter 23. Pondering Puddles

Jack Rodstrum sat in his car. The vision of the stiff human hand, reaching out amongst the red roses in the blue vase, was unnerving him. Stepping out of his car and into a puddle, he cursed his squeamishness. You're getting too old for this, he thought.

A voice shouted through the window, "Is that you Rodstrum?"

Rodstrum waved and hollered, "Hiya. Got a minute?" Cathcart reached the top of the stoop before Rodstrum could say anymore. In minutes, they were seated at his kitchen table. Both were more than glad to have someone to talk to about this circus troupe. Each had much to tell. Cathcart's wife brought beer and nuts; then tea and sandwiches, then brandy and cake. Still, they talked on.

In the end, both agreed something wasn't right with the police work surrounding the circus troupe. With Nevels' talk of racist criminal activity that was hushed up…they turned to the subject. It was well known certain police participated in racist activities. Just two years earlier, Cathcart investigated a constable's complaint about graffiti scrawled in the loo. He leaned in close to share the particulars.

"Jones, a white male, with two years on the force, bragged on social media about penning, 'Beware non-white rape gangs' in the ladies'. Owens, a black female, with one year on the force, added, 'Beware white rape gangs too.' So I issued a written admonishment to Jones for entering the ladies and defacing police property and an oral admonishment to Owens for defacing police property. Two days later, Owens got the boot, removed for conduct unbecoming a constable, but Jones got nothing further. I recall her church in Brimmerston protested the double standard to no avail. As the investigating officer, I told the brass her discharge was outrageous, but the only response I got was 'So noted.' Soon after, I was assigned to the night shift," finished Cathcart.

Rodstrum chuckled, "I was wondering how a rising star like you came to be on the night shift. Who made the call about Owens?"

Cathcart shook his head, "I've told you all I know."

Rodstrum ventured, "Seems like standards have slid in all sorts of places over the last six years or so. Used to be racism was frowned upon in public. I'm not a joiner, but it feels like civic groups aren't looking to diversify their membership like they once did."

Neither knew anything yet to report to higher ups or even to the press. It was just a series of incidents that didn't make sense, a hospital director's discrete gossip and a seemingly criminal lot wasn't being treated according to protocols. They needed a plan to get better answers.

Darryl walked briskly around the Bronx Botanical Gardens. He was thinking about his exposure from his time in Huffinfield. He could count on one hand the Huffinfield locals who had met him. And one of them was dead. The other four held fairly prestigious posts in the community. He had evidence of these four taking actions to cover up horrendous criminal activity. Perhaps he should dredge up old evidence from his computer banks and drop bits of it in the right person's lap. Perhaps he might even implicate Carmella.

Police would have access to the farmhouse. As of today, Rouben had cleared it of damning evidence. Darryl had full confidence in Rouben's abilities to clear it well. Drugs may remain in the kitchen; he wasn't sure Rouben would recognize them all. Fingerprints should be gone by now. He didn't know what had become of Bogdan. He needed to locate the triplets. Darryl would check with Otto on the status of the police records.

Carmella was recuperating at Nancy's flat in London. It had rained steadily since she arrived. She still had trouble sleeping, but the poisonous tea seemed to have left no permanent injury. Nancy was at work, leaving Carmella with hours to herself. She truly believed that circus troupe, or whatever they were, tried to kill her. She had no idea why. Remembering the blood gushing from the girl's cheek, and the older woman struggling to restrain the shrieking girl, and the dark glee of the observers…she shuddered.

Carmella spent hours on Nancy's exercise bike, trying to come to grips with her ordeal. She considered her visit to the farmhouse. She pondered the cast of characters: Darryl, dressed in black, biting into one of her cookies; the older man with a matching bow tie and cummerbund; the redheaded triplets in matching dresses; the pianist running her fingers over the keys without making a sound; and the little girl playing jacks. Other scenes floated in her mind and puzzled her. Did that little girl stuff jacks into her ears? Did the triplets twitter at her confusion? Did Darryl beam at her the whole time? Or did she imagine these scenes?

She did not imagine the open window at her home or the man who suggested they turn back from her house. Carmella winced at the thought of the police inspector being accosted in her rear garden and put in a burlap sack. Had she inadvertently done something to thwart this circus troupe? Did they want her real estate? She had been in Huffinfield almost a year without hearing a word about them. She hoped the police would obtain answers, if not for her, then for the bagged and bloodied Inspector.

Carmella heard a loud bang on the door. She jumped off the exercise bicycle and peered out the peephole but saw nobody. Upon opening the door, she spotted a letter in a puddle at the bottom of the stairs. Carmella picked up a damp letter tied to a wet rock. She took a photo of it. The envelope had her name on it. Carmella opened the letter and read:

We know you helped Solicitor Reed Crimson sell his ward's Huffinfield property at a loss. We know the sale obstructed a philanthropic organization's purchase at a much higher price. You pay 500,000 pounds Sterling or we report you to police and press. Electronic transfer to BeverlyHilltops@starstwinkle.com by tomorrow noon.

Carmella dialed Inspector Deighton's number and left a long message.

From a nearby sidewalk, the anxious triplets watched Camella pick up their letter.

From his third floor vantage point, Rouben watched Carmella open the door and pick up what looked like a rock and white paper and take them both inside. Within the next minute, Rouben texted, "Triplets located."

Chapter 24. Slithering Nightmares

On a bright morning, Darryl was skating on a large pond. In the far distance, he watched an ice fisherman pull in an empty line. As he pulled at his balaclava, the ice shattered under his feet so he jumped to firmer ground. But two sets of hands were on his shoulders pushing his face into the icy water through the hole in the ice!

Darryl awoke with a start. He rapidly read the flashcards in his mind. *If Otto could find him, others could find him. They could find Otto. Darryl needed to reach Swaeger before any of them. The triplets must be located. Would Rouben remain loyal? What of the jailed Ned? What confirmation that the six jailbirds are dead? Where was Helga? Given the number of corpses and the bloodied police inspector, the best approach with Carmella may be a campaign to discredit her.* By then, Darryl had packed his bag. He stepped out of his hotel at midnight.

It was a glorious day in April. Carmella was wearing a matching dress and Easter bonnet. She entered the church and felt thankful to be alive. She found her pew and knelt to pray. When she opened her eyes, she found herself surrounded by the circus troupe and it felt like something was on her head. In her shadow, she saw a bird, perched atop her hat. The crowd roared as the bird's beak moved toward her face and pecked out her eye!

Carmella sat up in bed and put her hands over her eyes. She turned on a night light to confirm she was alone. Such silly dreams rankled her. She sat for a bit and decided to regroup with a cup of tea. She put on her robe and found her way to Nancy's kitchen. She had just put on the kettle when Nancy joined her.

"Must have been more interesting dreams?" posed Nancy as she rummaged around a cabinet to find a package of ginger wafers.

Carmella shrugged. "I don't know what to say for myself," she confided, "This time they surrounded me in church, and a bird atop my Easter bonnet stretched down and pecked out my eye."

"That would wake me," grinned Nancy as she put three wafers on each plate. She considered, "At least they didn't chase you this time."

"If I see a doctor about this, they'll say I'm crazy," moaned Carmella.

"You could just say you need help to sleep," suggested Nancy.

They both knew Carmella would not be consulting a doctor. Soon, the tea was brewed and they both came down with a serious case of the giggles. Nancy quipped, "Perhaps you could write a comic strip about these nighttime visions? A comic book even…"

Carmella shook her head and insisted, "No, nothing less than a full blown novel will do."

Nancy's phone played a jig, announcing a text message. "You don't think it's the troupe at this hour," Nancy gushed. They stopped laughing.

"Oh, go see about it," cried Carmella impatiently.

Nancy reached for her phone. "It's from Gregg Armstrong, that lovely man whose grandfather is in hospital," she reported.

Carmella was relieved but agitated about fearing it might be that circus troupe. She considered, "It's awfully late. Is everything OK with his grandfather?"

Nancy put on her eye glasses and opened the text. "He writes 'the local newspaper suggests the circus troupe was involved with local racist elements.' He writes 'now deceased Solicitor Reed Crimson sold the Allen Road property to the troupe for much less than its estimated value."

Nancy paused, looked up from her phone and looked at Carmella. Then she continued. "He writes you are 'reported to have had prior business with that solicitor.' He writes, 'Thought you should know."

Carmella made a face, and exclaimed, "Who?"

Carmella didn't mention the photo to Nancy until another late night's cup of tea. Carmella drew the photo from her robe pocket and placed it on the table.

Nancy craned her neck as she asked, "What have you got there?"

"Reed Crimson," grimaced Carmella.

Nancy slid the photo closer to get a better look. Carmella and Crimson were just about cheek to cheek and he had his arm around her shoulder. With a raised eyebrow, Nancy inquired, "What? When? Where?"

Carmella shook her head and related, "As best I can recall, this was at a charity event in London. It was noisy and he was likely saying, pleased to meet you or some such, just in passing. Put with the letter, I'm sure they want to read more into it."

Nancy slowly nodded, "I certainly was adding more to it. So this came with the letter?

Carmella blushed, "I know I'm being foolish but you're the first I've told. This man died under suspicious circumstances, as I recall. I had nothing to do with him. But are they trying to set me up? Hopefully, it's my imagination."

"You need to tell Inspector Deighton," declared Nancy.

Carmella rubbed her shoulders and shook her head. "I don't know," she gulped.

Nancy spoke sharply. "Look at me. Whatever else you do, you are not wiring money to those people. This is ludicrous. Even if the photo found its way into The Times, it wouldn't be the end of the world."

Darryl moved fast upon discovering the triplets, sparing Carmella any chance of embarrassment.

Within a day of being taken by ambulance, the triplets were dead. The autopsy revealed they were poisoned with Novichok nerve agents, used by the Russian military. It was a very painful death, though the triplets were spared the knowledge that their extortion plot failed. Darryl was perplexed to learn the triplets died so quickly. Otto relayed an inquiry to Rouben, who promised a prompt report.

Hours later, Darryl arrived at the Staten Island Ferry landing to find Otto waiting on a nearby bench. Otto reported the triplets did not enter hospital until a full eight hours after their transport by ambulance. Darryl was less than pleased. He turned to Otto and through gritted teeth, advised, "Tell Rouben, I want him to confirm, go to the morgue and confirm three corpses belong to the triplets."

Jack Rodstrum glanced through Huffinfield's local newspaper, the Daily Slip. On the back page, the weather report was gray and his horoscope was dull. Turning the paper over, he had to blink. In the lower right corner, the headline read, "Local Lady Rids Shire of Continental Criminals." After seating himself at the breakfast table, Rodstrum involuntarily held his breathe as he read on. This scoop did not name a journalist. The police had no comment. He needed to tell Deighton none of this came through official channels.

Darryl's list for closing the farmhouse operation seemed to be dwindling until he read the Daily Slip's article, "Local Lady Rids Shire of Continental Criminals." What caught his eye was the mention of an extortion letter threatening publicity of her connections to the late, local solicitor Reed Crimson. Crimson finagled the troupe's purchase of the farmhouse. Why was Crimson being dredged up? If the triplets were responsible, it was too late to ask them now.

Darryl pondered if the news article might be of use. If he could tarnish Carmella's reputation, her allegations against the farmhouse may not gain so much traction. Darryl knew the troupe's purchase of the farmhouse was, in part, facilitated by the seller's preference not to sell to a charitable group seeking to aide Somali immigrants. How could he put this together to disparage Carmella?

Sitting in his office, Hospital Director Nevels read the news article, "Local Lady Rids Shire of Continental Criminals." He blanched and choked on his tea, getting the news page soggy and stained. Might this lead to questions about how the farmhouse came to be sold to that criminal element? Nevels raged at having signed Crimson's stack of documents. (Solicitor Crimson had come to him for a favor. He was sitting in Nevels' office and looking straight at him, implying he knew the hospital provided medical treatment to the black Brits "injured" on their holiday through the shire. Nevels felt vulnerable and signed a stack of Crimson's documents.) He was unhappy to see the deceased solicitor's name in a front page story about the people who purchased the farmhouse. Nevels reassured himself it was unlikely the story would go further. It would be best to remain calm, he thought.

Nancy was at work when she received the text from Gregg. "First page story this morning in the Daily Slip, 'Local Lady Rids Shire of Continental Criminals.' Check it out." At lunch time, she found the news story and sent it to Carmella with a note, "I want to hear all about this tonight!"

Carmella quickly read the news article and then slowly re-read it. It was accurate as far as she knew. No one had consulted her about the story. She wondered that it was attributed to no journalist. She left another voice mail message for Inspector Deighton. Carmella couldn't shake the nagging sensation the article may be part of an entrapment strategy. She did not transfer money to Beverly Hilltops.

Gregg received a phone call from Nancy. She told how Carmella received an extortion letter with a suggestive photo. Identical triplets were found writhing in pain at a tea shop, just a few blocks from her flat. Nancy asked if he thought it was too crazy to think there may be a connection between the letter and the triplets and the farmhouse.

Gregg responded, "I'm beginning to think nothing is too crazy anymore."

Deighton remained in hospital but was getting stronger. The doctors decreased his medications, enabling him to be awake more often. In checking his voicemail, he had three messages from Lady Carmella. A message from yesterday told of her receipt of an extortion letter. Today's two messages spoke of a photo of Reed Crimson being included with the letter and then of identical, female triplets succumbing to poison at a shop near Nancy's flat. Lady Carmella questioned if these were the same triplets from the farmhouse. Deighton gave a full update to Rodstrum.

Rodstrum met with Kevin Cathcart. He told him of the triplet connection and how the Consulate's package, on the Continental criminals, had been in the box of records left on Deighton's desk. Cathcart agreed to make an effort to locate the box. Cathcart told him per order of the Superintendent, the jailed troupe members were to be released. The administrative staffer, charged to relay the message to the jail, said all six troupe members succumbed to heart failure during the night. It was unclear if it was foul play, suicide or a bizarre coincidence. (Actually, Darryl ordered them shot with a gun that fired vaporized poison, which killed almost instantly upon being inhaled.)

Cathcart told Rodstrum how the Superintendent instructed all paper records of the troupe members' interrogations be destroyed, as it was already scanned into electronic record banks. All highly irregular, to say the least. They recalled how Deighton couldn't find any electronic records of the earlier investigations into the farmhouse troupe; they recounted his ordeal to find the box of paper records. They wondered if any record of the troupe's testimony and jailtime would exist in a month.

The next morning, the Daily Slip ran another front page story on Carmella, but this time, the news was not flattering. The article implied bigotry brought the criminals to the farmhouse, bigotry directly aided by Lady Carmella. The news recounted that Kingston Dove, a philanthropic foundation, assisting Somali immigrants, sought to purchase the farmhouse and its adjoining farmland. While those talks were ongoing, the land was quietly sold to the so-called circus troupe for a price, far less than the fair market value. Solicitor Reed Crimson handled the purchase of the farmhouse, property of his ward. Whether Solicitor Crimson assisted Lady Carmella in her desire to retire to a white enclave was uncertain. What was certain is Solicitor Crimson associated with civic organizations known to espouse slogans such as "It's OK to be White," even after rumors that one such organization applauded vicious race crimes against Black Brits.

Darryl was pleased the Daily Slip printed his anonymous letter as front page news.

Gregg dutifully alerted Nancy to the latest news though he made no comment on it. Nancy forwarded the news article to Carmella. At first, Carmella was devastated. Then she was angry. She would investigate this BeverlyHilltops@starstwinkle.com. She was determined to get an update from Inspector Deighton very soon.

Chapter 25. Deighton Gets Up and Goes Down

It was late afternoon and Inspector Mitch Deighton couldn't sleep. He was beside himself with questions. Not until he threatened to walk home, did the nurses let him out of bed. He was wheeled out to the window at the far end of the hall, where Deighton noticed Gregg Armstrong and at once recalled the Chief had assigned him to Reginald Atwater's case.

"Armstrong!" he hollered to the chagrin of his minder, who pushed the wheelchair. Gregg Armstrong bounded over.

"Inspector Deighton here," smiled Deighton, "How is your grandfather doing?"

Gregg looked at Deighton sitting in the wheelchair, covered with bruises and red scratches, with two black eyes, a neck brace, a leg in a cast and a white bandage wound around his head. Gregg's eyes widened as he recognized the police inspector assigned to Lady Carmella's case. "They say my grandfather is getting stronger, and hopefully will get home without much permanent injury," he replied.

Deighton motioned for Gregg to come closer. "It seems your grandfather's predicament and Lady Carmella's may be connected somehow."

Gregg noted the newspaper made that veiled implication. Deighton made a mental note to review the local newspaper. Deighton asked, "Do you think your grandfather might give me a few minutes?"

Gregg hedged, "I'll ask him."

"Much obliged," replied Deighton in as kindly a manner as he could manage. Gregg took his leave and Deighton went back to looking out the window, overlooking the hospital's garden. He heard nothing more and ultimately let the nurse return him to his bed. He had no luck in procuring the local newspaper; he would have to ask Rodstrum. Just after Deighton finished his evening meal, Gregg knocked on this door. He was pushing an empty wheelchair.

"He'll see you," announced Gregg. The nurse's aide bounded into the room and advised that the nurses would need to agree to moving Mr. Deighton anywhere. Almost an hour later, a nurse's aide pushed the wheelchair while Gregg escorted Deighton to his grandfather's room.

Reginald Atwater was lying supine on his bed. "He isn't good sitting yet," explained Gregg.

Atwater opened his eyes and looked at his grandson, who asserted, "I'll be right outside your door." Atwater gave him a faint smile.

Deighton started quietly, "Police Inspector Deighton here. Thank you for talking with me, Mr. Atwater."

"I haven't said anything yet," retorted Atwater.

Deighton nodded and proceeded, "I see somebody got the better of you. I was in a similar predicament just recently. I was bound and gagged and blindfolded, and stuffed into a suitcase overnight before being moved to a burlap sack and kicked into a ditch. What's your story?"

In a much softer voice than before, Atwater explained, "There was a car with a black family who stopped to fill up with petrol. A bookish-looking, black fellow attempted to pay with Euros and the cashier got indignant. The black man returned to the car and got Sterling from his missus. While he was gone, the cashier makes a frantic call saying this Leroy, without proper money, had gone out to his car to get something. When the man returned, the mechanics had come from the garage, each one grasping a decent length of metal pipe. One gritted his teeth and spit, 'the filthy jigs.' I say so they can hear me, 'Just let him go.' When the cashier pointed at him, the men with the pipes converged upon him. I was just in there to buy some smokes. I could see his family in the car. He was almost at the cashier's when he noticed the mechanics closing in. It was pitiful. I told 'em sharp to grow up and let the man pay. Then all hell broke loose."

"A man's gotta do what he's gotta do," intoned Deighton.

"No he doesn't," retorted Atwater.

Deighton tried again, "Are those mechanics the people threatening you?"

"No, they were just a lot of ordinary blokes caught up in the moment. They're not after me." Atwater lapsed into silence.

Deighton asked, "Do you know who is making threats against you?"

Atwater considered, "I've got a good idea. Wealthy types with too much time on their hands. They hear a story and take umbrage their kind isn't getting its due respect. I just didn't want to see it happen all over again. You follow?"

Deighton confessed, "I don't."

Atwater sighed, "Too bad." He closed he eyes as though dismissing Deighton.

Deighton nibbled, "Just one more thing. Do you know anything about hushed up crimes against a black family on holiday a few years back?"

Atwater opened his eyes. He looked hard at Deighton before answering, "There are other people who could tell you better than me."

Atwater closed his eyes and mumbled, "I need to sleep." He listened as Deighton left the room, maneuvering with one foot and pushing toward the door. He listened as his grandson said good night and left the room. Then Atwater opened his eyes wide and swallowed. Perhaps he said too much. His mind replayed the nightmare.

Atwater still had that pickled ear in a jam jar, as presented to him by the Gogglesgunshod Association for his part in the action. At the time, he was caught up in the mass frenzy, clamoring about defense of kin and country. At first he kept the pickled ear on a shelf in his den, as a matter of pride. After months of reflection, he realized he had taken part in despicable crimes. He could no longer bear to look at the ear.

He considered sliding the jar into a dark corner of the church, but he was too afraid.

He couldn't bring himself to discard the ear, but put it at the bottom of a tall, cardboard box full of old papers. He heaped his attic with fiberglass batt insulation, in such abundance that it rose past his knees. He stored the cardboard box amongst those pink rectangles of what looked like candy floss. He placed a few pieces of broken furniture around the box to give it the look of a junk pile. Atwater felt confident nobody would want to poke about the attic around the fiberglass insulation. That stuff makes you itchy.

Mitch Deighton told Jack Rodstrum about Atwater's story. Deighton wrinkled his nose and warranted, "The bits from Atwater and Nevels smack of a singular incident."

"Very well may be," uttered Rodstrum as his stroked his chin.

"As soon as I'm discharged," Deighton asserted, "I want to re-read that Consulate package."

Rodstrum tilted his head and darkly inquired, "Where again is that Consulate package?"

"Still in the box in my office," Deighton responded.

Rodstrum drummed his finger on the arm of his chair. Looking perplexed, he confided, "I had a chat with Cathcart late yesterday. He says your office was emptied and fumigated."

"My office didn't have any pests," protested Deighton.

Rodstrum sighed, "Makes you wonder where that box might have wandered."

Early the next morning, a bowie knife flew through the open window of Reginald Atwater's hospital room, missing Atwater by centimeters. The security guards raced to close the window. Witnesses saw someone hanging onto the lattice work along the hospital's exterior wall. Police had no suspects. Gregg Armstrong arrived mid-morning and criticized the hospital for its lackadaisical security. Hospital Director Nevels suggested Gregg take up his complaints with the police. Gregg sat by his sleeping grandfather and pondered what to do.

By late morning, Gregg phoned Nancy. He told of the knife barely missing his grandfather and Nevel's callous response. He mentioned seeing Inspector Deighton. Nancy asked, "Is Inspector Deighton still at hospital?"

Gregg responded, "I think he must be. He was in a wheelchair and looked bruised and battered, with a neck brace and a cast around his leg. I can't think he wouldn't still be here."

After a pause to take in that description, Nancy suggested, "Why don't you find Inspector Deighton and get his opinion on what happened to your grandfather and how best to respond?"

Gregg responded, "That's the best idea yet." After checking on his sleeping grandfather, the closed window, the guard standing at attention, and the two security guards by the door, Gregg left to find Inspector Deighton.

Nancy shouted, "Carmella, there was an attempt on Mr. Atwater's life this morning!" She related Gregg's description of Inspector Deighton's condition. Unbelievably, she and Carmella assumed he had escaped unscathed. Obviously, they had not thought that through.

Rodstrum stopped at hospital early that afternoon. He wandered into Deighton's room with a newspaper and tea. Deighton was sleeping so Rodstrum went to the visitors' lounge. He spotted Gregg Armstrong and approached him to see how his grandfather was coming along. Atwater was an old man to take such a beating, but he was a tough one.

"Mr. Armstrong," ventured Rodstrum.

Gregg jerked his head up from his paper and spoke. "Inspector Rodstrum! I'm so sorry about Inspector Deighton's sudden turn."

Rodstrum exclaimed, "Sudden turn? Would you fill me in?"

Gregg related, "From what I understand, Inspector Deighton has been listless since late morning. My grandfather was quite peaked by an article in the local paper and wanted to speak with the Inspector. I made inquiries to the nurse's station and learned he was presenting as lethargic."

"Is that so." said Rodstrum, more as a statement than a question. Rodstrum fumbled for his eyeglasses and grasped them in his hand as he strolled back to Deighton's room. Rodstrum read Deighton's chart. For the first time since he was admitted, it included the muscle relaxant, cyclobenzaprine, this morning. He seemed to be on the mend just yesterday. Would this new drug be responsible for Deighton's state? As Rodstrum was turning this around in his mind, a nurse bustled in and told him Deighton wasn't up for visitors.

"Too bad," shrugged Rodstrum. He asked, "Did you administer Inspector Deighton's medications this morning?"

"I did," asserted the nurse.

Rodstrum asked, "Do you know why he was given a muscle relaxant this morning? He doesn't seem to be reacting well to it."

"I just administer what's on the chart," she huffed.

Rodstrum pressed, "Would you know who prescribed it or where I could find who prescribed it."

"Come with me," she hushed. The nurse led him to the nurse's station. "This came in this morning," she whispered as she handed him a typed letter. "And he doesn't even have admitting rights at this hospital, but Director Nevels directed we comply with the letter." Rodstrum read a directive from a Doctor Miles Middleton, prescribing "30 mg. of cyclobenzaprine" for Mitch Deighton.

Rodstrum returned the letter and asked, "What did the treating doctors have to say about it?"

"They've called in sick, all of 'em," whispered the nurse as she shook her head. "Did you ever hear the like of it?"

Ignoring her question, Rodstrum asked, "Will any more of that be administered to Mr. Deighton?"

"Dr. Clemmer is due in later this afternoon and I'll leave that to him," replied the nurse.

Rodstrum thanked her and took his tea back where Gregg was engrossed in his notebook. Rodstrum sat next to him. When Gregg looked up, Rodstrum murmured, "I think he was drugged!" He told him of the letter prescribing thirty milligrams of a muscle relaxant.

Gregg asked, "What's the drug's name?"

"Cyclobenzaprine," responded Rodstrum.

"Spell it please," requested Gregg as he pulled his phone from his pocket.

Rodstrum pulled out his napkin where he had scrawled the name and read aloud, "C-Y-C-L-O-B-E-N-Z-A-P-R-I-N-E."

Gregg consulted Google and reported, "It says here, it is given in doses of five milligrams, ten milligrams, and twenty milligrams, and most take five milligrams." He gulped.

Rodstrum grimaced, "Doctor Clemmer is coming late this afternoon and hopefully, he'll put a stop to this medication."

Rodstrum switched gears and made his pitch. "Looks like Inspector Deighton will be having a long day. Do you think you grandfather might want to talk to me?"

"Let me inquire," sighed Gregg.

Dr. Clemmer didn't arrive. Gregg didn't return. Jack Rodstrum's head was reeling with questions.

Why did this unaffiliated doctor prescribe Deighton's new medication? Was Deighton being blamed for a leak to the press about the circus troupe being possibly Continental criminals? What happened to the box of records on the circus troupe? Why would the troupe members be released from jail when Deighton was in a cast and neck brace? Why would the paper records of the troupe members' testimony be destroyed?

He would seek out Cathcart. Perhaps between the two of them, they could make sense of it.

Chapter 26. Atwater's Attrition

Finally, Gregg Armstrong approached. "Inspector Rodstrum, my grandfather wants to speak to you. I warned him you take notes on napkins."

Rodstrum grinned, "I do keep a note pad in my pocket, but forget to take it out at times." Gregg escorted Rodstrum to Atwater's room. Two security guards were outside the door and another stood at the far side of the room. Gregg explained to Rodstrum that his grandfather wanted to speak with him privately.

When Rodstrum entered, he saw Reginald Atwater was flat on his back in bed. Rodstrum asked, "Can we help you up?"

Atwater gave a wry grin and responded, "These days, I'm best in this position. Thanks."

The interior guard moved to the door and paused. Atwater looked at his grandson and then Gregg moved toward the door, saying, "I'll be right outside your door."

Alone together, Atwater studied Rodstrum. After a minute, he grunted, "Have a seat. I don't recall we've met."

Rodstrum shook his head. "I'm Inspector Rodstrum, Sir. Inspector Deighton asked if I might help him on this case." After a short pause, Rodstrum sat in a chair next to the bed. Looking at Atwater, Rodstrum offered, "If you would prefer me from another angle, just say the word."

Atwater smiled faintly, "That'll do." He stared into Rodstrum's eyes and asked, "In what year did you join the police force?"

"It's been over thirty years now," asserted Rodstrum.

Atwater asked, "You always worked in Huffinfield?"

"Yes Sir," responded Rodstrum.

Atwater closed his eyes and murmured, "You'll be familiar with the local cast of characters then."

In a raspy voice, Atwater continued. "What I'm going to say, I have told no one before. I'm going to tell you, in large part, because I think it's only days or hours until they make good on their threats to kill me. They see me as a traitor, and they need to silence me so others don't have second thoughts after all these years." Rodstrum wanted to ask Atwater to be a bit more specific about who they were, but decided not to interrupt until Atwater finished what he wanted to say.

Atwater began, "It was some years ago, less than eight, more than four. It was a case of crowd mentality gone awry. We didn't have too much to drink. We didn't have any provocation. We were proud of our actions at the time. We did terrible things. It was a sunny day, as I recall." Atwater motioned toward his water glass and Rodstrum reached for it. Atwater held the straw, tipped his head upwards and took a long sip. Rodstrum returned the glass to the table and waited for Atwater to continue.

Atwater closed his eyes. "Somehow, Huffinfield got mention in a tourist brochure, cooing about the Centre's pub and pretty church and quaint footbridges. 'An idyllic country spot at the southern edge of Blinkingshire County,' it read. The shop owners were abuzz about Huffinfield's description as a bastion of true English tradition. Within a year, it turned sour. Sometime in the late spring, I believe it was. It was late afternoon on a weekend and three cars parked, all three full, and the bunch came tumbling out and headed over to Lillie's Pie Shop. They ordered pork pies and drinks, take away. Instead of appreciating the business, Lillie was enraged. I don't know if she was civil, but she made the sale and the group, a family group, headed over to Petunia Park for a picnic. When Lillie's husband, Clive Leeway, returned to the shop, she told him. And then it went like wildfire from there." Atwater lapsed into silence.

Rodstrum wasn't sure if he was still awake. After a long pause, Rodstrum cleared his throat and asked, "What did Lillie tell her husband that took off like wildfire?"

Atwater opened his eyes. "Lillie felt the bunch had made her shop unsanitary so people wouldn't want to purchase her pies. Clive is generally under the impression that England is under siege anyway. Between the two, they gathered a crowd, maybe two dozen, at the village pub where they wailed and carried on. The people on a picnic were black people. Huffinfield doesn't see many of those. People were in a huff about the affront to the sanctity of our English village. Somehow, within minutes, the consensus was these Black Brits had come to push us out of our homes and take over. Nobody was thinking clearly." Atwater shut his eyes and shuddered.

After a long pause, Atwater looked at Rodstrum and sighed, "It was a long time ago. But I'll tell you there were three black men and three black women. The rest were kiddies, maybe eight to ten years old. We found them in the park, just finishing their picnic. We surprised them. The children were thrown on the ground and then stuffed into the three boots. Minerva Cummington was left to keep watch while our crowd carried off the six adults to the pub. I can still hear the women screaming. Paul Foster tied a rope around each woman's neck and then tied them to a radiator. Mildred Pearson took the lead in throwing boiling water at the women. Then Constance Appleton cut off their hair. The three men were pinned to the ground where Dalton Payne methodically punched each of them unconscious. Then Tommy Hill directed how to prop up their bodies so each local man had a turn at them. As that came close to an end, Clive was pulling the roped women into the back room. I didn't go back there because Edgar Ward had me and Harvey West help him 'collect' the small fingers and small toes and one ear from each of the three men. We put our collection in a pile, and Reverend Jake mumbled a prayer over them." Atwater choked back a sob.

They remained in silence for a time. Clearly, Atwater believed what he was saying. Perhaps his old age had muddled memory with daydreams and crime reports. As the minutes passed, Rodstrum wondered if he had been dismissed.

Then a determined Atwater resumed. "The whole lot was taken by ambulance to this very hospital. No police asked questions. No report found its way to the news. We didn't stay especially quiet about it. I'll bet those Black Brits stayed quiet, happy to get away with their lives, if they did get away with their lives. I don't know! Sometime later, the Gogglesgunshod Association held a ceremony heralding our heroic defense of kin and country. With great ceremony, I was awarded a commemorative human ear. You see, these are the ones upset with me for sticking up for that black bloke at the petrol station. They have doctors, solicitors, influential businessmen…They'll get to me."

Atwater closed his eyes and mumbled, "I'm done talking today."

"Perhaps tomorrow," managed the perplexed Rodstrum. The ghastly confession rang true, except something like that would have made the newspapers.

As he rose to leave the shaking man on the bed, Rodstrum breathed, "I'll tell your grandson to come in."

Rodstrum was at the door in a matter of steps. "Your grandfather says he is done for today," he advised, before admonishing, "Keep security alert." Then Rodstrum strode toward Deighton's room, hoping Deighton was still breathing.

Mitch Deighton appeared to be sleeping. His chart didn't show any new medications administered since the morning. Rodstrum bowed his head and sighed, "Deighton, you deserve better." It was early afternoon, but the same nurse from the morning entered the room.

"Dr. Clemmer came early," she stated matter-of-factly.

"Is the doctor still here?" asked Rodstrum.

She nodded. "He's looking into the prescription by Dr. Middleton. Seems like the medicine's dosage was appropriate to an extended-release drug, but Dr. Middleton prescribed this dosage for three times a day, more for an immediate release version. The maximum daily dose for either version is thirty milligrams over the course of twenty-four hours."

After considering her reply, Rodstrum asked, "Has he had an overdose then?"

The nurse looked uncomfortable and replied, "I'm not the one to say. His blood pressure has dropped a bit. I've been instructed to monitor Mr. Deighton for any significant drop in blood pressure."

Rodstrum gulped, "Will he be lucid any time soon, do you think?"

The nurse shook her head. She added, "Dr. Clemmer should be available within the hour."

Jack Rodstrum took a brisk walk around hospital grounds and considered Deighton's predicament. How is it Hospital Director Nevels directed the nurse to administer Dr. Middleton's prescription? If Nevels was complicit in drugging Deighton, it would not do much good to make inquiries to him. He hoped this Dr. Clemmer was on the level. He slowly re-entered hospital and then remembered Assistant Director Minders.

Rodstrum headed toward the administrative offices, hoping to catch up with her before she left for lunch. As he turned the corner, he heard Nevels' voice coming from her office and retreated. He took the stairs to the twelfth floor, still determined Ms. Minders was his best hope.

From a distance, he saw a man standing by Deighton's bed. Rodstrum's heart jumped as his feet flew to Deighton's door. When the doctor looked up, Rodstrum took a step inside and quietly introduced himself, "Rodstrum here. I'm a friend. Is he doing any better than earlier today?"

Dr. Clemmers looked him over. "You are the one who inquired about his medication this morning, are you not?" Rodstrum nodded.

"It was an unfortunate decision and apparently an oversight, but I am hopeful your friend Deighton will pull through. Unfortunate again, his blood pressure has dropped significantly. Does he have a strong constitution?" asked Dr. Clemmers.

"Yes, sir, I think it's fair to say," Rodstrum replied and then blurted out, "Will you be changing the dose on this muscle relaxant?"

Dr. Clemmer shook his head. "I think it's best we discontinue this medication."

Rodstrum exhaled in relief. He hedged, "Is there any more that can be done to keep him safe?"

Dr. Clemmer responded, "I understand your concern. I'm not sure anyone means any intentional harm to your friend. For what it's worth, I will document my opinion for the record that any medication changes need to be approved by his treating doctors."

Dr. Clemmer sensed Rodstrum's unease. He considered how another patient on this hospital floor was receiving death threats from the local community. Dr. Clemmer sighed, "In an abundance of caution, I will order his transfer to the Intensive Care Unit. Given his apparent poor reaction to the cyclobenzaprine and his significant and sudden drop in blood pressure, we can keep a closer eye there that he doesn't go into shock.

Chapter 27. Asking Questions

Returning to the hospital's administrative unit, Jack Rodstrum sought Ms. Minders. He found her alone in her office. Ms. Minders looked at him for a long minute.

"I recognize you, Inspector Rodstrum! You gave a lecture on self-defense at a university program I attended a few years back."

"I hope it was helpful," quipped Rodstrum. Ms. Minders smiled and shrugged.

Rodstrum grinned back. "I was hoping you might give me a minute. I'm looking to get an understanding of a couple of hospital policies. It won't take long."

"You can ask but I may not have your answers," Ms. Minders asserted. More cordially, she beckoned, "Please be seated Inspector."

"Thank you, Ms. Minders." Rodstrum posed his question, "First, I was wondering about hospital policy toward doctors who aren't under contract to practice at this hospital. Would such a doctor be able to treat a patient at this hospital or prescribe medications even?"

She replied. "Generally no. There may be special circumstances where one of our doctors may consult with an outside doctor at the request of a patient. We have a full staff of doctors in most all specialties, even in this small rural hospital. Any consultation of outside experts would be at the behest of the team treating the patient and would generally be pre-approved by the administration." Ms. Minders looked at him expectantly.

Rodstrum looked up. "Yes, thank you. And just one more question. When patients are transported to this hospital by ambulance, are records kept of any treatment administered here?"

"Yes and yes," replied Ms. Minders.

"For how long does the hospital keep those records?" asked Rodstrum.

"That's a third question! We keep the records for fifteen years before archiving them, permitting their retrieval even after that." Ms. Minders tilted her head, "What's this all about?"

"Thank you Ms. Minders," grinned Rodstrum as he rose from his chair. "Just connecting the dots, that's all."

Back at his favorite pastry shop, Rodstrum pulled out his laptop and conducted a search for Dr. Miles Middleton. This doctor retired at a young age and served several terms as Treasurer of the Gogglesgunshod Association. Rodstrum read over the list of Association Officers for the last eight years. He noted that six years earlier, the current Police Superintendent Sykes had been Vice President of the Association. He didn't find Hospital Director Nevels among the office holders. He learned the Gogglesgunshod Association was the charitable unit of the Blinkingshire County's Business Association. Its fundraising activities resulted in generous donations to the local hospital. Six years earlier, the Association hosted an awards ceremony. Atwater was among those recognized.

Rodstrum wondered again if there could be something to Atwater's story. Rodstrum knew he needed help and looked up the contact information for the Independent Office for Police Conduct (IOPC). Its main function---to investigate allegations of serious police corruption---might make IOPC best able to discern whether police had covered up any crime. The more he considered it, Rodstrum realized he wasn't sure enough of his facts and what would need to be included in his allegation. Cathcart was just the one to know such details.

Lady Carmella reached out to her philanthropic contacts in an effort to find the Kingston Dove Foundation, referenced by the Daily Slip. After obtaining a referral as a potential resource for the Foundation, she arranged to meet with the Foundation's Public Relations Officer. It was her first outing since fleeing to Nancy's home. As though she was still at university, Carmella found herself staring into Nancy's closet wondering what outfit she wanted to borrow. She selected a light blue dress and a pair of navy pumps. Then she helped herself to a strand of pearls and a small gray clutch. Carmella liked what she saw in the mirror.

Lady Carmella arrived at her one o'clock appointment. The receptionist ushered her into a small conference room overlooking a small park. A secretary bobbed her head in the door and announced the Public Relations Officer would arrive shortly. Minutes later, the secretary entered the room with a tray of tea and shortcakes. She poured a cup of tea for Lady Carmella and then left to check on the absent Public Relations Officer.

Carmella looked out the window and considered what she wanted to accomplish. First, she wanted to confirm she had not been involved in any plot to thwart the Foundation's purchase of the farmhouse…she didn't think she had been.

Marcus Wakefield bounded into the room, all apologies for keeping her waiting. Her first impression was that of an animated pair of black-rimmed glasses galloping atop a black bow tie. She accepted his apology and thanked him for agreeing to meet with her. Marcus thanked Carmella for the copy of the Daily Slip news article referencing the Foundation. He already read it as part of the general newsfeed, and the story intrigued him. He was unfamiliar with the Foundation's prior efforts to purchase the farmhouse, and he was more than surprised to receive word from her that morning.

Marcus related he took over as Public Relations Officer just last year so he asked the Communications Director, the prior Public Relations Officer, if she would join them. Rosemarie Carruthers wouldn't be available for the next half hour but in the meantime, he would be happy to explain the Foundation's purpose, history and future goals. Without skipping a beat, Marcus did just that.

Marcus was interrupted when a redheaded fireball burst through the door. As she pulled up a chair, Rosemarie gushed, "Marcus! Oh you must be Lady Carmella." Carmella was struck by the matching temperaments of Rosemarie and Marcus. She wondered if she might get an opportunity to speak today.

Rosemarie suggested Marcus get more tea. In a hushed voice, Rosemarie explained she had found just the person who could answer her questions. "Brad Leveler is a barrister who has done work for the Foundation. He was privy to the selection of Huffinfield as a Foundation site. Brad should be here in a bit, but I'll fill in whatever I'm able for you in the meantime."

Marcus returned to the table and reported, "Brad says it might take him a bit; he is pulling pertinent records."

Marcus looked at Carmella. "He says you will likely want to look through them."

Marcus looked at Rosemarie, "What's this all about?

Rosemarie responded, "All I recall is the Huffinfield property was listed for sale. The Foundation made an offer. Then the seller came back with a list of questions about our intentions for the property. Brad had the lead for the Foundation in the talks. The next I recall is being asked for the Foundation's comment on the quick sale of the property to another group."

The secretary knocked, opened the door and announced, "Barrister Leveler is on his way from reception."

Brad Leveler was tall and athletic. He had a spring to his step. His face was a square jaw under an aquiline nose and two medium blue eyes. His sandy brown hair, sprinkled with gray, touched his collar. His tweed suit looked well-worn and his shoes were a cross between a dress shoe and a walking shoe. His button-down collar and narrow tie looked like he may have been wearing them for the past twenty years. Brad Leveler said. "If I may, let me be frank. The Foundation targeted the Huffinfield property with the hope of counteracting the extreme racist elements within the community."

He noted Carmella's raised eyebrow and asked, "Are you not from the area?"

Carmella explained she was a Londoner who had retired to Huffinfield in the last year. She stated she had seen no evidence of racism and thought the populace, in general, seemed rather chipper. Brad Leveler retained a blank expression as he nodded.

After a pause, Leveler continued. "For perspective, I'll use a specific incident. Approximately six years ago, a Black British family, traveling on holiday, stopped for a bite in Huffinfield's Centre. The local people terrorized them, multiple counts of aggravated assault and battery, mayhem, aggravated rape, and child abuse. All family members were treated in London's hospitals after being transferred from the local hospital. The family barely escaped with their lives and was understandably afraid to speak out. When one of the victims subsequently died in questionable circumstances, the others were vehement about not pursuing justice for their mistreatment."

"I can't believe it," Carmella murmured. Marcus and Rosemarie remained silent.

Brad responded. "It's all documented."

For the next ninety minutes, Carmella skimmed through affidavits from doctors, social workers, child psychologists, surgeons, hairdressers, dermatologists, and trauma counselors. She noted an anonymous donor, Troward, paid for these services.

Chapter 28. Tension Takes Its Toll

Lady Carmella's meeting with the Kingston Dove Foundation left her perplexed. Reviewing the Foundation's box of records, in the presence of a chastened Marcus Wakefield, was uncomfortable. After she departed the Foundation's offices, she took a taxi to Bond Street. Carmella wandered about the shops while her mind replayed her life. She felt alone, as though she had stepped through the Twilight Zone, leaving the clerks and customers in another dimension. She pondered her move to Huffinfield.

In the evening, Carmella returned to Nancy's empty flat. With the Foundation's records still swirling around her mind, Carmella wondered if she may be in danger. She bolted the door and headed for the kitchen to make a cup of tea. She was waiting for the kettle when she heard the apartment door unlock. Carmella was panic-stricken and couldn't move while she listened to the approaching footsteps. At the last minute, she grabbed her empty tea cup, ready to use it in self-defense. Nancy came into the kitchen. Carmella stood up, feeling weak in the knees.

"I have a dress just like that," mocked Nancy.

Carmella tumbled back onto her chair and whispered, "Did you bolt the door?"

Nancy ran to bolt the door. She returned to the kitchen and hissed, "What is going on?"

Carmella heaved her shoulders and shook her head. "I'm so scared."

Nancy pulled a chair next to Carmella. "Tell me everything," she coaxed.

Much later that night, Nancy made arrangements for a three-day jaunt to Paris. Nancy was concerned about Carmella's mental health. After this hellish week, it would be good to get away from the pall cast by the circus troupe and the rest of Huffinfield.

On that same day, Darryl reached out to the Kingston Dove Foundation, or rather he engaged a London solicitor, by the name of Hughes, to make contact with the Foundation. After conveying the current owner's shock and condolences upon learning their purchase had stymied the Foundation's plans, the solicitor mentioned the property was for sale, with a special price, in consideration of the Foundation's prior purchase attempt. After a brief huddle with the Executive Board, the President phoned Emily May, the Foundation's solicitor, whose subsequent phone call with the seller confirmed a Tuesday closing. By late Friday, the Foundation's President forwarded the draft Purchase and Sale Agreement to alert Barrister Brad Leveler.

On Saturday morning, Jack Rodstrum visited his family in Chester. Deighton's close call had reminded him of life's fleeting nature. His family members thrilled to see him. Rodstrum's return trip was filled with nothing but good feelings and blaring radio music. Upon approaching Huffinfield, he turned off the radio and remembered Deighton. Rodstrum collected his thoughts and headed straight to Cathcart.

Cathcart, Privitt and Wiley sat stone faced around Cathcart's kitchen table and pondered the police response to Deighton's attackers. It wasn't right and left them feeling vulnerable. At almost eight o'clock, Cathcart's wife greeted Rodstrum at the door. She invited him in and announced, "Another one's come to the party." After giving Rodstrum a pint and Cathcart a quick peck on the cheek, she teased, "Don't wait up," before departing the flat.

Straight away, Rodstrum told the trio of Deighton's lethargy and drop in blood pressure and his current placement in the Intensive Care Unit.

"You heard how the brass directed the release of the six circus troupe members?" asked Wiley. "And the directive to destroy the hard copy records of their statements?" asked Privitt.

Cathcart interjected, "Yes, I told him that and about the six concurrent cases of heart failure at the jail."

"Any clue as to why?" asked Rodstrum.

Cathcart replied, "Not a one."

Wiley asked, "Do we know whether the records on the six troupe members were destroyed yet?"

"They were not," asserted Cathcart. He admitted, "They're under lock and key." The others grinned. A long silence fell upon them. "What I want to know---how did the Daily Slip get its scoop?" asked Privitt.

"It sounded spot on," declared Wiley.

"The brass are ape shit about it," grimaced Cathcart.

Rodstrum shook his head. "I thought it was one of you. Now I'm stumped. Maybe Atwater? Deighton's kept mum, but I have a notion he was given an overdose because people suspected it was him."

Privitt raised an eye brow, "Did you say maybe Atwater?"

"I'll bet it's that so-called circus troupe," wagered Wiley. Just the thought made everyone feel uncomfortable.

Rodstrum sighed and stretched a bit. "I may as well tell you about Atwater's story." Rodstrum closed his eyes to regroup. When he finished, the hum of the refrigerator filled the room.

Finally, Privitt broke the silence. "Mike Parish retired all of a sudden right around that time and moved his family to Somerset. I wonder if he could tell any bits about it?"

"Wouldn't the hospital records show who was treated for what?" asked Wiley.

Rodstrum related his meeting with Ms. Minders.

Cathcart noted, "We should have paper files of any such incident in the same locked room where Deighton found the farmhouse files. I'll look into that."

Rodstrum looked up. "That reminds me, any luck on locating the box removed from Deighton's office as part of the fumigation protocol?"

Cathcart responded. "I believe I spotted it in the Chief Inspector's Office."

"Why don't we put a bunch of cockroaches in his office so it'll need to be fumigated?" suggested Privitt.

Cathcart smirked, "Anyone know where we can find a load of cockroaches?"

Early on Sunday, Otto updated Darryl. Rouben confirmed the three corpses belonged to the triplets. The ambulance staff were sacked after the triplets died. Investigators found the triplets spent six unattended hours in an ambulance van. The workers contended they saved the lives of six fellow Brits by not pausing to transport the three foreigners. (They did, in fact, respond to six heart attack victims in between bringing the triplets to the hospital dock and transporting them to hospital.)

Darryl and Otto finalized plans for the upcoming sale of the farmhouse property. Otto dredged up the deed, listing the purchaser as the ZXY Corporation. They decided not to change the name at this late hour. Otto was charged with clearing the Foundation's purchase check and transferring funds to a Swiss bank account. Rouben was to conduct a final sweep of the farmhouse premises, with specific instructions to clear all vegetation from the rear of the herb garden. Darryl had yet to find Helga.

On late Sunday morning, Deighton was transported from the Intensive Care Unit to his same twelfth floor room. Rodstrum checked in at eleven o'clock and found Deighton in good spirits, with all signs of lethargy gone. Rodstrum had much to relate from the last forty-eight hours.

Neither man had seen the Sunday Daily Slip. On page three, the news article entitled, "Racist Rage Escapes Justice," suggested leading county residents had been involved in heinous, criminal acts against Black Brits, crimes the police had ignored and buried.

In the early afternoon, there was a loud commotion on the twelfth floor. Upon investigation, Rodstrum learned a rock had shattered Atwater's window. On this rock, drawn in heavy black ink, was a swastika. The security guards refused entry when Rodstrum attempted to check on Atwater.

Soon after Rodstrum had finished relating the matter to Deighton, they heard Gregg Armstrong in the hall, raising his voice to the security guards. Rodstrum left to investigate. He learned the security guards were under orders to allow no visitors until the rock situation had been investigated. Rodstrum went to the nurse's station and requested the nurse advise the Director that Atwater's grandson wanted to see his grandfather now. Within minutes, the guards relented and let Gregg into his grandfather's room. Gregg had not seen Sunday's Daily Slip either.

On Monday morning, Darryl met Swaeger's cruise ship on its four o'clock arrival in Boston. Swaeger himself disembarked from the vessel at five o'clock. Attired in a tailored men's suit, he looked nothing like his persona of the last five years. The two men let themselves be taken up in the morning rush hour. Finally, they stopped at a diner for breakfast. Glumly, Darryl looked around and decided it would be an appropriate place to meet death. Swaeger observed his mood and assured him they had survived worse. Both ordered the Trucker's Breakfast. Swaeger looked at Darryl expectantly and inquired, "What's the plan?"

Just before six o'clock on Monday morning, a shoe box unloaded a heap of cockroaches, which were corralled under the door and into the office of the Chief Inspector. The cockroaches were very discrete.

Just before nine o'clock on Monday, Rodstrum returned to hospital to check on Deighton. He noticed Gregg Armstrong pacing in the visitor's lounge. Rodstrum approached and asked what was wrong. Gregg paused, "They want to put a spinal brace on my grandfather and transport him to a rehab hospital."

"At his age, why would they want to do that?" wondered Rodstrum.

Gregg seethed. "The shattered window! The security guards! My grandfather says it's prompted by a news article in Sunday's Daily Slip. I don't know any good reason. He received more blood just yesterday. Not all his cuts have closed yet."

"Calm down," counseled Rodstrum. "Is your grandfather still here?"

Gregg nodded. "Still finishing his breakfast. I couldn't sit still when I heard the news so I came out here."

Rodstrum recommended Gregg notify Lady Carmella about this turn of events. He promised to see what he could do and set off for Ms. Minders' office.

Gregg sent a text to Nancy. He wrote about his grandfather's plight and the article in Sunday's Daily Slip. Nancy read his text as she was packing to return home from Paris. "Poor Gregg," she sighed, "he has had no respite." She showed the text to Carmella, who read it and paused.

"That does it!" Carmella declared, "I'm returning to Huffinfield."

Chapter 29. Digging Deeper

Tompkins Hospital didn't transfer Reginald Atwater on Monday. Gregg was convinced high jinks were afoot, and it was all Atwater could do to talk Gregg into leaving him to go to work. Atwater was sorry this sordid affair had taken such a toll on Gregg.

In Monday's issue, the Daily Slip included an article following up on Sunday's allegations of racist crimes in Huffinfield. It featured an adamant denial by Milton Alcorn, a former long-term member of the Town Council. Mr. Alcorn demanded the names of those seeking to sully Huffinfield's good name. Police Superintendent Sykes was quoted as saying "If crimes like that happened in Huffinfield, the perpetrators would be in jail now." Chief Inspector Jenkins was quoted as saying, "Police will be conducting a record check." The pub's owner, Curtis Field, claimed no knowledge; he was quoted as saying, "I would've remembered that." Atwater read the article and knew what he had to do.

When Gregg returned to hospital at mid-day, his grandfather was ready for him. "I'm so glad you've come," declared Atwater. Gregg looked at him expectantly. Atwater warned, "I've got something to say and it won't be pretty." Two hours later, Gregg headed toward the offices of the Daily Slip to deliver his grandfather's letter to the editor.

The sale of the farmhouse was proceeding at a fast clip. The London Solicitor Hughes selected a London real estate agent to meet with Kingston Dove Foundation representatives at Monday's inspection. He apologized for not having the time to engage a local agent. Darryl was amused---a London agent was perfect as she would know nothing of the property.

Otto suggested they use that same real estate agent to ensure compliance with smoke detectors and the like while she was onsite. He suggested waiting until after the closing to notify the utility companies. The Swiss bank account was open and ready for funds. Otto noted there was still a question as to the whereabouts of Bogdan.

Time was growing short. Darryl wondered if the triplets might have taken Bogdan with them on their exit from the farmhouse.

Brad Leveler opened his email to see the news about the Foundation's intent to act on its former plan of creating a presence in Huffinfield. He researched the Foundation's database on hate crimes and came across the recent case of Reginald Atwater, a badly beaten elderly gent, who had taken the side of an outnumbered Black man being attacked by a group of pipe-wielding white locals. The report noted the Black man's terrified family watched from the car as the man's body was thrown out the door and bounced off the pavement. Clearly, the location still merited attention. He wrote to the Foundation's president, wholeheartedly endorsing the plan for a Huffinfield presence. Leveler then contacted three of the victims of the attack from years back, hoping to arrange a group meeting about the project.

Rouben cleared the mess left by the police in their search of the farmhouse. He emptied all drawers, closets and cabinets, vacuumed the rugs and arranged a few pieces of furniture on the first floor. Rouben dug up the rear herb garden and buried the yanked plants in the back woods.

Rouben went to Bogdan's room and looked in his closet. He saw no crevice. After a thorough inspection, he found nothing. He kicked the closet wall in frustration and stumbled upon a hidden door, leading to the decomposing body of Bogdan. Rouben hauled him out and that night, buried him under the mound of a recent burial at the local cemetery.

Jack Rodstrum rose early on Monday and travelled to Somerset, determined to speak with retiree Mike Parish. He pulled up at Parish's address to find a neat bungalow, a bit pricier than what most constables could afford. Rodstrum rang the bell. Parish, himself, answered. Recognizing Rodstrum, he inquired, "Inspector Rodstrum, what brings you here?"

"I was hoping to find you," grinned Rodstrum, observing Mike Parish was still gregarious and athletic.

"You found me!" responded Parish.

"Might I have a few minutes of your retired time?" asked Rodstrum.

Parish stepped outside the door and suggested, "Perhaps we could take a walk around the block?"

Once they reached the sidewalk, Parish asked, "What's this about?"

Rodstrum furrowed his brow. "I'm hoping you might be able to fill me in on what happened to a family of Black Brits, who stopped for pie in the Centre some years back." Parish's face remained blank. When Parish didn't respond, Rodstrum asked, "Do you know anything of it?"

Parish looked bothered but responded, "I do. I'll tell you what I know. But I signed a confidentiality agreement so if you ever say I told you, I'll deny it."

Rodstrum shrugged, "What have you got?"

They walked in silence for a few minutes. Then Parish started slowly, "It was a bit before five in the afternoon when there was an anonymous call saying an ambulance was needed at the pub. What was interesting is they requested six ambulance vans and the town only had one. That stuck in my mind. I set out to see what was afoot."

They walked a bit further in silence. Parish shook his head and continued, "I still remember the loud wails from the three women and the smell of blood. The three men's heads were drenched in red blood. The women's necks were roped by a single piece of cord. One of the women was shrieking, 'in the boot,' over and over again. At the time, it was too much to take in. Over the years, different details have come to me. Now I don't know if they were real or if I've imagined them."

Parish paused and then recounted, "The one ambulance arrived. The woman, who was now sobbing something about the boot, became violent and the people at the pub laughed. That's when I noticed a good two dozen locals, sipping their pints and looking at me. It was then that Tommy Hill shouted, 'Somebody tell Minerva she can come back in.' The crowd chuckled at that. Lillie Leeway headed off and I followed her. Minerva Cummington was standing outside Lillie's shop and there was pounding coming from the boots of three cars parked along the sidewalk. The cars weren't locked so I opened the boots and found six screaming children, scared out of their minds. I radioed for help."

Parish wiped the perspiration from his brow. He took two slow breaths before resuming, "When I returned, all six adults from the pub, and they were all Black, were on the ambulance floor. The shrieking woman was now unconscious. The medical technicians, Brian Bates and Alfred Norton, swore they didn't touch any of them. By now, the children were approaching. I tried to hold them back but they saw the adults, such as they were, and ran to them."

Parish pouted his lips and arched his back. "I watched the ambulance doors shut with the whole lot of them stuffed inside. Then I got a call from Headquarters saying to return to the office. I explained I needed to take names and ask questions. I was told others would be charged with the investigation and I was to return to the station immediately. So I got on my bicycle and set off for the station."

Parish crossed him arms. "This is where it gets even stranger," he whispered, "Once I arrived at the station, I was sent to the Chief Inspector's Office but the Chief Inspector wasn't there. It was Superintendent Stebbins sitting behind the desk. He told me the town had been spared great harm by the good citizens of Huffinfield. He told me if I wanted to enjoy my retirement, I was not to relate what I had seen or heard to anyone. He asked if I understood. Then the

Superintendent says as I was nearing retirement, I may as well retire now. He hands me an envelope and says this will hold you over until your pension is processed. Then he says, you can keep the uniform, and then he says, you're dismissed."

Parish stopped at his gate, concluding, "I got home, told the wife everything. She took one look in the envelope and says we're moving far away from this town, and that's what we did. That's all I know. And you didn't hear it from me."

It was late Monday afternoon when Lady Carmella visited Inspector Deighton. "The poor man is truly a sight," she later told Nancy. But Deighton was in good spirits and graciously welcomed her visit.

"You seem to be progressing well, Inspector Deighton," murmured Carmella.

Deighton smirked, "I suppose I'll live." Then he vouched, "I have noted each of your messages."

Carmella interrupted. "I do apologize for not having realized you had been badly throttled. I suppose I was too wrapped up in my own drama at the time."

Rather than conceding how it puzzled him why she demanded action from his hospital bed, Deighton beamed, "No apology necessary." He shifted the conversation, "I read in the news you single-handedly rid the shire of the nasty lot."

"The Daily Slip doesn't seem keen to confirm its news before printing," Carmella mused, "I'm actually hoping to speak with their news room in an effort to sort out its recent mentions of my name."

Deighton considered and then commented, "They're always looking for content."

Carmella sighed, "What I still don't understand is the reluctance of the police to go after the circus troupe. Can you help me with that?"

Deighton confided, "Between you and me, I don't understand either."

Carmella winced and then pulled a detective novel from her purse. "Something to speed your recovery," she announced.

"Say, I have an idea," said Deighton. He reached for his phone and dialed.

"Beatrice Butterfield please."

After a pause, Deighton continued, "Hello Bea. Mitch Deighton here. In hospital and reading every word of the Daily Slip. Hey, I was wondering if you considered interviewing Lady Carmella. She was mentioned in those stories about the circus troupe and then about Reed Crimson. Might be interesting to hear what she has to say." Deighton paused again and then teased, "Just a thought from someone with too much time on his hands. Thanks Bea."

He grinned at Carmella and hinted, "I wouldn't be surprised if the local press requests an interview!"

"Well done," declared Carmella, and she left Deighton with his new book.

At the police station, the Chief Inspector's Office was being prepared for fumigation. Nobody noticed when the box, lying on the floor and mostly hidden by the Chief Inspector's desk, went missing. A cursory inspection confirmed the box held the records on the circus troupe. On Monday night, those documents were scanned into an electronic file named, Jones #AR-01-FH-18-CT, and saved to the archived records folder, ensuring it was lost for the most part. The box returned to its prior obscurity in the locked storage room.

Chapter 30. Desolate Dread

Accountant Delilah Banks clenched the message in her hand, and her mind went blank. As if an air bag had jettisoned and enveloped her, she floated in an empty white space. Slowly, she recognized she was sitting alone at her desk in her London office. Still stunned, she read it again. Her secretary had penned a message from Mr. Bradford Leveler, calling from the Kingston Dove Foundation and asking for a return call.

His call could mean only one thing. He wanted to ask her to share her nightmare. She had been clear she wasn't up to the task. But two years had passed since he last called. Perhaps he didn't understand that time didn't heal all. Delilah Banks put the note into her purse and pushed it out of her mind. She had business depreciations to calculate.

After work, Delilah took the Tube and disembarked at a station near a school gymnasium. Her two children were playing a coed game of basketball this evening. She didn't take her beautiful children for granted. After two years of battling social service agencies to keep them, she had won. Her children may be scarred, but they were definitely in recovery. Delilah felt her feet treading upon the pavement. She hoped she was in recovery.

Delilah's life had been fairly predictable until that day, a bit more than five years ago. She and her cousins were taking a long weekend in the English countryside. Their three family cars paraded through beautiful vistas, with occasional stops to skim stones or take walks. On the second afternoon, without warning, she was caught up in a nightmare. By the end of that month, her husband was dead, her children were raging and she was cowering at the sound of a telephone.

She found her way onto the bleachers. The game started and her children gave her big smiles. She forced herself to smile back. She started to feel shaky. She hoped the sensation would go away soon.

"Hey," a woman's voice boomed as a hand squeezed Delilah's shoulder. It was her cousin.

"Hi Rose," grinned Delilah. Rose settled herself next to Delilah, waved at the children and placed her folded coat on her lap. Rose's two children were playing too.

Delilah looked around and spotted another cousin. "Nicki's on her way," she pointed. Rose looked like she was about to speak but then waited for Nicki. She didn't have to wait long.

"Excellent location," Nicki beamed before looking out and shouting, "Go get 'em team," at no one in particular. Nicki's two children were playing too.

Nicki sat next to Delilah, gave her arm a squeeze and whispered, "Good to see you Cousin." She reached across Delilah and squeezed Rose's hand.

Nicki declared, "I love game nights." Delilah and Rose grinned. Their cousin was a one-woman cheerleading squad.

At half-time, Rose pulled her cousins close and scowled, "Did that Leveler call you today?"

"My secretary took a message from him," admitted Delilah. Nicki pulled out her phone and saw he had left her a voicemail message.

"How is it he can't understand we want to put that behind us?" asked Nicki.

"After what our families have been through, it's outrageous," agreed Rose.

Delilah remained silent, but her cousins railed until the game resumed. At the end of the game, Rose pulled them into a huddle again and directed, "We need to focus on moving forward. Delilah, you are finally back on your feet. Don't let this shake you. If you feel you're getting upset, you call us. Stay away from Leveler." Delilah nodded.

Delilah took her children, ages twelve and fourteen, to McDonald's to celebrate the game. She watched more than listened to their excitement.

She remembered how they had switched off to become embittered truants. On a journey full of frustrating false starts, she had found them compatible therapists, special school programs and helpful medications. Now, only the biweekly group therapy remained of that regimen. Delilah hoped nothing ever turned them around again.

Later that night, Delilah pondered her solitary bed. Her Glen was dead. It was all well and good for Nicki and Rose, they still had husbands with whom to share their feelings. Her anxiety triggered by Mr. Leveler's message frightened her.

Perhaps talking about what happened might be healing. She pondered the insanity it might unleash. Perhaps if she was looking at another breakdown, the Foundation could help her or at least find support for her children. She would return Mr. Leveler's call.

The next day, on her lunch hour, Delilah called. When Leveler answered his phone, she disconnected.

That night, Delilah Banks tossed and turned in her bed. Her thoughts raced: *It's a nagging secret but it isn't a secret, is it? I never chose for my race to define me. Does my silence serve as an enticement for them to doubt my intellect, to deny my humanity? My attackers defined me by my race. Kicked me, spat on me, grabbed my children and stuffed them in a boot, tortured me, tortured my loved ones, raped me, jeered at me…a legacy from the slave trade…a culture and heritage that lets people blink and call it the way of the world. History argues for some degree of skepticism anything I'll do might change that. Shall I move on then and stay mute when my outrage threatens my sanity? What about that nest of bigots? Do those animals fondly reminisce about the day and how they tormented me? No, they likely don't think of me at all. It was just another day in their neighborhood. Here I am, irreparably damaged. I will not be silent.*

Delilah sat up. Minutes later, she opened her laptop and addressed an email to Rose and Nicki. Though always close to her cousins, overcoming the Huffinfield attack intertwined their lives like never before. She couldn't talk to Mr. Leveler without talking to them first.

She wanted to speak with her cousins in person, but Delilah knew that wouldn't be easy. Nicki worked as a Nurse Practitioner and no matter how many times Nicki explained the pattern of her hospital schedule, Delilah still couldn't guess her days off. Rose worked a nine to five weekday schedule as a Project Manager at an architectural firm, but Rose could disappear for days while troubleshooting an overdue project.

Delilah herself loathed the thought of taking time off from work. Her coworkers clearly thought she had overplayed her crime victim card, with her extended leave of absence years back. Mending relations at the office was an ongoing project.

Delilah decided to ask when they could meet for an evening meal. She wanted to say why she wanted to meet but didn't want to say much.

She typed, "I want to talk to Leveler and wanted to discuss." With a sigh, Delilah pressed the send button.

Chapter 31. The Daily Slip Goes Viral

In the early morning, Beatrice Butterfield of the Daily Slip phoned Lady Carmella, who consented to a three o'clock interview at the library. In preparation, Carmella re-read the news articles; made a timeline of events; selected her attire and took a walk.

In New York City, Darryl enjoyed his late breakfast. Earlier that morning, Otto reported Rouben found and buried Bogdan's body. The farmhouse sale seemed imminent. The home inspection went smoothly; the municipality certified the smoke detectors. The local bickering, about the hushed up crimes toward the Black Brits on holiday, distracted from news of the impending sale. Darryl reviewed his mental checklists as he finished his coffee. The circus troupe caper was on track for closure.

Jack Rodstrum spent the morning drafting his complaint to the Independent Office for Police Conduct.

Inspector Deighton was anxious to look at the day's newspaper. He overheard hospital staff going on about this morning's news but was unable to get any straight answers. Finally, Rodstrum arrived with the newspaper. Rodstrum had not given the Daily Slip a glance. Deighton skimmed through the pages. On page four, he found Reginald Atwater's letter to the editor.

In a hushed voice, Deighton read aloud: "I am writing to corroborate the earlier report of racist crimes. Unfortunately, I was a participant. A family of Black Brits on holiday stopped in our village for a picnic of local pies. There were three men, three women and the rest were children. At Petunia Park, the children were thrown on the ground and then stuffed into the boots of their three cars parked next to Lillie's Pie Shop. Minerva Cummington kept watch on the cars whilst we others moved to the pub. Paul Foster tied a rope around each woman's neck and then tied them to a radiator. Mildred Pearson took the lead in throwing boiling water at the women. Then Constance Appleton cut off their hair. The three men were pinned to the ground where Dalton Payne methodically punched each of them unconscious. Then they were repeatedly propped up so each local man could have a turn at them. Clive Leeway pulled the roped women into the back room. I didn't follow because Edgar Ward had me and Harvey West help him cut the small fingers and small toes and one ear from each of the three men. Reverend Jake mumbled a prayer over the severed body parts. The Gogglesgunshod Association held a ceremony heralding our heroic defense of kin and country. I was awarded a commemorative human ear. So help me God. "

The two men remained silent for a time. Rodstrum exhaled, "That takes the pressure off me having to relate his reminiscence."

"Go check on Atwater now," snapped Deighton.

Rodstrum rose and headed out the door. At almost noon, Atwater's door was closed. Rodstrum strode over to the nurse's station. Rodstrum whispered, "Is everything OK with Mr. Atwater today?"

The nurse raised her eyebrows. "His door is closed because a doctor is examining him. Dr. Miles Middleton made an unannounced visit; Director Nevels instructed me to let him to see Mr. Atwater. Against the doctor's express wishes, the duty nurse accompanied him. Our protocols don't let hospital staff see Mr. Atwater without an escort so we weren't making an exception for this outside doctor."

"Did Mr. Atwater agree to seeing Dr. Middleton?" asked Rodstrum.

"I think they knew each other," responded the nurse.

"Hope he's safe," murmured Rodstrum.

After reporting about Atwater, Rodstrum described his visit with retired Constable Parish. Deighton was dumbfounded.

Rodstrum concluded, "And to top it off, Parish says he'll deny telling me any of it!"

After a long pause, Deighton remarked, "Nobody will believe you if you tell them Parish told you such a tale anyway."

Rodstrum quipped, "Even I can hardly believe it."

Deighton asked, "What became of the medical technicians, Brian Bates and Alfred Norton?"

"They're on my list," assured Rodstrum. "And there's another thing. I spent the morning drafting a complaint about police corruption to the IOPC. You are welcome to review it. I want Cathcart to go over it and make sure it covers all the required points."

"Cathcart is the one," agreed Deighton.

At two o'clock in the afternoon, at a London bank, the Kingston Dove Foundation closed on its purchase of the Huffinfield farmhouse. Within an hour of the closing, the sale proceeds were deposited in a Swiss bank account, courtesy of Otto.

Brad Leveler read and re-read Reginald Atwater's letter to the editor in the Daily Slip. He pinned a Tweet about it on the Foundation's Twitter account.

At three o'clock in the afternoon, Beatrice Butterfield waited at Huffinfield's library for Lady Carmella. Butterfield considered herself a no nonsense businesswoman, who knew how to sell a newspaper. It was all about being relevant, even if that meant being up-to-date on the local gossip. She pondered her upcoming subject. This Lady Carmella was new to the area; she may not understand how things worked in Huffinfield yet.

Carmella carefully selected a lilac, linen dress and a triple strand of pearls for her interview with the local press. After entering the library, she could not fathom why she chose this outfit. She listened to her gray heels resounding loudly on the library's hardwood floors.

Though retirement came with a modicum of liberation, an interview with the press flaunted all decorum. Not entirely sure the interview was a smart decision, Carmella despised the fretful voices in her head.

Carmella knocked discretely on the open door. "Ms. Butterfield?" she inquired.

Butterfield rose and smiled at Carmella and told her, "Please call me Bea." Butterfield ambled over to close the door and thanked Carmella for agreeing to the interview.

Carmella took a seat near the closed door and studied Beatrice Butterfield. Her auburn hair was impeccably coiffed. She wore a turquoise silk dress over no-nonsense, navy pumps. Butterfield's wide, brown eyes seemed to miss nothing. Carmella sensed this reporter was more business-savvy than she let on.

After an exchange of pleasantries, Carmella tried to focus the conversation. She stated, "I have been reading your newspaper for almost one year now. Little did I dream I would find myself mentioned on the pages."

"Well, that is one of the factors to consider when moving to a small place like Huffinfield. Not much goes unnoticed," grinned Butterfield.

Unamused, Carmella remained quiet.

"Our readers will want to know who does your hair, it's very stylish," gushed Butterfield.

Carmella put up her hand and declared, "I'm not here about me."

"Everyone likes to be noticed now and then," coaxed Butterfield.

Carmella paused. This woman was tone deaf. She tried again, "Your paper has referenced my name more than once this week. That is notice enough."

Beatrice Butterfield found this Lady Carmella a bit tedious. Pleasantries were wont to continue a bit longer in the country than in the city, she supposed. Butterfield tried again, "Your name did pop up more than once, didn't it? Well, now we can get your perspective."

Carmella straightened her spine, which had been quite straight already. "For the record, I did make a police complaint about the circus troupe living in the farmhouse at the end of Allen Road, but I had no idea who they were. I am not sure how they came to leave the premises. That's one topic I would appreciate being cleared up.

Butterfield tipped her reading glasses onto the tip of her nose and took notes in shorthand, capturing Carmella's every word. She knew how to report accurately even though it was a bit old fashioned nowadays. "So let me make sure I understand, you didn't know the circus troupe people were criminals and don't know how they came to leave the premises. What led you to file your complaint with the police?" Butterfield inquired.

Carmella replied, "On a walk, I saw a group of adults laughing at a young girl, being pecked by a bird tethered to her hat, while a woman held the girl's arms so she couldn't protect her face. When I sought to intervene, they were hostile toward me so I returned home and contacted the police."

Butterfield looked up. "The girl had a bird tied to her hat and the bird was pecking the girl's face, is it?"

Carmella nodded affirmatively. Beatrice Butterfield was getting more than she had hoped possible. She would have to send flowers to Mitch Deighton at hospital. Butterfield ventured, "Did you have any more contact with the circus troupe?"

Carmella continued, "I believe they drugged me."

Butterfield indicated she should go on.

Carmella instantly regretted raising the matter. "The police told me it was a circus troupe practicing their acts and what I saw was not truly what it seemed. I made cookies and brought them over to the farmhouse as a good will gesture. I accepted their cup of tea and the next I knew, I was on my back stoop, going in and out of conscious."

"That is quite curious," tempered Butterfield.

Carmella interjected, "I would rather not speak of it more as the matter is still under police investigation."

Butterfield murmured, "Of course."

Carmella folded her hands and took a deep breath. "There is more I want to say. I did not participate in any effort to obstruct the Kingston Dove Foundation's purchase of the farmhouse. I am not aware of any effort to obstruct that purchase. I only met the solicitor Reed Crimson in passing. The photo showing the two of us together was at a fundraising event, quite loud and he was likely saying something like, 'Pleased to meet you.' We had no relationship, professional or otherwise."

Butterfield pouted. "I suppose people can read whatever they like into a photo. We can post your note about it. I saw it merely as showing who you were and there was a photo with one of our own too. You do understand?"

Carmella gave her a faint smile and continued. "There is another thing I would like noted for the record. The newspaper references racist crimes. I have read denials and I have read a confession. For the record, I have seen proof enough of the racist crimes against Black Brits by Huffinfield residents."

"Oh my," uttered Butterfield. After a pause, she inquired, "What did you see?"

Carmella had not considered she would be pressed for specifics. She responded, "I have seen affidavits by caregivers and service providers. I have no doubt they were put through hell when they stopped for a picnic in Huffinfield."

Butterfield looked at Carmella and sharply inquired, "Did you see these affidavits before moving to Huffinfield?"

Carmella could feel herself start. With effort, she retained her composure and responded, "No. I saw them just this week. I would rather not say more about it at this juncture."

Butterfield tilted her head. "Perhaps another time," she suggested.

Lady Carmella left her interview with Beatrice Butterfield wishing she had merely written a letter to the editor.

By this time, Brad Leveler's Tweet had gone viral, as had Atwater's letter to the editor, as had the Daily Slip!

Week Three

Chapter 32. Monday Goes Crazy

At approximately four o'clock in the afternoon, the receptionist at Tompkins Hospital informed Brad Leveler that Mr. Atwater wasn't allowed visitors. A piqued Leveler asked to speak to her supervisor. The receptionist telephoned Assistant Director Minders and asked if she wouldn't mind speaking with Mr. Leveler.

Mr. Leveler proceeded to Ms. Minders' office; the receptionist gratefully watched him go away.

Paula Minders muted her conference call connection when Leveler arrived at her door. "Please come in," she beckoned.

Leveler went straight to his point. "I am here from London to speak with Reginald Atwater. Surely, there must be a way to make this possible."

"Let me phone his grandson and you can speak with him," Minders responded as she dialed Gregg Armstrong's telephone number. Minders told of his grandfather's visitor. Gregg advised he should arrive in ten minutes to evaluate the visitor.

Minders looked up at Leveler and beamed, "Mr. Armstrong will be here in ten minutes." She motioned she needed to reconnect the audio to her teleconference. Leveler left her office to wait for this Gregg Armstrong at the hospital entrance, where he practiced his deep breathing.

Gregg approached the entrance. "Mr. Leveler?" he inquired.

"Yes, Brad Leveler. You're Armstrong?"

"I am," Gregg stated as he shook Leveler's hand. "What brings you to see my grandfather?"

Leveler replied, "I work with the Kingston Dove Foundation. We're looking to raise local awareness of racism and encourage practices to foster tolerance. I read your grandfather's letter and wanted to talk to him about our project and see if he might want to work with us."

"I'm not sure you'll find he's inclined to do that," smiled Gregg, "But you can ask."

"Then I can see him?" asked Leveler.

Gregg sighed, "There has been more than one attack on my grandfather's life at this hospital. Let's speak with the Hospital Director and get his blessing if we are to let you see him today."

The Director wasn't in. Minders was hesitant to bend the protocol, but agreed Leveler could see Atwater if she and Gregg accompanied him. Having reached this consensus, the trio took the elevator to the twelfth floor. Minders stopped at the nurse's station to request the visitor log. Gregg and Leveler watched from a distance. Minders creased her brow and mouthed "Oh dear."

Gregg Armstrong was at the nurse's station in a flash. Leveler followed. Gregg demanded, "What's going on?"

Minders blanched. "It's about your grandfather's medical status." She looked at Leveler.

"You can say whatever it is in front of him," Gregg prompted. His gut feeling was Leveler might be more of a support than a threat.

"Your grandfather was diagnosed with dementia this morning," Minders whispered.

Gregg was upset. "What? Why was he even being screened for such a thing? He's as sharp as a tack. What doctor proffered this diagnosis?"

The nurse at the nurse's station looked at her computer screen and slowly read aloud, "Dr. Miles Middleton made the diagnosis."

"Who is that?" Gregg demanded.

Minders hesitated. "He isn't affiliated with the hospital, but I know certain patients like to deal with him anyway. We generally let it go on if the patient requests it and the treating doctors don't raise any objection."

"I'll bet it's got to do with his letter," exclaimed Gregg.

"This is the first I've heard of it, Mr. Armstrong. I'm so sorry," Minders breathed.

"If you saw him this morning and he seemed the same as when you saw him last month, I suggest we proceed with the plan to visit your grandfather together," suggested Leveler.

"Yes, let's go," agreed Gregg. Minders nodded her agreement and signed all three of their names on the visitors' log.

Gregg knocked on the door and announced, "You have company today." The internal guard stepped into the corner.

Leveler stepped in. "Mr. Atwater, sir, I'm Brad Leveler. I work with the Kingston Dove Foundation. The Foundation…"

"I know of your Foundation," interrupted Atwater. "Hello Mr. Leveler. Hello Ms. Minders. Why has Gregg dragged you both here?" Atwater looked at his grandson.

Gregg quickly explained. "Mr. Leveler came from London just to see you, but his visit goes against the security protocols. He seems like an honorable man and has come a long way so I talked to Ms. Minders about how we might make his visit possible. Ms. Minders and I agreed Mr. Leveler could visit with you only if he agreed that we could come along. Here we are."

"That's the sum of it," agreed Minders.

"Well, Mr. Leveler, please state your purpose then," requested Atwater in a pleasant tone.

Leveler took a letter from his suit pocket as he explained. "The Foundation is looking to start a conversation, to raise awareness of inadvertent acts of racism. After reading your letter to the editor in the Daily Slip, I was hoping you might help us."

"Ah," considered Atwater and he took a sip of water.

Gregg couldn't restrain himself any longer and blurted, "Grandfather, do you know Dr. Middleton wrote in your record this morning that you have dementia?"

"The bastard!" exclaimed Atwater. He shook his head. "No, this is the first I've heard of it. Middleton claimed he was just stopping in for a quick visit." Atwater closed his eyes and muttered, "That beats all."

"Hey, I'm your only approved visitor. How did Middleton get in?" demanded Gregg as he looked at Minders. She was at a loss for words.

Atwater looked at Minders too. "Why don't you see if the nurse's station has news to enlighten us?"

Minders left the three men alone in the room with the security guard.

Leveler cleared his throat and addressed Atwater. "You mentioned Dr. Middleton was paying you a visit. Do you two know each other?"

Atwater replied, "We certainly do. Middleton is a past or current officer in the Gogglesgunshod Association. They issued me an award a few years back. I swap small talk with Middleton from time to time."

Gregg looked at the floor. "Grandfather, that is just the sort of person you want to avoid at the moment."

Atwater responded, "With this recent news, I quite agree. But I never would have suspected duplicity from him. And Middleton is a medical doctor so I didn't think twice about him walking the halls."

Minders returned to Atwater's room with a report. "The computer record shows the morning nurse put a note…the unaffiliated Dr. Middleton arrived to see Mr. Atwater at ten minutes to ten o'clock and Director Nevels gave permission for Dr. Middleton to see Mr. Atwater at ten o'clock." She looked at Atwater and asked, "Did you request a visit of any kind with Dr. Middleton?"

"No," replied Atwater. "I just returned to bed after washing up and he bounced in, all casual, with a 'there you are' comment."

Leveler interjected. "Ms. Minders, what is Tompkins Hospital's involvement with the Gogglesgunshod Association?"

"The Association is very generous in making donations to our hospital," she responded. "It conducts fund-raising activities and donates locally."

"I would like to speak to my grandson alone, if you don't mind," grimaced Atwater.

"Certainly," stated Minders.

Leveler held out his envelope to Atwater and asked, "May I leave this for your consideration?"

"Please do," replied Atwater.

"Wait for me in the visitor's lounge, if you would Mr. Leveler," suggested Gregg.

Linda Chickering, the News Editor for Porter Public, a weekly magazine, read Brad Leveler's Tweet and determined this Huffinfield story merited attention. Chickering decided to send her Assistant Political Correspondent Susan Daly and her Domestic Affairs Correspondent Tom Valley. Resources were tight, but given the sensitive nature of the allegations, she was sure a two-person team would yield more information. Chickering hoped the story might trigger a wider discussion about racism in the country; she noted this goal on her budget ledger.

Carmella phoned Nancy about her disastrous interview with Beatrice Butterfield. "She must think I'm looney," she moaned.

Nancy squealed at Carmella's imitation of Butterfield's voice, "Our readers will want to know who does your hair."

"Tell me you didn't tell her," mocked Nancy.

"Why did I tell her I made them cookies?" Camella groaned.

Nancy declared, "It isn't fair how you get all the fun!

Chapter 33. More to Mull Over

Over tarts, Jack Rodstrum updated Kevin Cathcart. Cathcart promised to check the police response to the rock shattering Atwater's window. Handing over his letter to the Independent Office for Police Conduct, Rodstrum solemnly stated, "I was hoping you might review it to see if I've covered all the requirements." Cathcart promised he would.

Rodstrum was determined to find the medical technicians, Brian Bates and Alfred Norton. By mid-afternoon, he discovered the two were cousins, living at their elderly aunt's home on the edge of Huffinfield. They were gardening when he arrived. Clara Crumb, the aunt, answered the door and invited him in. She was a slip of a woman and her ruffly apron looked like it could go around her more than once. Brian and Alfred entered through the back door to find their aunt pouring Rodstrum a cup of tea.

"Here come my nephews," Clara smiled. She turned toward her approaching nephews.

"Go wash your hands before you step near my tea," she admonished. They turned.

Rodstrum leaned back in his chair. "Lovely," he murmured as he sipped his tea and enjoyed Clara's floral perfume.

The two men approached again and their aunt stepped up. Clara explained, "Inspector Rodstrum has a few questions for you."

"Mr. Bates and Mr. Norton," greeted Rodstrum as he stood to shake their hands.

Rodstrum said, "I hear you two are emergency medical technicians for the local ambulance service, is that right?" The two men nodded.

Rodstrum continued, "There has been an allegation of racist criminal activity from some years back. Did you get a chance to read the letter to the editor by Reginald Atwater?"

When the men remained silent, their Aunt Clara piped up, "I read it aloud to them twice already."

"We've heard there are newspaper people asking questions around town," stated Bates.

Rodstrum asked, "Did you bring the ambulance around to the pub and take away a family of Black Brits, children and adults?"

"Yeah," responded Norton.

"Where did you take them?" asked Rodstrum.

"Tompkins Hospital," asserted Bates.

Rodstrum inquired, "To the best of your knowledge, what happened to those people?"

Norton replied, "Once we pulled up at hospital, we put each adult on a stretcher and took them to the emergency room."

Bates added, "Then we asked the receptionist to have the Social Worker come around to look to the children."

Rodstrum asked, "How many children were there?"

Norton replied, "Six in all. They were a bit bruised and in shock but doing much better than the bloodied adults."

"How did you fit all the people into the one ambulance van?" asked. Rodstrum.

Bates responded, "We didn't. The crowd came out of the pub, a bit menacing they were. They backed us up against the side of the van and rather roughly put the six adults onto the van's floor. The children came a bit later and ran to the adults in the van. The crowd closed the back door of the van, and we got away as fast as we could."

Norton added, "We didn't want to leave any of the Black people with that crowd either. It wasn't clear how they came to be so bloody, but nobody came forward to suggest it was an accident."

Bates noted, "There was a police constable on the scene, but he seemed as stunned as we were."

Norton stated, "After the Social Worker came for the children, the Hospital Director Nevels came to us, put a wad of currency in our hands and told us it was best not to speak too much about the matter."

Bates commented, "We knew the police constable saw as much as we did, so it didn't seem like a bad idea."

"In my fifteen years on the ambulance, it was the strangest call," declared Norton.

Bates observed, "And we still don't know what happened to those people at the pub or why the children were all banged up. There was no car crash or anything we could tell that would have explained it."

Norton confided, "The anger of the crowd who put them on the floor of the van was a big clue, but nobody ever said."

In the late afternoon, Rodstrum stepped into Deighton's room with two cups of tea to find Deighton in a wheelchair.

"Feeling chipper today, are we?" smirked Rodstrum. He looked around to see a huge basket of multi-colored flowers.

"From a secret admirer," Deighton confided. He took his tea and related how he overheard from hospital staff that Dr. Middleton had "diagnosed" Atwater as having dementia. "More like he's started thinking clearly," sputtered Deighton, "It's the letter to the editor!"

Rodstrum interjected, "Let me start before I forget." He told of finding the ambulance technicians and of Cathcart's agreement to review the IOPC complaint.

Deighton took another sip of his tea and leaned back in his wheelchair. "I had a short talk with our man Nevels today."

"I'm listening," grinned Rodstrum.

Deighton recounted. "I gave it to him for letting that Dr. Middleton prescribe me a medication. Told him it was enough to make me want to leave without being properly discharged, if only to avoid additional mischief."

Deighton raised his eyebrows. "Nevels went on about it being an administrative error. I interrupted and demanded, 'Just what is your involvement with the Gogglesgunshod Association?'"

Rodstrum tilted his head. Deighton scowled, "Claims he has no involvement. All he would say is the Association has a history of being very generous to the hospital."

The Daily Slip featured a prominent back page article on Beatrice Butterfield's interview with Lady Carmella and reprinted the photo showing Lady Carmella with Solicitor Reed Crimson. Butterfield related Lady Carmella and Solicitor Reed Crimson got to know each other at a party, but Lady Carmella was adamant she had not obstructed Kingston Dove Foundation's purchase of the Allen Road farmhouse. Butterfield revealed Lady Carmella is very secretive about who does her hair. She noted Lady Carmella intimated she is a hardcore drug user.

About the Circus Troupe at the farmhouse, Butterfield reported Lady Carmella had confided how she once had reported the troupe to the police for being quite mean to her, had brought homemade cookies to the farmhouse to make amends, and had no idea why the circus troupe disappeared. She noted Lady Carmella objected to the troupe's treatment of children and the manner in which they served tea.

Butterfield ended the piece, reviewing the recent conflicting statements on alleged racist events in Huffinfield's Centre, implying she asked Lady Carmella to comment. Butterfield reported Lady Carmella averred she had "proof enough" of racist crimes against Black Brits by Huffinfield residents; Lady Carmella was quoted as saying, "I have no doubt they were put through hell when they stopped for a picnic in Huffinfield."

After reading the article, Carmella groaned and quickly put the newspaper down to avoid reading it a second time. She put on her walking shoes and set off on a long, brisk walk.

Darryl was pleased with the smooth closing on the farmhouse. The Foundation's check cleared, providing a good deal of liquidity. After much internal debate, he decided to continue the services of Rouben and Otto. He had Swaeger's provision list for work on incoming purchase requests. Darryl was not finished with the Lady Carmella character, but a damaging story was spilling forth without his help. He was baffled at not finding Helga.

Chapter 34. Porter Public Investigates

On Tuesday, Porter Public reporters, Tom Valley and Susan Daly, drove toward Huffinfield. (Neither had heard of the place before reading Brad Leveler's Tweet.) On the drive, they wondered aloud if the Atwater letter was a hoax. The local paper's mention of racist crimes seemed to corroborate Atwater's letter, but a former city councilor described the reports as slanderous and police had no comment. By mid-morning, Tom and Susan arrived in Huffinfield's Centre.

Susan's first stop was at the local pub. Curtis Field, the longtime owner, looked up and greeted her. Susan introduced herself and asked what he could tell her about Mr. Atwater's letter to the editor. Curtis Field poured a shot for Susan. As an afterthought, he poured one for himself.

After a quick gulp, he slowly confided, "Sometimes the patrons imbibe a bit too much. You would be amazed to hear what's been said to have happened here. I've known Atwater for years, a nice chap. Best to let his delirium go by the wayside. He's been at hospital all last week, you know."

Susan swallowed her shot. "Poor man," she murmured. She reached for her wallet.

"It's on the house," Field announced, surprising himself.

Tom's first stop was at Lillie's Pie Shop. After Tom introduced himself and stated his purpose, Clive Leeway snarled, "Get out!" Tom braced as Clive came around the counter. Before Tom reached the door, Clive himself stormed out. That left Tom with Clive's wife Lillie, a curvaceous blond. To make amends for Clive's affront, Lillie fussed over Tom. As she wrapped up a complimentary meat pie, she confided Clive wasn't sleeping well lately.

"Any Black customers in my shop! I would remember that!" assured Lillie Leeway. Tom thanked her for the pie, and Lillie wished him good luck with his report. Tom noted she was eager to reach for her phone.

When Tom stopped at the library to inquire if Ms. Cummington was volunteering that day, the front desk librarian waved him toward the stacks. He approached slowly and noted the scent of furniture polish. All was quiet. Finally, he spied a woman, thin with cropped hair and wire rimmed spectacles, re-shelving books from a cart.

As he approached, the woman looked up and prompted, "You're that news writer, aren't you?"

He smiled, "Tom Valley. Porter Public."

"Lillie told me you'd likely be around. I'm Minerva Cummington. Did you want to talk to me?"

Tom smiled. "Yes. Can we talk here?"

"Depends on what you want to talk about," replied Minerva. Without waiting for an answer, she returned to shelving books.

Tom took out his pad and tried again. "Excuse me, Ms. Cummington. Did you get a chance to read the letter by Reginald Atwater?"

"I did," declared Minerva. "I can barely believe that twit mentioned me by name. People have lost all sense of civility these days."

Tom continued, "Did you see a Black family stop at Huffinfield for pies?"

"I did not," declared Minerva. She added, "I didn't see them in the pub either."

Tom asked, "Did you see Black children get stuffed into a boot with the door slammed shut on them?"

"I did. I'm taking no more questions on that." Minerva looked up and down the stacks and shelved another book.

"Did you see the doors of an ambulance outside the pub close shut on adults and children inside?"

"I did. The adults were already in there but I saw the children run in, of their own volition."

Minerva moved her book cart toward him and mumbled, "All through in this row."

Tom asked, "Did you see any blood in the ambulance or in the pub?"

"Yes and yes," responded Minerva as she pushed the cart of books.

Tom asked, "Where were the children before they were put in the boot?"

Minerva replied, "In Petunia Park."

Tom asked, "Were the children in the park with adult supervision?"

"Yes, there were six adults," intoned Minerva as she pushed another book into place on a shelf.

Tom asked, "How did you come to see the children and adults in Petunia Park?"

Minerva winced, "Lillie and Clive Leeway were over at the pub, carrying on like we were being invaded. We followed them to the park mostly to shut them up. When we got to the park, those people were on picnic."

Tom asked, "How did the children come to be put in the boot?"

Minerva paused to recall, "Some of the men put 'em in. I didn't put them there."

Tom asked, "How was it the adults went from the park to the pub?"

Minerva considered the question and answered, "They walked. At least they weren't carried. They were caught up in the crowd. I didn't go to the pub with them."

Tom asked, "Did they want to go to the pub?"

"I can't say what's going on in other people's minds," Minerva retorted.

Tom continued, "In that ambulance outside the pub, were the people inside the ambulance Black people?"

"Yeah, I think so." She paused. "It's time for my break," Minerva panted as she pushed the cart around him. "I've said all I've got to say. Good day."

Susan stopped next at Heavenly Hairdoos. The shop's hairdresser, Constance Appleton, had one customer and shouted from the back. "I'm just about ready to put her under the dryer, I'll be right with you." Susan took a seat and waited.

In minutes, the hairdresser approached. She had short, bouncy hair and a round face made up like a runway model's. She wore silver-tipped, black flats over her polka dot silk stockings. A coral salon smock covered the rest of her.

Appleton greeted Susan. "Morning. Are you one of those news writers from Porter Public?"

"Susan Daly, Porter Public," Susan introduced herself.

Ms. Appleton noted, "Lillie told me I'd likely be hearing from someone. Do you want your hair cut?"

"No, thank you. I've been sent to follow up on the letter by Reginald Atwater. Did you get a chance to read it?" asked Susan.

Appleton laughed, "There's not a soul in Huffinfield hasn't read it. I'm Connie Appleton. What can I do for you?"

"I'm interested in whatever you remember about this incident in Mr. Atwater's letter," shrugged Susan.

Appleton came around the counter, sat next to Susan and confided, "It all happened in an instant and when it was done, it was as though it couldn't have happened. You know what I mean?"

"Maybe," hedged Susan. "What happened, as far as you know?"

Appleton blew out her cheeks and considered the question. She put her arm on the armrest and leaned toward Susan. In a hushed voice, she related, "Clive and Lillie Leeway entered the pub, wailing and carrying on about a boatload of Black Brits infesting the town, making the food unsanitary, taking over the park, about to contaminate the public loo…"

Appleton shook her head. "It was a dull day and they were probably given more attention than they deserved. We all rolled down the same hill of anger and fear. The pub emptied out as the two of them led the way to Petunia Park. In a far corner, there was a group, three couples and a half dozen kiddies, finishing up a picnic."

She paused, but then continued. "The next thing I honestly remember is the women were in the pub and howling in pain, hot grease or something was being thrown at them. To calm it down, I said let me cut their hair instead. That seemed to stop the worst of it but then Clive pulled the three women in the back, and I don't want to think what happened. Their men were flopped on the pub floor like they had fallen a long way. When they sliced their ears off, I left and went home. I don't know anymore."

The customer under the dryer yelled that it was too hot. "I gotta go," moaned Appleton as she rose and scrambled toward her customer.

"Thank you," muttered Susan as she headed for the fresh air.

Tom Valley stopped at Miller's Mechanical. When he asked for Paul Foster, Mr. Miller directed him toward the yellow tractor at the far end of the yard. "You'll find him under that."

Tom strode past the many parked cars and onto the mud where the tractor stood. He saw no one. Tom looked around the tractor and loudly inquired, "Paul Foster?"

"Hold a minute, that's me," said a voice. From under the tractor, a muscular man in a t-shirt, splotched with grease and mud, slid into view. He looked at Tom inquiringly. "I'm Paul Foster. Who are you?"

Tom introduced himself and stated, "Excuse me for interrupting your work, but if you would indulge me for a bit, did you get a chance to read the letter by Reginald Atwater?"

"It would be impossible not to have read it by now," asserted Mr. Foster. "My name was right there in print. I wasn't overly pleased to see that, I'll say."

Tom pushed ahead. "What happened that day, as far as you know?"

Mr. Foster thought about that for a minute. "I don't know."

Tom asked, "Did you see any Black people in Huffinfield that day?"

"I believe I do recall that, yes," responded Mr. Foster.

"Where were the Black people when you first remember seeing them?" asked Tom.

"Petunia Park," replied Mr. Foster.

"What were the Black people doing in Petunia Park?" asked Tom.

"Don't know," replied Mr. Foster, "but it looked like they were having a picnic lunch."

"Did any Black children get put in the boot of a car?" asked Tom.

Mr. Foster nodded. "Yes. Two children each in three boots, as I recall."

Tom asked, "Who put the children in the boot?"

"It wasn't me," declared Mr. Foster. "I don't rightly remember, but I believe they were heaved in so it was probably a bloke who put 'em in."

"Did you observe any Black women in the pub?" asked Tom.

"I did," replied Mr. Foster, "But I don't know their names."

"How did they get in the pub?" asked Tom.

"I do not recall," replied Mr. Foster.

"At any time, were the women tied up?" asked Tom.

"No," replied Mr. Foster, "They were waving their arms around so I wouldn't say they were tied up."

"Were there any Black men in the pub?" asked Tom.

"Three Black men," replied Mr. Foster.

"Did you observe anyone punch or hit or poke any of the Black men?" asked Tom.

"I think I did, but it has been some years now so I wouldn't swear to it," replied Mr. Foster.

"Were the women taken to the back room of the pub?" asked Tom.

"Yes," replied Mr. Foster.

"What happened in the back room?" asked Tom.

Mr. Foster shook his head. "Others might be able to help you out more than me. I don't even remember what I had for supper last night. I need to get back to work." He turned and slid back under the tractor.

At the entrance to the botanical garden, Susan found Dalton Payne, the town groundskeeper. Payne, a large, sunburnt man, was intent on trimming shrubbery. After getting his attention, Susan explained Porter Public was following up on Reginald Atwater's letter. Dalton Payne squinted his eyes, and huffed, "I'm not talking to you."

Susan ventured, "Why is that?"

He snarled, "I'm not talking to you. Follow?" He turned, raised his shears and resumed trimming.

Susan stopped at the Office of Mildred Pearson, Chartered Accountant. The receptionist called to Pearson's office and then related, "She says she can give you five minutes. It's the third door on the right."

Susan thanked the receptionist, walked down the hall and knocked at the door.

"Yes, come in," beckoned the voice from inside. When Susan opened the door, a stately woman rose from behind her desk and walked toward the table in the corner of the room, so Susan headed there too.

After introducing herself, Susan explained, "I've been sent to follow up on the letter by Reginald Atwater. Did you get a chance to read it?" asked Susan.

"I did, " declared Mildred Pearson, facing her from across the table.

After a short pause, Susan ventured. "As you are mentioned by name, I wanted to get your take on Mr. Atwater's recounting."

Pearson looked Susan up and down and then confided, "A bit more colorful than the reality, but there was a grain of truth to it. They weren't welcome here."

Intimidated by Pearson's gaze, Susan floundered, "What happened that day?"

Pearson bristled. "Here's for your follow-up. We don't want their kind here. We want to preserve our world for our children. We won't let them come in here and take over. We were protecting what little we've got. And it worked, no more have come."

Susan posed, "What of the reports that town residents subjected Black Brits to torture?"

Pearson scoffed, "Let them stand in fear."

Susan was silent for a moment.

In an officious tone, Pearson said, "My time is valuable, Ms. Daly. Please see yourself out."

Susan stammered, "Thank you for your time," as she headed out the door.

Tom stopped at the home of Tommy Hill, a retired plumber. Mrs. Hill pointed upward and told him her husband was on the second floor porch.

On the porch, Mr. Hill smiled when Tom asked about the events in Atwater's letter. "I was concerned everyone get a fair chance to get involved," nodded Mr. Hill.

"What do you specifically remember happening that day?" pressed Tom.

Mr. Hill shrugged. "It was pretty much how Atwater said it was. He's a straight arrow, that one." There was a long pause. Mr. Hill ventured, "Both Atwater and I were given commendations by the Gogglesgunshod Association; we each got a jam jar with one of the ears too."

Tom inquired, "What is the Gogglesgunshod Association?"

"They raise funds for different charities. They give a good sum to the local hospital each year." To emphasize this was public information, Mr. Hill added, "It's reported in the paper."

Tom thanked Mr. Hill for his time. On his way out, Tom asked, "Do you recall who was tending bar at the pub that day?"

Mr. Hill frowned, "Travis Sillman. He clerks at the hardware store."

Susan stopped at the Simple Super, the supermarket where Edgar Ward worked as the manager. She found Mr. Ward in his office and noted his broad-shoulders and thinning hair. Standing in the doorway, Susan introduced herself and stated her purpose. He beckoned her in.

From behind his desk, Mr. Ward pointed at a shelf and sneered, "See that jam jar sitting on the shelf? Go on, take a close look."

Susan bent close to look at the jar and saw a human finger suspended in clear liquid. Satisfied she understood what she was looking at, Mr. Ward declared, "That's what I've got to say. Now move out, if you please, I've got work to do."

Tom found Travis Sillman unloading large bags of bird feed in aisle three of Harry's Hardware. Tom introduced himself and stated his purpose. Sillman quietly turned away and put another bag on the shelf. Turning to face Tom, Sillman gave him a hard look and growled, "Take it elsewhere."

"Right," muttered Tom as he walked away.

By chance, Tom found Harvey West, a retired bus driver, sitting on a bench in Petunia Park. When asked about Atwater's letter, Mr. West harrumphed. "It's a shame, you know. Those people are just like us, trying to eke out a life around here. I did what I did to keep my head down. You don't want to find yourself on the other end of Dalton Payne's fist."

Tom asked what Mr. West recalled of that day. Mr. West lamented, "I've been working for years now to recall nothing of that day. Sorry lad."

Tom nodded his understanding and stayed seated on the bench. After a long pause, Mr. West ventured, "I will say, Atwater is an honest man." Tom made a mental note.

Tom remained on the park bench a bit longer, in case Mr. West added anything else. He admired the park's greenery, approximately two hectares with a paved path along its perimeter and through its middle. The park featured an ornate fountain, a sundial and a scattering of war monuments. It was a picture of serenity.

Mr. Harvey stirred and offered, "Every place has its share of odd characters; might be inbreeding to blame." He shook his head and fell quiet again.

Susan rang the bell at the residence of the Reverend Jacob Applegate, the local pastor. A middle-aged man, wearing a white shirt and navy tie, answered the door. Reverend Jake, as he was known to his congregation, looked upon Susan with benign amusement. He clasped his manicured hands in front of his chest and responded, "It may have happened. I just don't recall. If I remember anything, I'll let you know."

Susan and Tom met at their car. Susan declared, "There's definitely something here."

Tom sighed, "Unnerving how normal they all look.

Chapter 35. Under Attack

Assistant Director Minders reported to Director Nevels that Mr. Atwater's letter to the editor was everywhere in the news. He didn't register much interest until spending the afternoon fielding phone calls about Atwater's safety. At day's end, Nevels raged to Minders about Brad Leveler's Tweet. Minders looked up and stated, "The immediate goal is to handle ourselves well. I suggest we make no more exceptions to the protocols." Nevels glared and left without a word.

Within minutes, the receptionist phoned to report that two Porter Public reporters wanted to speak with Mr. Atwater and refused to go away. Minders closed her eyes and responded, "I'll be right there."

Minders escorted the two reporters to the twelfth floor, where she found Atwater's grandson Gregg huddled with Leveler. Turning to the reporters, Minders explained, "You'll have to get his grandson's permission. This is Mr. Armstrong." She took a seat, relieved Nevels was unaware of Leveler's presence. Gregg rose to consult his grandfather. Leveler remained behind, peppering the reporters with questions.

Gregg returned and advised his grandfather would be delighted to speak with them. Ever since the dementia diagnosis, Atwater seemed open to talking to anyone who would listen. Minders collected the reporters' credentials for the visitors' log. When she returned, she suggested it may be better if she stayed in the hall, as it would be quite crowded with so many. In truth, she was too tired to fake it.

As the Porter Public reporters were interviewing Atwater, eight men, bearing spades and pitchforks, marched past the receptionist and into the elevator. The receptionist pressed her security button and phoned Minders' office but it went to voicemail. The receptionist phoned Nevels and shrieked, "We're under attack."

Nevels quit his office and ran to the first floor lobby. "I see no one at all," he stormed.

The receptionist pointed. "They took the elevator. There were eight of them with pitchforks and long spades. Do you think they're going for Mr. Atwater?"

"Call Security," snapped Nevels.

"I pressed the button," she wailed.

Nevels turned back toward her and shouted, "Then call the police. I'm going to the twelfth floor. When you find Ms. Minders, tell her to ring Mr. Armstrong." Nevels sped up the stairs.

By the time he reached the twelfth floor, the security guards were in hand-to-hand combat with the men bearing pitchforks and spades. Two nurse's aides and a nurse crouched under the desk at the nurse's station. Minders had taken up a floor lamp and was brandishing it from a safe distance. Leveler and Armstrong knocked down the two militia members who entered Atwater's room. The reporters ducked behind Atwater's bed. Atwater, himself, was holding up his cell phone and taking a video of whatever he could see. Deighton, swabbed in bandages, bearing a neck brace and a leg cast, was pushing his wheelchair with one arm, closing in on the scene and brandishing what looked like a cricket bat. "Where did he find that?" wondered Nevels aloud, just before a pitchfork missed his head and caught his shoulder instead. He was in the thick of it when the uniformed constables arrived.

Jack Rodstrum stopped by Deighton's hospital room early the next morning with the newspaper. With everything going on yesterday, it was only this morning he read Lady Carmella's "Exclusive Interview" with the Daily Slip. He showed it to Deighton.

"Hence my flowers," Deighton chuckled.

"What?" replied Rodstrum.

Deighton motioned him closer and lowered his voice. "I have bigger news. Last night's visitors included an armed militia, I call them that, not only because they wore 'Armed Militia' t-shirts, but they waged battle with pitchforks and spades." Deighton gave Rodstrum a play-by-play description of what he knew before concluding, "By the time the police arrived, at least a half dozen people were lying on the floor, unable to get up."

"Is Atwater all right?" gasped Rodstrum.

Deighton nodded. "Indignant as hell, but otherwise OK."

"Where was Nevels?" asked Rodstrum.

"He arrived after the fighting began but was in the thick of it when a spade hit him on the head. Last I saw, Nevels was on the floor." Deighton paused, "I don't know how he is now."

"Who were the blokes in the t-shirts?" asked Rodstrum.

"It was a party of eight assailants," stated Deighton as he reached for his notebook on the nightstand. He opened to a page inked over with writing and put on his eyeglasses.

"Quite an eclectic lot, all locals," Deighton muttered as he ran his finger down the page. "There was Dalton Payne, the village groundskeeper, one of them mentioned by Atwater. Travis Sillman, the former juvenile delinquent who does odd jobs about town."

"I know him," assured Rodstrum.

Deighton continued. "There was Clive Leeway, from Lillie's Pie Shop where Atwater's story began. There was Samuel Granville, the younger brother of Mildred Pearson, mentioned in Atwater's letter to the editor."

"How do you know he's her brother?" asked Rodstrum.

"I went to school with him," replied Deighton. "That's four so there's four more," calculated Deighton as he squinted over his scribbles. "We had John Wells and Nathan Marsh, two mechanics from the garage that sent Atwater to hospital. And two more that don't seem to have prior connections. Ethan Gardner is a stone mason. Neil Clarkson is unemployed and a member of the local Veterans Breakfast Club. That's eight."

"Did police arrest this militia?" asked Rodstrum.

"The police took a report. I thought I heard Privitt there, but can't be sure.

After another hospital breakfast, Atwater was skimming through the Daily Slip and saw his name on page four. "Reginald Atwater, at age eighty-one, was diagnosed with dementia, poor man." He blinked. He went back to the beginning of the article. That weasel Alcorn was trumpeting the phony diagnosis as proof that no racist crimes were committed in Huffinfield. Atwater seethed and calculated Alcorn wasn't much younger than eighty-one. Atwater was determined to get his mobility back and fast. He was picturing the clout on the head he would give that Alcorn.

Gregg texted Nancy to tell of the armed attack on his grandfather. He invited her to phone if she wanted to hear more. Nancy phoned at lunch. Gregg told her of the armed militia and the newspaper report about his grandfather being diagnosed with dementia and how that apparently settled it about his allegations. Gregg wanted Nancy to know, given Carmella's quote about racist crimes in her interview. Nancy thanked him for the update.

Later that afternoon, Nancy texted Carmella. "It may be safer in London. You know you are welcome. Call me."

At approximately two o'clock in the afternoon, Nevels' concussion subsided. He found himself in a hospital bed. He thought for a moment and recalled the pandemonium on the twelfth floor. He wondered how Minders fared. He wondered how Atwater fared. He rang the nurse's bell.

The nurse bobbed her head in the door and asked, "Everything all right?"

Nevels nodded, "Yes, but…"

"Then let me get Ms. Minders," interrupted the nurse as she disappeared.

Five minutes later, Minders knocked on Nevels' door. Nevels beckoned, "Come in, Minders."

Minders looked at him and sighed, "Are you OK?"

Nevels declared, "Yes. I'm OK." He quickly added, "How did it go last night?"

"You fought valiantly," assured Minders. "The police took two of the militia away and six unconscious ones were put in hospital beds on the second floor. Mr. Atwater is fine. His grandson is unscathed but furious. The security guards handled themselves well, only minor cuts and bruises there. The newspaper called, but I haven't called back yet. That's the long and the short of it."

Later in the day, Rodstrum found Minders in her office. Rodstrum greeted her, "Ms. Minders, Inspector Deighton tells me you were a valiant trooper last night!"

Minders smiled, "Mr. Deighton was no wallflower himself."

Rodstrum inquired about Nevels. "Over the worst of his concussion," confided Minders. Rodstrum asked about Mr. Atwater. Minders replied that Atwater was fine.

Rodstrum leaned in her doorway and nonchalantly inquired, "Did the militia members regain consciousness?"

Minders nodded her head. "All eight?" he queried.

"All in hospital," responded Minders as she held up six fingers.

"Did the police arrest the other two?" asked Rodstrum.

"They took them away is what I saw," pondered Minders. She ventured, "They were accosting the police so I assume there will be charges."

"Will the six in hospital be discharged soon?" asked Rodstrum.

Minders shook her head and whispered, "Not today anyway."

Rodstrum straightened. Before leaving, he added, "Good to see you well, Ms. Minders."

Darryl monitored Huffinfield and was exceedingly pleased with its progress. Still, he could play on that Carmella woman's fears. Perhaps a local militia might confront her?

Reginald Atwater spent the day writhing in aggravation about the news report saying he had dementia. He would produce his evidence to show he wasn't crazy.

When his grandson stopped by after work, Atwater told him the whereabouts of the jam jar and his Certificate of Commendation. Gregg looked at his grandfather and smirked, "I'm not going to retrieve those for you. That stuff makes you itchy."

Atwater grinned, "I taught you well." After a pause, he added, "Just remember they're in the attic if I'm gone and anyone wants proof of what I'm telling you."

Gregg confided, "I think those Porter Public reporters obtained more than enough corroboration."

Atwater became still and asked, "What's that?"

"What?" asked Gregg.

"Open the window more," Atwater directed, "It's coming from outside."

Gregg went to the window. "It's about twenty people holding candles and singing," he reported.

After listening for a few minutes longer, Atwater suggested, "Perhaps the nurse's station knows what's going on."

"I'll ask," shrugged Gregg.

At the nurse's station, Gregg found himself in line. Inspector Deighton was in his wheelchair and waiting for an answer. In a hushed voice, the nurse confided, "From what I can gather, it's local residents holding a candle light vigil for the six militia members in hospital after last night's attack on Mr. Atwater."

"For the love of Pete," exclaimed an exasperated Deighton. He turned to see Gregg behind him. "I'm very sorry," is all he could think to say.

"Who are they?" asked Gregg.

"Take a photo for me and I'll see what I can tell you," replied Deighton.

In minutes, Deighton was peering at Gregg's phone. "Could you email me this photo?" asked Deighton.

"Sure," replied Gregg. "My grandfather's looking over the photograph now. Any surprises I should prepare for?"

"The Police Superintendent, for one," stated Deighton as he studied the faces. "Did those assailants last night get arrested and charged?"

"Nothing in today's paper," responded Gregg. "Hopefully, we'll find out tomorrow."

Deighton nodded, "I'll keep an eye for it." He groaned, "Be forewarned, Reverend Jake is holding a candle."

Gregg bowed his head. He returned to his grandfather's room and sent a text message with the photo about the candle light vigil to Leveler. Leveler immediately texted the photo to the Porter Public reporters.

Before long, Gregg sent the text to Nancy as well. The vigil keepers made him feel lonely. He could only imagine how his stoic grandfather was feeling.

Chapter 36. Candle Light Vigil

After opening Brad Leveler's text, the Porter Public reporters requested names for the faces in the photo. Leveler set off.

He spotted the crowd outside of the hospital's main entrance and parked at the carpark's edge. Leveler heard the crowd singing and recognized the church hymn, "I Vow To Thee My Country." He pulled a random piece of paper from the glove compartment and wrote down the title. He counted eighteen men and women and judged them mostly middle aged. They were holding nine-inch, white tapers. He didn't recognize any of the faces in the dim light.

Leveler walked toward the crowd and the singing stopped. A man stepped forward to talk about unity and preservation of sacred trusts. It could have been about anything. Leveler stood with the crowd and caught the eye of the woman next to him. "What is he going on about?" whispered Leveler.

"It's Reverend Jake. We're here to say prayers for the brave men who stood up for the cause last night and landed in hospital. They meant to do in Atwater but…"

"Shhh" hushed a man next to them. He looked at Leveler very unkindly. Leveler quickly ducked inside. He took the elevator to the twelfth floor to distance himself from the vigil holders. He headed toward the visitors' lounge but was stopped by Mitch Deighton's wheelchair.

"Did you just come in the main entrance?" demanded Deighton.

"I did," replied Leveler.

"Where's your candle?" asked Deighton.

"I'm not with them," replied Leveler.

"What did you make of them?" asked Deighton.

Leveler replied, "Reportedly, they're here to say prayers for the men hospitalized after trying to 'do in' Mr. Atwater."

"They told you that?" asked Deighton.

Leveler replied, "When I asked, the woman next to me said so. She said the Reverend Jake was addressing the crowd. The man, standing next to us, shushed her and glared at me. It's all I know."

"Poor Mr. Atwater," mumbled Deighton. "He must feel awfully alone."

Leveler asked, "If I show you a photo, do you think you identify any of the faces?"

Deighton nodded, "I know them all."

Carmella phoned Nancy that night. Carmella was adamant she wasn't running away again. "Then take good care and be extra careful this next week," admonished Nancy.

Carmella told Nancy how she was working around the clock to find the circus troupe. It was as though they had vanished. Nancy suggested that might be a fortunate event. Carmella was determined to visit the farmhouse to see for herself. Nancy made her promise to wait for the weekend so they could go together.

The next day, Jack Rodstrum was reviewing his IOPC allegations when Kevin Cathcart phoned. Rodstrum asked, "Did you get a chance to look at my allegation?"

Cathcart answered, "Yes but I want to look at it more. Do you have a minute?"

I do," replied Rodstrum.

Cathcart proposed, "Let's meet at the McDonald's near the gym in a half hour."

"I'll be there," replied Rodstrum.

At the McDonalds, Rodstrum and Cathcart huddled over their Big Macs. Rodstrum looked at him expectantly. Cathcart shook his head, "It's bad."

Cathcart took another huge bite and Rodstrum resigned himself to waiting.

"Wiley and Privitt responded to a call for help at hospital last night - armed militia storming in and making for Atwater's room. They got there and found mayhem. Only two of the assailants were conscious when they arrived, and those two put up a struggle with spade and pitchfork. Unbelievable, right? They took the two conscious ones to the station, booked 'em and filed a report showing eight militia members had attacked, with the Hospital Director unconscious after a spade whacked his head. There was blood on the floor." Cathcart paused, put his BigMac on the table and bit his lip. Rodstrum waited.

Cathcart took a deep breath before continuing, "The Police Superintendent came in at four o'clock in the morning. Odd enough, right? Then almost immediately, Superintendent Sykes demanded the charges be dropped against the attackers, the two at the station be let go, the records of the questioning be destroyed, and Wiley and Privitt be put on indefinite sick leave! She asked me to provide the ledger which recorded the booking of the two militia members." He paused and pushed an envelope toward Rodstrum.

Cathcart stated, "I'm giving these paper files to you for safe keeping. There's a report, five statements, photos and the constables' affidavits."

Rodstrum took the envelope and asked, "Is this the only copy?" Cathcart shook his head.

Cathcart promised to give Rodstrum his comments and additions on his IOPC complaint at the pastry shop the next morning. "I'll be there," promised Rodstrum.

Jack Rodstrum was at the pastry shop early the next morning. He took his usual order to a far table. Kevin Cathcart was in the door just as Rodstrum started his tart. In short order, Cathcart was emptying a large envelope onto the table. Rodstrum winced at the scribbled comments covering his draft, but he grinned when Cathcart presented an updated complaint with post-it notes showing where to sign.

Rodstrum returned all the papers to the envelope before asking, "What news on the militia being booked?"

Cathcart still didn't know if the six hospitalized assailants were booked. He explained, "The booking ledger is missing. I can still see the record of the two being booked the night before. I'm not sure that isn't an oversight. Armed assailants storming a hospital, then being let go without notice to a magistrate or a bail hearing? Irregular, to say the least. Given the context of the situation, it feels sinister. I hope you send the allegation soon."

"Today is the day," declared Rodstrum.

Mindful of local tensions, Rodstrum drove far from town to post his IOPC complaint.

It was mid-afternoon when Rodstrum stopped at hospital to update Deighton.

"What! No tea? You're fired," Deighton declared. Rodstrum stormed out and went directly to the cafeteria. When he returned, Deighton had moved from his bed and into his wheelchair.

"That's more like it," huffed Deighton. After ensuring his cup of tea was up to snuff, Deighton recounted the candle light vigil." Rodstrum was flabbergasted.

"You'll never guess who was there," taunted Deighton.

"Dr. Miles Middleton?" guessed Rodstrum.

Deighton shook his head. "No. He did not put in an appearance. But two faces of note were our own Police Superintendent and Reverend Jake."

"Unbelievable," gasped Rodstrum.

Deighton continued, "And today's Daily Slip reports on a militia storming hospital, Atwater unscathed, Nevels felled unconscious, six militia in hospital and two taken to police station and booked."

Deighton picked up the paper and put his finger on a line of text. "Chief Police Inspector says No Comment.' That fits, doesn't it?" he huffed.

Deighton flipped the newspaper on the bed, and brightened, "Fortunately, the paper included Ms. Minders' statement, commending hospital staff for its professionalism and relating that Hospital Security successfully repelled the 'eight assailants bearing spades and pitchforks."

"Go Ms. Minders!" cheered Rodstrum.

Deighton picked up the newspaper again. He held it up and scowled, "Another kick is the article implies that instead of the militia, Porter Public is to blame for this manifestation of rage. Claims Porter Public is stirring up the community. Such rubbish."

Rodstrum smirked, "Calm yourself. You got your flowers, didn't you?"

Rodstrum related his own news. Deighton chuckled about his road trip to mail the IOPC complaint.

Upon leaving for her morning walk, Carmella snatched an envelope, addressed to YOU, taped to her front door. She unfolded the sheet of white stationary to find one typed line: meddling makes me mad – lies leer lovey – move maybe – desist or death. She retreated, locked the front door and doubled checked the back door's lock. Enraged at her fear, she paced.

Carmella considered the facts. Someone left the note on her front door. She unlocked her front door and marched around the house, looking for any sign of those responsible. She found nothing. She didn't know what to make of this. Was it reasonable to construe this as a death threat? Nancy would have a fit if she told her. She put on the kettle for a cup of tea and resumed her pacing. She found her phone and arranged to visit Inspector Deighton later that morning.

Lady Carmella stepped off the hospital elevator and strode toward Inspector Deighton's room. He was sitting in his wheelchair and waiting for her.

"Good morning, Inspector Deighton. Looking on the mend," greeted Carmella.

Deighton grinned and welcomed her. "What news?" he prompted.

Carmella took the envelope from her purse and handed it to Deighton as she related, "This was taped to my front door this morning."

Deighton grabbed his eye glasses and pulled the letter from the envelope. Carmella leaned on the window sill.

"I don't know what to do," she confided.

"Have you reported this to the police?" asked Deighton.

"I'm reporting this to you, Inspector Deighton. I have to say my faith in the local police was a bit shaken by its treatment of the circus troupe."

"But you trust me?" asked Deighton.

She responded slowly, "You put yourself in harm's way to check on me, I suppose." She paused and declared, "Yes, I do trust you."

"Thank you," said Deighton.

Carmella asked, "Is it reasonable to construe this as a death threat?"

Deighton nodded and asked, "Do you have any idea about who might be responsible?"

Carmella frowned. "I don't know. My interview for the paper corroborated Mr. Atwater's letter." She paused, then blurted, "Perhaps the circus troupe?"

Deighton shrugged. Absorbed in deciphering the text, he muttered, "Open to interpretation, but a death threat."

Beatrice Butterfield appeared in the doorway. "My, but I hope I'm not interrupting," she minced.

"Not at all. Come in Beatrice," responded Deighton.

"Good morning, you two," greeted Butterfield.

"Ms. Butterfield," Carmella briefly tipped her head upward in acknowledgement.

"Do call me Bea," responded Butterfield. She looked from one to the other and burst out, "What's this about a death threat?"

Deighton interjected, "Did you hear about the candle light vigil for the armed men who came to pitch battle outside Mr. Atwater's door? Unnerving and quite nasty, it was."

"Where were you?" asked Butterfield.

"Charging up the hall in my wheelchair, my cricket bat at the ready," declared Deighton.

"How did you come to have a cricket bat?" inquired Butterfield.

"My local team brought it to cheer me as I'm not going to be at practice soon," responded Deighton.

Butterfield stamped her foot. "Damn, I should have checked with you before sending the news to print. The Daily Slip reported on the militia's assault, you know. I'll send you a copy."

"Bless your heart," replied Deighton.

Butterfield was not so easily deterred. She repeated, "Now what is all this about a death threat?" She looked at Deighton sharply, "You know I'll learn of it somehow."

"You have a way, you do," agreed Deighton and he looked Carmella.

Carmella bit her lip and took on a sullen look. Sure Butterfield would learn of it, she divulged, "I found an anonymous letter at my front door this morning."

At that moment, a nurse bustled into the room. It was time for Deighton's medications. Visitors would have to wait outside. Carmella jumped at the chance for escape, entered the stairway, and closed the door behind her before Butterfield even finished admiring Deighton's flowers.

"Weren't you all about the Circus Troupe when now it's all about Atwater's letter?" she posited.

"Real life rarely wraps itself into a neat movie plot," shrugged Deighton.

At almost noon, Director Nevels checked on Atwater and then proceeded to Deighton's room. Deighton was in bed but noticed Nevels in the doorway and beckoned to him. Nevels stepped inside his room and commended, "Inspector Deighton, you were the picture of an undaunted hero the other night, pushing your wheelchair with one arm and getting ready to brandish a cricket bat with the other. The picture lingers in my mind. Very impressive, I wanted to say."

"Thanks Director Nevels," replied Deighton. He added, "You weren't looking all that bashful yourself!"

"Quite the night," Nevels declared, before turning on his heel.

That evening, Carmella phoned Nancy to tell her of the death threat. Nancy wanted her to return to London, but Carmella remained firm.

Chapter 37. Community Invitation

In London that same evening, Delilah Banks and her two cousins supped at their favorite Thai restaurant. Delilah listened to Nicki's plea that she stay away from the likes of Leveler. Nicki reminded her any ensuing publicity might reach her children, and none of them wanted her children sucked back into that vortex of hurt and loss. Delilah's stomach churned as she thought of the hell her children had endured. She pictured the school fights and the report cards and the police visits and the car accidents. After eighteen months of enduring their property destruction and self-harm, she knew she was blessed her children seemed to have returned to some semblance of normalcy.

Before Delilah could respond, Rose added, "And none of us want you to be further injured." Delilah looked at her cousin Rose, whose pretty face had been widened by surgery to conceal disfiguring scars from third degree scalding. Nicki had undergone painful hair transplants to fill in the bald patches on her scalded skull. Delilah herself had permanent scarring on both shoulders. The gang rape had left each of them traumatized and unable to bear more children. The shaky fear at the slightest thing, the marital discord, the loss of her husband, the nightmares, the thwarting of career goals, the quiet at holiday meals…there had been injury.

Nicki leaned in and softly stated, "Some things we can't forget but still bear repeating. Delilah, those people attacked us in the light of day, as though it was the right and proper thing to do."

In a hushed tone, Rose fumed, "None have been held to account."

"Nobody was held to account for the Tulsa Massacre, Rose. Don't go there with me," warned Nicki.

Rose continued, "My point is the Huffinfield gang is dangerous and connected. The police officer didn't help us. The hospital didn't want to know what happened. Clearly, these people, these criminals, aren't contrite about inflicting their senseless rage. Why wouldn't they do it again?"

Delilah nodded and quietly added, "That's why I need to speak up. Tell me I'll still have your support if I do."

"Group hug," Nicki demanded. They each extended their arms to close their circle and squeezed each other's hands tightly.

At the Independent Office for Police Conduct, the intake clerk was undecided on the proper subject box for Rodstrum's multi-faceted complaint. He placed the letter in his supervisor's inbox with the note: "The subject of the allegation is unclear."

That morning's Daily Slip included an article on page three, reporting on a candle light vigil held outside the main gate at Tompkins Hospital as a group of sixteen to eighteen people, praying for the truth to prevail. Upon reading the article, Deighton was miffed. "You might think they were Hare Krishnas, the way it's worded," he muttered.

Late that morning, Brad Leveler made arrangements for a community meeting to discuss racism. Given the statements by the Porter Public reporters and the hospital attack by armed assailants, Leveler didn't believe it was too soon to act. The Foundation's Executive Board agreed. One of the mob victims agreed to an audio interview about her experience. Leveler intended on airing the interview while playing a slide show of the town center scenes. He selected a list of fact sheets to make available. It was unclear whether the farmhouse was up to code for a public meeting or if the school auditorium might be the better venue.

The IOPC's website warranted a verbal or written notice of receipt within twenty-four hours. Postal tracking showed a response was overdue. Rodstrum phoned to learn IOPC had no record of his allegation. Rodstrum countered that the tracking data showed delivery. The representative suggested he send it again. Rodstrum made another copy, signed it and again traveled two hours away to post his complaint.

That afternoon, Deighton saw Gregg Armstrong in the visitors' lounge and wheeled a bit faster. "Mr. Armstrong, good to see you," he greeted.

"Good afternoon Inspector Deighton," responded Gregg. "Let me introduce you to Brad Leveler from the Kingston Dove Foundation."

"Well met," declared Deighton as he reached out his hand.

"Thank you again for identifying the candlelight vigil participants," replied Leveler.

Deighton responded, "We should have phoned a report into the Daily Slip. The coverage was horrendous." He turned to Gregg. "How is your grandfather holding up?"

"He is better, thank you. Mr. Leveler here is looking to hold a community meeting to raise awareness on racism. He is with the Foundation that purchased the Allen Road farmhouse."

"There should be a notice in tomorrow's paper," asserted Leveler.

"Laudable," retorted Deighton. "You say a Foundation purchased the farmhouse at the end of Allen Road?"

"Yes, Kingston Dove Foundation," replied Leveler.

"Did you have much contact with the seller?" asked Deighton. Leveler shook his head.

"I'm pretty sure it was the seller who put me in hospital," mentioned Deighton.

"What put you in contact with the seller," asked Leveler.

"Investigating a complaint against them," responded Deighton. He looked at Gregg and asked, "Is your grandfather planning to attend this community meeting?"

"I don't see how he could. On the other hand, nothing he does would surprise me," responded Gregg.

"We need someone to set the record straight," suggested Deighton.

Gregg nodded, "I'm looking forward to the upcoming issue of Porter Public."

Deighton looked at him quizzically. Gregg confided, "They sent reporters to investigate earlier this week."

"You don't say," replied Deighton.

In a phone call, Deighton told Rodstrum about Brad Leveler. He related, "Not only does he say Kingston Dove Foundation purchased the Allen Road farmhouse, they want to have a community meeting about racism."

Rodstrum arrived at the Registry of Deeds within thirty minutes of closing time, time enough to confirm the ZXY Corporation's sale of the farmhouse to the Kingston Dove Foundation.

After supper, Rodstrum checked his email to find notice of the IOPC acceptance of his complaint. Rodstrum was dismayed to read IOPC's investigation into Huffinfield Police would not start for another six months. He phoned Deighton to relate the runaround by IOPC and the six-month backlog. Deighton responded, "It's up to us to preserve the evidence until then."

The next morning, Brad Leveler scanned the Daily Slip for notice of the upcoming community meeting. On page two, he found mention of Lady Carmella's receipt of a death threat. Continuing to turn pages, he spotted a small boxed announcement on page five. "The Kingston Dove Foundation invites you to a Community Meeting on Encountering Racism." Leveler was relieved.

Darryl was pleased to read of the anonymous death threat to Lady Carmella.

In the early afternoon, Leveler contacted Lady Carmella to personally invite her to the community meeting. She agreed. When Nancy heard, she insisted on joining her. Nancy sent a text to Gregg saying she and Carmella would be attending.

Atwater spotted the community meeting invitation and decided to attend. Once he finished breakfast, he demanded to be put in a wheelchair to try sitting. (He had been flat on his back for more than two weeks.)

Chapter 38. Group Song

With two days until the community meeting, Reginald Atwater gritted his teeth and watched the clock from his wheelchair. Though sore, he could manage thirty minutes of sitting. He figured his endurance would improve if he took it slowly. It wasn't easy getting old.

The next day, Porter Public's report on Huffinfield hit the newsstands. Porter Public reprinted Atwater's letter and juxtaposed its investigative findings with quotes from the Daily Slip. A sideline reported on the candle light vigil for hospitalized militia members with a photo of the candlelight vigil, captioned with the name of each participant. Porter Public insisted Huffinfield's narrative mirrored the national problems of racism and overlooking racism.

Beatrice Butterfield read the article with concern. After reviewing each issue of the Daily Slip since the publication of Atwater's letter, she was relieved to note each comment, naysaying Atwater's allegation, was attributed to a specific individual.

Gregg brought a copy of Porter Public to his grandfather. Reginald Atwater read the entire article while sitting up in his wheelchair.

Constance Appleton read the article before placing the magazine on Heavenly Hairdoos' coffee table. She was pleased to see herself quoted.

In a fit of spite, Milton Alcorn purchased the remaining magazines at the local pharmacy and chucked them into a recycling bin. Unable to find a copy anywhere in Huffinfield, Jack Rodstrum drove to the next town over and purchased two copies; he gave one to Mitch Deighton.

In the late afternoon, Rodstrum visited Kevin Cathcart's flat. Cathcart invited Rodstrum into the kitchen where he was making his "lunch" for the nightshift.

"You know," confided Cathcart, "I wasn't sure you had it right about the sale of the farmhouse." He paused before continuing, "You were correct on all counts. Police had not finished searching the premises. Inexplicably, there was an order to suspend the search. I don't see why the farmhouse wasn't impounded."

"Not only is the farmhouse sold," imparted Rodstrum, "but they almost held this community meeting there."

Cathcart pondered as he sliced his sandwich. "We need someone with time and access to go through those records Deighton unearthed. Perhaps he remembers something to provide a clue."

"I'll raise it with him tomorrow," responded Rodstrum.

"The Chief Inspector looks stricken whenever questioned about it. I think he knows something," revealed Cathcart.

Rodstrum smirked. "On a brighter note, I'm looking forward to seeing Privitt and Wiley tomorrow. I'll be sure to ask about this mysterious sickness that has put them on indefinite sick leave."

"Where are you seeing them?" asked Cathcart.

"The community meeting on racism sponsored by the Foundation. It's at the school auditorium." After a pause, Rodstrum suggested, "The tiny notice in the Daily Slip was easy to overlook."

Cathcart looked closely at Rodstrum before confiding, "I am quite aware of the upcoming public meeting. It was the topic of a conference call yesterday. Mark me, the Superintendent wants a force in riot gear outside the school building, should these 'incendiary philanthropists' instigate violence. That's what she called them."

"Sounds like she wants a race riot," said Rodstrum.

On the day of the Community Meeting, Atwater's doctors were adamant it was too soon to discharge him. After a huddle with his grandson, his doctors relented to his night out, but stipulated Atwater's trip away from his hospital bed would remain undocumented. Concurrently, Nevels insisted Atwater sign a waiver of liability.

Bearing the latest issue of Porter Public, Nancy arrived at Carmella's house to join her at the community meeting. "What's this?" asked Carmella.

"You can flip through it in the car," assured Nancy. "Did you know Gregg Armstrong and his grandfather are planning to attend?"

"Can Mr. Atwater even get out of bed?" asked Carmella.

"He's in a wheelchair, I hear," responded Nancy.

They pulled into the school's carpark at five minutes before the start time. "It looks like a good crowd," commented Nancy. Carmella was engrossed in the Porter Public article.

"Come on," urged Nancy.

Reginald Atwater hired a security unit (four plain clothesmen) to accompany him to the community meeting. His grandson Gregg was by his side. They sat to the side as none of the pre-arranged seating would accommodate a wheelchair. At their angle, Director Nevels was in view, as was Constance Appleton, Mr. and Mrs. Tommy Hill, Clara Crumb, Harry of Harry's Hardware, Mr. Miller of Miller's Mechanics, and Joey from the pastry shop. The two Porter Public reporters sat on either side of their editor, Linda Chickering. Nancy and Carmella sat perpendicular to Atwater and Gregg. Beatrice Butterfield took a seat next to Carmella.

Brad Leveler looked out. It wasn't a packed house, but it was a sizable crowd. He reviewed the use of the equipment with the logistics person for the third time and hoped the presentation would play without a glitch. The Foundation's Executive Board filed into the audience. It was time to begin.

Fifty minutes later, the scheduled program was over. People were fairly silent but had participated when asked. He hoped it had been a learning experience. Leveler did not invite questions. He didn't want to mar the receptive vibes he was getting. Nobody seemed to want to ask any questions, not even that Butterfield character.

The Foundation's President approached the stage. He thanked everyone for coming and suggested they end the evening by joining together to sing "Amazing Grace." The sour School Superintendent pointed to his wristwatch. The President nodded his understanding and amended, "Unfortunately, our time at the auditorium seems to have expired. Please join us in song at the entrance to the carpark in ten minutes. Thank you for coming."

The crowd slowly filed out. Carmella was a bit relieved and a bit disappointed she wasn't asked to speak. Atwater appeared amused by the proceedings. Constance Appleton caught up with Butterfield and beamed about such a wonderful program. Butterfield beamed back and they walked out shoulder to shoulder, in conference.

Gregg explained to Nancy that his grandfather needed to use a back exit, as the school's front entrance was not wheelchair accessible. "We'll come along with you," declared Nancy.

As they left the auditorium, they could hear the crowd singing. When they exited through the school's back door, they heard people screaming and sirens blaring. Carmella was glad to be next to Atwater's security unit. Gregg offered them a ride home. Nancy wanted to see what was happening, but she accepted Gregg's offer rather than risk the chaos.

Engaged in song, the people didn't notice the dozen police encircling them. In a coordinated action, police raised their water hoses and attacked with violent streaming water. The first ones knocked to the ground were soon joined by others seeking to help them. A soaked Brad Leveler tweeted about police violence against peaceful gatherings. Chickering watched while hunched aside of her car. Her reporters recorded portions of the incident from various angles and wrote the names of those taken in ambulance vans. Rodstrum and Wiley and Privitt were soaked but reached their cars. From his car, Nevels, who had no intention of joining in group song, watched in amazement.

The off-duty medical technicians, Bates and Norton, waited for their Aunt Clara. At the entrance to the carpark, Clara Crumb was frozen in place and bawling her eyes out. Rodstrum spotted her from his car. He ran back for Clara and took her inside the school, where he waited with her until she regained her wits. Clara phoned her nephews and arranged to meet them at the school's side door. Rodstrum accompanied her to their car. By the time he returned to the carpark, it was as though nothing happened.

In a statement to Butterfield that evening, the Police Superintendent stated there was no permission granted for a public gathering in the carpark. The former councilman Alcorn phoned Butterfield, applauding the police response to those troublemakers from London. Mildred Pearson tweeted: "Foundation reserved school for one hour but into second hour, crowd wasn't dispersing; who knows what may have happened if police didn't act!"

Bates and Norton took their still stunned Aunt Clara to hospital and met Butterfield in the waiting room. Butterfield asked their elderly aunt what she thought of the police reaction. Clara quipped, "Our singing wasn't that bad." Atwater returned to hospital unscathed. Constance Appleton's YouTube of the police reaction went viral.

Reginald Atwater lay on his hospital bed. He wasn't sure whether he would spend his final years in prison, but he was relieved his nightmare was finally being shared.

Week Four

Chapter 39. Reactions Reverberate

Sunday's Daily Slip sold out before Jack Rodstrum could get a copy. With two cups of tea, he visited Mitch Deighton in hospital. Rodstrum told of the community meeting, the Police Superintendent's reference to "incendiary philanthropists" and the riot police using water hoses on the group of less than fifty people, who had been singing, or at least mouthing the words. Deighton responded, "I hope to read all about last night and see live photos when the next Porter Public hits the newsstands."

Rodstrum noted, "Mr. Atwater attended in a wheelchair and thankfully missed the fire hoses."

"What prompted the firehoses?" inquired Deighton in a tone of disgust.

"Clara Crumb, from the outskirts of town…she suggested they didn't like our singing," mused Rodstrum.

"Was she there? She must be ancient!" exclaimed Deighton.

Rodstrum responded. "She was in attendance. More curious, her nephews gave her a ride but stayed outside in their car."

"It will be interesting to discover the repercussions of last night. I put nothing past Huffinfield," murmured Deighton.

Tommy Hill and his wife stayed silent about their Saturday evening excursion until Sunday midmorning when the wife commented, "Not a word in today's Daily Slip about all that last night."

"Likely went to print prior to the meeting," commented Mr. Hill.

The wife pursued it. "Beatrice Butterfield was in the audience. Did you see her face when that fire hose sent a stream onto her hair?" She chuckled and quipped, "I feared for the copper for a minute."

Mr. Hill grimaced, "I am speechless at being attacked like that." He shook his head and muttered, "I don't know what this world is coming to."

After a pause, the wife ventured, "The audio clip from the Black Brit was sobering."

"That it was," agreed Mr. Hill. They spoke no more of it.

Constance Appleton spent most of Sunday chatting about the community meeting. In the afternoon, while highlighting Lillie Leeway's hair, she exclaimed, "That Brad Leveler is to die for!"

At that, Lillie wished she had attended but confided, "Lee would have gone into conniptions if he even thought I went." She giggled, "And he would have seen me in your YouTube!"

"Did you see it?" squealed Appleton.

Lillie nodded and smirked, "Did you see Bea Butterfield's hair?" They both fell into uncontrollable laughter.

News Editor Linda Chickering took a brisk walk on Sunday morning to put her thoughts in order. Upon her return home, Chickering decided Huffinfield's community meeting deserved its own article in Porter Public.

Beatrice Butterfield reviewed Lady Carmella's letter to the editor and decided to print it later in the week. She had her own story to tell and wasn't about to compete for her readers' attention. The more she thought about the fire hoses ruining the results of her expensive excursion to the London hair salon, the more outraged she became.

This was not the England she knew. Butterfield worked on her special editorial late into the night.

On Sunday evening, the Groundskeeper Dalton Payne was on his eighth pint. To his disgust, Connie Appleton's YouTube was all the talk at the pub. Payne drummed his fingers. Surveying the remnants on his plate, he foraged for chips.

When Travis Sillman walked in the door, Payne motioned to him. Sillman sat across from Payne and crooned, "Gonna be a nice bit of weather this week. Good for business, eh?"

Payne didn't hear him. He was thinking as hard as he ever did. "That Foundation meeting last night," he puffed, "it needs a response."

In a disapproving tone, Sillman muttered, "What are you talking now?"

Payne flattened his hands on the table and leaned in. "What if the militia was to pull its t-shirts out of the laundry and ride again? We could smash windows at Miller's Mechanical and Harry's Hardware, eh?"

Sillman shook his head and whispered, "Mate, we almost got jail time and I work at Harry's Hardware." He leaned closer and declared, "I am not in, no way."

Payne flung his plate in Sillman's face. Without even wiping off Payne's fish batter, Sillman quit the pub. Payne drummed his fingers on the table, oblivious to the shattered plate on the floor. Patrons carefully ignored his table. Curtis Field decided the clean-up could wait until closing.

On Monday morning, Nevels gave Minders a play-by-play description of Saturday night's events. "The victim telling her story was powerfully moving," Nevels declared. Minders looked at him wide-eyed, hoping he would spare her the details.

Sam Wiley and Pete Privitt visited Mitch Deighton at hospital. Deighton was pleased to see them and joked, "I hear you're on sick leave. Nothing contagious, is it?"

"I have notified the Department that to the best of my knowledge, I have no health impediment. What a crock!" asserted Privitt.

Wiley smirked, "Since we didn't get called into work on Saturday night, we were at that Foundation's community meeting. What a time!"

Privitt interrupted to relate, "Rodstrum, soaked like a water rat, ran back through the fire hoses to fetch an old lady, Clara Crumb. She was frozen with fear, though I think they were taking care not to knock her over. So Rodstrum took her back inside and got her safely on her way through another exit. Bet he didn't tell you that!"

Deighton shook his head and demanded, "What else did he leave out?"

After Porter Public's news report and the police riot response to the community meeting, the Independent Office for Police Conduct opened its investigation sooner than scheduled. Rodstrum phoned Deighton and Cathcart with the news.

That evening, six militia members were discharged from hospital to their homes. The police didn't call them and they didn't call the police.

On Tuesday morning, the Daily Slip featured Butterfield's editorial. She praised the courage of the picnic victim who agreed to speak of her attack in Petunia Park. She floated the idea of tax rebates, considering the police failure to address the heinous crimes against Black Brits traveling through Huffinfield. She registered her horror at the fire hoses streaming all around the shaking Clara Crumb and asked, "Who were the police protecting?" She noted the absence of Reverend Jake.

Butterfield suggested influential residents supported the death threats against Reginald Atwater, following his intervention in defense of an innocent man, and then upped the ante when Atwater wrote his letter to the editor. She questioned the prevailing level of civility in Huffinfield that permitted an armed militia to storm a hospital. She questioned, "How is it the police response to the armed militia storming Tompkins Hospital resulted in no arrests, when none of them got away?" She questioned the Police Superintendent's participation in a candlelight vigil in support of armed assailants.

At the Hill home, Tommy's wife spotted Butterfield's editorial and read it aloud. "She must have read Porter Public's report," commented the dour Tommy.

"I tell you she's still seething about her ruined hairdo," replied his wife.

At the Leeway home, Clive finished reading Butterfield's editorial, rolled up the newspaper and smashed it on the dining room table, before kicking the leg of a nearby chair. "Anything the matter Dearie?" inquired Lillie.

Clive made a face and grumbled, "That Bea Butterfield is a raving idiot."

He picked up his phone and dialed Milton Alcorn's number. In less than a minute, he spoke, "Morning, did you read the editorial page?"

After a pause, Clive stated, "Agreed, I nominate you to write a rebuttal." Lillie was relieved Clive wasn't going to ask her to write it.

Brad Leveler marveled at Butterfield's editorial, an amazing change of tone for the Daily Slip. In a voicemail message, he commended the editor but suggested using "mob victims" instead of "picnic victims."

Nevels had Tuesday's Daily Slip opened up before him. He was beside himself about Butterfield's editorial. He kept re-reading one line, "How is it Tompkins Hospital treated these victims but registered no report to authorities of obvious assault and battery?"

Late Tuesday morning, Rodstrum headed to the hospital's Administrative Unit and found Assistant Director Minders in her office.

"Good morning, Ms. Minders," Rodstrum said.

Minders looked up from her notebook and grinned, "Good morning, Inspector Rodstrum."

"As I recall, six of those militia members were hospitalized. Any of them discharged?" asked Rodstrum.

"All six, all last night," revealed Minders. After a pause, she related, "We sent them all home."

Rodstrum nodded knowingly. "Thank you for your time, Ms. Minders," he murmured.

Chapter 40. Executive Planning

IOPC's paperwork on allegations of police corruption in Huffinfield progressed to its Investigations Unit. That morning, a clerk from the IOPC contacted Jack Rodstrum to schedule his in-person interview. The same clerk issued written notice to Police Superintendent Sykes, informing her of IOPC's investigation into confidential allegations.

The next day, the Daily Slip printed Lady Carmella's letter, in which she asked: Had there been an attempt to obstruct the purchase of the farmhouse? Who was Reed Crimson and why are people suggesting she was acquainted with him? Is the circus troupe somehow involved in the racist crimes? How was it the circus troupe resided on Allen Road for years and then vanished? Now that Kingston Dove Foundation owns the farmhouse, has anything in Huffinfield changed?

In a subsequent letter to the editor, former councilman Milton Alcorn suggested Lady Carmella was an outsider who knew nothing, Beatrice Butterfield had been bought off by friends of Reginald Atwater, and the Kingston Dove Foundation was a subversive, left wing organization looking to undermine Huffinfield's way of life.

In his letter to the editor, Harry of Harry's Hardware Store declared, "The militia, who attacked Mr. Atwater in hospital, stole the pitchforks and spades from my inventory."

Mr. Miller of Miller's Mechanics wrote his own letter, announcing, "The three cars of the picnic victims were towed to my shop some years back, and the cars remain available to the lawful owners."

Nevels had been reading each new letter with interest. He phoned his personal solicitor and scheduled a meeting. He regretted signing that stack of documents for Reed Crimson those years ago. He suspected Crimson kept records and filed reports for Gogglesgunshod Association members on a multitude of dubious schemes, to hide profits and justify bankruptcy declarations. Had Nevels implicated himself?

Nausea swept over Travis Sillman when he read Harry's letter. Sure his gig at Harry's Hardware had ended, Sillman told Payne he was onboard for the militia's next action.

Following the Foundation's community meeting, Mr. Miller terminated Foster's employment at Miller's Mechanicals, leaving Foster open to re-enlisting in the militia.

With the spades and pitchforks stashed in his shed, Clive Leeway was raring to go. That made four. Leeway instructed Foster to sound out Edgar Ward. Leeway, himself, would ask Reverend Jake to confer with the two mechanics about continuing on. Neil Clarkson entered the pub a bit later and Foster filled him in. Clarkson declared he was in and agreed to speak with Samuel Granville about joining. Sillman was charged with procuring safety goggles.

In response to the week's news, the Gogglesgunshod Association called a meeting of its Executive Board.

From New York City, Darryl read the Daily Slip. The local people were covering all the bases, as far as he could tell. The police failed to conduct more than a cursory inspection of the farmhouse. Prior to the closing, he directed all walls and furniture be wiped down so few if any fingerprints remained. As far as he knew, neither the police nor the new owners knew of the farmhouse's hidden passages. Otto cleared the police electronic system of pertinent records. Darryl's efforts to locate the paper records proved unsuccessful. He had a hunch the police couldn't locate them either. Perhaps he would send Rouben for another look.

Jack Rodstrum welcomed Trenton Storrs and Bill Walters of the IOPC to his home. In a recorded interview, he swore to tell the truth under penalty of perjury. After four hours, Rodstrum felt tired but satisfied. Bill Walters found Rodstrum to be a credible witness, who provided enough detail to justify further inquiry.

Under the leadership of Dalton Payne, the reconstituted militia donned their black t-shirts and emerged into the dark hours. With their spades and pitchforks, they smashed the windows of Harry's Hardware and Miller's Mechanical. When they turned toward the pub to celebrate, out-of-town police arrested them.

At a special meeting of the Gogglesgunshod Association's Executive Board, not much was spoken during the roast beef and Yorkshire pudding. After dessert was served, Milton Alcorn banged his spoon on the table and demanded, "How is it the Foundation purchased the farmhouse and we needed that Carmella Lady to tell us?" The others around the table gave him hard looks.

The Executive Board's Chairperson, Victor Lloyd, frowned and admonished, "We'll discuss these matters in due course." The meal was completed in sullen silence. Finally, the six men of the Executive Board retired to the drawing room.

Alcorn muttered, "Am I permitted to speak now?"

Ignoring him, Lloyd announced, "Gordon Butler will provide a timeline of recent events. If you please, Mr. Butler." A man in his sixties, of impressive girth, rose. As he shuffled his notes, the others slunk in their stuffed chairs, dreading a laborious litany. Twenty-five minutes later, Butler, confident he had done his part for the evening, returned to his seat.

Denis Chapman, pulled his phone from his coat pocket and silently read a text. "There's been something else!" he informed the group. He slowly read aloud, "The Brimmerston Police have booked six Huffinfield residents for smashing the windows of Harry's

Hardware and Miller's Mechanical." After a short pause, he looked up and added, "No names released as yet."

Brian Turner gasped, "I'll be dashed."

They debated into the night before reaching a consensus.

Mr. Butler would persuade Dr. Miles Middleton to part with an embalmed cadaver, and arrange its deposit in the Foundation's farmhouse. Mr. Palmer would encourage the town solicitor's write-up of criminal charges, sufficient to freeze the Foundation's assets. Mr. Alcorn would inquire into the arrest of militia members and engage Mildred Pearson to stage a vigil for the jailed militia. Mr. Turner would visit Hospital Director Nevels, to emphasize the importance of denying these picnic-victim stories. Mr. Lloyd would see the Police Superintendent confirmed no evidence existed to link the circus troupe with criminal activity. Mr. Chapman would ensure Lady Carmella reconsidered her choice of Huffinfield as a retirement destination. Mr. Butler would suggest to Atwater that his refusal to recant may jeopardize his grandson's wellbeing. At every opportunity, all would discourage cooperation with Porter Public.

Even Alcorn left the meeting with a sense of satisfaction.

Beatrice Butterfield suspected Porter Public would run another article about Huffinfield. She was determined to get the better scoop. She tracked the known confidents of Solicitor Crimson. She spoke to those who complained the loudest against the circus troupe. With homemade tarts in hand, Butterfield visited Brad Leveler and received a tour of the farmhouse. With following up on leads and making connections between hints and disavowals, she forgot to run any mention of the IOPC investigation. (Don't ask how she knew.) Tomorrow, she promised herself.

Outside the townhall, approximately twenty people joined Mildred Pearson's candle light vigil for the jailed militia. Butterfield demanded to know if Pearson obtained a permit for the public gathering. When

Pearson fumbled, Butterfield retorted, "I'll take that as a 'No, you didn't.'"

Butterfield walked over to the lone copper, who was leaning on the park bench and sipping a hot drink. She addressed him and asked, "Where are your fire hoses this evening?"

Constable Goddard straightened as he responded, "I just follow orders, ma'am."

Butterfield pursued it. "Do your superiors know about this public gathering?"

Constable Goddard replied. "Yes ma'am. They sent me over here to make sure no unsavory types accost these local citizens on parade in the dark."

Butterfield turned on her heel and left. The constable exhaled in relief but did not return to leaning on the park bench. He stood tall and hoped his photo wouldn't be printed in the Daily Slip.

At dawn, the newly installed alarm system at the farmhouse on Allen Road was sounding. The exterior walls of the structure were alight with blinking red lights. Brad Leveler awoke to the cacophony and the security monitoring company's report that police were on route.

Police walked around the building and found a door with a busted lock. They asked if anything was missing. Leveler, still in his bathrobe and slippers, didn't have an answer. He asked if they would accompany him while he looked around. The Foundation didn't have much in the building, but he wasn't sure whether anyone might have entered. Leveler and the police walked about the first floor.

Leveler opened up the cabinets and closets. When he opened the coat closet nearest to the back door, a nude manikin fell out. It looked like it came from an Arts and Crafts Store window. "That manikin wasn't there before," he protested. The constables returned it to the closet. Leveler demanded they remove it. Though disinclined to take it, they judged Leveler was likely to win any debate. The police removed the manikin and took their leave. While Leveler watched, they stuffed the manikin into the boot of their police car and secured it with a shock cord. Leveler did not see the police car stop at the end of the drive. There, the police dumped the manikin behind the overgrown Himalayan Lilac bushes.

Later that morning, Police Superintendent Michelle Sykes held a press conference. Butterfield asked for her comment on the IOPC's investigation. Sykes responded, "I was brought into this job to clear out corruption, and I take umbrage at the suggestion I am party to a cover-up."

Mr. Lloyd was in the audience and asked about the circus troupe's criminal activity. The Police Superintendent maintained, "We have no evidence to link the circus troupe with criminal activity."

Following up, Butterfield inquired about the six circus troupe members booked for the kidnapping and attempted murder of Inspector Deighton. The Police Superintendent paused to grimace before responding, "The inspector was accosted by unknown assailants. No further comments please. I'm late for my next meeting." She quickly walked out, with her entourage in tow.

Lloyd was satisfied. Butterfield noted she was overdue to pay another visit to Mitch Deighton.

Shortly after the Porter Public reporters returned to town, a constable directed them to move their car, insisting it blocked a private drive. They returned to their car and confirmed it was parked alongside a curb. On closer inspection, they found all four tires slashed. Their editor, Linda Chickering, sent a colleague to fetch them.

Chapter 41. Carnage and Umbrage

Lady Carmella awoke to carnage---two heads of sheep dogs on her front step and their bodies by her mailbox. When she called the police, the dispatcher connected her to voice mail. The morning passed without any police response to her message. Flies hovered over her stoop. Carmella called Inspector Deighton.

Mitch Deighton answered his phone to hear Lady Carmella's anxious voice, relating the horrendous scene on her property and the lack of a police response. Deighton explained an inspector should conduct an onsite investigation, take photos, ask questions and note any clues as to how the dog parts came to be there. He promised to follow up. Carmella agreed to be patient.

Deighton phoned the morning desk sergeant, Jane Tines, to inquire about Lady Carmella's report. She declared it was the first she heard of it. Deighton asked what he could do to get this moving. Tines promised to sort it. Within minutes, Tines pulled the dispatcher records from that morning to find Lady Carmella was put through to the voicemail line for cat retrieval requests. Tines printed Carmella's message and the dispatcher recording. She put the paperwork in the Chief Inspector's inbox with a post-it, advising, "Needs Action."

At approximately two o'clock, the rookie Inspector Donald Dibbs presented himself at Carmella's front door. She found Dibbs taking photographs of the carnage on her stoop. Dibbs introduced himself and asked her to please explain why the dogs were decapacitated. Carmella was incensed. She informed Inspector Dibbs she had contacted the police in hopes they would be able to provide answers. In an effort to be helpful, Dibbs noted the mail carrier would not remove the detached bodies set by the mailbox. Carmella asked for the name of Dibbs' superior. He stiffly responded, "I report to the Chief Inspector."

After confirming she had no further information, Dibbs put away his notepad. With a bit of a shrug, Dibbs muttered, "Good day to you then."

Carmella gasped, "Is that all you are going to do? Who is going to remove the carnage?"

Dibbs bit his lip as he considered. "Homeowner's responsibility, ma'am."

Dibbs warned, "Violations of the Animal Welfare Act can carry a jail term of fifty-one weeks in prison, ma'am." Dibbs strode back to his car. It was dawning on Dibbs his promotion to Inspector meant he could no longer rely on a partner's expertise.

Carmella watched Dibbs' car pull away. She was dumbfounded. She phoned Nancy and left a frantic voicemail message: "I'm not crazy! I awoke to find two beheaded sheepdogs, with their bloodied heads on my stoop. I phoned the police and hours later, Inspector Dibbs came by to tell me I could get jail time for violating the Animal Welfare Act. I'm going to see Inspector Deighton before the police return."

Carmella was at hospital by three o'clock. Deighton listened to her report. Deighton had never heard the name Dibbs. He called Jack Rodstrum and arranged for him to remove the carnage that afternoon.

On her way out, Carmella ran into a distraught Gregg. "Is your grandfather all right?" she asked. Gregg shook his head and almost walked into the wall. Carmella invited him for a walk around the carpark. He silently followed her.

Finally, Gregg disclosed, "I came early to see him because I had plans after work. When I arrived, I found my grandfather in great pain and gripping a piece of paper in his hand. I called for the nurse and dislodged the paper." Gregg paused and didn't seem able to continue.

"Where is your grandfather now?" asked Carmella.

"In the intensive care unit," gulped Gregg, "Minutes ago, the doctors successfully dislodged a razor blade he swallowed."

"I didn't know they could do that," whispered Carmella.

"It was endoscopic intervention with the use of an over-tube under general anesthesia," replied Gregg.

Carmella looked at him quizzically. He explained, "It's what the doctors told me just minutes before you found me."

"Are you sure it wasn't an accident?" asked Carmella. Gregg shook his head and pulled the note from his coat pocket with a shaking hand and showed it to Carmella. It was an anonymous note, threatening harm to Gregg if Atwater didn't recant his "story about the picnic victims."

"Come with me," she directed.

She knocked on Deighton's door and announced, "Inspector Deighton, you need to hear this." Once Gregg entered Deighton's room, she raced home to meet the retired Inspector Rodstrum.

In spite of his full schedule, Director Nevels agreed to lunch with Mr. Turner of the Gogglesgunshod Association. Like prior lunches, this one moved at a snail's pace. What made the day worse is after enduring the lunch, Nevels learned Mr. Turner wanted to discuss "business matters."

Back in Nevels' office, Turner closed the door. "This won't take long," he promised. He took a seat at the far table and waited for Nevels join him.

Turner leaned in and said, "Troward, the Executive Board has requested I convey their gratitude for the good works done at this hospital."

"Very kind," accepted Nevels.

"The Board has asked me to impress upon you the Gogglesgunshod Association's expectations." He cleared his throat. "You understand my meaning?" asked Turner.

"That we strive to operate in an efficient and humane manner?" suggested Nevels.

"Of course that," Turner peevishly replied. He tried again, "We expect your support in denying these picnic victim stories."

"Was I invited to this picnic?" quipped Nevels.

Turner interpreted this as an affirmative response. "Very good," he asserted. As he rose, Turner muttered, "Be sure the staff and electronic records are in accord."

"We strive to be accurate," retorted Nevels.

Turner wasn't keen on Nevels but other than his demeanor, Turner found nothing on which to fault him.

At five o'clock, Nevels received a full report on Atwater, including reference to the anonymous threat clenched in his hand. Nevels directed Minders to consult the log of those entering Atwater's room that morning. He suspected Turner. Nevels was insulted by Turner's request to lie. He never lied, but he didn't always tell everything he knew. At this juncture, Nevels regretted keeping quiet.

Beatrice Butterfield stopped at hospital to bring news to Mitch Deighton. He was in bed and about to tell her he was too tired to talk when Butterfield told how Superintendent Sykes said he was accosted by unknown assailants. His adrenaline soared. In a hushed voice, Butterfield asked, "Weren't your attackers part of that circus troupe at the farmhouse on Allen Road?" Deighton recounted how he came to be at hospital. Given his update on Reginald Atwater's state and the carnage on Lady Carmella's stoop, Butterfield decided she owed Deighton another basket of flowers.

After attending the Huffinfield Police Superintendent's press conference, Bill Walters sent IOPC personnel to impound the police records on the circus troupe. Unfortunately, those records weren't to be found. Bill Walters phoned his office and requested the IOPC Solicitor's Office apply for a search warrant. He wanted to find Deighton's report, the testimony of the deceased circus troupe members at the time of their booking and any report about the picnic victim affair.

Within the hour, Darryl learned of the impending search warrant and decided it was time to locate the records. He arranged for Rouben's entry into Huffinfield's police station at two o'clock that morning. In an abundance of caution, Darryl directed Otto to review the electronic records to ensure no supplemental entries had re-entered the police data banks. He requested a list of those clients of "taxidermy cadavers" from the farmhouse. He wanted to know who he could lean on.

Meanwhile, Rodstrum completed his inspection of Lady Carmella's grounds and removed the sheepdog remains. Carmella pressed Rodstrum for his thoughts on the whereabouts of the circus troupe. With ten troupe members dead and another in jail, Rodstrum posited the rest might be on another continent by now. Carmella hated to think they slipped away but dreaded to think they didn't. Upon his departure, Rodstrum suggested, "A thorough inspection of the farmhouse might reveal something."

Alone again, Carmella noticed a text from Nancy: "If you won't come here, I'm going to you. Leaving tonight and should arrive by eight o'clock this evening."

After a grueling day, Gregg Armstrong knew what he had to do. He went to his grandfather's home. In the attic, he sank into fiberglass batting as he strode toward a junk pile. He spotted a cardboard box and discerned it was filled with paperwork. Downstairs, Gregg reviewed the contents of the box. Among the papers, he found a Certificate of Commendation from the Gogglesgunshod Association. Under the papers, he found the jam jar. He took photos. He sent a copy to Nancy, a copy to Beatrice Butterfield and a copy to Porter Public's News Editor Linda Chickering.

Milton Alcorn drove to the Brimmerston Police Station. While unsuccessful in obtaining access to the militia members, he did succeed in scheduling a meeting with the Officer in Charge for the next day.

That evening, Victor Lloyd called to check on his efforts. After Lloyd rebuked him for squandering his time, Alcorn bowed his head and wondered why he worked so hard for the likes of Lloyd. As he saw it, he had worked and waited more than enough for the Gogglesgunshod Association's respect. In his heart, he knew there was no respect coming. When he next raised his head, Alcorn found he had been polishing his shoes for almost an hour.

In New York City, Otto sat at his computer. Huffinfield's police records system showed no records linked to the Allen Road farmhouse. But a search for "circus troupe" showed entries in the archived records; these files were no longer in the police database. Where were they?

While Deighton practiced his toe exercises, an orderly delivered a second basket of flowers from Beatrice Butterfield. It was still early when Rodstrum arrived with two cups of tea. Deighton looked at him expectantly. "You have news?" he asked.

"Maybe," replied Rostrum as he set out the tea. "First before I forget, the IOPC wants to interview you. They'll be contacting you to schedule. I told them all I could think of. Bill Walters is in charge, but he seemed to observe more than anything else. A young fellow, Trenton Storrs, handled the interview. Cathcart says Walters has a record of outstanding work."

Deighton patiently nodded his head. Rodstrum sipped his tea and suggested, "Perhaps you could learn more about their plan for the investigation?"

Deighton agreed to try and then urged, "Now tell me why you're here so early."

"New flowers?" asked Rodstrum. Deighton rolled his eyes.

"OK, I may have news. See what you think." Rodstrum leaned in close to Deighton's bedside and lowered his voice. "I've been talking to Cathcart. Someone went into the storage room, the one kept locked by order of the Superintendent. So Cathcart snuck in and gave it a quick look; he didn't see the box on the circus troupe but had to get out quickly when he heard someone in the hall. He'll look more tonight."

"How is he sure someone went in?" asked Deighton.

Rodstrum suppressed a chuckle. "He had a small piece of thread at the door jam. When he saw it was pulled, he checked the video for the hallway. The lights were turned off and the door opened for seconds and then closed again. We were trying to figure who on the force might be that sly."

Deighton ventured, "Maybe Wiley, but he's on sick leave."

Porter Public's reporters, Tom Valley and Susan Daly, returned to Huffinfield in a chauffeured car. Susan started by meeting Lady Carmella on a bench by Petunia Park's fountain. Tom started with Harry of Harry's Hardware and then proceeded to Mr. Miller of Miller's Mechanical. Susan checked in with Constance Appleton before meeting Brad Leveler by the church. Tom finally reached Milton Alcorn, and Alcorn maintained he would be delighted to meet.

Later that afternoon, Tom and Susan arrived at hospital to find Mr. Atwater was in the Intensive Care Unit, but his grandson Gregg related finding the anonymous note, threatening to harm Gregg unless his grandfather recanted.

As Deighton maneuvered his wheelchair toward the visitor's lounge, he saw a dejected Gregg Armstrong and greeted him. Gregg was glad to have company. Gregg said he didn't feel confident the police were paying proper attention. Deighton confided he had a pending interview with the Independent Office for Police Conduct. Gregg asked him to share the anonymous threat. Deighton asked if he had shown it to the local police. Gregg shook his head, "Not after seeing the Police Superintendent at that candlelight vigil."

Deighton didn't know what to say, but agreed to tell the IOPC.

Linda Chickering opened an email from her boss Steve Willard. In disbelief, she read: "Huffinfield filed a libel complaint, contending Porter Public concocted the Picnic Victim story."

That evening, Beatrice Butterfield dined with Lillie Leeway. Lillie despaired about Clive's arrest for Malicious Destruction of Property and Accepting Stolen Goods. Because the whole stupid lot had resisted arrest, he was also charged with Assault and Battery with a Dangerous Weapon. By the second bottle of wine, Lillie confided she was not paying Clive's bail to have him storm around the house about his predicament. In a charm offensive, Butterfield assured Lillie this was a smart decision.

Stifling a sob, Lillie tapped her index finger on the table, and maintained, "He brought it on himself, charging around with a stolen pitchfork, smashing the windows at Harry's Hardware and Miller's Mechanical. They did nothing to him, but he was livid they showed up to the community meeting, the one where police used firehouses on people."

Lillie remembered the hose drenching Bea's hair. To squelch the awkward moment, she sniveled, "Clive brought it on himself."

"He did, didn't he," soothed Butterfield. Within minutes, Butterfield obtained the names of the other militia members. She learned Samuel Granville reneged on his promise to participate in smashing windows and Mildred Pearson procured the militia's matching t-shirts. Lillie sniffled that as far as she knew, nobody stepped forward with bail for any of the so-called militia.

Butterfield cooed, "So Clive has company!"

They both ordered the rhubarb crumble.

Troward Nevels couldn't sleep. He wanted to make a statement to someone. But to whom? The local police were out of the question. The Care Quality Commission didn't seem appropriate. Perhaps that Brad Leveler from the Foundation…but he was barely staying afloat these days. Porter Public seemed too extreme. Not Bea Butterfield. Perhaps that Inspector Rodstrum might have a suggestion.

Nevels had his double-spaced, five-page statement ready to share. He felt certain it was imperative to have his statement delivered to the appropriate people before the Gogglesgunshod Association had any inkling he might talk. Over the past two weeks, Nevels had come to acknowledge, that which he previously pushed aside, the dark side of the Association's nature.

After a long day, Brad Leveler took his cognac to his makeshift office for a final check on his email. He was leading a group discussion in London the next day to determine the Foundation's next steps. People here didn't recognize racism, and recognition needed to be a first step, he thought. The Foundation needed a strategy. In response to his report on the manikin falling from the closet, he received an inquiry as to what the police had gleaned from the manikin. Leveler made a note to contact the police in the morning.

Late that night, Bill Walters was reviewing the record and listing the events leading to the allegations of police corruption. There was this so-called circus troupe and a potential cover up of its alleged crimes. It seemed settled in the news the troupe was responsible for severe injury to a police inspector. Only two weeks later, did the Police Superintendent deny this circus troupe's responsibility. How was the farmhouse sold before a thorough search after the alleged crimes?

What about the alleged obstruction of the sale of the farmhouse? Rodstrum said he followed up on multiple calls about the troupe in its first two years at the farmhouse. The records for that work didn't appear in police files. Walters listed Brad Leveler and the Night Desk Sergeant Kevin Cathcart as potential witnesses.

Where was the police response to Lady Carmella's recent allegations against the circus troupe? The Chief Inspector implied the responding inspector, Deighton, was not well enough to talk. Rodstrum told him he and Deighton spoke daily. Where were the records of police responses to the assaults on Mr. Atwater? The Chief Inspector couldn't give him a straight answer on who was working that.

Then there was the whole affair with the picnic victims. The Police Superintendent denied it ever happened. Several residents held otherwise. The Chief Inspector ordered a record check more than a week ago, but still didn't have answers. Rodstrum maintained the reporting Constable received an early retirement.

Police reaction to the candlelight vigils and the community meeting posed their own concerns. The Superintendent had not seen fit to investigate the use of fire hoses. There was unsubstantiated talk the Police Superintendent had attended one or both candlelight vigils. He made a note to look for photographs. He didn't know where the beheaded canines and the manikin fit in. It was problematic that police records failed to mention either.

Chapter 42. Finding Connections

That morning's Daily Slip was packed with news. On the front page, Butterfield reported on the IOPC investigation into police corruption. Sykes was quoted as saying: "no evidence of criminal activity linked to the circus troupe" and "Inspector Deighton was attacked by unknown assailants." Butterfield recounted the mystery of the manikin confiscated by police at the Foundation's farmhouse. She raged about the discovery of two decapacitated sheepdogs on Lady Carmella's stoop.

On page three, under the article listing the Horticultural Club's awards, Butterfield commented on Mildred Pearson's presence at a candlelight vigil for Huffinfield residents, who were under arrest for smashing the windows of local businesses. Did Pearson want their matching t-shirts returned? Why was Samuel Granville absent from the second militia action? What happened to the Huffinfield Police on that night of militia destruction? Did Brimmerston Police recover the nine pairs of safety goggles reported missing by Harry's Hardware?

At the top of page five, Butterfield commented on the community meeting and noted the sobering experience recounted by a picnic victim. She called it odd that with a full ten minutes remaining to the allocated hour, the School Superintendent insisted the people exit the school auditorium before a closing song. "Wasn't that picky?" she protested. Butterfield maintained it was high time the townspeople learned who ordered the police to set fire hoses on the community song, but ordered protection for the candlelight vigil.

On page six, under Simple Super's weekly price specials, Butterfield demanded to know about this Dr. Miles Middleton, who almost killed Inspector Deighton, by prescribing a medication without the consent of his treating doctors. She questioned why Hospital Director Nevels gave his approval to administer this prescription?

On the back page, under the Horoscope listing, Butterfield raised questions about what she had not been able to confirm, the libel charges. "Did the Town Council vote to use town coffers to sue Porter Public for libel when we all know everything it printed was true? What records do we have of any debate? Where is the voting record?"

Daily Slip readers took note.

Bill Walters read that morning's Daily Slip. He resolved to discover what was happening in Huffinfield before the IOPC brass replaced his team. Publicity always led to artificial time constraints. Walters made another cup of tea. He counted prospective witnesses. It would be a long slog.

Milton Alcorn felt good. He gave a straight story to that Porter Public reporter. He let Bea Butterfield know about the Town's libel complaint. Now he was off to Brimmerston to meet with the Police Officer in Charge, likely whoever pulled the shortest stick. Even if it wasn't informative, the meeting would fulfill his obligation to the Gogglesgunshod Association.

Brad Leveler was put on hold for eleven minutes before being connected to the Morning Desk Sergeant, Jane Tines. For the third time that morning, he explained how police were at the farmhouse in response to something setting off the security system and found a manikin in a downstairs closet. As she pulled up the incident report on her computer screen, Sergeant Tines wondered why she had not heard of this before. She found the notation and slowly stated, "I see here the police responded to the farmhouse that morning…it doesn't seem to mention a manikin."

Trying to stifle his mounting frustration, Leveler recounted how the police asked if anything was missing and how he asked the police to accompany him so he could safely ascertain if anything was missing. He explained, "I wasn't sure whether someone had entered the farmhouse and was still inside, you know?"

"Of course," assured Sergeant Tines.

Leveler continued, "Then in the downstairs closet toward the rear of the farmhouse…when I opened the door, a life-sized manikin tumbled on top of me. I assume whoever, set off the security system, put it there. At first, the constables wanted to return it to the closet. I insisted it be removed; I wasn't sure if it might be stuffed with drugs or other contraband."

"Good thought," noted Sergeant Tines. She paused a bit and then advised, "I don't see any reference to the manikin in the electronic file system. Perhaps the pen and ink report may be more helpful. Let me make a note of it and follow up with the responding constables. We'll be sure to get back to you within the next two days."

"Thank you, Sergeant Tines." Leveler was irritated. After he disconnected, he huffed, "Two days to follow up!" Then he realized he had yet to pen a thank you note to Ms. Delilah Banks.

That same morning, Jack Rodstrum was alighting from his sleeper car in Edinburgh, where Reed Crimson's younger sister, Penelope Crimson, resided. Rodstrum wasn't sure she would talk to him, but he could do worse than a day trip to Edinburgh. (He was retired. What else did he have to do? Of late, this rationale had carried him far.)

After climbing the steps from the train station, he found a still and empty city. Even the Wimpy's had yet to open. Rodstrum looked at his GPS; he was an hour's walk away. He walked toward 56 Frybell Lane and hoped Ms. Crimson was awake.

His destination, a low brick building, looked uninviting. He bounced onto the landing and rang the bell. A tall and lanky man, smelling of cigarette smoke, came to the door.

Rodstrum said, "Good morning. My name is Rodstrum from Huffinfield; retired police, looking for a Penelope Crimson, I'm hoping to get information on her brother Reed."

Irritated, the man mumbled, "I'll get her," and shut the door. Within minutes, a bright-eyed woman with red curls appeared.

"I'm Penelope Crimson," she announced.

"Ms. Crimson," started Rodstrum.

"Call me Penny," she interjected and asked, "Do you want to tell me about my brother?"

Matching her hurried pace, he responded, "Name's Rodstrum, retired Huffinfield police, and I was hoping you might be able to fill in bits about your brother for me."

She looked him over and chuckled, "I need to be at work in an hour. If you wait for me to finish getting ready, we can talk on my way to work. I walk, take the bus, walk and then take another bus."

"Very kind of you," responded Rodstrum. She nodded and closed the door.

Minutes later, Penny reappeared and moved briskly down the steps and onto the sidewalk. Rodstrum kept up and learned she knew of the circus troupe. Rodstrum mentioned it was unfortunate that all known members were dead.

"What about Father Ned from Essex Parish?" Crimson asked.

"Ned?" asked Rodstrum.

Crimson filled him in about train workers finding Father Ned bleeding in an Edinburgh train. "At hospital, they discovered his identity," she finished.

Rodstrum's eyes widened. "That's right. I had forgotten him!"

Crimson declared, "Ned Carraway is in jail somewhere. I would have noted any report of his death. I used to work for his cousin so I've followed the news closely."

Rodstrum asked, "How did your brother come to sell that property to the circus troupe?"

Crimson sighed. "My brother wasn't one for the ladies, if you know what I mean. He fell hard for this debonair man called Darryl. I don't know the details, but in the midst of the brouhaha over the impending sale to the Foundation, Reed introduced me to a man he was just gaga about. I believe that man convinced him to undersell the property to the circus troupe. Maybe he was even involved with the circus troupe; I don't know. I do know he was much smarter than my brother, very charming and had a slight accent, Russian or something Eastern European. I would've fallen for him too."

They hopped onto the second bus. Crimson held onto a pole and turned toward Rodstrum. "You know what! I might have a picture of the two of them together."

"Your brother and that man?" Rodstrum looked hopeful.

"Tell you what," Crimson promised, "I'll look tonight and if I find it, I'll send it to you. Where can I send it?"

At Huffinfield's local graveyard, two gravediggers arrived in the early morning to dig a grave for an infant, to be buried atop the grandfather's recent grave. They had not dug far when they discovered a corpse of a large man wrapped in a sheet. One called their boss and the other called his neighbor, Sam Wiley. Wiley arrived first and took photos of the corpse. The grave diggers estimated it was buried a good week earlier. Wiley suggested they re-wrap the putrid corpse. The police arrived just as the gravediggers finished re-wrapping it. As if on cue, Wiley made himself scarce. After all, he was on sick leave.

Linda Chickering entered Steve Willard's office with a tall pile of documents. She was in her ninth year as News Editor. On her heels, came Mortimer Ely, in his twelfth year as the magazine's House Solicitor. Libel complaints were part of the business. Chickering did everything Ely directed be done to prepare for such situations. Still, she wasn't sure what their response would be to running the follow-up article.

Three hours later, Chickering felt relieved. Ely was satisfied the libel charge would not go far. Both Willard and Ely were on board with the follow-up article, including photos of Mr. Atwater's commendation and jam jar.

Chickering notified her reporters. Porter Public would not be intimidated by water hoses and specious libel claims.

That same morning, Darryl learned the police discovered Bogdan's corpse. Just as disturbing, Otto's queries on the circus troupe showed matching entries in Huffinfield's archived police records. Darryl stormed down Ninth Avenue and considered what he knew. The triplets were sloppy. An unidentified corpse was open for inspection. Circus troupe files remained in police archives. Police took statements from seven troupe members. The sacked Inspector was recuperating. Rouben removed the police records on the troupe, but their location remained unknown. Huffinfield's local newspaper twice printed the deceased Reed Crimson's photo. Police confiscated a "life-sized manikin" from the farmhouse. Attention to the town's racists was calling attention to the circus troupe's purchase of the farmhouse. Helga was missing. Ned was in prison. Darryl determined it best to wait and watch.

At ten thirty, Mitch Deighton was in his wheelchair. He combed his hair, something he didn't do much in hospital. He wondered if he should head toward the second-floor conference room, reserved for his IOPC interview.

"Inspector Deighton?" greeted a measured voice outside his door.

"Yes, come in," replied Deighton as he craned his neck to glimpse at the speaker. Two men stepped into his room. Both were tall and wore tweed jackets; one was noticeably older. After introductions, the three men proceeded to the elevator.

Two hours later, Deighton paused. "Don't go. There is more I think you may want to know. I just need water."

Bill Walters sent his assistant Trenton Storrs to get three bottles of water. Squinting at Deighton, Walters remarked, "There's more, is there?"

Deighton reached into the side pocket of his wheelchair. "I can't let you leave without giving you this." He handed the anonymous threat that Gregg Armstrong had removed from his grandfather's hand. Deighton related how a militia, in matching t-shirts, bearing pitchforks and spades, had pitched battle on the twelfth floor. He noted the candlelight vigil for the wounded militia members, attended by more than a dozen people, included the Police Superintendent. He showed Walters the photos taken by Gregg Armstrong and Brad Leveler.

"Then this threatening message came in. A bit over the top, even for the stoic Mr. Atwater," sighed Deighton.

"Sounds like your hospital stay was anything but dull," quipped Walters. Storrs entered with three bottles of water.

"Not a dull day," agreed Deighton. "I get reports from Lady Carmella, who mistrusts the police. Breakroom talk from the station finds me. I've heard local confessions. I almost died from meddling by Dr. Miles Middleton, who, for unknown reasons, prescribed me medication."

He sighed, "I hope you will be speaking with Chief Inspector Gerald Jenkins. Carol sits right outside his office and if she isn't too scared, she may have something to say. The Night Desk Sergeant Kevin Cathcart is a sharp one; if you ask him the right questions, he can provide detailed information. I don't know if Superintendent Sykes put any of her questionable edicts in writing, but you might look for directives to destroy paper files or emails excoriating subordinates for acting without her prior approval."

Deighton paused and noted, "Records might be the corker in your investigation. Seems the Superintendent locked up the paper files and rarely gives permission to unlock them."

Deighton finished his water and added, "Two more things. The Consulate's package suggests the circus troupe is a group of hardened criminals, wanted on the Continent. And mark my words, the Gogglesgunshod Association has a major part in this lunacy."

"Could you tell us a bit about the Association," queried Walters.

Jack Rodstrum spent his morning locating Ned Carraway. Once he learned Ned was at Millipede Prison in Northern Scotland, he spent the rest of the day trying to schedule a visit with the prisoner.

The forensics report on the anonymous corpse buried atop the fresh grave made news in faraway places. The DNA matched a wanted criminal, Horatiu Bogdan, from Romania. The National Crime Cracker noted his corpse was discovered in Huffinfield.

Victor Lloyd phoned Milton Alcorn to suggest they have lunch. A suspicious Alcorn agreed. As they waited to be seated, Alcorn told Lloyd the militia members were having a fine time in Brimmerston's jail with chips and lemonade and penny poker. When Lloyd grimaced, Alcorn smirked. As lunch progressed, Lloyd attempted to state his purpose. Alcorn gleefully reminded him there would be no business to interrupt the meal.

After the blueberry crumble smothered in custard, Lloyd suggested it may be a good time for Alcorn to submit a letter to the Daily Slip. "A tidbit to cast suspicion on the Kingston Dove Foundation. Perhaps a reference to the manikin in the closet?" drawled Lloyd.

Alcorn huffed, "It's already assumed an outsider put it there. I'm not about to implicate myself." Lloyd's response was stymied when the server arrived. Once the server turned away, Alcorn thanked Lloyd for the meal. He rose and departed into a crowd of people before Lloyd could say more.

At hospital, Beatrice Butterfield looked for Director Nevels. His car was in the carpark but he wasn't in his office or in the cafeteria. In fact, Nevels saw her enter and hoped to avoid her. He was on the twelfth floor, chatting with the window company representatives about replacing the patched window in Atwater's room. Butterfield stopped by Deighton's empty room. Waiting for the elevator, she heard Nevels' voice and abruptly walked toward it. "Trowie Nevels, I've been thinking about you," she declared.

Nevels forced a faint smile, "Beatrice!"

Butterfield walked up to him and asked, "Might I schedule a bit of your time this week?"

Nevels surrendered. "I'll be free in a minute. We can talk in my office."

Lovely," replied Butterfield.

He joined her at the elevator bank and they chatted about the weather until reaching his office. After settling in, Butterfield started slowly, "I'm not sure how often you get to glance at the Daily Slip."

Nevels interjected, "I never miss an issue. You should be proud of it." The office secretary came in the open door with two cups of tea. Nevels thanked her and asked her to close the door on her way out.

Butterfield grinned. "Have you been keeping up with the so-called picnic victims?"

Nevels looked at her quizzically. "You don't think it does their ordeal a disservice to refer to them as 'picnic victims?'"

Butterfield was on the defensive. "Well, I hadn't thought…I suppose I was too caught up in devising a memorable headline. I'll keep that in mind for next time."

Nevels ventured. "Did you have a few questions for me perhaps?"

"Yes, I do," Butterfield replied. She took out her note pad.

"You can make a recording if that's easier," offered Nevels. As a longtime reader of the Daily Slip, he figured a recording would decrease, though not eliminate, his chances of being woefully misquoted.

"A wonderful idea," responded Butterfield. She opened her purse and pulled out a recording device. She pressed the record button.

"Did your hospital treat these Black Brits who were packed into the ambulance at the pub?" asked Butterfield.

"I wasn't at the pub," clarified Nevels. "I do know we treated six bloodied adults and called services for their six crying children."

"Did they arrive conscious?" asked Butterfield.

"The three men were unconscious, but the three women were conscious," replied Nevels.

"To the best of your knowledge, what happened that these people landed in hospital?" asked Butterfield.

"The Emergency Technicians stated a constable was present when they picked up the lot. You would get your best answer there," replied Nevels.

"How long did they stay at this hospital?" asked Butterfield.

"The six adults stayed for three days. The children were taken away upon arrival. I believe they were driven to a relative's home in London."

"Were the adults discharged?" asked Butterfield.

"Transferred to a London hospital, closer to their families," replied Nevels.

"Did anyone ask you to keep their presence at hospital quiet?" asked Butterfield.

"It was an unspoken expectation, I believe." responded Nevels.

"Whose expectation was that?" asked Butterfield.

"It was some time ago," replied Nevels. Butterfield squinted her eyes and fixed him with an intense stare.

Nevels squirmed and replied, "If memory serves me right, it was Reed Crimson who visited my office."

"Did Reed come on his own behalf or on behalf of another?" asked Butterfield.

"I seem to recall it was in his capacity as a solicitor," drawled Nevels.

"Who did you understand he was representing? Who wanted the group's time at hospital hushed up?" asked Butterfield.

"The names of Brian Turner, Denis Chapman and Gordon Butler, come to mind," admitted Nevels.

"Does the hospital have records of the medical treatment administered?" asked Butterfield.

"We should have something in the archives," winced Nevels.

"Did Reed mention why his people wanted the lot's time in hospital kept quiet?" asked Butterfield.

"I understood they thought it would lead to bad publicity for Huffinfield," stated Nevels.

"Did you ask what happened to them after you transferred them?" asked Butterfield.

"Some things are better left alone," replied Nevels.

Butterfield paused. Now, she understood. "So…Turner, Chapman, Butler…you were concerned about donations from the Gogglesgunshod Association."

Nevels raised his eyebrows and tilted his head.

Butterfield sipped her tea. "Just a few more questions, Trowie."

Ten minutes later, Nevels announced he had work to do. When they rose, Nevels walked over to his desk drawer and pulled out a town council brochure from years back. Nevels handed it to Butterfield and suggested, "Perhaps you'll find this useful."

The brochure referenced the Kingston Dove Foundation under the caption, "These people want to change our local ways." Butterfield thanked him and put the brochure in her purse.

The next day, Bill Walters received correspondence from the London law firm of Less and Moore, retained by Police Superintendent Sykes. Less and Moore conveyed its client was distressed to learn of corruption charges leveled against the Huffinfield Police; vouched it was a top level organization, maintained no knowledge of police misconduct, denied and resented any inference of personal wrongdoing, and noted the incidents referenced in the allegations occurred either prior to her appointment or during her off hours. The correspondence advised communications with their client should be directed to Less and Moore.

Walters sent a furious email to his home office. He requested Legal respond to this law firm to specifically explain this is an internal police investigation, for which Police Superintendent Sykes is required to make herself available and honor the proffered search warrant. Walters seethed. He only requested the search warrant so he wouldn't have to fight with the locals. Now he feared it may be used to imply an external investigation. Walters put on his coat and told Storrs, "I need to take a walk." In fact, he needed to calm down.

Sergeant Jane Tines reported her findings on Leveler's manikin to the Chief Inspector. Jenkins dismissed her with a curt, "Thank you, Sergeant."

Bill Walters presented Jenkins with a copy of his search warrant. "The Police Superintendent is absent from the office and I was directed to you," he advised.

Before Jenkins could reply, Walters asked, "Where do you keep police records?"

Jenkins silently cursed being left to explain the Superintendent's questionable actions to the Independent Office for Police Conduct. Bill Walters was looking at him intently.

Jenkins cleared his throat and ventured. "If you will allow me, the Superintendent, in an effort to encourage our use of the new electronic records system, has pulled the records from their various file cabinets, boxed them and secured them. I, personally, am uncertain about their secured location or who, other than Superintendent Sykes, has access."

"Odd," responded Walters. "Do advise your Superintendent that I have a search warrant authorizing my access and would appreciate no further delay."

"Of course," replied Jenkins.

Walters continued, "In the meantime, please be so good as to provide the electronic files on the so-called circus troupe living at the end of Allen Road."

Knowing the electronic file system didn't work, Jenkins fumbled, "You'll want a private office."

"Your desk will suffice," retorted Walters. "If you would, please pull up the appropriate files before leaving."

Jenkins countered, "If I may suggest, why don't you use Inspector Deighton's office?" He added, "My Administrative Assistant Carol will assist you in accessing whatever files you wish."

Walters rose and looked expectantly at Jenkins. Jenkins pressed the button on his phone for Carol, but received no answer. Walters gave him a hard look. "After you, Chief Inspector."

Jenkins grabbed his set of keys. On route, he spotted Carol coming from the loo and motioned to her. Jenkins announced, "Carol, IOPC will be using Inspector Deighton's office. Here's the key. Please assist him to access the records he needs." Jenkins turned and fled.

Chapter 43. Lost and Found

Chief Inspector Jenkins fielded a phone call from Inspector Jeff Cutler, assigned to follow up on the manikin. Cutler reported, "I found it. It was behind the hedges just as the constables said. Shall I bring it in, Sir?"

"Yes, do," responded Jenkins. Another tough explanation in the making, he feared.

Inspector Cutler opened the boot and stepped into the wet greenery. The thing was slippery and the whole bit seemed unyieldingly firm. It would not fold to fit in the boot. He put his arms around the torso, heaved up and pushed it through the rear car window on the driver's side, and then maneuvered it diagonally so the feet would go through the open, front passenger window.

Cutler noted the time and returned to the hedge to take a few photos. Cutler followed protocols as a matter of self-protection in his job.

Cutler reached the police station without incident. He noted a few odd looks as he walked into the building with the manikin over his shoulder.

On route to the evidence locker, Cutler left the manikin in the hallway while he stopped to use the men's. When he returned, the manikin was gone.

In Deighton's hospital room, Rodstrum sipped his tea while Deighton scanned the Daily Slip. Deighton pointed to Victor Lloyd's letter claiming the Kingston Dove Foundation was a nefarious bunch. "Nothing gracious about that one," murmured Deighton.

Rodstrum sighed, "I scheduled a visit with our Parson Ned for three days from now. He's in Millipede Prison."

Deighton shuddered, "That's a harsh place."

Rodstrum pulled a photo from an envelope. "I'm hoping to show him this."

Deighton leaned in to see a photo of Reed Crimson and a cosmopolitan-looking man, fair skinned with dark hair.

Rodstrum pointed at the photo. "It's Penny Crimson's photo. She says the man was involved with her brother Reed at the time of the Circus Troupe's purchase of the farmhouse. Perhaps Ned can tell us something about him."

"Well worth the trip," approved Deighton. "I'll be rooting for you. Perhaps Ned can tell you why they put me in a sack."

Bill Walters, even with Carol's help, was stymied in searching for Rostrum's files on the circus troupe. Carol confided, "I have never been able to retrieve any electronic records more than six months old from the date of my query."

Walters asked, "Have you reported it to the Information Technology Unit?"

Carol grinned. In hushed voice, she responded, "Oh yes, many times and will likely keep on reporting it. You see, the software company, the ones who installed the national record system for Huffinfield, is owned by a cousin of a Town Councilor. The adjustments needed to make Huffinfield's antiquated computers compatible with the national records system have created many glitches. New bugs are regularly discovered, creating a good deal of business for the Town Councilor's cousin."

Walters pursed his lips.

Carol beamed, "On the bright side, I have very little filing to do these days."

"What do you do with the paper files now?" inquired Walters.

"I was filing them in the empty file cabinets. Then the Superintendent wanted certain paper records destroyed. I went through and pulled all those files." Carol grimaced. "Then she wanted all paper files destroyed."

"Did you destroy them?" asked Walters.

"I couldn't bring myself to shred them. Just between you and me, I asked the Night Desk Sergeant Kevin Cathcart to take the documents for me. He's a lovely young man. So I keep the documents in an envelope and hand deliver them to Sergeant Cathcart when the envelope becomes full."

"I see," noted Walters.

"Just remember," cautioned Carol, "Officially those records have been destroyed, per order of the Superintendent."

"Quite!" Walters agreed.

He and Carol tried various search queries. The Information Technology Specialist had taken the day off. Undaunted, Walters put his home office Specialists on speaker phone to offer advice. Three and a half hours later, he had quite enough of trying. He thanked Carol and she left for lunch.

In an email, Walters informed Superintendent Sykes he expected access to Huffinfield's records. Storrs advised him of scheduled interviews with Constables Sam Wiley and Pete Privitt later that week. Walters told Storrs to pick him up at the police station. So the day wouldn't be a complete loss, Walters wanted to pay a visit to Lady Carmella.

Chief Inspector Jenkins was not so lucky to escape the police station. He received a frantic phone call from Sergeant Tines. A parole officer was having a nervous breakdown in the break room. Jenkins wanted to call an ambulance, but he proceeded to the breakroom, hoping whatever was happening could be addressed in a confidential manner. The police didn't need more bad press at this moment.

When Jenkins arrived on the scene, he found Parole Officer Russ Wilkinson with his face on the table. Jenkins approached and demanded, "Wilkinson, explain yourself." Wilkinson's shoulders heaved as though he may be sobbing. Jenkins circled around him, not wanting to exacerbate the situation. Finally Wilkinson looked up.

"It's the young Gates, sir," gasped Wilkinson. "He reported to me as a juvenile for two years. The last I heard he was picking himself up, accepted to the Farm and Circus Program for Disadvantaged Youth at the farmhouse on Allen Road. When I saw him, I…"

"Take your time Wilkinson," soothed Jenkins. "Where did you see him?"

"Next to the downstairs loo, leaning against the wall," choked Wilkinson. He looked up in despair at Jenkins.

"I didn't know what else to do so I picked him up and brought him here," breathed Wilkinson.

Jenkins looked about. Next to the refrigerator was what looked like a manikin, red-haired and explicitly nude.

Jenkins walked to the breakroom door and saw Tines nearby. "Get Inspector Cutler, please," directed Jenkins.

In New York City, Otto waited to meet with Darryl. He sat on the steps of the New York Public Library on Fifth Avenue and watched the crowds of people approaching from three directions. When Otto glanced up at the huge stone lion at the side of the steps, he discovered Darryl looking at him. Darryl motioned with a quick tilt of his head to follow him. They walked toward the park.

"Yes?" queried Darryl, without turning toward Otto.

Otto took a deep breath before replying, "I received a message from Rouben. You recall asking Rouben to remove the police files on the farmhouse?"

Darryl kept looking straight ahead but nodded once. Otto reported, "Rouben told me he had the files but didn't know what to do with them. So I said, 'destroy them!' Rouben replied, 'Nothing is off the table.' I didn't engage him further but instead contacted you."

Darryl was incredulous. They walked on a bit. Finally, in a nonchalant tone, Darryl responded, "I'll handle Rouben from here. You need do nothing else."

"Very good then," sighed Otto.

With a faint smile, Darryl managed, "Thank you, Otto." The path separated and the two men went their different ways. As he walked away from Otto, Darryl's face became as threatening as a black storm cloud.

Lady Carmella welcomed Bill Walters and his assistant Trenton Storrs. She told them what she knew of the circus troupe, the misfortunes of Inspector Deighton and Mr. Atwater, the crime documentation compiled by the Kingston Dove Foundation, the police reaction to the Foundation's community meeting, and the police response to the decapacitated sheepdogs on her property. Carmella suggested Walters speak with Gregg Armstrong to get his impressions of the police response to the death threats and assaults on his grandfather.

Almost two hours later, as Walters and Storrs were readying to leave, Carmella stopped them.

She declared, "What continues to haunt me is what became of the circus troupe after Inspector Deighton was taken to hospital? They had been at the farmhouse for years and then disappeared. Not a word on why they left or where they went or how they quit the premises so quickly…that is not the way of this small town."

"I'm getting that impression myself," quipped Walters.

Seeing Storrs's perplexed face, Carmella said, "I have a hunch the answer may lead to information pertinent to your investigation."

"That may be," posited Walters.

Storrs disagreed but said nothing.

It had been two days and Brad Leveler still had no news about the manikin. Undaunted, he phoned the police to obtain a copy of the police report on the security breach at the farmhouse. Sergeant Tines told him he would need to complete a request form, available at the station, and noted the fee would be five pounds. When she said nothing about the manikin, Leveler recounted his prior inquiry and asked for an update. Sergeant Tines replied, "We have it, but no final report at this point. It's been frightfully busy."

The next morning, Chief Inspector Jenkins, received the key to the storage room from the Police Superintendent. He gave it to Carol with instructions to assist Walters to the extent she could.

Carol found Bill Walters and escorted him to the storage room. Carol chatted as they walked along the hall. "After Inspector Deighton learned the Information Technology Specialist could find nothing in the electronic records, he had a difficult time trying to get the paper files, nobody could say where they were. But you aren't interested in all that."

"You have me riveted," Walters assured her.

Pleased with his response, Carol explained. "Back when the paper files were squirreled away, the Chief was out sick. Upon his return to work, his questions about their whereabouts were ignored. I remember Inspector Deighton gave me a written request, addressed to the Chief, for access to the paper records. The Chief immediately forwarded Inspector Deighton's request to the Superintendent. We received the request marked 'Approved' but nothing about the records' whereabouts. Once we learned where to look, it took me ages to get the key."

Walters sighed. "And I thought I was being given the runaround. It appears I'm indebted to Inspector Deighton."

"Perhaps," agreed Carol. She unlocked the door. After peering inside, they both stood in disbelief at the mishmash of piled high, unmarked boxes.

Chapter 44. The Long Slog

Brad Leveler's London meeting stretched over two hours. While they didn't nail down a solid plan, they brainstormed a few good ideas. Back at the farmhouse, he looked over his notes. Possibilities included: a concert on the green featuring educational booths; adult education classes; teaching tolerance in local schools, an international fair to celebrate the world's diversity; partnering with a London civil rights group to develop a series of community forums, and police education on recognizing and addressing race-based crimes and crowd behavior. They discussed an immigrant cooperative, but determined more ground work was required to prepare the community. Leveler poured himself another cup of coffee and plunged into developing a strategy.

After lunch, Leveler sat and wondered if Gregg Armstrong and Lady Carmella, and perhaps Inspector Deighton, would be interested in lending their support. This assignment was too big for one person, and they each had a unique perspective. He phoned Lady Carmella and asked if he might stop by to talk about his project. To his relief, she sounded enthused and invited him to visit later that afternoon.

By two o'clock that afternoon, Bill Walters and Trenton Storrs, with Carol's help, had doggedly made their way through many file boxes but had yet to come across any on the circus troupe. Walters called time for lunch and told Carol they would resume the search the next morning.

Storrs and Walters proceeded to Joey's Pastry Shop to meet Constable Privitt. They placed an order and selected a back table. Within minutes, Pete Privitt walked over to their table. "You IOPC?" he asked.

As Rouben strolled along the riverbank, he noted a male jogger coming toward him. He squinted his eyes as he walked into the wind. He did not like the look of that jogger but stayed on the path. That was a mistake.

Reginald Atwater returned to his twelfth floor hospital room with its newly installed windows. He asked the nurse if he could see Inspector Deighton. The nurse promised to run it by the nurse's station. Minders was consulted and approved.

Within the hour, Deighton was wheeling his way into Atwater's room. Atwater was sitting up in bed. After sparse pleasantries, Atwater closed his eyes. Deighton waited.

"I wanted to tell someone what happened. The day I was put into the Intensive Care Unit, I received an anonymous note, threatening to harm my grandson if I didn't recant my letter to the editor, you see?" Atwater reached for his water glass.

"I definitely do," responded Deighton. "You know, your grandson found that note in your clenched fist and gave me a copy and I gave it to the Independent Office for Police Conduct, out here investigating police corruption and the like."

"So this is old news," muttered Atwater.

Deighton shrugged and took his travel backgammon set from the side pocket of his wheelchair.

Jack Rodstrum packed an overnight bag for his trip to Millipede Prison. He couldn't bring himself to search the internet for the face in Penny Crimson's photo. It was as though he didn't want to see what he might find. Or more like he didn't want the face to find him. He printed out his approval to visit Ned Carraway. His train was scheduled to leave at eleven o'clock from London that night, but he was leaving early. He wished he knew why, but something was telling him people didn't want him to speak with Ned. He left his car in the drive and walked to the desolate bus stop.

That evening, Ned Carraway was told he was to have a visitor the next day. Ned didn't like the sound of that. He had confessed to nothing. He was merely charged with crimes, yet he was in a high security prison, in solitary confinement. From everything Ned knew of the criminal justice system, this was highly irregular. Did an old victim have connections? Were they still trying to get him to talk about the sale of human cadavers? Ned didn't sleep that night.

After two days in the Brimmerston Town Jail, Travis Sillman wanted to return home. Sillman had nobody to pay his bail. The mean sounding charges were enough to make a body despair. A possible escape hatch might be the information Sillman could share. He had done a few jobs for the goon working weekend security; he could slip a note out with him. If nothing else, Sillman would remind people of his existence.

Constance Appleton left a voicemail message for Beatrice Butterfield. She claimed to have news and asked Bea to stop by her shop the next morning.

Full of anticipation, Butterfield arrived at Appleton's hair salon the next morning, just as it opened.

"Bea," Appleton squealed when she saw her enter.

"What's all this about Connie?" asked Butterfield.

Appleton sat in the row of chairs by the door and motioned for Butterfield to sit next to her. "I have news," she teased.

Butterfield knew better than to change Appleton's mood. "I'm all ears," she promised.

Appleton reached into her bra and pulled out a department store receipt. "Tah dah," she gloated as she handed it to Butterfield, who looked at it in puzzlement.

"The other side," directed Appleton. Butterfield turned it over and saw a list of names.

"You are holding a list of the police constables holding fire hoses in the school carpark. Maureen Todd's brother was one of them and she spilled the scoop while I frosted her hair." Appleton preened, "Am I good?"

Butterfield nodded, "So good, Connie, thank you."

Butterfield folded the receipt and put it in her purse. She stood and declared, "Now we'll find out who gave them orders to do what."

"Always a pleasure," gushed Appleton.

Butterfield murmured, "Always," before letting herself out.

Police Superintendent Sykes arrived at work early that morning. The high-priced legal firm of Less and Moore merely advised her to tell the truth, as best she knew it. "Idiots," grated Sykes. She wanted advice on how to tell the truth in a way to exculpate herself from wrongdoing. She needed someone with Reed Crimson's wide view of ethics.

Bill Walters and Trenton Storrs returned to the storage room with Carol at eight o'clock in the morning. They opened countless boxes but found nothing on the circus troupe.

At one o'clock in the afternoon, Walters knocked on the Police Superintendent's door. He found Sykes sitting behind her desk, facing her solicitor from the Law Firm of Less and Moore. Walters introduced himself and stated the purpose of the investigation. The Superintendent's solicitor interjected, his client denied and resented any inference of being involved in misconduct.

"So noted," responded Walters, "But I have a few preliminary questions." Walters requested the whereabouts of police records on the community hearing, the militia at hospital, and the windows smashed at two local shops.

The Superintendent avowed, "When I was appointed, the Town Council charged me with eradicating corruption."

"Have you found any?" quipped Walters.

Sykes gave him an icy stare and responded. "With regard to the incidents you mention, those all happened outside my work hours. The

Night Desk Sergeant Kevin Cathcart would be best able to speak to those incidents."

Walters made note and proceeded. "At a recent press conference, you denied that the so-called circus troupe, from the farmhouse at the end of Allen Road, was responsible for the assault and battery on Inspector Deighton. Members of the circus troupe were arrested at the scene, booked and questioned. How is it you came to learn they were not responsible?"

"I have full faith in the reports of my subordinates," responded the Superintendent.

"Did a subordinate report to you that the circus troupe members had been cleared of suspicion?" asked Walters.

The Superintendent looked Walters in the eye as she responded. "At the moment, I don't recall how that came down. It was over a week ago. A good deal happens in a police department each week."

"I have noted the weekly police blogs in the Daily Slip," grimaced Walters, "Quite a few cats rescued of late."

"If there is nothing else," sniffed the Superintendent.

Walters exhaled slowly and persisted. "I am seeking the police records on the circus troupe, recently of the farmhouse on Allen Road. Your staff people are unable to locate the electronic files. I have wasted eight hours going through unmarked boxes of records in your storage room. I trust you will be able to provide those documents in the next twenty-four hours."

'We'll do our best, of course," murmured the Superintendent.

"I would appreciate a status update at eight o'clock tomorrow morning," persevered Walters. The Superintendent indicated she understood.

Walters addressed the unintroduced solicitor, "Again, please coordinate the scheduling of the Superintendent's interview with my assistant Trenton Storrs."

Storrs brought the car around and Walters got in. "I told them twice now to speak with you about scheduling the Superintendent's interview."

Storrs sighed, "If I don't hear anything by mid-morning tomorrow, I'll call Less and Moore."

Sam Wiley and Pete Privitt paid a visit to Mitch Deighton at hospital. They swapped their impressions of the IOPC investigators. Given how the brass could twist things, they harbored little hope the IOPC would weed out corruption. None of them could guess what provoked the use of fire hoses at the community meeting. As far as they could recall, that had never been done.

"Not even when the local vet was caught poisoning French Poodles," piped Privitt.

"And that was the most violent rioting Huffinfield has seen in modern times," asserted Wiley.

"Should we take bets on whether the Superintendent attempts to place blame on the Chief Inspector?" smirked Deighton.

Wiley shrugged. "I wouldn't wonder if she tries to blame Privitt and me, and we've been on mandatory sick leave the whole time!"

The Daily Slip printed a letter to the editor by Travis Sillman. He praised Mildred Pearson's generosity in providing the militia t-shirts; suggested somebody check on Samuel Granville, seeing he didn't show up for militia duty; commended Harry's Hardware for donating goggles to the militia; and asked for help in sorting his bail.

Harry took a deep breath after reading Sillman's letter. Then he fetched a pen and paper to write his rebuttal.

Walters and Storrs pulled into the carpark at Tompkins Hospital. Gregg spotted them and bounded over. "Afternoon to you. I spoke to my grandfather. He's looking forward to speaking with you." Gregg led the way.

Two hours later, Bill Walters concluded the interview with Reginald Atwater and confiscated Atwater's jam jar. He noted, "I do believe the owner of this ear might want it returned."

"Fair enough," mumbled Atwater. Walters wondered who that owner might be.

Brad Leveler and Carmella had a productive meeting about the Foundation's next steps. Leveler presented her ideas to his Executive Board and obtained their approval. Carmella suggested a biweekly installment in the Daily Slip featuring success stories in overcoming and overturning racism. The Executive Board wanted him to continue efforts on approaching the survivors, of the Huffinfield mob assault, for permission to publish their statements.

That evening, Chief Inspector Jenkins pondered how to avoid being implicated in the Superintendent's madness. In the last week's allegations of mob violence and armed militia attacks, the Superintendent insisted she would assign Inspectors to these matters but made no assignments. The Daily Slip quoted Sykes as saying she was appointed "to clear out corruption." The only corruption complaint he could recall was the complaint against then Junior Inspector Sykes.

Only when readying to leave did Jenkins realize he had yet to address the manikin, or worse, the preserved corpse of an unfortunate young man. The day shift had mostly gone and the night shift was mostly yet to arrive. "Damn," he muttered. Jenkins strode to the breakroom. The manikin had not budged from where Wilkinson put it. Jenkins carried it to his office. Desperate to leave work, he stashed it in the corner, grabbed his coat, and locked his office door.

Troward Nevels took that afternoon off from work. He put a copy of his written statement in his safe deposit box, the same box in which he kept his will. After deciding to hand-deliver a copy of his statement to the Kingston Dove Foundation, he couldn't find Brad Leveler. Nevels made himself a roast dinner, as if it might be his last meal. Later, as he sipped brandy and stared at the fire, Leveler phoned. When Nevels told him he wanted to meet, Leveler offered to present himself at Nevels' home. To his own surprise, Nevels agreed.

Jack Rodstrum was exhausted, but glad to be far away from Millipede Prison. Though Ned Carraway remained silent, Rodstrum felt certain Ned's enraged face recognized the man in Penny's photo.

When the bus pulled to his stop, Rodstrum stepped onto the street, unlit by the broken street light. After two blocks, he reached his front door. As he inserted his key, he noted a scratch on the steel plate. He froze. Someone had been inside his flat. Rodstrum put down his bag and looked around. Wanting sleep more than anything, he turned the key and stepped inside. Upon flipping the light switch, he saw an unmarked cardboard box on his coffee table.

In New York City, Darryl was beside himself. Though he searched, he was unable to find any clue to the whereabouts of the police records. Reportedly due to a timing glitch, Rouben's demise preceded any efforts to press him for information. He didn't trust that Rouben was truly dead, but that contractor was definitely dead.

Chapter 45. Body Surfing

Mildred Pearson sat at her office computer. Upon opening her Twitter account, she slowly typed.

Save our way of life! Kingston Dove wants Marxist rule. Atwater's Picnic People are liars. Deep State IOPC overriding our police. Moxie militia still in jail. Please join us at Huffinfield Town Hall on Saturday @9AM, before it's too late.

She read it, counted the characters and pressed the button to publish her Tweet. She hoped her brother Sam would make good on his promise to drum up crowds for Saturday.

Carol arrived at work to find she was copied on the Superintendent's email to the Chief Inspector, directing the circus troupe records be on her desk by twelve noon. Chief Inspector Jenkins called in sick that morning. Carol contacted Desk Sergeant Tines to get the storage room key from Jenkins' locked office. Tines unlocked the door. Upon entering, they spotted the manikin, stashed in the corner, next to the Chief's flip chart.

"I was wondering what had become of it," sighed Tines.
Later that morning, the Superintendent directed Carol to place a call to Walters, advising that Huffinfield Police were on track to meet his deadline.

Jack Rodstrum rose from bed and made coffee. Only then did he peek into his living room and confirm the box on his coffee table was real. Inside the box, he found police records on the circus troupe.

Concerned Porter Public would produce another article on Huffinfield, Beatrice Butterfield doubled down on her local coverage. In an effort to appear neutral, Butterfield scattered the sensitive news throughout the Daily Slip pages.

The careful reader could discern: The Superintendent ordered the use of water hoses on the community song participants. After tripping the Allen Road farmhouse alarm, an intruder deposited a manikin in a closet. Racist fears drove the Town Council's opposition to Kingston Dove Foundation's earlier attempt to purchase the farmhouse. Mr. Atwater received another anonymous threat. Police Superintendent Sykes denied any evidence linking the circus troupe to criminal activity. Militia members were charged with Destruction of Property, as well as Assault and Battery with a Deadly Weapon against Police. Inspector Deighton revealed details of his kidnapping by the circus troupe.

Bearing two cups of tea and the Daily Slip, Rodstrum stopped to visit Deighton. It was mid-morning. Deighton smiled when he saw him.

"Relieved Millipede let you out. Is Porter Public on the stands yet?" began Deighton.

"Not until Saturday," responded Rodstrum. "But you are featured in the Daily Slip!"

"Until I read it, I'll have no idea what that rag says I've said," grumbled Deighton.

"It sounds good to me," noted Rodstrum as he handed over the newspaper.

"Tell me everything," directed Deighton.

"Where to begin?" sighed Rodstrum. He related his visit with Ned Carraway and the cardboard box placed on his coffee table.

Deighton gave an inverted whistle.

"I was hoping you might have helpful advice," complained Rodstrum.

"Give the IOPC a copy of Penney's photo. They may be able to find a link with the circus troupe." Deighton added, "Be sure to explain the photo wasn't included in the box of records."

That afternoon, Desk Sergeant Kevin Cathcart reported to work early. Walters and Storrs had moved his interview ahead while they waited for the Superintendent' s solicitor to confirm their client's availability. "She's paid to be here each day, isn't she?" muttered Storrs.

"We'll get to her," Walters assured him. "You'll note she provided no status update on the records."

"She's directed Carol to produce them!" countered Storrs.

Walters checked his messages and related, "The home office reports the other fingers and toes have been confiscated."

Storrs grimaced, "After all these years."

Knocking on the open door, a wiry man announced, "I'm Cathcart. You wanted to see me?"

"We do," replied Walters, "Please come in."

By the end of that afternoon, Carol was still looking for police records on the circus troupe. After preparing an update for the Superintendent, she put on her coat, pressed the send button and made a dash for the door.

Beatrice Butterfield inserted Harry's letter to the editor into the next day's copy. Harry denied making donations to the militia. "Stolen goods is what they are," maintained Harry.

At seven o'clock that evening, Storrs and Walters thanked Sergeant Cathcart for his cooperation. Walters directed Storrs to schedule an interview with Constable Goddard. While Storrs was packing up, Walters checked his messages. He returned the call from retired Inspector Rodstrum and accepted his invitation to witness his discovery. Opening the message from the Law Firm of Less and Moore, Walters read aloud: "Our client will be available at the police station at nine o'clock tomorrow morning."

Storrs and Walters went directly to Rodstrum's flat. Rodstrum told how he discovered the box. Walters donned a pair of plastic gloves and opened the box. Just as Rodstrum described, he found the police records on the circus troupe. In response to Walters' surprised look, Rodstrum arched his back and asserted, "I compiled most of those files. I ought to recognize them." Walters and Storrs confiscated the box.

It had been a long day, but the Police Superintendent's interview was up next. They stopped for a snack and took a booth. As Walters was looking over the menu, Storrs was flipping through the Daily Slip. After they placed their order, Storrs read aloud Butterfield's report. Walters told Storrs to make a note to interview Beatrice Butterfield.

The next morning, Storrs and Walters arrived at the police station at eight o'clock. Walters informed Carol they would pause their search. Pleased at that, Carol suggested the lifelike manikin in the Chief's Office might be Leveler's manikin. Walters recalled being told Carol knows much. She had said recent records were retrievable in the electronic records system.

Walters asked Carol for the records on the booking of the circus troupe members, subsequent to the discovery of Inspector Deighton in the ditch. Within minutes, Carol located the records and selected the print option. Walters sent Storrs for coffee. As he and Carol waited for the records to print, Walters asked Carol about this manikin in Chief Jenkin's office.

By the time Chief Inspector Jenkins arrived, Walters was sitting outside his office door, pouring over papers and sipping hot coffee. Walters gave him a few minutes to get settled and then knocked on his door. "Good morning Chief Jenkins. Would you be so good as to tell me about what you are keeping in the corner?"

Jenkins flinched. He motioned Walters into his office. "Have a seat," suggested Jenkins.

Jenkins told him what he knew, starting from when he fielded a query from Desk Sergeant Tines, who was looking to respond to Brad Leveler.

After Walters left his office, Chief Inspector Jenkins fumed at the carelessness he and other staff exhibited toward the manikin.

Jenkins called in the constables, who were responsible for removing the manikin from the farmhouse. He called in the Inspector sent to retrieve the manikin from the bushes. He even spoke to Brad Leveler about how he had come to find the manikin in the farmhouse. Finally, Jenkins sent the manikin to the Forensics Specialist and set about creating his own report of the proceedings.

Bill Walters and Trenton Storrs exchanged glances as they sat waiting outside the Police Superintendent's office. The scheduled start time came and went. Finally, the door opened. They entered and didn't emerge until two hours later.

"She has no knowledge and she has been advised not to address this matter---I'm fit to be tied," scoffed Walters. "We'll turn it over to Legal and let them stomach her," he sputtered.

"Well, we did get some express denials on record," noted Storrs to the glum Walters. "For instance, Sykes stated she had no knowledge of the circus troupe members being questioned, but we have her emails directing the destruction of the paper files for that questioning. And we have her emails blasting the Desk Sergeant for having the suspects questioned without obtaining her prior approval. In the big picture, it's more than we had before."

"We'll study what we've got, and I'll bet we'll find more," agreed Walters. "We have not seen any records on that questioning. Make a note of that," directed Walters.

"What I find astounding is rather than kick this against the door of her Chief Inspector, she is reaching down to the Night Desk Sergeant," pondered Storrs.

"Wonder what's happened between those two?" mumbled Walters. "It's as though Sykes wants us to believe the Night Desk Sergeant outranks her." Walters rubbed his eyes and griped, "She claims to get information from subordinates, can't identify those subordinates…and her steely silence about the candlelight vigil!"

"Dodgy," observed Storrs.

Carmella's phone showed an unopened message. "Carmella, I hit the jackpot! It's too hot to tell on the phone. Why don't you skip out and visit me this week?"

Carmella finished listening to Nancy's voice mail message for the second time. She bristled, "Really, does Nancy think I have nothing better to do?" But she didn't have much better to do and time was dragging. Though barely three weeks since she first spotted the circus troupe, it felt like three months. Hopeful about Nancy's promised news, Carmella packed an overnight bag. While in London, she may as well take in a show.

Porter Public hit the newsstands. Rodstrum purchased a copy at the corner store. He took it over to Joey's Pastry Shop to see what it had to say before relinquishing it to Deighton. Rodstrum chuckled as he flipped through the photographs showing the evolution of the community song to the community shower.

Beatrice Butterfield examined the most recent issue of Porter Public. They had covered Atwater's turn for the worst and noted an anonymous threat found in the unconscious Atwater's hand. She was pleased they had not described it as an attempted suicide. The poor man had been through enough. The other bit of news was the Independent Office for Police Conduct had confiscated Atwater's jam jar, containing a human ear. What she found more thought provoking was a quote from Milton Alcorn, "Gogglesgunshod isn't willing to concede we are in a new century; that's the long and the short of it."

That week, expert cook Amy Medwin was made redundant from her decades long post at Dr. Miles Middleton's home. More annoying, she was replaced by her assistant, a mere girl with no culinary arts education. Medwin consoled herself with a review of the latest in culinary news.

At the Huffinfield Library, Medwin ran into Tommy Hill's wife, who told how the Independent Office for Police Conduct confiscated Tommy's jam jar with the floating ear, gifted to him by the Gogglesgunshod Association.

"I never thought gifting a piece of another's body was Christian," maintained Mrs. Hill. Medwin nodded her agreement.

As Medwin opened the latest issue of Baking Heaven, it was the questionable body pieces in her former employer's study that held her attention. Perhaps the Independent Office for Police Conduct might be interested.

In London, Lady Carmella stopped at her favorite coffee shop. She found her favorite seat, overlooking the Jean Miró artwork. She scrolled the theater options.

Nancy came bounding into the shop. Within minutes, she joined her cousin. "What news?" urged Carmella.

Nancy grinned and related how she missed her last cookbook club meeting that night they stumbled about in the dark shed. Carmella urged Nancy on.

Nancy leaned closer. "Well, Giles Hopson, an older man in my cookbook club, asked me where I was last time, and I told him I was visiting my cousin in Huffinfield. It turns out, Giles is a retired Interior Designer who has made several home visits to Huffinfield clients. I told him about the strange events unfolding. He seemed quite interested. When he got home, Giles did a bit of checking on Huffinfield. Says the talk of jam jars with human ears triggered his memory of a local doctor, Miles Middleton."

Nancy paused to collect her thoughts and sip her coffee before continuing, "Giles and I went to lunch yesterday. According to Giles, Dr. Middleton is the Police Superintendent's maternal great uncle. This doctor has done work for the Gogglesgunshod Association, what Giles described as a local civics club with a history of involvement in the English Eugenics Society. He showed me photos of what looked like various body parts as well as two entire bodies. Giles called them cadavers; they were male nude bodies, one black and one white. He says he took the photos in Dr. Middleton's home and says he'll send me copies."

"Do you think I've retired into a nest of racists?" gasped Carmella.

"I'll bet we've only seen the tip of the iceberg. Still no idea how the Circus Troupe fits in," murmured Nancy.

Nancy toyed with her spoon and confided, "I'm thinking if we share this information with Huffinfield locals like Gregg Armstrong and Inspector Deighton, or even Bea Butterfield, we might stir up the pot."

Brad Leveler re-read Nevels' statement for the umpteenth time. It was what Nevels left unsaid that Leveler found unsettling. Leveler scanned the statement into the Foundation's electronic records and made a hard copy for the box of Huffinfield case records. Given the police conduct at the community meeting, Leveler could understand why Nevels didn't contact the police, but he wondered what Nevels expected him to do with it. Leveler left a message for Bill Walters, hoping to get his advice.

It was mid-afternoon when Walters called. He scheduled an interview with Leveler for the following morning.

Walters caught up with his associate Trenton Storrs just in time for Constable Goddard's interview. Goddard maintained the Police Superintendent, herself, had directed him to the town common, to stand watch over the candlelight vigil, "lest any ne'er do well try to create trouble" for the participants. Goddard volunteered that Superintendent Sykes was making his work difficult, by insisting he use an electronic records system that rarely worked.

"So noted," declared Storrs.

Walters and Storrs left the station early and returned to their hotel. They carefully reviewed the box they had removed from Rodstrum's coffee table. Storrs scanned each page into his laptop.

Rodstrum's meticulous records on the circus troupe were full of detail. Both took copious notes, just in case they went missing again. The reception desk's phone call interrupted their work. "They say it's a package for you," said Storrs.

"On my way," muttered Walters. He was a bit perturbed to be interrupted but mildly curious. The receptionist handed him a sealed envelope, addressed to "IOPC." As he walked away, Walters opened the envelope and read Amy Medwin's words.

At the pub, Rodstrum sat with Privitt and Wiley, swapping stories of embarrassing moments in policing. Rodstrum walked home, relishing his pleasant mood. As he approached his flat, he noticed the shades were drawn and a light was on. Knowing he left the blinds up and turned off the lights, Rodstrum stopped and turned. He jogged a few blocks before calling the police. The dispatcher recognized him and kept him on the phone while the neighborhood night watch headed toward his flat.

Rodstrum found a bench at a bus stop and waited. His shock began to dissipate. It was possible he left a light on and conceivable he pulled the shade. Rodstrum was jolted back to the present when the dispatcher reported, "Looks like your flat is in a shambles."

Within a quarter hour, Privitt's car pulled up to the bus stop and the car window opened. "Hop in," directed Privitt. He drove Rodstrum to his home and guaranteed the sheets on the guest bed were clean.

In New York City, Darryl gnashed his teeth. After finding nothing in the hidden laboratories at the farmhouse, Inspector Deighton's flat, Carmella's home, Beatrice Butterfield's office, Linda Chickering's office, and even Reginald Atwater's attic, he had bet Rodstrum's place was spot on. Darryl paced. Conceivably, Rouben did destroy the police records.

Chapter 46. In the Soup

Bill Walters and Trenton Storrs arrived at the Kingston Dove Foundation's farmhouse at eight o'clock in the morning. Brad Leveler met them at the door and showed them into the kitchen, where a pot of tea and homemade scones awaited. "Just fit your laptop wherever it works best for you," he advised Storrs.

As Walters and Storrs settled themselves at the table, Leveler flipped through a pile of papers looking for Nevels' statement. He handed the statement to Walters and remarked, "As promised." He motioned toward an electric outlet and Storrs plugged in his laptop.

Walters glanced at the statement. "Thank you," he said as he placed it in a large envelope. "Have you permanently moved to Huffinfield?"

"Not at all," responded Leveler. "I'm merely attempting to sort things before the Foundation moves program-based staff to the facility. With the politics, being as they are, the Foundation is looking to get things smoothed out."

"I see. What would 'smoothed out' look like?" asked Walters.

Leveler sucked in his cheeks as he considered. He replied, "They are hoping to get answers about the prior obstructions to their attempt to purchase the farmhouse, obtain a reckoning for the Black Brits victimized by a local mob here, and begin a conversation on race relations."

Leveler grabbed a scone. "Help yourself," he invited. "I am glad you are interviewing me. While I'm not from here, I have been witness to multiple incidents I believe may have bearing on potential police misconduct."

Walters poured himself a cup of tea and asked. "Can you give us a brief summary of what you've witnessed?"

Leveler related the highlights. He was at hospital for the armed militia's attack. He stopped at the candlelight vigil in the hospital's carpark. He told how Reginald Atwater came to learn of Dr. Middleton's dementia diagnosis. He saw the shattered window pane in Atwater's hospital room. He chaired the Foundation's community meeting that ended with police turning water hoses on the participants' song. Atwater told him about getting an award for his part in a mob attack on Black Brits.

Leveler maintained the Police Superintendent's presence, at the candlelight vigil, spoke volumes, as did Huffinfield Police absence at the time of the vigilante militia's arrest by Brimmerston Police. Finally, he told of the police response to the housebreaking and a manikin being stuffed in a closet, adding, "I had to insist that police remove the manikin from the premises!"

That same morning, Lillie Leeway approached the Brimmerston Police Station. Life was better without Clive, but now five dead mice were visible in her cellar and dozens of maggots had hatched into flies. Lillie wasn't touching the mice. After chasing the extra-large flies with her fly swatter for two nights in a row, it was time to bring Clive home.

That same morning, Amy Medwin took pains to use a facial mask, to give her face a youthful glow. She put on a Sunday dress and rehearsed her sentences to ensure she used proper English in responding to the Independent Office for Police Conduct. At her suggestion, Walters and Storrs met her at a Wimpy's in the next town over.

Medwin told them she had been a cook at Dr. Middleton's home for over a decade. No need to be specific and reveal her age, she decided.

Walters stated, "We've both read your letter Ms. Medwin. If you will be so good to talk of how you came to know what you wrote?"

Medwin took a sip of tea. She would have preferred to add sugar but didn't want to call unnecessary attention to herself, so she didn't.

"Yes, I'll do my best," she responded. She told how the doctor didn't have much luck keeping housekeepers.

"From bits and pieces, I gathered there was discomfort with the medical-looking items strewn about the house. Years ago, after a time without a housekeeper, the doctor suggested I tidy his home. That is when I spotted things. Human-looking body parts floating in glass jars. Life-sized human reproductions with their private bits uncovered. Sights you don't easily forget," she said.

Walters asked, "Did you happen to take any photographs?"

Medwin shook her head but ventured, "I do know of a former housekeeper who posted photos on Facebook a few years back." She reached into her purse and pulled out a recipe card on which she had neatly printed the housekeeper's name and contact information.

She handed the card to Storrs and stated, "I didn't see the photos were still on her Facebook page, but I'm sure she would have kept them." Medwin searched their eyes.

Walters replied, "That will be sufficient." Medwin was relieved.

Carmella and Nancy shared their information, gleaned through Nancy's cookbook club acquaintance, with Inspector Deighton, Gregg Armstrong and Beatrice Butterfield. They shared the photographs of what looked like jarred body parts and two life-like male reproductions. Butterfield promised to ascertain whether Dr. Middleton was, in fact, the Police Superintendent's maternal great uncle. Gregg stated his grandfather once mentioned the Gogglesgunshod Association's connections with the English Eugenics Society. It was all news to Deighton, but he promised to make inquiries.

Chief Inspector Jenkins received the Forensics Specialist's report on the manikin. Fingerprints, other than Parole Officer Wilkinson's, were no longer recognizable. Relieved his prints weren't mentioned, Jenkins resumed his reading. The lab analysis found the manikin was human. Approximately two years earlier, the body had undergone treatment similar to taxidermy; the list of chemicals used on the body included two chemicals unavailable to the general public. The report concluded by requesting guidance as to whether the body should be forwarded to the morgue and the public notified of the death. Jenkins told the Forensics Specialist to secure the body and pause on notification until further instruction. Given his suspicion the Superintendent may be biased against the Kingston Dove Foundation, Jenkins did not consult her. Instead, he left a message for Bill Walters, asking if this may be evidence pertinent to the IOPC's investigation.

At the end of the day, Bill Walters finally reached Dr. Miles Middleton and even better, scheduled a meeting with Dr. Middleton for the next day. Dr. Middleton telephoned Victor Lloyd about Walters' scheduled meeting and coldly remarked, "I thought you were going to take care of this."

Early that evening, Lloyd emailed a letter to the editor, saying it was interesting this manikin seemed to pop up at the farmhouse only after the Kingston Dove Foundation moved in. He questioned what diabolic science the Foundation may be pursuing in the Huffinfield farmhouse. Lloyd was pleased with his handiwork.

Gregg found himself facing a new threat to his grandfather's safety. "I'm ready to go home," declared Atwater to his worried grandson.

"Please don't say that to the nurses yet. Don't you think you may be safer here?" asked Gregg.

"Safety has never been my guiding light," Atwater staunchly responded. In more gentle tones, he added, "I can't hide out forever. I can walk as long as I use a walker. A few wheeled additions to the house, and I'll be right enough."

"With the upcoming demonstration on Saturday, the misfits are picking up steam. I would feel better if the IOPC removed the Police Superintendent before you go it alone." Gregg shrugged, "I just have a bad feeling about this, that's all."

Atwater was frustrated, but merely stated, "How about a game of chess?"

Gregg reached for the chessboard and set it up. He tried again, "Did you hear how Inspector Rodstrum's flat was ransacked this week? And they say the manikin stashed in the farmhouse was a human taxidermy mount. Huffinfield is experiencing abnormal activity of late."

A resigned Atwater muttered, "I'll give it another week but that's all I can promise,"

"Thank you grandfather," Gregg winked, "I'm still not letting you win this time."

The next morning, Victor Lloyd's letter to the editor was printed in the Daily Slip. Police Superintendent Sykes read Lloyd's letter with concern. Late that morning, she sent a memorandum to the Evidentiary Unit, directing the manikin be destroyed. The Evidentiary Unit notified the Forensics Specialist, who notified Chief Inspector Jenkins, who notified Bill Walters. Jenkins sent a memorandum to Superintendent Sykes. He related Leveler's repeated inquiries about what the manikin might reveal regarding the housebreaking at the farmhouse, and he suggested there may be ramifications if the manikin was destroyed. Superintendent Sykes phoned Jenkins to say she was aware and her order stood. Jenkins updated Walters.

Walters confiscated the manikin and took it into custody. He sent a hurried explanation to the Superintendent via email: "Given the manikin was taken as part of a Huffinfield police response to a housebreak, IOPC justifies our confiscation of the manikin to preserve it as evidence of police conduct." (Specifically, the Independent Office for Police Conduct confiscated the manikin because of its status as a human corpse, but Walters didn't want to show his hand to the Superintendent.)

Superintendent Sykes sent a rash reply. "I see you are seizing on another opportunity to countermand my directives."

Walters sent a summary of events to his home office and recommended it move to protect evidence. He recommended the Superintendent be relieved of her duties with pay while the investigation proceeded. To appear impartial, Walters recommended suspension with pay for Night Desk Sergeant Cathcart, the official named by Superintendent Sykes as responsible for the lacking police responses. Within hours, Storrs reported to Walters that the home office accepted both recommendations.

A grimacing Walters sighed, "Now we're in the soup!"

Chapter 47. Jail Break

In Brimmerston, Travis Sillman was sliding into a laundry van and stepping into an empty laundry bag. He crouched and rolled onto his side. He was safely behind ten other bags of laundry. Someone was coming with even more laundry. The stench intensified. The doors slammed, the ignition turned over and the van moved.

Clive Leeway was taking his morning break from the counter at Lillie's Pie Shop and read Lloyd's inflammatory accusations against the Kingston Dove Foundation. He tore the letter from the page and kept it for sharing later at the Pub.

Brad Leveler finished reading the Daily Slip. He dutifully scanned and forwarded Victor Lloyd's letter to the Foundation's Board of Directors. The insistence on this nonsense was wearing on him. He banged his fist on the wall next to his bedroom closet and the wall slowly creaked open, revealing a lit hallway. Pushing a chair against the wall opening to safeguard his exit, he investigated and found himself in an empty laboratory. He pushed open drawers and cabinets. Everything was spotlessly clean. The lingering smell of chemical cleansers indicated it had not been long empty. He returned to his bedroom, kept the wall propped open, and called Bill Walters.

Jack Rodstrum and Mitch Deighton were taking their morning cup of tea in Deighton's hospital room. "I'm ready to get home once I can hobble upstairs," declared Deighton, "They tell me I've got at least another week."

"Patience is a virtue," Rodstrum intoned. "The police are done with my flat but it's a mess."

"I've been pondering your predicament, and I believe I have good news," announced Deighton.

"Go on," urged Rodstrum.

Deighton continued, "A fine lady, Amy Medwin, recently was made redundant. I took the liberty of chatting with her the other day. She would be happy to assist. She and I have agreed on the fee. All you need do is say, yes."

"What fee?" asked Rodstrum.

Deighton shrugged. "I've already paid it. She was short on dough. Just say the word and she'll help out."

"Thank you." Rodstrum exhaled. "So what do we have this week? Lloyd's letter, a forensics report finding the manikin is a corpse, and IOPC's confiscation of body parts. I can't help but think these bits are going to line up at some point."

"Truly," agreed Deighton. "I have no idea what happened to that circus troupe, the ones who aren't dead, that is. I see no recompense coming for the mob victims. The hotheads won't give it a rest."

"I have news!" Rodstrum slapped his knee. "Kevin Cathcart received word last night, he's suspended with pay until IOPC finishes its investigation."

"Cathcart?" gasped Deighton as he scrunched up his face in consternation.

"Go figure," quipped Rodstrum.

"Well, tell him to come visit me then," demanded a petulant Deighton. It was difficult to see how the situation could become more tangled.

Walters and Storrs stood before a classic Tudor house, almost hidden at the end of a long drive. Storrs knocked on the door. Dr. Miles Middleton invited them in and escorted them to his den. After a brief introduction, Storrs confronted him with the photographs alleged to have been taken in his home. Dr. Middleton smirked, "Interested in science, are you?"

"Might we have a tour," asked the wide-eyed Storrs.

Dr. Middleton looked at the time. "Perhaps a short tour," he agreed.

Sure enough, it was just as the photographs presented. Walters paused at a human form near an exceptionally ornate bookcase. "Would you look at that?" Walters murmured.

Dr. Middleton intoned, "Sixteenth century."

"I'm more interested in the body," directed Walters.

"Oh, I purchased that and one other, years back. Terribly lifelike, but totally dead," chuckled Dr. Middleton.

"Where did you get this?" asked Walters, trying to hide his irritation.

Dr. Middleton paused and looked at it with Walters. "A local vendor; I believe it has local origins too."

"Did it come with documents?" asked Walters.

"A bit of a history. That's what interests me," confided Dr. Middleton, who added, "I like to know about parentage and education. It makes all the difference."

"In what way?" asked Walters.

"Come now," scoffed Dr. Middleton.

"Is the body really from a human who used to be alive?" ventured Storrs.

"But, of course," snapped Dr. Middleton.

That clinched it. Walters reached into his pocket and removed his phone. He pressed a speed dial button. "You may enter." The front door to the residence burst open and heavy boots stormed in.

Dr. Middleton looked at Walters and murmured, "We'll see who has the last word."

It was three o'clock and Clive Leeway had yet to return from lunch. Lillie wondered if she had wasted good money on paying his bail. She called Constance Appleton to ask if she had seen Clive. "He's in the pub, love," cooed Appleton.

"Bless his cotton socks," replied Lillie. She hung up the phone with a heavy heart. Lillie cleaned up for the day without Clive and figured she may as well get used to it. That man was bent on getting himself into trouble.

The Independent Office for Police Conduct sent the manikin and the Consulate package to the National Crime Cracker (NCC), as its Headquarters wasn't keen on being the keeper of material evidence outside of police misconduct investigations. The NCC seemed pleased to get both. Not much later, they posted an international All Points Bulletin (APB) seeking information on Darryl. Within the hour, Otto opened the APB.

The six o'clock news caught Lillie Leeway's attention. It was about a Huffinfield mob attack at the farmhouse on Allen Road. Lillie's jaw dropped open. Dalton Payne was leading a dozen other pub regulars, including Clive, up the drive. They marched and held flaming torches and shouted, "Shove your science." They were met by a steely-faced Leveler and a police line. A SWAT team ran toward them from behind. Porter Public reporters were at the scene, vainly trying to coax an explanation from Payne.

Lillie threw up her hands. She opened her computer and started an email to the Rent-A-Husband business in the next town over. She felt sure she could negotiate a deal cheaper than what she paid for Clive's room and board.

If the news anchor knew what was happening around town, he wouldn't have given so much air time to Dalton Payne and his mob.

That afternoon, Travis Sillman made his way to freedom from the Brimmerston jail. Once in Huffinfield, he set straight to work. First, he knocked on Milton Alcorn's door. When Alcorn opened the door,

Sillman laid him flat and emptied his wallet of cash. Next, he set a roaring fire in the basement of the Gogglesgunshod Association's meeting place. At the supermarket's carpark, he slit the tires on Edgar Ward's Mercedes Benz. With a pile of rocks, he knocked out all the back windows on Mildred Pearson's house. Using the service door to Harry's Hardware, he entered and appropriated a can of red spray paint, a can of pop and a packet of crisps. After a short walk, he used the spray paint to scrawl "Lesbo" on the hood of the Police Superintendent's white Lamborghini and added some choice words onto her windshield. Feeling satisfied, Sillman caught the bus out of town.

After returning from the farmhouse fray, Chief Inspector Jenkins confronted the handiwork of Travis Sillman. It was quite late by the time Jenkins left work.

Kevin Cathcart started his nightshift to find Dr. Miles Middleton, a prominent resident, left waiting most of the day, ready to be questioned and booked. Middleton answered his questions with cold courtesy and returned to the holding cell. Reflecting on that task, Cathcart realized the Superintendent was angling to destroy his career by way of the IOPC investigation. His shift passed slowly, full of dreadful Sykes apparitions. In the morning, Cathcart's head throbbed as he left to start his mandated leave of absence.

Week Four

Chapter 48. Brass Interviews

Last year, Michelle Sykes was appointed Police Superintendent at the age of thirty-two. Granted, she presided over a district with more sheep than people, but still, she was young for the job. Her mother's family was influential in town and her father's family was wealthy. It piqued her they shared neither their influence nor wealth with her. Even so, her loyalty to her family came before her job. Certain relatives lived on the edge of respectable legality. Protecting them had created a few squeamish moments. But overall, Sykes was proud of her tenure.

Sykes considered her options and concluded she didn't need this job, but she wanted it. Her suspension from work made her thirsty so she drank long and hard. When Trenton Storrs sent an email trying to schedule a follow-up interview, he received no response. When IOPC Legal demanded her cooperation, Sykes' solicitor withdrew. (Like Storrs, the Law Firm of Less and Moore was unable to reach its client.) Storrs sent a certified letter to Superintendent Sykes.

After opening his letter, Sykes phoned Storrs to sullenly say they could come to her home if they wanted to speak with her. She was surprised at his eager response and quickly jumped into the shower.

Later that morning, Bill Walters and Trenton Storrs pulled into the drive leading to a quaint Elizabethan house. A bit too many Hosta plants, but otherwise the grounds were pleasing. While Storrs admired the checkered patio blocks bordering the carport, Walters wistfully eyed the weeping cherry tree. Storrs turned off the ignition, jolting them back to their mission.

Superintendent Sykes admitted them to her home. Smirking, she watched Walters and Storrs commandeer her dining room table. Storrs turned on a tape recorder and recited a list of topics they hoped to cover. Sykes rose and took a writing pad from the cupboard. Returning to the table, she penned a quick outline for her remarks. In her current state, she relished the limelight.

An hour later, Sykes appeared to be slurring. "I was hired to address and remove corruption from the local police ranks. I have taken steps. You will note the placement of Constables Wiley and Privitt on extended leave. I feel certain I am closing in on Night Desk Sergeant, Kevin Cathcart."

Sykes gulped and hastened, "I never would have let him on the force. It wasn't my decision to hire him."

Storrs looked at her quizzically.

"Perhaps I've said too much," murmured Sykes.

"Is there anything else you believe to be pertinent that we haven't touched upon?" asked Walters. Sykes shook her head.

On their drive to the police station, Walters expressed his disappointment with the low level of detail from Sykes. He grimaced, "We'll note her apparent lack of sobriety."

Storrs was upbeat and asserted, "We have much more than we had starting out."

Storrs recounted, "Sykes became the Vice President of the Gogglesgunshod Association when nobody else would accept nomination for the office. Claims she never took much interest in Association activities and her family were longtime members. As Vice President, she was mostly the mouthpiece for her great uncle, Miles Middleton. Yes, she did present, what looked like, a human ear floating in a jam jar, to Reginald Atwater. She did not ask from whence it came. She knew nothing of the mob victims. Yes, she was a Police Inspector at the time of the alleged crimes."

"Keep going," encouraged Walters.

Storrs grinned and continued, "Sykes never met the circus troupe. She was unclear whether those apprehended for injuring Inspector Deighton were connected to the circus troupe. She did not recall ordering the destruction of evidence regarding the troupe's arrest and questioning. She did recall complaints about the circus troupe when it first moved to town. Said Inspector Rodstrum investigated and suggested the Chief Inspector might be better able to speak to the investigations."

Storrs bit his lip as he considered what was next. "Sykes asserted she attended the candlelight vigil for militia members. Claimed Atwater was lying to make Huffinfield look bad. Sympathized with the militia members though disagreed with their methods. She knew of no white supremist sympathizers in Huffinfield. At the demonstration in support of the militia, she thanked participants for supporting local police. Pleaded ignorance about the manikin stuffed in the farmhouse closet. When confronted with her directive to destroy the manikin, she claimed she was looking to downplay its existence more than have it destroyed. Said she was stressed about the investigation and suggested her staff may have misunderstood her directives."

Walters added, "And about the use of firehoses, Sykes was adamant---it was a lawless group and her duty was to protect public property. She cautioned that Porter Public was owned by a group of discredited communist sympathizers. Claimed to be unfamiliar with any human specimens or models on display in Dr. Middleton's home."

Storrs sighed, "I'm ready for lunch."

As he waited for the investigative team, Chief Inspector Jenkins was glum. He considered the awkward questions on the manikin, how he snitched on the Superintendent to save the manikin from destruction, his failure to find any record of the alleged mob violence in town, and the failure to relocate the circus troupe records. Jenkins cringed as he wondered what the Superintendent, with her penchant for spouting fantasy, might have told them. Carol interrupted his squirming to inquire if he wanted to contribute to a charitable golf tournament.

Carol was on her way from Jenkins' office when Storrs and Walters arrived for their scheduled appointment. She offered to make them a fresh pot of tea. Jenkins exhaled and beamed at her. "That would be lovely," he replied before beckoning Storrs and Walters to the round table in the back corner of his office.

"Before we begin," stated Jenkins, "let me say I try to carry out my duties while paying the utmost respect to Superintendent Sykes. She was a Junior Inspector, reporting to me, when the prior Superintendent Stebbins suddenly died. The Town Council picked her, over me, to be the new Superintendent." Jenkins clammed up and bit his upper lip.

"Curious staging," commented Walters.

Carol came in with the three cups of tea and left them to their meeting. Storrs turned on the tape recorder and recited the points they wanted Jenkins to address.

Jenkins took a sip of hot tea and said, "I don't know much about the circus troupe except they were a curious lot. Retired Inspector Rodstrum investigated a multitude of complaints. Rodstrum was a fine Inspector, better than most. When his investigation showed a serious disregard for the law by the troupe, it garnered attention in odd circles. The Gogglesgunshod Association, a group of London scientists and a pack of society war horses, all raised objections to Rodstrum's work."

He continued, "Superintendent Stebbins and I discussed these objections. He was adamant we would not be intimidated. A week before his death, Stebbins directed Rodstrum's investigations be 'closed, that's an order.' I directed Rodstrum to close the investigations. Stebbins was as strong as an ox. His sudden and unexplained death gave me pause about my personal safety as well as Rodstrum's."

Jenkins picked up his tea cup and put it down. He asserted, "I had no knowledge of the alleged mob violence against Black Brits. If you read the papers, you know just as much as I do, except I do know

Constable Mike Parish was given an early retirement package around that time. I assumed it had to do with health reasons and didn't see it my place to pry."

Storrs pressed, "Looking at recent violent crimes, what is your view of the police response?"

Jenkins hedged, "Perhaps we didn't do as much as we could have."

Jenkins paused to collect his thoughts. He said, "Subsequent to our discovery of the roughed-up Inspector Deighton, we booked and questioned circus troupe suspects. Subsequent to the hospital attack, we booked and questioned the militia suspects. Superintendent Sykes determined the charges were in error. Another thing, she has been eager to make us less dependent on paper files and has opined staff are reluctant to let go of paper. This is important because the electronic records system doesn't work. In her defense, I'm not convinced the Superintendent understands this. I have raised my concerns to her, both verbally and in writing, in these past three weeks since its inception."

Storrs said, "A sampling those written communications would be helpful."

Walters added, "Seeing Inspector Deighton has been in hospital, why weren't any of his cases reassigned?"

Jenkins shrugged, "The Superintendent herself reassigned Inspector Deighton to Mr. Atwater's case. I didn't see it my place to change her assignment."

Chapter 49. Revealing Signs

Exhausted from dealing with her smashed windows, Mildred Pearson remained undeterred as she pulled up to the Town Hall. A good number of people promised they would participate in the demonstration. Given the suspension of Sykes, she wondered about any police presence. Given the blue skies, surely Heaven was on her side.

Pearson saw her brother jogging toward her. She jumped from her car and asked him to remove a wooden box from the boot. Samuel Granville set the box in the middle of Petunia Park and sat upon it. He softly pleaded, "You don't have to go through with this."

Pearson snapped, "Get off my podium."

Pearson was relieved her three dozen faithful arrived by nine o'clock. Reverend Jake made an appearance to bless the gathering. By nine-fifteen, the chant of "No justice, no peace," could be heard in Lillie's Pie Shop.

To no avail, Lillie Leeway protested Clive's departure to join the demonstration. As he slammed the door, Lillie screamed, "Get jailed again and you'll rot there."

Clive fell in behind the library aide, Minerva Cummington, whose folded hands clutched an upraised sword. Beside her was the supermarket manager Edgar Ward, bearing a "Defend Huffinfield" sign, duct-taped onto a heraldic shield.

At half past nine, three buses arrived with people from across Blinkingshire county. A large box was set next to each bus door. As passengers filed out, they reached into the box for a sign.

These demonstrators held signs with a myriad of messages, including: Atwater is a Race Traitor, Support our Police, Picnic Victims Lie, Kingston Dove wants to Brainwash You, First Huffinfield-Then England, Stop London Meddling, Free Brave Militia, Carmel Carmella,

Stop the Lies, Porter Public Fakes News, Defend Our Heritage, and Protect our Families. Rather than join in Pearson's prepared chants, these demonstrators were more inclined to roar "Yeah," in response to her local group's recitations, lending an unruly air to the activities.

Passersby approached to investigate the parading crowd, but quickly tired of the noise. Police Superintendent Sykes appeared as a guest speaker. After thanking the crowd for its support of Huffinfield Police, Sykes body surfed up and down the crowd.

Beatrice Butterfield stood on a bench and raised her phone to take photos. She noted Clive Leeway was out of jail. She counted the locals in attendance at fifty-two, with some watching the protest rather than protesting. She noted the police presence, only two constables ambling about the perimeter.

The demonstration came to an abrupt end at eleven o'clock when the three bus drivers blew high-pitched whistles. As their passengers returned their signs to the boxes and climbed onto the buses, Pearson thanked everyone for their support and promised to keep them posted. The two police constables estimated the crowd at two hundred. Butterfield counted one hundred and fifty.

Once the crowd subsided, Butterfield spotted Milton Alcorn. She asked what he thought of the demonstration.

"Hogwash!" he harrumphed.

"Didn't you get the sign you wanted?" Butterfield inquired sweetly.

Alcorn rolled his eyes and snapped, "I could tell you news."

"I'm all ears," promised Butterfield, and she took out her recorder. Alcorn talked of the Black Brits who were attacked years back. He related exactly what body parts were given to whom and told her just this week, the Independent Office for Police Conduct confiscated the bestowed body parts.

"Don't believe me? Just ask around," urged Alcorn.

Butterfield asked if he wasn't the same man who contended the picnic victims were a lie. Alcorn looked forlorn as he confessed, "I stood out in front for them, even though it got me no respect, because I wanted to be part of the elite. Now I don't want any part of them."

Butterfield didn't press him. She was too busy picturing the Sunday front page photos of the body-surfing Sykes.

Amy Medwin finished sorting Rodstrum's flat. She guessed about where to put most items, but at least it would give the poor soul a start. She put on the kettle and walked about admiring her work. As she dallied with her cup of tea, Rodstrum arrived home. "Oh, just resting my feet," stammered Medwin.

"This place looks better than it has for years," maintained Rodstrum.

"Don't you hesitate if they mess it up again," grinned Medwin. "You're a retired copper, right?" She didn't wait for his answer. "Did you hear about the APB for Darryl somebody from Huffinfield?"

"I did not," replied Rodstrum.

"How did you come to know Mitch Deighton?" he ventured.

"He walked beat in Brimmerston along my dead Tommy long time you know," replied Medwin. She silently cursed her sloppy rendering of the English language.

Chief Inspector Jenkins received a communication from the NCC, advising its agents would take Dr. Middleton into custody later that day. In an unenviable position and unable to get further information, Jenkins sent a confirming email and copied the Superintendent.

Within the hour, Jenkins accepted a call from the Superintendent. Before he could say a word, she bawled, "Jenkins!"

"Here," was the best he could muster.

"What the hell do you mean by arresting Dr. Middleton?" she demanded.

"Good afternoon Superintendent Sykes," he replied.

"Well?" she snarled.

Jenkins related, "The National Crime Cracker directed we arrest him earlier this week, and they'll be taking over from here. That's as much as I know."

Sykes disconnected.

What Jenkins didn't know was the NCC matched several human hairs on the "farmhouse manikin" to Dr. Middleton's DNA. Combined with the photos of a similar item in his home, and Middleton's own testimony, the evidence implicated Middleton in the unsolved disappearances of young men in the Huffinfield area.

When Brad Leveler called to inquire about the manikin, Desk Sergeant Jane Tines responded, "The National Crime Cracker has it; I can tell you no more."

Later in the week, the Daily Slip printed a letter from Superintendent Sykes. Sykes lambasted police for arresting Dr. Middleton. She claimed it was a tragic mistake by those who don't understand science.

Chapter 50. Chit Chat

In New York City, Otto slid a large manila envelope toward Darryl and reported, "This morning, an updated photo was added to the APB. It's of you and Reed Crimson."

"Curious," pondered Darryl. Not only had the box been found by the NCC, but someone connected to Huffinfield had provided an update.

He gazed in amusement at Otto devouring his cheesecake. Otto caught his gaze and gushed, "The blueberry is very good!"

Leaning in, Darryl advised, "I'm concerned about what else Rouben may have left for discovery. Today, I want you to see the doctor about a new set of prints."

"I'll see him today," nodded Otto. This would be his third set of artificial fingerprints.

"Keep me informed, snapped Darryl. Then he rose, picked up the manila envelope, and pushed his way through the busy crowd.

The Daily Slip reported on Travis Sillman's jail escape and the ensuing chaos and it dominated lunchtime at Huffinfield's Pub.

As patrons munched on the salad of the day or the shepherd's pie special, a consensus evolved it would be better to ignore Sillman now he was gone. The scuttlebutt was Sillman smashed the windows on Mildred Pearson's house and slashed the tires on Edgar Ward's car. No clear consensus arose on what happened to Alcorn. Some said it was Sillman. Some speculated it was Victor Lloyd. Others suggested Alcorn may have suffered a stroke as he was hospitalized.

Many presumed Alcorn set fire to the Gogglesgunshod Association headquarters. Some said it was Sillman. A significant number suggested insurance compensation may have swayed the likes of Victor Lloyd. Sillman, Alcorn or Lloyd? When asked for his opinion, Curtis Field recommended the dessert special.

Absent from the discussion was talk of Police Superintendent Sykes. She didn't tell anyone about the spray paint on her Lamborghini, but immediately garaged it.

At Tompkins Hospital, Milton Alcorn regained consciousness and realized full-on pain. Noticing his distress, a nurse called the doctor, who increased Alcorn's medication. Alcorn didn't wake until the next day.

By then, most suspected the inner circle of the Gogglesgunshod Association was responsible for Alcorn's condition. Common sentiment held it was pitiful the way he had been used. Even Atwater felt a tiny tender spot growing in his heart for him. Deighton checked in once he learned Alcorn was able to sit up. Alcorn appreciated the kindness.

Deighton was wheeling his way from Alcorn's room when he spotted Lady Carmella in the visitor's lounge. After respectable pleasantries, Lady Carmella asked, "Would it be prudent to involve Scotland Yard at this juncture?"

Deighton replied, "We're not quite London. The Regional Organized Crime Unit, LAMB CHOP, has jurisdiction in our area."

Lady Carmella nodded.

Deighton stated, "You wanted to know why people didn't want Kingston Dove in town. Milton Alcorn is in hospital and in a prime place to know points of information we wished we knew." Deighton sat back in his wheelchair.

"But is he trustworthy?" asked Carmella.

Deighton considered, "I'm not sure he'll tell us everything, but I'm confident he'll be on the level with what he does tell us. Give it another day, and then I'll ask what he knows."

"It's the best plan to come along," replied Carmella. She reached into her handbag and handed him another paperback detective story. "I wanted to mention I'm hiring a Private Investigator to track down the Circus Troupe," she murmured.

Deighton paused. "You know, Jack Rodstrum has a photo of the man you described as Darryl." He later arranged to get a copy of Penney Crimson's photo to Lady Carmella.

Carmella hired Private Investigator Stanley Marbles. He came with high recommendations and much experience. She related her encounters with the Circus Troupe. Marbles didn't say much but left with Penney Crimson's photo.

Marbles used his connections to obtain airport security footage. After applying the latest in facial recognition software, he found Darryl had taken a flight to New York, less than a week after Lady Carmella's farmhouse visit. Marbles booked a flight to New York.

By the next evening, Deighton had enough information to write a book. Milton Alcorn was a font of knowledge. Deighton scribbled: *Per Alcorn, Gogglesgunshod Association was convinced Kingston Dove wanted a Liberian refugee shelter at the farmhouse, and was not keen on this idea. Gogglesgunshod assisted in the smooth sale of the farmhouse to Reed Crimson's client, an alternative buyer. Knows nothing of the circus troupe. Reed Crimson was not "officially connected" with Gogglesgunshod.* Deighton gave up scribbling and counted the remaining items on his fingers before falling asleep.

The next morning, after thanking Rodstrum for the cup of tea, Deighton recounted, "So according to Alcorn, the librarian Minerva Cummington has a son who married a Black Brit. She hasn't seen her son since the night he announced his engagement. That was the same night her now ex-husband threw her son out. Strangely, she is still friendly with the ex-husband but militantly against Black Brits."

Deighton took a deep breath before continuing, "Alcorn says the accountant Mildred Pearson is estranged from her daughter. It seems the daughter became enamored of a Black Brit, and Mildred informed her she could not condone their friendship. Then the daughter divorced her husband and ran off with the Black Brit, taking Mildred's only grandchild with her. She has been enraged ever since. Alcorn says her brother Sam Granville enables his sister's twisted wrath. Says Granville funded the early retirement of Constable Mike Parish."

Deighton shook his head, "Alcorn says the store manager Edgar Ward didn't get into the college of his choice and remains convinced he was passed over for Black Brits with lesser qualifications. He says the mechanic Paul Foster is a trust fund baby with a grandmother who emigrated from South Africa, where she grew up enamored of Apartheid."

Rodstrum mumbled, "You can't make this up, right?"

Deighton sipped his tea and continued, "Alcorn says Clive Leeway was made redundant in a plant restructuring. Lee claims the plant kept on Black Brits, with less seniority. So these Huffinfield residents have strong views on race relations."

"They're racists, you mean to say," corrected Rodstrum.

"Right," agreed Deighton as he checked the door was shut.

"There's more," added Deighton, in a conspiratorial whisper.

Deighton confided, "According to Alcorn, then Junior Inspector Michelle Sykes discovered her boyfriend was having an affair with Kevin Cathcart. But we'll never know the truth because the boyfriend died soon after in a car accident. Cathcart was married at the time so he isn't talking."

Rodstrum pursed his lips and commented, "That would explain much."

Deighton snapped, "We all know it isn't his work ethic feeding her abhorrence of the man."

Before leaving, Rodstrum told Deighton of the APB for a man named Darryl. He added, "The man in Penney Reed's photo, I'll warrant. Any word from Lady Carmella's PI yet?" Deighton shook his head.

In New York City, Darryl received game-changing news. The Bosnian Government granted blanket immunity to its former State Security Service Chiefs. As former Chief of the Special Operations Unit, Darryl was exonerated for murders, persecutions and deportations of citizens. The United Nations acquitted his former superior and announced no plans to prosecute Darryl. Consequently, his threat level plummeted in the eyes of the law enforcement community. The NCC rescinded its APB. Darryl still had many enemies, but this meant a substantial drop in bounty hunters.

That same day, Otto reported the National Crime Cracker confiscated a cadaver, that sounded like the triplets' work, from the home of Miles Middleton, who was now under arrest.

Darryl had been content to track the ebb and flow of Huffinfield's discord, but Middleton knew enough to be dangerous. Closing out the English farmhouse would require closer attention.

Mr. and Mrs. Tommy Hill paid a visit to Milton Alcorn in hospital. They brought him a plate of Mrs. Hill's homemade cookies. "How's our favorite Town Councilor?" greeted Tommy. Alcorn smiled, pleased to have company.

Upon departing hospital, the Hills found they had a flat tire. Brad Leveler was walking from his car when he noted their distress. "Anything I can do?" asked Leveler.

Startled at first to see a stranger, Mr. and Mrs. Hill found their courage and looked Leveler in the eye. Tommy spoke up, "Looks like I've got a flat and with my back being as it is, we're going to need help."

"Have you a spare in the boot?" asked Leveler.

"We do," piped up Mrs. Hill.

"I can change a tire. If you want, I'll be happy to put on your spare." Leveler looked at the two silent, unmoving people.

"How much will you charge," Mrs. Hill asked quietly.

Leveler considered. "Your presence at the community meeting being presented by the Kingston Dove Foundation next Thursday, six o'clock, at Town Hall. What do you say?"

The wife looked at Mr. Hill and nodded affirmatively. Tommy mumbled, "Thank you kindly," as he opened the boot.

Upon his arrival in national custody, Dr. Miles Middleton demanded to see his solicitors. The first day, the wireless networks and telecommunications systems were hacked. Nothing happened. On the second day, the building was emptied in response to a bomb scare. When Middleton returned to his cell in the evening, the guard explained business would not restart until the next day. On the third day, his solicitors were contacted. Given the evidence, the magistrate refused to set bail. Dr. Middleton turned to Plan B.

Two Executive Board members, Denis Chapman and Brian Turner, paid a visit to Milton Alcorn. Alcorn's physical therapy was scheduled to start, prompting a nurse to escort the two of them out. Imploring the therapist not to rush, Alcorn confided, "I well may have to toss them once they return."

The young therapist looked Alcorn up and down and asserted, "I believe you are up to the task, sir."

After thirty-five minutes of cooling their heels, Chapman and Turner returned to Alcorn's door. Turner knocked on the open door and asked, "May we have a word?"

Alcorn nodded.

"We were in the neighborhood and thought we'd pop in," Chapman explained.

"I see," Alcorn responded. Given their sullen faces, Alcorn doubted that was genuine.

"We, and the full Board, are extremely sorry to hear of your accident," continued Chapman.

"What makes you call it an accident?" inquired Alcorn.

"Just what did happen to you?" asked Chapman.

"Who's asking and why?" retorted Alcorn.

"Whatever happened to you," continued Chapman, "we are hoping you will be clear the Association had nothing to do with it."

"Is that so?" stated Alcorn. He added, "I read in the paper the Association's building caught fire."

"It was a lowdown thing to do," fumed Chapman.

"I expect so," agreed Alcorn.

"Surely that was rash," ventured Turner.

"I daresay you may live to regret it," muttered Chapman.

"Excuse me?" inquired Alcorn.

Peeved, Chapman droned, "Let me be brief, Alcorn. We've come to obtain your signature attesting that the Association was in no way involved in the physical attack against you." With that burst, Chapman took an envelope from his jacket, removed its contents and unfolded it.

"Get out," hissed Alcorn.

"Once we have your signature," taunted Chapman.

"I'm not signing anything. Now get out," growled Alcorn.

Chapter 51. Bon Fires

After a quick and curious plea bargain, Dr. Miles Middleton was transferred to a posh prison. Darryl was waiting for him. After reading the doctor's plea bargain, Darryl was surprised the doctor was as much sought after for drug trafficking as for murder.

Brad Leveler was still in his bathrobe when the doorbell rang. He looked out the window and spied two vehicles in the drive. He pulled on his trousers as he hopped down the stairs. He opened the door to a man, who held out a badge and announced "National Crime Cracker."

In the next hour, four NCC agents used a myriad of tests to examine the empty lab and, upon Leveler's suggestion, examined the closet from which the manikin fell. Leveler sent a report to the Foundation's Board.

Lillie Leeway was getting her highlights freshened up. She mentioned her efforts to compose an advertisement for help, as Clive seemed to have developed a penchant for jail. Appleton laughed but grew contemplative when she heard the sort of help Lillie was seeking.

Appleton suggested, "You know who might be a good fit…what about Amy Medwin?"

"I don't think Amy would touch a mouse, do you?" retorted Leeway.

"I think she would and what's more, people would assume you had her helping with the cooking instead of discovering you're scared of dead mice!" asserted Appleton.

Brad Leveler phoned Lady Carmella to offer her a part-time Grant Writer position with the Kingston Dove Foundation. Carmella accepted. She phoned Nancy with her good news.

Victor Lloyd was busy, busy churning out fiction to be exact. Somehow, Lloyd learned the National Crime Cracker was interested in the farmhouse now that Kingston Dove owned it. That was a helpful tidbit in suggesting Kingston Dove was involved in a nefarious scheme to taxidermy human bodies. Lloyd had a way of mixing in just enough truth to convince a small part of the population he might be on to something.

With the free time from his mandated sick leave, Sam Wiley volunteered with Soccer for Youth at Risk, part of the county's community program. Parole Officer Russ Wilkinson also volunteered.

Wilkinson told Wiley about his former parolee, Stuart Gates. He painted a picture of a troubled youth who seemed to have matured while on parole, and then entered the Farm and Circus Program for Disadvantaged Youth. Wiley listened. Wilkinson recalled, "I spotted his face first and recognized him straight away. It seemed unbelievable, but I knew it was Gates. He was dead stiff, leaning upright against the wall."

Wilkinson continued, "Today, before the game started, I received word Gates is being transported to the Meeks and Mire Funeral Home today."

Full of remorse, Wilkinson related, "Gates had no family. I wish I had sought out Stu before finding his corpse. I…" Wilkinson was at a loss.

Wiley bit his lip. He didn't know Wilkinson well. Wiley finally managed, "It wasn't your fault. I'm sure Gates would have considered you one of the better parts of his life. That's the truth."

Soon, the return of Stuart Gates was all over town. Victor Lloyd wailed about the sad fate of young Gates. He took umbrage at the

Foundation's reference to Gates as a manikin. Somehow, many overlooked Lloyd's own reference to this "manikin." Lloyd joined with Reverend Jake to arrange a memorial service. Russ Wilkinson attended and gave a eulogy for Gates.

Paula Minders accompanied her aunt to the mid-afternoon memorial service. On the way home, her aunt was teary eyed about the vileness of the Kingston Dove Foundation. Minders pulled the car over and turned to her aunt. "Aunt Sophie, all they have is a lot of hot air holding up their speculation and innuendo."

"Don't you read! It was in the newspaper," gasped her aunt.

Minders placated, "That's right. I read that too. That was Victor Lloyd's letter. Within two days, the Kingston Dove Foundation had its own letter printed, denying all Lloyd's accusations."

Minders paused and grinned, "I read the newspaper."

"But dealing in human cadavers!" huffed the aunt.

Minders pointed out Lloyd was President of the Gogglesgunshod Association, now known to have distributed human body parts in jam jars. Minders hoped her aunt would reconsider the source and substance of the wild claims about the Kingston Dove Foundation. But the aunt continued to upbraid Minders. For her part, Minders stopped listening right around the time her aunt called her heartless. Silently, Minders turned on the ignition and drove toward the aunt's home. She could hardly wait to get her aunt out of the car.

Clive Leeway was another town resident steamed up by Victor Lloyd's antics. After the memorial service, Clive borrowed his cousin's tractor and crashed it into the Foundation's farmhouse, smashing the bay window into the middle of the parlor. Clive fought to unjam the gears as he muttered, "Nobody is going to use my friends and family for lab specimens."

After sending a team to subdue the tractor-wielding Leeway, Chief Inspector Jenkins took three deep breathes. He arranged to have Clive Leeway held in the Brimmerston jail. He gave instruction to impound the tractor as soon as practicable. Hoping Clive didn't do more damage, Jenkins left for the farmhouse. He couldn't afford any stupid mistakes.

Jenkins watched a constable jump onto the tractor to reach the crazed Clive. After a brief struggle, the tractor was disengaged. Once Clive was off the tractor, a constable moved it a safe distance away from the farmhouse.

Chief Jenkins told Brad Leveler he was adding police surveillance to the farmhouse until they got to the bottom of this smear campaign against the Foundation. Jenkins suggested he contact his insurance company straight away.

Porter Public was soon on the scene and preparing for a photo shoot when Beatrice Butterfield arrived. She noted Jenkins' departure and remained until Porter Public left. She offered her condolences to Leveler, who asked if she wanted to join him for a cup of tea. "I would be delighted," she replied.

Through the window opening, a dusty breeze flowed into the farmhouse. Wondering when the insurance company might arrive, Leveler opened a tin of butter cookies and devoured five cookies before noticing Butterfield's observant eye. He asked if she heard about the APB on the circus troupe member Darryl. She had. He wondered what linkage, if any, the circus troupe might have to the local racists.

Butterfield replied, "That circus troupe kept to itself."

"What was it doing with a laboratory?" asked Leveler and then quickly described his discovery of a concealed room behind a wall.

"It's not what you would generally connect with a circus troupe," agreed Butterfield, before demanding, "Are you going to show me this secret room?"

"Of course," said Leveler as he rose. Butterfield was right on his heels.

Chief Inspector Jenkins phoned Bill Walters. He reported finding security camera footage showing a man removing the circus troupe box from the storage room. That same man had gone missing after being apprehended as an accessory to the attack on Inspector Deighton.

The day's Daily Slip included a small box ad for the Kingston Dove Foundation's second Community Meeting. At hospital, Paula Minders added it to her June calendar. Atwater was looking forward to it. Jack Rodstrum showed it to Deighton. They were definitely going. Editor Linda Chickering decided Porter Public would be attending. Bill Walters sent notice of the second Community Meeting to his Headquarters, which forwarded it to the National Crime Cracker, which assigned two agents to cover the meeting.

The pub was a bit rowdy that night. A jug band played. Dalton Payne and Neil Clarkson celebrated their liberation from the Brimmerston Jail. Brad Leveler stopped in for a beer. Curtis Field looked at Leveler and looked at Payne. He made the command decision to break a bottle over Payne's head at the first sign of trouble.

Leveler sat at the counter and made a list of those he wanted to personally invite to the upcoming community meeting. One of those people, the pub owner, was looking directly at him. Leveler waved Field over and invited him to attend.

"Who me?" asked Field.

"With a prominent position in town, such as yours, it would mean a lot to have you in attendance. Can I count on you?" coaxed Leveler.

Curtis Field was reluctant, but at the same time, curious. "Sure, put me down," responded Field.

"Great," replied Leveler. He ventured, "Did you ever get to know any of the so-called circus troupe that lived in the farmhouse?"

"I did not," declared Field. He added, "I do know Edgar Ward had some sort of business arrangement with them. I believe he rented a greenhouse on the property. You might ask him."

Beatrice Butterfield put on a second coat of hairspray before setting out for the second Community Meeting. Given what happened the last time, it seemed prudent. She knew Porter Public would be there. After hours of considering which angle the Daily Slip could cover best, she decided to focus on the local reactions to the meeting.

By the time Butterfield arrived at the Town Hall, it looked like a stellar turnout. She noted the pub's owner, Curtis Field, was milling about the crowd. She spotted Connie Appleton with Amy Medwin and Lillie Leeway. Mr. and Mrs. Tommy Hill sat with Harvey West. She made a note to ask for their reactions tonight. Lady Carmella and her cousin Nancy were in the front row. Reginald Atwater and his grandson Gregg were entering the hall. Inspector Deighton was seated with former Town Councilor Alcorn and retired Inspector Rodstrum. She made a note to get Alcorn's reaction too. Butterfield spotted Porter Public staff and gritted her teeth.

A well-spoken young man took the stage to set forth the evening's goals. In the audience, Dalton Payne and Neil Clarkson raised a ruckus, talking over the presenter. Constables, posted at the Town Hall doors, escorted them outside.

On a video screen, one of the women, who had been accosted in Huffinfield while on a picnic, recounted her ordeal. Reginald Atwater, Tommy Hill, Constance Appleton, Lillie Leeway and Harvey West, all relived the day with her. Toward the end of the video, fire trucks clanged as they clamored up the street. A few people jumped up to see what was happening and ran back shouting, "Fire!" People left their seats to investigate. A bonfire soared up from the middle of Petunia Park. Soon, many gathered on the Town Hall steps, watching the fire.

Huffinfield Constables arrested Dalton Payne and Neil Clarkson for setting the bonfire.

The constables became distracted when the stream of onlookers obstructed the fire fighters' access to the hydrant. Immediately, Payne and Clarkson returned to feed the fire. A subsequent scuffle ensued when the constables sought to stop them. Porter Public Reporter Susan Daly shook her head in disbelief.

As the crowd watched, the fire fighters put out the fire. Leveler rubbed his brow, wondering if it was possible to regroup.

As the crowd's attention to the fire started to wane, Leveler spied Kingston Dove volunteers moving through the crowd, holding placards that read, "Join us for Tea and Tarts after meeting." Within minutes, the majority of the crowd shifted back toward the doors of the Town Hall.

The crowd headed to the basement where refreshments were generally served after Town Hall events. The basement had no public address system. Leveler frantically pleaded with the resident technician to rig an amplifier. The technician grimaced.

Within ten minutes, a podium and working microphone were carried into the basement. Leveler's heart leapt. The technician shrugged, "It's a flash, rabbit out of the hat, maneuver, but it might hold up."

Leveler motioned to the Executive Board that they were able to amplify. The President of the Board stepped up to the podium. He rapped for attention and then addressed the room.

"Now that we've all had a taste of uncertainty and fear, where the situation was quickly resolved, we may better understand our video speaker's ordeal, where instead of resolution, the matter proceeded to get worse. It's not that some people are better than others. It's more that people's fears can trigger defensive tactics that hurt and harm others. We need to help ourselves, consider the available information, so we can be less afraid when encountering unsettling situations. When we lessen our fear, we can increase our tolerance, and maintain our civility. With that hope, we at the Kingston Dove Foundation, invite you to continue your attendance on this journey, to discuss what may be quite uncomfortable topics."

He paused to read the crowd and finished, "Please continue with us. Your presence matters. Thank you, good neighbors."

The Foundation's President stepped away from the podium. Leveler breathed a sigh of relief. He wanted to hug the Board Member who suggested the refreshments. He felt a hand on his arm. It was Mr. and Mrs. Hill, the couple with the flat in the hospital carpark.

Mrs. Hill smiled and told him, "We wanted to make sure you saw us."

Leveler thanked them for coming. Mrs. Hill noted, "It was a shame about the disruption, but you had a good turnout all the same."

Tommy Hill confided, "I was at the pub that day and it was just like that lady told it. I got a jar with one of the husbands' ears from the Gogglesgunshod Association for my part."

"A human ear, you say?" exclaimed Leveler, "What does one do with the likes of that?"

Mrs. Hill interjected, "It set on the bookshelf for years until the National Crime Cracker collected it last week."

Tommy Hill sniffed, "Took it right off the shelf!"

Mrs. Hill huffed, "I always said it wasn't Christian to gift a human body part. When I asked Reverend Jake about it, he said it was complicated. So I let Tommy keep the ear on the shelf."

"What did you gather he meant by 'complicated?'" asked Leveler.

Tommy Hill harrumphed, "Those preachers are experts in talking forever without saying a damn thing."

Mrs. Hill posited, "Reverend Jake may have been trying to say just because a person does a bad thing, it doesn't make him a totally bad person. His brother was indicted for human trafficking. That could have weighed on him."

Tommy Hill added, "His brother wasn't found guilty. It was something about being a subcontractor to provide housekeepers, landscapers, childcare, and that sort of work."

"It's hard to say where people are coming from until you walk a mile in their shoes," suggested Leveler.

"The tarts are quite good," commented Mrs. Hill.

"I'm so glad you think so," replied Leveler, before adding, "Thank you both for coming tonight." He watched Mr. and Mrs. Tommy Hill move away and shuddered at how incredibly normal they looked. Silently, Leveler gave thanks to his deceased uncle for teaching him how to change a flat.

Within the hour, Leveler shared his newly obtained information about Reverend Jake with Gregg and his grandfather. Atwater maintained the indictment, against Reverend Jake's brother a few years back, was common knowledge. Leveler mentioned how Curtis Field told him Edgar Ward rented a greenhouse from the circus troupe. Atwater mumbled, "They say Ward made a bundle on marijuana. You could use a greenhouse for that, couldn't you."

Before the night was through, Gregg shared both these tidbits with Nancy, who shared them with Carmella, who shared them with Deighton, who shared them with Rodstrum.

Rodstrum wondered at the absence of Clara Crumb. He noted Nevels' absence. He found it odd Curtis Field attended but Reverend Jake didn't.

Minders attended the community meeting. She found the video disturbing and remembered the head nurse mentioned some untoward comment that Minders wrote off as gossip from a disgruntled employee. Now, she feared she may have contributed to the Town's failure to protect the rights of the mob victims. Upon returning home, Minders posted a note on her refrigerator to guard against another convenient lapse of memory.

Curtis Field was unprepared for the woman in the Foundation's video. "A bit of horseplay by a few regulars," is what Sillman had said about the blood on the floor. This woman described torture. In his pub! Field was inclined to believe this woman. Taken with Atwater's letter and the Porter Public news article, Field was shaken.

Two NCC agents blended with the crowd. The agents watched every move of Leveler and the Kingston Dove Foundation's Executive

Board, prime suspects in the investigations of missing persons and cannabis distribution.

Chapter 52. Bits and Pieces

Superintendent Sykes received a phone call. Her great uncle, Dr. Miles Middleton, was found dead, hanging from a cord in his cell. After a pause, Sykes asked that the body be sent to Meeks and Mire Funeral Home, where Dr. Miles had prepaid his funeral. As she put down her phone, she noticed her hand shaking. Sykes had never been close to her great uncle, but she was shaken by his death and shocked by the manner of it.

Lady Carmella received an email from Private Investigator Stanley Marbles, requesting she confirm a photo subject's identity. She confirmed it was Darryl. Marbles advised he soon should have finger prints. Carmella phoned Inspector Deighton to inform him Mr. Marbles had located Darryl in New York City. Deighton reported the news to the Chief Inspector, who reported it to the NCC.

Stanley Marbles entered the sidewalk deli. He sat at the counter and ordered a cup of coffee. He watched Darryl rise from his booth and disappear through the door marked "Men's Restroom." Once the door closed, he walked over to Darryl's booth and quickly returned to his counter seat with Darryl's water glass. Within seconds, Otto sat on the stool next to Marbles and softly said, "You should be more germ-conscious."

Otto barked, "Waitress, a new glass of water for my friend." Marbles was distracted and in that instant, Darryl's water glass crashed onto the floor.

"Harry," yelled the waitress. The cook groaned and walked toward Marbles with a mop.

The waitress poured water into a new glass as she demanded, "What's all this fuss about?" Marbles found himself alone as he apologized for the mess, paid for his coffee and noted Darryl's table had been cleared. Finding the men's was empty, a wary Marbles left the deli.

Jack Rodstrum paid a visit to the former, longtime Town Councilor Milton Alcorn at hospital. Alcorn was pleased to have company. (Over the years, Alcorn grilled Rodstrum about the circus troupe and rumors of cannabis production around town and repeated graffiti on the Town Hall. They developed an amicable relationship of sorts.)

After swapping choice reminiscences, Rodstrum stretched his shoulders and ventured.

"You remember Reverend Jake's brother Carlson?" asked Rodstrum. Alcorn nodded.

Rodstrum continued, "I seem to remember Carlson was arrested for human trafficking some years back. Is that right?"

Alcorn considered the question and replied, "Carlson Applegate was arrested in Dorset for human trafficking of Black Brits. I'm not sure how that turned out, but no charges were brought against Reverend Jake. At the time, people debated whether the Reverend would be implicated. That's all I know, but I'll bet there's more to it."

The conversation meandered. Rodstrum leaned in, and related he heard Curtis Field made mention of Edgar Ward renting a greenhouse from the circus troupe. "Wonder if Kingston Dove Foundation rents it to him now?" queried Rodstrum.

"I have no proof," declared Alcorn as he bit his lip, "but I believe Ward is connected to the cannabis market that persists in circling Huffinfield."

"What makes you think that?" asked Rodstrum.

"If you look back over the last five years, it seems more people around this town are driving cars beyond their means. I'm not saying they can't be in hock up to their ears, but still. Ward, himself, drives a Mercedes Benz. He's single and a supermarket manager. OK, so maybe that's not news. But look at those who socialize with Ward."

Alcorn expounded, "I've watched Travis Sillman polishing a new Harley Davidson. That young mechanic Paul Foster drives a Porsche. The ambulance driver Norton is driving a Ferrari, and the librarian Cummington gets a Rolls-Royce from her no-good ex-husband!"

"Conjecture, but a fair point," murmured Rodstrum.

Alcorn continued. "You mentioned Curtis Field earlier as having commented on Edgar Ward. He came to the Town Council seeking a loan for his pub. We didn't approve it because his balance sheets left much to be desired. No crime there, just a poor credit risk. Within that month, I see Field driving around town in a Bentley. Why would someone like that be looking for a business loan? Or did his financial picture drastically change somehow?"

Alcorn shook his head, "I know, conjecture. But it's odd."

"Maybe you should tell the Independent Office for Police Conduct?" Rodstrum suggested, and added, "If I recall correctly, it was then Junior Inspector Sykes who purchased a Lamborghini. Of course, we all assumed it was an inheritance."

Alcorn raised his eyebrows and harrumphed. "That Walters wants to talk to me. Maybe I do have something to say to him."

Rodstrum returned from the cafeteria with two cups of tea and found Deighton.

"Lady Carmella says her PI located the man in Penney Crimson's photo," announced Deighton.

"I won't hold my breath on that one," Rodstrum said.

While they swapped small talk, Deighton skimmed the pages of the Daily Slip and found a snippet of interest under the recipe for "Easy Butter Biscuits." He thumped his finger on the page.

"Something of note?" inquired Rodstrum.

Deighton shrugged and related. "Bea says she received a tour of the Allen Road farmhouse and noted a number of concealed entrances. Says Chief Inspector Jenkins had no comment when asked if those provided any clues on the circus troupe's exit." He paused and muttered, "That's because the police never searched them!"

"I think she made her point," opined Rodstrum.

Clara Crumb visited Milton Alcorn at hospital in the mid-afternoon. He thanked her for bringing a plate of lemon cookies. He munched on a cookie to be polite as well as to stay awake. Clara mentioned she didn't know what to think about the Kingston Dove Foundation's science experiments on humans. Alcorn felt a surge of remorse. He sat up straighter as he sought to set the record straight. Thirty minutes later, Clara left and Alcorn fell asleep. As she waited for her ride, Clara decided to attend Kingston Dove Foundation's next community meeting.

In the late afternoon, Mitch Deighton phoned Rodstrum to say it looked like he would be discharged the day after next. Rodstrum promised to visit the next day. Deighton gave him an excuse to be at hospital, and Rodstrum had a feeling Director Nevels might have information on Carlson Applegate.

The next morning, as Rodstrum entered hospital, he encountered a distraught Samuel Granville, badgering the front desk for information. "I know she was taken away in an ambulance; I want to see my sister."

In a calm voice, the receptionist responded, "Please Mr. Granville, your sister was transferred and you need to wait to hear more from a doctor."

"Where is she?" Granville demanded.

The receptionist looked at him sternly and replied, "I've already said more than I should. I'll call upstairs and let the medical team know you are here and want someone to answer your questions."

"Unbelievable," Granville bellowed as he left the desk and began to pace.

Rodstrum ducked into the elevator and stopped at the second floor Administrative Unit. The second floor receptionist told him Assistant Director Minders wanted to speak with him.

Upon arriving at Minders' door, without even a greeting, Rodstrum heard himself asking, "Where is Mildred Pearson?"

"The Clifford Unit at Lester Hospital," quickly whispered Minders.

Rodstrum gasped, "The psychiatric unit?"

Minders sighed and whispered, "A breakdown."

Jack Rodstrum paused at the entry to the Hospital Director's corner office.

"Still on the case?" Troward Nevels inquired sourly.

"Might be," responded Rodstrum, before adding, "Mind if I come in?"

Rodstrum asked Nevels what he knew about Carlson Applegate. After a long pause, Nevels muttered, "I would rather not see this in the Daily Slip." Nevels rose and shut his office door.

"Confidentially," Nevels warned. He paused again, as though considering how to begin.

After a long exhale, Nevels confided. "I had an eight-month affair with Carlson Applegate. He seemed easy going, supportive and full of energy. Slowly, as the months went on, I noticed bits and pieces about his business affairs that gave me pause. By the time I ended our relationship, it was clear Carlson did not want the Kingston Dove Foundation in town, offering a potential refuge for his workers. I'm not sure what led to his arrest in Dorset, but I did come to know the tragic life stories of certain workers employed by Carlson." Rodstrum fixed him with a curious look.

Nevels fixed Rodstrum with a look of his own and quietly continued. "Olivia from Ghana, no papers, working illegally and turning over her pay to Carlson, who kept her safe from her husband. Clint, from Liberia, had parents who fled the civil war, and Carlson shipped his family to London as gardeners. Delly escaped slavery in

Mauritania and arrived in England by way of Egypt; Carlson set her up working as a care attendant to elders. These workers were grateful to Carlson. But I believe Carlson was taking cruel advantage of their circumstances."

Nevels hung his head. "I have no proof, but I believed justice was served when I learned Carlson was charged with human trafficking. I can't prove it, but I'm certain Curtis Field was involved, providing transport for Carlson's workers. According to local gossip, the pub was behind in its rent. After connecting with Carlson, Curtis Field purchased the building."

Nevels looked up. "That's all I have to say, but I don't know anything."

The hospital discharged Reginald Atwater. Pleased to be home, he made himself a cup of tea, sat in his easy chair and looked out his window. Minutes after finishing his tea, Atwater was roused by cracking noises and noted yellow spots appearing in quick succession on his windows. He went to the door and spotted Minerva Cummington throwing the remains of her carton of eggs. He held his phone to take a video of the event and sent it to his grandson, asking how to send it to the police. His grandson Gregg responded in a text message, "I'll handle it."

It was Town Councilor Milton Alcorn's second day at home. So far, he had a morning meeting with Bill Walters, and now he was expecting Beatrice Butterfield of the Daily Slip.

Butterfield brought a plate of sandwiches and Alcorn put on the kettle. At his kitchen table, they nibbled and recounted town events. Butterfield asked about his departure from the Gogglesgunshod Association.

"You know my second wife, Althea, was first cousin to the Executive Board's President for life. We were married for four years and that is how I became involved with the Association. Truth be told, the whole lot was a bit too pretentious for the likes of me. But I liked their charitable work. Once my wife died, I should have reassessed my place in that group, but I ran headfirst for them instead. Now, I'm done with them."

Butterfield asked about the talk of criminal charges. Alcorn scowled, "Let me enjoy my lunch first."

Butterfield took another sip of tea. She asked if he had heard the talk about Mildred Pearson having a mental breakdown.

Alcorn took another sandwich and considered, "I don't know that I've heard that, but I do know she was in a tizzy the other day. From what I heard, Millie was ranting about keeping Black Brits away from Huffinfield."

Butterfield harrumphed. Alcorn confided, "She can be a bit much at times." Butterfield nodded.

Alcorn continued, "So her neighbor points out how Millie used a Black Brit landscaper until a couple years back. According to a confidante of the neighbor, her eyes popped, she quit yapping and ran inside her house, she did."

Week Five

Chapter 53. Row Your Boat

On Saturday, Porter Public hit the newsstands. Photographs showed two Huffinfield residents in a tug of war with police over feeding a bonfire. Bea Butterfield saw their story highlighted the victim's narrative on the video but included a bit of the crowd's reaction. Former Town Councilor Milton Alcorn was quoted as saying, "Mistakes were made." Surely one of the year's understatements, thought Butterfield. Brad Leveler was quoted as saying, "Turnout doubled from the first meeting." Porter Public commented on Reverend Jake's conspicuous absence.

Butterfield was saving her report on the second Community Meeting for the Sunday edition. Saturday's Daily Slip took note of other local happenings.

This week's round-up: Minerva Cummington arrested for throwing raw eggs at Reginald Atwater's front windows; Lillie's Pie shop owner files for divorce after spouse lands in jail for third time in three weeks. Gogglesgunshod Association requests the Crown press arson charges against its own Executive Board Member Milton Alcorn; Alcorn denies arson and says Gogglesgunshod Association should be taken to court for Assault and Battery on his person. Police Inspector Mitch Deighton was discharged from hospital, after almost three weeks since his injury in the line of duty. Police Superintendent Michelle Sykes remains on paid suspension, pending IOPC investigation.

Brad Leveler found the Saturday Daily Slip's roundup under the local school's Spelling Bee results. He was learning how to read this small town newspaper. Leveler reflected on how it was only after Lady Carmella accepted the Grant Writer position, that he learned of her work for financial institutions and its emphasis on charitable fundraising. His stay in Huffinfield was challenging his assumptions about the town and its people.

Michelle Sykes drove her spotless Lamborghini to Reverend Jake's home. Hoping to discuss funeral plans for her great uncle, she walked toward his door. Before she could knock, the door opened and Curtis Field's red face pushed past her. "The Reverend is inside," he huffed over his shoulder. She turned to watch him jog toward a motorcycle parked on the street.

The door was still open. Sykes knocked on it and hesitantly called, "Reverend Jake?"

"Here," was the reply from far inside the house. She stepped inside and noticed the house looked empty.

After waiting a bit, Sykes announced, "I can come back later." Just then, Reverend Jake stepped into the room.

"Michelle, so sorry about your Uncle Miles," greeted Reverend Jake.

In the Sunday edition of the Daily Slip, the second Community Meeting was front page news. Butterfield gave a play by play account of what it was like to be in the audience: seeing the horror of the attack through the victims' eyes, rushing outside in response to shouts of fire, watching two residents' struggle against police to feed a bonfire, enduring the loud clang of fire trucks, feeling the mist from the spurting water blown on the wind, moving to regroup inside at the promise of food, listening to the Foundation's quick follow up during tea and tarts, and interacting with neighbors. She covered reactions to the entire evening, some somber and some comical. Her photos emphasized the community coming together.

Butterfield looked at her work and looked at Porter Public's. Both were worth reading.

In New York City, Otto and Darryl met at Battery Park. Darryl set a quick pace as they walked down First Street. Otto told Darryl of Dr. Middleton's apparent suicide in prison. Darryl replied, "You have something else?"

Otto reported on the Chief Inspector's discovery of security camera footage, showing Rouben removing the farmhouse records. Otto added, "Police identified Rouben as the man who went missing after being apprehended for the roughing up of the police inspector!"

"Keep me informed," Darryl snapped before he abruptly turned a corner and disappeared. Darryl's survival instincts pounded on his brain. It didn't make sense that a slick operator like Rouben wouldn't destroy the security camera footage. (He didn't know that in response to the erratic edicts from the Police Superintendent, Desk Sergeant Cathcart installed an alternate security camera.)

Inspector Mitch Deighton returned to work, on desk duty. He found the Chief had not reassigned Reginald Atwater's case, even though Deighton was hospitalized on the day he received the assignment. By his second day, he was looking forward to escaping the office on his morning break. Deighton hobbled over to the pastry shop for a cup of tea. He spotted Jack Rodstrum at a back table with Sam Wiley and Pete Privitt. Deighton pulled up a chair. They chuckled at Deighton being found medically fit to return to work while Privitt and Wiley were still on sick leave, by order of the Police Superintendent.

Deighton leaned in. "I'm trying to finish up the paperwork on Lady Carmella's incident. She talked of a boat house on the far side of the pond. Who owns that anyway?"

Nobody knew, but Wiley and Privitt volunteered to have a look.

In the early afternoon, Privitt and Wiley took a friend's row boat to the far side of the pond. They pulled onto the shore and set out along the wooded trail. About ten minutes later, they heard movement. Beyond the bend, they spotted a small cottage. They carefully approached to watch Edgar Ward removing boxes and loading them onto a dolly. Then Ward locked the cottage door and pulled the dolly along a perpendicular path toward the water. They could make out a boat within a hundred paces.

Wiley and Privitt ran back to their rowboat and moved it to a space concealed by scraggly trees. They listened as a loud motor turned over. In the nick of time, they ducked behind the trees to watch Ward's boat motoring to the pond's far shore. Ward debarked, moved a pickup truck close to the boat, unloaded the boxes, hitched the boat to the truck and sped away.

"Got that?" asked Privitt as Wiley put down his phone.

"Every bit," replied Wiley, "I'm forwarding it to Bill Walters. I don't want to muck up IOPC's investigation by forwarding it to local police."

Bill Walters forwarded Wiley's video to his Headquarters, where it was immediately forwarded to the NCC.

NCC agents, already in town, were alerted to IOPC's reports, and soon stopped Ward's truck. The agents identified themselves as "law enforcement" and spoke to him about the correct way to connect a boat trailer to a truck. Ward exploded and told them he had no time for them. The agents phoned in the incident to Huffinfield Police as they gave chase. The agents cornered Ward's truck at the end of a barricaded tunnel. Huffinfield police caught up, and the agents advised they suspected Ward was transporting contraband. The responding constables opened a box and found cannabis. By then, Ward and the constables' vehicle had left the scene.

Chief Jenkins put his head in his hands. Once he opened his eyes, he sent reinforcements for the stranded constables, sent two cars to apprehend Edgar Ward, and told Carol to pull all reports from former Junior Inspector Sykes. Jenkins sent an email to Bill Walters, saying he would have pertinent information by the end of the day.

In the late afternoon, Jack Rodstrum phoned Kevin Cathcart. It turned out Cathcart was hosting a card party with Sam Wiley and Pete Privitt in attendance. Rodstrum left to join them.

When Rodstrum arrived at Cathcart's flat, Wiley was giving a play by play description of their row boat adventure. Privitt noted, "Odd that after two years at a store manager job, Ward became independently wealthy; but we just assumed it was an inheritance."

Rodstrum asked, "So did Ward rent a greenhouse from the circus troupe?"

Wiley recalled, "There was talk once of a cannabis route in the vicinity of the Allen Road farmhouse."

Cathcart stated, "If I'm not mistaken, then Junior Inspector Sykes opened an investigation on that and closed it a week later, finding no supporting evidence."

"Yes, I remember that," Privitt chuckled and added, "That was just weeks before she first drove the Lamborghini to work."

Wiley laughed, "I hope the IOPC takes note of that one."

Rodstrum shared the news about Reverend Jake's brother Carlson being charged with human trafficking. Cathcart stated, "The judge dismissed the case after scheduled witnesses for the prosecution failed to appear at trial." He added, "I know because my cousin lives in Dorset and followed Carlson's trial for the local news."

Wiley banged his fist on the table. "Wait a minute," he whispered.

He sat back in his chair and looked at the ceiling. He drummed his fingers. Gathering his thoughts, Wiley mused, "This is the part about the mob victims that's been haunting me, but I couldn't put my finger on it. Huffinfield had a few Black Brits, regulars in town, before Carlson's arraignment. Gardeners, eldercare, childcare, all day-laborers, they were. Then that stopped. Reverend Jake in the pulpit and Curtis Field at the pub, both took up the drumbeat of 'us against them' after that. You know what I mean?"

Nobody did know exactly what Wiley meant, but they dwelled on it for the rest of the afternoon.

The next morning, Carmella awoke to the sound of an explosion. She looked out the window to see her detached garage destroyed and still burning. Determined not to flee, she was relieved to see the fire trucks arrive before the fire spread.

That afternoon, Deighton learned Private Investigator Marbles was found dead and the subsequent coroner's finding was death from heart failure. Given the morning's events, he drove to Lady Carmella's home to deliver the news.

That evening, Nancy sent a news clip from New York's Daily News, a story from Chinatown about sanitation workers finding a nude corpse, later identified as Stanley Marbles from the UK, in an alley dumpster, located three blocks from the Brooklyn Bridge. Shaken, Lady Carmella was determined to get answers.

Ned Carraway was scheduled for trial later that year. Authorities remained baffled at his silence on cannabis production. When the NCC agents, investigating cannabis production, crossed paths in Huffinfield with LAMB CHOP, the Regional Organized Crime Unit (ROCU), investigating missing persons and the alleged sale of cadavers, it prompted attention to the deceased Dr. Middleton's plea bargain. The pressure mounted to find Darryl.

Even if police did look in New York City, Darryl was unrecognizable with his now sandy hair. His nose job and new fingerprints were courtesy of Swaeger. This new look was not in response to Mr. Marbles, but in response to a police investigation, opening in the former Soviet Bloc, on former secret police, those state spies used for political purposes. A local news journalist in Prague asked why it took so long for the Interior Minister to address the issue. Darryl couldn't help but grin.

Otto didn't care for Darryl's new look, but he was careful not to say.

Chapter 54. Unwanted Visitor

With Herculean effort, Lady Carmella managed to schedule a visit with Ned Carraway in Millipede Prison. Still reeling from her garage explosion and Mr. Marbles' fate, she wanted to know what sort of threat, if any, she faced from the circus troupe. Ned was her best link.

On a gray Thursday morning, Nancy drove her to the prison, but the rules let her accompany Carmella only as far as the outlying carpark. Nancy promised, "I'll be right here waiting for you."

Carmella took a deep breath and muttered, "Right," before resolutely opening her car door. Nancy watched her walk toward a guard booth, provide her visitation document to a uniformed official, and step up to a dark platform where a train car was waiting.

At the end of the line, guards escorted Lady Carmella off the train. She entered a large, gray structure. It was eerily threatening, even entering of her own volition. She waited in one room and then another. Both had white, bare walls and sparse, spartan furniture. Finally, a new guard arrived to escort her, this time to a narrow booth with a window on its far side. She was told the prisoner would arrive shortly.

Five minutes later, Carmella could hear chains clinking on the hard floor. When he came into view, she saw Ned had a guard at each manacled arm. She watched as he was placed in a seat before the window. His face was hard and mean. For a time, they both looked at each other.

Carmella broke the silence. "My name is Carmella and I live near Allen Road in Huffinfield. Weren't you a resident of the farmhouse at the end of Allen Road?"

Ned remained silent, though his savage demeanor softened.

Carmella tried again. "I think about them often," breathed Carmella and she looked into his eyes. Ned was silent. Carmella had assumed he would be glad to have a visitor. Ned didn't look pleased at all.

Carmella decided to be candid. She folded her hands and stared at them hard before looking at Ned and confiding. "Their memory haunts me. Can you tell me, is that circus troupe still out to get me?" Ned remained silent and still.

A guard moved into view. Carmella's heart jumped. Was her scheduled visit being cut short?

Carmella implored, "Please, I must know, are they lying in wait for me?" and then paused to wait for his response. Ned remained silent. The guard too remained silent. She switched tactics.

"Just tell me that and I'll leave you in peace," Carmella promised. Ned's face remained impassive. Carmella faced down the dread that this visit was a terrible farce.

"You saved me, don't you remember?" pleaded Carmella as her eyes swelled.

With a faint smile, he softly spoke. "They were a bunch of hornets. Don't you worry, they've lost their sting now." Ned motioned to the jailer he was ready to return to his cell. It was the first Ned spoke since his incarceration.

Bill Walters re-read his report summary for the umpteenth time. He knew IOPC Legal would rather tear it apart than risk having to defend its findings. He drew on his years of experience to consider each of the bombs they would lob in his direction. He checked again to confirm each finding addressed all required elements. He cross-checked the report's statement of facts with the exhibits. (Walters made a note to commend Storrs for his work on the exhibits.) He was convinced the report's bricks and mortar were solid. But he didn't feel good about it.

Later at the gym, the reason dawned on him. The report needed a backstory to make sense of it. Loathe to go beyond his investigation's purview, Walters considered adding a background section to the summary or a few, well-sourced exhibits on context (the circus troupe, the mob victims, the cannabis farming, the missing youths, the citizen militia, and the drenched community sing-out). A glimpse of the craziness within Huffinfield might better reveal the impact of police inaction.

Back at his desk, Walters instinctively knew this was a bad idea. He concentrated as he munched on his carrot sticks. Perhaps one exhibit, entitled "Community Context," with a timeline, might serve his purpose.

With a grimace, Jack Rodstrum watched the two suits walk toward his door. Law enforcement, from the look of them. Pleased they waited until that Medwin lady sorted the place, Rodstrum opened the door to an outstretched arm holding a badge. "Enter," Rodstrum muttered before retrieving his coffee.

After thirty minutes of questions about his investigations into the circus troupe, a vexed Rodstrum put up his hand and announced, "Perhaps I can make this easier for you. I have never been on the take."

After a pause, the lead NCC agent asserted, "We still need to ask these questions."

"Just leave enough time for me to provide you with information that may actually prove helpful," Rodstrum grunted.

Before departing, the lead agent asked, "Do you have any other information you believe to be pertinent?"

Rodstrum responded, "A bit of background first. The Gogglesgunshod Association is peppered with a dozen disgraced medical doctors, notorious for their connections to the London Eugenics Society." He noted their blank stares and added, "Look it up."

Rodstrum continued, "Between four and six years ago, Black Brits were not an uncommon sight around Huffinfield. You would see them as gardeners and housekeepers and the like. The local Reverend Jake Applegate has a brother Carlson. Carlson's employment agency was a big player in procuring day laborers. Sometime, about six years ago, Carlson was hauled into court on charges of human trafficking.

The case was dismissed when the prosecution's witnesses failed to appear in court."

The agents looked at him with glazed eyes.

"Stay with me," Rodstrum encouraged, "Sometime after that, the Black Brit labor force around Huffinfield disappeared. Could be Carlson turned to a different occupation. I don't know. I'm just saying that's what happened. And when it did, Reverend Jake and the local pub owner Curtis Field, at about the same time, raised questions about the veracity of Black Brits and implied they were best avoided. And they are two influential people in town so it should be noted."

Rodstrum sighed, "Then you likely know as much as I do about the picnic victim saga that has been in the local newspaper and featured in Porter Public. Though you may want to talk to retired Constable Mike Parish and the ambulance technicians Bates and Norton."

Rodstrum creased his brow and said, "The grocer Edgar Ward was likely renting a greenhouse for cannabis at the farmhouse on Allen Road when it was owned by the so-called circus troupe. Ward drives a Mercedes Benz. You can guess about who else was involved by the gap between their legal income and their choice of motor vehicles. I learned about that later. The current Superintendent Sykes was assigned to investigate cannabis production around the farmhouse. So a number of people had a vested interest in protecting the landlord, the circus troupe."

"It seems likely the circus troupe included a few hard-core criminals. By now, many have shown up dead, but missing actors may have remained local. I tried talking to one Ned Carraway, now in prison, but got nowhere. I provided the IOPC with a photo of the one most involved in procuring the farmhouse. A concealed laboratory in the farmhouse looks like it was used by the circus troupe. A human corpse was stuck in a first-floor closet after the new owner took possession. When the circus troupe lived in the farmhouse, they ran a Farm and Circus Program for Disadvantaged Youth. The recently discovered corpse belonged to Stu Gates, a youth who had participated in this program."

The agents looked overwhelmed. Rodstrum said. "Just a bit more. A local doctor, now deceased, had human corpses, preserved in the same manner, on display at his residence. This doctor was also involved in the Gogglesgunshod Association. Police Superintendent Sykes served as Vice President of the Association during the Picnic Victim Saga. The current President, Victor Lloyd, is spearheading a smear campaign, painting the new owners of the farmhouse as responsible for the corpse and suggesting the new owner conducts scientific experiments on humans. This is even more bizarre when you consider the Association gifted body parts of known living humans."

Rodstrum stretched out his legs and concluded, "That's it. It may not all be connected, but I believe the different factors feed each other."

After a pause, an agent asked, "What led you, as a retiree, to all this sleuthing?"

Rodstrum replied, "First, a friend and fellow Inspector was badly beaten by the circus troupe. That reminded me how my investigations were shut down. In the news, Police Superintendent Sykes announced no evidence linked the circus troupe to criminal activity. I saw no police action on physical threats to Mr. Atwater in hospital. My friend almost died when a physician walked in off the street and prescribed him questionable medication. And of course, my flat was turned upside down."

Shortly after the NCC agents left Rodstrum's apartment, they consulted with their LAMBCHOP ROCU counterparts investigating missing persons and the alleged sale of human cadavers.

The week was otherwise uneventful until Saturday.

On Saturday, the pub was closed; a notice hung on the door that read, "Under renovation and Under new management." Without any notice, Curtis Field was gone.

That Sunday, a visiting vicar preached, amidst many questions on the whereabouts of Reverend Jake.

As baffled as anyone, Beatrice Butterfield was determined to get the scoop before Porter Public.

In Somerset, retired constable Mike Parish slouched in his easy chair, closed his eyes and declared, "Mary, I'm not moving."

His wife sat hunched forward on the couch and faced him. She repeated, "We need to leave. I don't want to spend the rest of my days with a convict husband."

"For the last time," grated Mike, "I merely took orders from Superintendent Stebbins."

"Who is now dead and can't vouch for you," cried Mary as her hands slid from her lap to grasp her knees. She softly pleaded, "No, Mike. We need to leave. You saw Porter Public. You must see your predicament. We can move to Spain."

"Mary! I'm not going anywhere," growled Mike.

The doorbell rang. Mike rose to open the door to three men in dark suits. The front man's outstretched arm held up a badge. "National Crime Cracker," he announced, "And you're Michael Parish?"

"I am," said Mike.

Mary ran into the kitchen.

In record time, the Independent Office for Police Conduct issued a report finding police corruption in Huffinfield and copied the NCC. Walters was relieved. He could only assume the NCC's interest helped to advance the report.

Chapter 55. Missing in Action

As part of its investigation, the NCC brought in Carlson Applegate, ostensibly for questioning on additional claims of unpaid salaries. Based on Jack Rodstrum's information, the agents noted Carlson's deceased father had been a prominent member of the London Eugenics Society. More curiously, Carlson appeared to have wholly different fingerprints from those recorded years earlier. When asked, Carlson claimed his prints were doctored by a pianist at a Huffinfield farmhouse.

The next day, Carlson was found hanging from his TRX Suspension Trainer. In a handwritten note, he admitted to human trafficking and keeping people in servitude. According to Carlson: he appropriated all salaries in return for food and shelter, Curtis Field provided transport for the workers, and his brother Jake convinced unwitting families to trust in the promise of a new life. Carlson also named Helga Nikitina as an accomplice. Carlson vowed he was truly sorry and asked his wealth be distributed among a list of workers. Carlson apologized if his campaign to label his black workers as untrustworthy had contributed to the crimes against the picnic victims.

The NCC issued international All Points Bulletins for Jake, Curtis and Helga.

"Never was all that smart," grumbled Jake as he read the internet news of his brother's death. Upon deciding to retire to Belize, Jake emptied his bank accounts, used Carlson's passport to fly to Mexico, and made his way overland to San Juan. Jake figured the note of a suicidal loser couldn't seal a case against him.

Curtis Field felt sure the prior human trafficking allegations against Carlson were true. He did not have firsthand knowledge of the workers' plight but did know Carlson Applegate paid him a fortune for driving a van. Instinctively, Field knew not to ask questions. He didn't want to answer questions either. When Reverend Jake informed him that Carlson was to be questioned again, Field moved fast to liquidate his assets. He took the bus to Dover, boarded the ferry to France, and opened Carlson's email from Paris. Without looking back, Field headed for Brussels.

Unbeknownst to the NCC, its international All Points Bulletin for Helga yielded results. Helga, the former farmhouse cook, was working on a cruise ship. Instead of pink, her tall hair was blue. While the cruise ship was docked in Budapest, undercover NBSZ agents detained Helga. She was never heard from again.

With the sudden departures of Reverend Jake and Curtis Field, Huffinfield was in an uproar. Rumors of kidnapping and ransom demands spread like wildfire. After reporting on Carlson Applegate's suicide in the Daily Slip, Beatrice Butterfield hoped people would calm down. But instead, many residents felt duped and betrayed.

Troward Nevels contacted Brad Leveler and asked if the Kingston Dove Foundation might organize a grief support group for those who had known Carlson's workers, but didn't know of their plight, or perhaps turned a blind eye. The Foundation retained an impressive list of counselors for a six-week program, open for free to Huffinfield residents.

The Foundation's standing in the Community began to solidify, in spite of Victor Lloyd. Lloyd did not appear to have any notion of abandoning his newly found "prominence." At least weekly, he spoke at rallies; tweeted obnoxious slurs; and worse, encouraged others' anti-social tendencies. Brad Leveler finally convinced the Foundation's Board that the likes of Lloyd would not walk away quietly. He obtained approval to take action.

According to Brad Leveler's weekly report, he merely hand-delivered a letter, in which the Kingston Dove Foundation threatened to bring an action for slander and libel against Victor Lloyd. Within the next week, Lloyd's rants against the Foundation petered out, following his public admission he may have been "confused." It was later noted Lloyd personally paid for repairs, necessitated by Clive Leeway's crashing a tractor through the bay window of the farmhouse.

After two weeks in hospital, Mildred Pearson was discharged from the Clifford Unit. Over a lunch of fish and chips, Beatrice Butterfield quizzed Milton Alcorn on Mildred Pearson's whereabouts. Alcorn acknowledged speaking with her brother, Samuel Granville, who said Pearson was engaged "in some sort of outpatient program." Alcorn maintained he didn't know the particulars.

"It must be difficult for him to see his sister like that," sighed Butterfield.

Alcorn confided, "Sam holds Millie is on the mend, especially after a warm letter from her daughter." He leaned in and whispered, "Their first communication in years!" Butterfield nodded knowingly.

Edgar Ward was indicted for cannabis production with intent to distribute. Minions of Edgar Ward's cannabis empire were gabbing to anyone who might listen. Stories abounded to the point where one might think Ward was acting under duress, put upon by the foreigners in the farmhouse. It didn't appear Ward was making any effort to dispel the stories. More intriguing, Facebook commentary by NCC clerical staff, suggested charges of aiding and abetting were pending. Darryl smelled a plea bargain in the works.

Darryl considered the evidence. Crates of cannabis loaded from a secluded cabin on the pond, Ward's erratic transport of those crates, and Ward's discontinued electronic deposits to a bank account owned by the ZXY Corporation. It was unclear whether the more outlandish tales would hatch "witness statements." The greenhouse and cannabis fields were the most damming evidence to connect the Farmhouse to Ward's illicit business. Curiously, the NCC did not conduct a protective sweep of the greenhouse and abutting fields. (Perhaps that was a call for Police Superintendent Sykes, but she was under suspension. Chief Inspector Jenkins did nothing.)

Darryl wasn't one to get his hands dirty, but given the last botched contract jobs, he prepared to return to Huffinfield. Darryl skimmed his mental catalog for Practical Thermodynamics. With the right wind conditions, a fire would spread quickly in the farmhouse fields.

On a Sunday afternoon, Butterfield dined with Connie Appleton and Lillie Leeway. They chatted about Edgar Ward's predicament. Appleton huffed, "What made them pick this year to act like it was illegal?" With their well-placed businesses, Appleton and Leeway knew all the players and their various roles in Ward's cannabis business. Butterfield made a mental note to interview each of them about what they knew.

Inspector Deighton met with Lady Carmella to close out his investigation. He explained the circus troupe included hardened, wanted criminals, many of whom had died since her initial complaint. Though police did not apprehend those unaccounted for, she could rest assured that her activism prompted the recent All-Points Bulletin for the ringleader and his girlfriend. (In fact, that was Darryl and Dr. Swaeger.) Deighton promised to let her know if he learned of their apprehension, but wasn't hopeful. The Arson Unit determined a pipe bomb demolished her car garage, but police had no leads.

A barely recognizable Darryl arrived in Huffinfield to await the proper breeze. A watchful pair of eyes spotted him.

The next day, the town was under a gray haze. Fire fighters from all over Blinkingshire County worked to extinguish the fast-moving fire in the cannabis fields at the end of Allen Road. Lady Carmella set off for a long ride in her new Bentley and hoped the fire wouldn't spread to her newly-built garage. By mid-morning, most everyone in Huffinfield was feeling quite relaxed and thinking about lunch.

Darryl returned to New York City.

Later that year

Chapter 56. Enough Already Huffinfield

The Independent Office for Police Conduct detained Michelle Sykes pending her arraignment on corruption charges. The Town Council appointed Chief Inspector Gerald Jenkins as acting Police Superintendent. In his first official act, Jenkins authorized Kevin Cathcart, Sam Wiley and Pete Privitt to return to duty. Upon Cathcart's recommendation, the electronic records system was shelved, pending updated computer capacity.

Having come together for the investigation, Jack Rodstrum and Mitch Deighton rekindled their friendship. They met regularly on Thursday nights at the pub, where they heaped rave reviews on the new owner's Roast Beef Special.

Lady Carmella obtained two grants for the Kingston Dove Foundation. One grant provided funding for programs to teach tolerance and foster diversity in the Blinkingshire County's school system. Another grant funded training for Huffinfield's first responders on how to respond to racially-motivated crimes.

Police closed the case on Travis Sillman, not spotted since his escape from the Brimmerston Jail.

Former Town Councilor Milton Alcorn resumed playing billiards with Reginald Atwater.

Nancy Mapother enjoyed a romantic relationship with Gregg Armstrong, eighteen years her junior.

Ned Carraway went on a hunger strike and died in hospital. Penny Crimson emailed the news to Jack Rodstrum, who informed

Deighton and Carmella of Ned's fate. Lady Carmella said a prayer for him.

The Kingston Dove Foundation filed a court action on behalf of the mob victims against the Gogglesgunshod Association for the distribution of their body parts. Within weeks, the parties reached a settlement agreement, in which the Association agreed to make a generous contribution to Royal Riot Against Racism.

Delilah Banks accepted a promotion at work. Her children thrived. Her cousins Nicki and Rose continued providing support and encouragement.

The National Crime Cracker filed charges upon discovering eight additional taxidermy youths in Blinkingshire County residences. All were identified as participants in the Farm and Circus Program for Disadvantaged Youth. Huffinfield's visiting vicar presided over the group's memorial service. Paula Minders drove her Aunt Sophie to the service, and both came away with their conflict behind them.

Sadly, the National Crime Cracker's investigation yielded no information on the human-trafficking victims, ensnared by the Farm and Circus Program for Disadvantaged Youth.

With Connie Appleton's expansive knowledge of the local cannabis industry, and a few salient points added by Lillie Leeway, Beatrice Butterfield investigated, more to confirm than discover, the workings of Edgar Ward's far-reaching cannabis empire. She published a series of six installments in the Sunday edition of the Daily Slip. Police subsequently questioned a number of local residents.

In a letter to the editor, Victor Lloyd took umbrage with police investigations into local residents' involvement in the cannabis trade. He called it an obscene use of the criminal justice system to prosecute good citizens for helping their neighbors. Those with loved ones facing criminal charges were quick to agree.

Butterfield's series brought her a national award in journalism. (Though residents liked to see one of their own receive recognition, the award stoked consternation among Huffinfield's reading public, familiar with Butterfield's reporting.) Linda Chickering, News Editor at Porter Public, sent Butterfield a congratulatory bouquet of flowers.

Butterfield's journalism award left Lady Carmella with a feeling of dread. Despite her repeated denials of involvement with Reed Crimson, it was complicated. When Crimson stood accused of embezzling funds from a charity in her portfolio, she relented and agreed to serve as his character witness. Soon after, the charges were dismissed. Still, Carmella preferred their photo not reappear in the Daily Slip. After confiding to Nancy, they decided if Butterfield ever asked, Carmella would simply claim she forgot.

The Gogglesgunshod Association dissolved. In the same month, the defunct Association's Executive Board formed the Heron's Guild to take over the Association's charitable activities. The Heron's Guild hired the public relations firm of Beak and Brine to reframe the town narrative. As talk show hosts discussed Huffinfield's challenges upon being designated as a travel destination, Porter Public continued its efforts to illuminate the need to address racism.

After many months, it looked like the Crown would press charges of Affray, Assault and Battery, Rape, and Child Abuse, in response to Delilah Banks' ordeal. Then the Heron's Guild retained a law firm, skilled in legal hopscotch, and what seemed straight forward now appeared muddled. When pressed, the Crown averred the police investigation was ongoing. Nothing further happened in Reginald Atwater's lifetime. He died just short of his eighty-second birthday.

Darryl marveled at his success in New York City's underground, where he found much call for the gifted Doctor Swaeger's skills. Both agreed it had become a bit dull in the English countryside. As they supped, they relished their new life in a SoHo loft, looking onto an urban skyline. Swaeger raised his glass and toasted, "He, who doesn't take risks, doesn't drink champagne."

Minutes later, a spray of bullets crashed through their loft's window. Through an infrared monocular, former KGB Agent 99 admired his work. Satisfied, he etched two more lines onto the barrel of his Mini Uzi. Police sirens wailed in the distance. "Amateurs," scoffed Rouben, before disappearing into the night.